The Brittle Riders

Book Two

Bill McCormick

Azoth Khem Publishing
July 2017
Rocky Mount, Virginia

AN AZOTH KHEM PUBLISHING PUBLICATION

3rd Edition (revised)

ISBN: 1-945987-04-9
ISBN-13: 978-1-945987-04-5

Azoth Khem Publishing
70 Foxwood Drive
Rocky Mount, Virginia   24151
Tel: (540) 352-8457

www.azothkhempublishing.com

Ordering Information:
Quantity sales and special discounts are available on quantity purchases by U.S. and International trade bookstores and wholesalers. For details, contact the publisher at the address above.

Printed in the United States of America

Book Two

P'marna was as nervous as a small before her first kiss. It had been five Full Suns since the fall of Anapsida and she'd been much busier than she would have thought. Her Queen had been as good as her word and had invited N'leah to stay with them in their new home with the Dwellers of the Pit. And she had when she could, but it had been two full seasons since they'd last been together. However, in just a few cliks, she'd be here again.

She nervously paced the entranceway of the new, albeit insignificant, palace Elder Urnak had built for Queen A'lnuah and her burgeoning court. Small, that is, compared to the Minotaurs', it still could hold one thousand brands. The spurs of her heels made a soft clicking sound which was augmented by her tapping the talons of each toe against the new stone. She hadn't realized how many new appointments would need to be made after the war. The Succubi had lived on the fringe for so long they'd been forced, by necessity, to pare any diplomatic staff down to its bare essentials. Not counting the number of brands who were needed to staff even a small palace, now there were ambassadors, trade representatives, couriers and more who were all needed to deal with each warren and the lands of the new Lord Südermann.

The new Lord Südermann was nice, like her father, but had only been fifteen Full Suns old when she'd assumed power. As well trained as she was she had no actual experience. And, unlike her predecessors, she'd been the first Südermann who'd been denied the opportunity to work alongside her father for her two Full Sun apprenticeship. It had been a very delicate time for a while. P'marna had been dispatched to deal with the young lord on several occasions back then because it was felt she had a gentler way about her. P'marna didn't know if it was true or not, but she and the adolescent Südermann had gotten along very well. To the horror of her guards, they'd even managed to play a couple of games of skizzi-ball behind the palace.

Greko, now a 6th Level Dweller of the Pit since his appointment to the council and clearly being fast tracked to be an Elder, spied P'marna and smiled. He, too, knew N'leah was coming and how much those visits meant to the Queen's courtesan. He walked through the palace entrance and over to where she was pacing in a tight circle.

"There are easier ways to drill a hole, you know. You could get a BadgeBeth or a shovel, either would be quicker."

She hadn't seen him coming, actually, she hadn't been paying attention to anything at all, and was completely startled by the sound of his voice. She turned, absently adjusted her skirt and blushed.

"Am I that bad?"

"Being diplomatic, yes."

They both laughed and P'marna draped an arm over the burly Minotaur.

"Come, let me get us both a drink. I need to calm down and you need to lighten up."

She led them into an antechamber where a servant, those were new too, took their order and scampered away.

"So, tell me friend Greko, why do you look so dour?"

"I wish I knew," he mumbled, "trade has been good, the new army of the Plains is truly formed now and with the Gaping Canyon now the Great Lake, agriculture has become stable and profitable. But, Geldish and his Brittle Riders have been making wider and wider forays into neighboring lands and have been very quiet this last Full Sun.

"There is nothing specific I can point to, but when those five start keeping secrets no good can come of it."

Their drinks arrived and they sipped them for a moment until the servant left.

"I have known N'leah since we were smalls. If there

was something threatening the Plains she would tell me."

"Would she?" wondered Greko, "She is now bound to the Temple of Azarep and even more closely to her fellow riders. They may deem the knowledge too important to share. Or they may be waiting to be sure of something they only suspect. She is not the same femme you stole kisses from behind a barn."

"How did you know about that?" she squealed, her face turning beet red.

He laughed and sipped his drink before answering.

"Well, you're both from Anara. Nothing there but barns and houses and no one's daring enough to steal kisses in a house where they could be caught. It was just a guess, but an accurate one I see."

P'marna straightened her unruffled skirt once again and thought. N'leah was older now and battle hardened. While she'd been at the battle, N'leah had been in it. Her many wounds were a testament to that. And while the two were very close she'd caught her, more than once, staring at the ceiling when she should have been sleeping.

She cherished those evens, snuggled on N'leah's strong shoulder with her wing draped across her body. She'd never felt more comfortable, and more secure, than she did at those times. Still, Greko could be right. There was much N'leah kept to herself these turns.

She shook off her doubts.

"If there is something they only suspect, then I applaud their secrecy. There's no need to cause panic needlessly. Other than that, I stand by what I said, there is no way N'leah would keep something a secret if it posed a real threat."

Greko pondered her statement and finally nodded.

"N'leah fought valiantly against the Naradhama and Xhaknar. Her whole life, since she met Geldish, has been dedicated to keeping the Plains safe. I believe you are right. Nevertheless, there is something brewing and it troubles me not to know what it is."

"Have you tried asking Geldish?"

Greko nodded.

"Twice, in fact. I may as well have asked him to don flesh and do the Aklop for all the good it did me."

P'marna giggled at the image.

"I'll broach the subject with her this even after we've eaten and rested."

Greko nodded, finished his drink, turned to leave then stopped.

"One more thing."

"Yes?"

"You look stunning in that outfit, quit fiddling with it."

He smiled as he left and she looked down to discover she'd been worrying her skirt with her fingers. She quickly smoothed it out for the seventeenth time and decided to catch up on some paperwork for her Queen until N'leah arrived.

If she didn't do something to take her mind off N'leah she'd end up rubbing holes through the fabric.

Geldish sat on the grass outside the temple and marveled at what he saw. It mattered little he'd seen the sight many times over the last five Full Suns, it still held his gaze.

After Anapsida fell the Kgul had moved above ground and the Wolfen had asked to be allowed to stay and build their own warren on the lands. Karrish, Makish, and Elzish had agreed readily enough since the temple had been a lonely place for far too long. Zrrm, whom Geldish had long stopped thinking of as just another Din-La, had opened a trading post next to the stables and turned it into a major concern.

Some Kgul and Wolfen smalls were playing a game

with a twelve-sided ball, laughing and screaming as they ran back and forth. Geldish had no idea what the rules, if any, were, but he enjoyed watching them play.

King G'rnk, Pack Lord of the Wolfen, a title he was still having trouble getting used to, sidled over and sat down next to him.

"It is amazing to see so much joy after what we endured, don't you think?"

"I think we endured what we did just so we could see this much joy. For me, sights like this make it all worthwhile."

"I agree. To be honest, even seeing it I have trouble believing it. I keep fearing it's all just images in smoke and a strong wind will come and blow it all away."

Geldish nodded but said nothing. They sat for a little longer, listening to the sounds of innocent delight, and then Geldish excused himself and headed back to the temple.

He walked into the kitchen area and grabbed himself a snack. He saw Zrrm sitting with Karrish playing a leisurely game of Ti-Zam. His sons were old enough now to mind the post and he liked to give them a couple of cliks each turn to do that without supervision. It was his way of showing trust and they loved him all the more for it.

After a quick exchange of pleasantries, he strode past the idol, across the main chamber, and headed for the library. He walked straight for the journal he'd been keeping on his water reclamation project and began adding notes.

He'd wanted to salt the clouds, which would have been easiest, but had no feasible way to do so. The Succubi, even if they could have stayed at the altitudes he needed for as long as was required, could still only carry about twenty-five pounds each. That thought brought him back to H'laar's brilliant cannon balls. A shell would be filled with hydrogen then covered with Krolnk's explosive paste and then covered again with another thin shell to bind it all together. Each ball barely weighed more than two pounds.

But when the explosive ignited the hydrogen which, in turn, ignited any remaining explosive, the effect was pure devastation. He wondered idly how H'laar was doing. He knew he'd been promoted to Lieutenant in Charge of the Royal Mantis Guard after Elaand had been promoted to Colonel. Then, as he thought of Elaand, he smiled. He hoped the old bug was doing well.

He went back to his notes. Using his body's natural control over magnetism he'd begun polarizing the air at the far north end of the Gaping Canyon. There was more moisture there, even if it was colder, and he needed to have as much as possible to start with. He knew, before the gen-O-pod war, there'd been water in Gaping Canyon. He also knew Xhaknar had made his Mayanorens dig massive tunnels which forced the water to drain out to the south, flooding vacant lands. What was left, when he was done, had simply evaporated over time. The life-giving moisture and rains it created were gone. The smell from all the dead fish and drying plants was horrendous. That memory would never leave him.

His initial effort had only earned him a cloud about the size of an infant kgum. But he kept adding to it and adding to it, breaklight after breaklight, over the course of three full seasons, until it became self-sustaining. This he unleashed into the canyon and let nature follow its course.

His foremost concern was it wouldn't stop. He had a plan in case that happened, but it hadn't been needed. As the water levels rose the cloud finally spent itself and dissolved into the waters whence it came.

Now, for the last four Full Suns, the Din-La, with help from the Fish-People, had been resupplying fish and plants into the waters. It was an enormous task, one which would take many more Suns, but he could tell it was already reaping rewards.

This turn he'd spied a school of fish, the Din-La called them Blue Gills, which were much younger than the last stocking. That meant they were breeding.

He'd then floated over the lake and, reaching out with his mind, found stable patches of life scattered throughout. Not enough to be a balanced eco-system, but a very good start to building one.

He finished marking his map with all the points where he'd detected life, closed his notebook and decided to show it to Zrrm. Maybe, by consulting with the Fish-People, they could figure out what was missing and begin filling in the gaps.

With that cheerful thought in mind, he exited the library humming a peculiar tune and went back to the kitchen to talk with Zrrm.

Anapsida was a dramatically changed place. The Mayanoren had all left when they heard of Xhaknar's demise. The Naradhama, who were essentially an effete class of elitists once the military and the slaves were gone, were trying their best to grasp the concept of working for their keep. The slaves had been freed and placed in homes in various villages. Some later moved to the warrens to take jobs where they could.

The blood fountain was destroyed and all evidence of Xhaknar's tortures burned. The arms factory, when found, was razed to the ground. They had no need for inferior weapons and no desire to have slaves do the work.

After Xhaknar fell and the soldiers of Rohta's Warriors had regrouped, they'd hit Anapsida like a monsoon. They'd swept through every crevice, every cranny, every cubbyhole they could find erasing all memories of Xhaknar and his evils.

Once those tasks were accomplished they'd lowered the taxes and set up a Din-La trading post. Then they'd found an underground river and used it to set up a hydroelectric plant. By combining that power with the new solar panels - courtesy of Lord Südermann - that were soon attached to every available roof surface, within one Full Sun, Anapsida, once the blight of the Plains, glittered like a jewel. The new Lord Südermann sent technicians and workers to assist in the project and they were pleased with how well the brands of the Plains picked up on the technology. And those who didn't could still string wires and lay cables with the best of them. The work went better than anyone had hoped.

The palace, now cleansed, became the home of the Elder's Council. They even hired a couple of former Naradhama slaves to work as greeters and write down any concerns the citizens might have. It took them a while to grasp the concept their new bosses wanted to hear complaints as well as compliments. But, once they cleared that hurdle, issues began being addressed promptly.

The Council, which had only planned on meeting once or twice a season, had its hands full and became a permanent part of the warp and weft of every citizen's life.

Some of Lord Südermann's more adventurous younglings took up residences around the walls and soon the population was as polyglot as any ever imagined before.

Before crime could become an issue, the Council conscripted the surviving members of the Naradhama army into an effective police force. They had to be taught some self-restraint, since beating someone to within an inch of their life for every perceived infraction wasn't as productive as they might have wished, but within two Full Suns, they were an accepted and useful part of normal life.

The one thing which caught the residents of the Plains by surprise was how quickly the Naradhama took to naming themselves. Well, that and how odd the names were they chose. Having no basis or family histories to work from they just chose names at random out of news sheets and dictionaries. It was very hard for folks to keep a straight face when they were introduced to someone claiming to be Effluvia of the House of Dingle, a former weapons master of the Naradhama.

But they managed as best they could, for the most part.

The courtyard, once the home of Xhaknar's military might, became an ongoing bazaar run by the Din-La. With subtle encouragement from Geldish and Lord Südermann, new gadgets and technologies were proudly available for sale. If the Din-La had given up the secret of the radio, they still had many others. Plus, they found folks liked being able to get news from the other warrens as it was happening, so they set up one channel and dedicated it to that. From breaklight to even-fall, it would broadcast all the news from each warren and then from even-fall to breaklight it would broadcast music. Soon every tavern and every shop on the Plains had a radio tuned to that frequency. And, where the infrastructure could support it, so did many homes.

The Din-La were taken aback when some of the shops and taverns began asking how much it would cost for them to get a mention between stories. But not for long. Soon their radios were making them even richer with a ten sepi-clik mention going for half a golden.

By the fifth Full Sun, Anapsida had completed its transition from calamity to a dream.

Elzish and Makish were strolling through the grove. Much to their delight they'd discovered they enjoyed their new tenants. They'd been isolated for far too long. It wasn't until the arrival of the Wolfen, and the emergence of the Kgul and, even, the insertion of a small contingent of Din-La, they'd noticed they'd missed living, sentient, beings.

Even the uncomfortable, yet innocent, questions from the various smalls delighted them.

It was during their conversation with a Wolfen small named N'glar, just after the war, they became aware the Plains had a problem. The darling little femme had asked the most innocuous question possible and it had set off a chain of events which had ended up spanning four Suns.

"What's going to happen to the sna-Ahd weasels and pit-people now that the sands are going away?"

That was a very good question.

And there was no good answer.

No one had a clue how many of the creatures were strewn across the Plains. But they had a pretty good idea where they were. They tended to congregate about halfway between Anapsida and the Minotaur's realm. They stretched from two to three kays south of Go-Chi all the way down to about ten kays north of the lands of Lord Südermann.

It took several meetings with the Din-La and their ecology experts but, finally, a plan was devised to herd the creatures and help them migrate to the wastelands north of Lord Südermann's realm and well east of the mountains.

There was a vibrant ecosystem there with plenty of food and no threat of armies marching over them on their way to or fro. They could thrive there. Who knew? Maybe some turn they may join as citizens of the world.

The Din-La seemed to think it was possible long Suns from now.

The herding process had been difficult but mostly due to logistics. The creatures, themselves, seemed to enjoy it.

The Din-La had set up a scrimmage line of wagons over four hundred kays long. Each wagon was spaced about a kay and a half from the next and all were laden with food and tiny bells. They'd long known the creatures were attracted to the sounds of bells.

They had no idea why. That secret had probably died with Rohta.

They marched only in the dark. The creatures were very uncomfortable in the light. Other than that the weather seemed to bother them at all. Raging heat, blistering cold, none of it. They'd just keep moving happily along.

Not all of the creatures followed. About ten percent stayed behind. They seemed to like their changing surroundings. The herders decided not to force the issue.

To keep the warrens from panicking they'd made sure to provide turn by turn updates of their progress and let everyone know about the reasons for the move. The entire process became known as N'glar's Adventure. Since that was as good a name as any, and it at least had the benefit of being relatively accurate, the Din-La made sure to use it whenever they could.

But after four Suns, and Rohta knows how much expense, the creatures were repatriated. Displaying, Din-La provided, images of them frolicking in their new home became a fad for a while.

That fad seemed to be fading now and Elzish and Makish were privately glad. The creatures were far from adorable.

Ben el Salaam quickly thanked Allah the Most Merciful for getting him here safely and then, sitting on his steed and staring at the scenery, began to wonder exactly where "here" was. When the Din-La trading post in his village had announced the fall of Xhaknar five Full Suns ago, it had been met with skepticism. But, now, with new items showing up from the Plains in almost every shipment, it was determined the rumors had to be checked out.

He'd decided to take the safest route to the south and then come up to the youngling pass and use it for cover until he could cut north again. But the youngling pass was now a river. And a wide one at that. Worse still, he could see barges on it, so that meant he'd likely be detected if he followed the shore until he could cross.

The land, which Ben had surveyed almost fifty Full Suns ago, was now lush and on its way to being luxuriant. His steed huffed and he patted it absently on the neck as he considered his options.

There weren't many. Certainly, none which were useful.

He pulled his magnifying goggles out of his saddle pack and looked up and down the river. About two kays to the east was a dock and it looked as though it had a ferry.

No way around it then, spy or no spy, he'd have to mingle with the local populations. That would not be easy. His brand, like the Minotaurs, had been bread from bovine stock, but unlike the Minotaurs, his brand had feet instead of hooves and was far less muscular. They'd been bred to be functionaries but had learned to be farmers well enough after the war.

And some, like Ben, had even learned to be warriors. But no one with sight would mistake him for a Minotaur. He tried to think of a useful lie if asked where he was from and decided there weren't any. If asked, he'd tell the truth and just say he was here to check out the possibilities of trade. That was close enough to the truth Allah would not strike him dead.

He turned his steed to the east and began heading towards the docks. Less than half a clik later he came upon the entrance to the ferry and read the sign. It would cost him a tenth of a golden to cross. That was as fair a price for a ferry as he'd ever seen so he dismounted and walked to the hut where he assumed he'd have to pay.

A tall Succubus came out to greet him. She was wearing a simple breast wrap and loin cloth but still looked as though she could give Ben a fierce battle if it came to that. However, she turned out to be extremely gracious and gregarious. When asked where he was from he answered, in the manner he'd recently agreed with himself, and was surprised to see her smile even more.

"We welcome new business on the Plains. Keep your goldens and take the path to the left when we get across. That will take you towards Anapsida. It's about a seven turn journey, but once there you can register with the Elder's Council and they'll take care of all your needs."

She went on like that for the entire crossing and then, after Ben had remounted his steed, gave it a playful slap on the rear and wished him well. One thing was clear to Ben as he rode down the appointed path, Xhaknar was well and truly gone. There was no way a fringe dweller would have been working for a living under his rule.

A few cliks up the road he came across a wagon train also heading to Anapsida. Lacking any useful plan he asked to join them and was immediately welcomed.

They might be infidels, according to his Imam, but they were really nice infidels. Ben felt he was going to like it here. He smelled hope at every curve in the road.

Four really smart Mayanorens stared at sheet after sheet of print outs. When they'd arrived five Full Suns ago, they were surprised to find the facility in as good of condition as it was. They'd soon realized it had been built to be self-sustaining. Except for two small rooms, where the machinery had broken down, everything was pristine. As foretold by the ones who'd sent them on this mission, they'd found the notes of the makers readily enough. Within a season they were ready to decant one of the super soldiers.

The process had gone exactly as ascribed in the notes and, using a secondary method they'd found for speeding up the steps to sentience, they had a fully aware super soldier in one Full Sun. He called himself Dagnar. They'd come to realize the super soldiers got their names from their tank designations. Dagnar had been DG-nr 1793. The 'nr' stood for non-replicating. Xhaknar had been in tank XHK-nr 2034 and Yontar had been in tank YNT-r 1305. Yontar would have been able to replicate had a super soldier with a uterus been decanted.

They found it all interesting, but not enough to care.

Dagnar had proved very useful in many regards. When the Mayanoren refugees from Anapsida and the garrisons began showing up he had them completely organized and settled in just ten turns. After that, they'd cleaned and ordered the hothouse the original four had ignored since it was too much work to fix. Within twenty more turns, they had a functioning garden and access to plenty of produce. Hunting parties were arranged to provide the meat.

Now, with other smart Mayanorens able to assist, they'd really begun pouring over the voluminous amounts of paperwork, looking for a solution to the problem that brought them here. In that effort Dagnar was useless. He claimed he could feel Yontar from time to time and even let him share his senses, but that was all. There was just no way for him to clear his mind enough to allow Yontar to take over.

Now, though, they'd hit on a possible solution. They would decant another YNT tank and leave it non-sentient. Then, with Dagnar's guidance, Yontar should be able to overcome the empty mind and slip his bonds in the nether realm. A simple solution to a complex problem but one that would, and should, work.

Dagnar informed them Yontar approved and the work was begun.

And the sheets they were staring at so assiduously were telling them the results. For three turns the meters and dials had remained almost flat. A blip here, a blink there, but nothing to indicate transference had occurred.

Now, however, the readings had gone off the charts. The body, wisely secured by Dagnar the instant it was decanted, was now twitching and bucking in its restraints. Something had clearly happened, but what? Was Yontar back in full or had they merely doomed him to another type of lingering death?

They looked again at the print outs and decided there was no way to know right now. In a few turns they'd have their answers, good or ill, so all they could do was wait.

They assigned a couple of not-so-smart Mayanorens to guard the door and retired to their chambers to do exactly that.

Yontar felt as though his mind was being sucked through a straw. Every fiber of his being, for lack of a better word, was being ripped asunder and peeled apart. The pain was worse than any he'd ever encountered or even imagined. But he was unable to stop it and every sepi-clik it just grew more intense.

Finally, unable to withstand the agonies anymore, he attempted to retreat to the nether realm. But that, for some reason, was denied him. The vortex he was in was too strong. He tried to push forward to end this one way or another, but the straw he was being sucked through only allowed so much in at one time. He was trapped in a litany of tortures.

He began to feel blackness closing in around him. The edges of what he could perceive were now hopelessly blurred. Flashes of images and lights dominated his vision. Pain seared through him, each lance more white hot than the one before, and, eventually, and somewhat gratefully, the darkness became complete.

King Gornd stood in the palace parapet, looked around the turret's walls and beamed. His BadgeBeth had done an exemplary job. The exterior wall was built of stone and mud, fused by the workers into a product harder than steel. The palace itself wasn't very big, but with most of his brand living underground, it didn't need to be. Granq, Sland's brother, had led the construction efforts and approved all the designs.

There were stables for the deisteeds, two courtyards for common use and a smaller one with a garden for Gornd and his invited guests to relax in. As built, the palace could easily house three thousand brands. That was enough.

Around the palace were many farms which had sprung up when former Naradhama slaves had arrived and, with the assistance of BadgeBeth citizens, begun cultivating the newly fertile soil. The former slaves worked hard and appreciated their freedom. Gornd, for the most part, left them alone. They brought in fresh meat and produce to the, now ubiquitous, Din-La trading post and traded for goods and services that made their lives easier.

The Naradhama mingled freely with the BadgeBeth and life was better for all involved. With the Elder's Council having formed a true army of the Plains, all he needed was a token guard to handle ceremonies and some basic police duties.

He preferred that. He was not one to complain about life being too peaceful.

By now a full two-thirds of his brand had regained the old talents for working the soil. He, alas, was not among that number. Try as he might all he could accomplish was getting dirty. He'd given up several Suns ago and settled into the routine of running his developing warren.

He heard voices running around one floor below him and smiled some more. His smalls must be back from their lessons. They were bright and funny and constantly getting into mischief. Which was fine with Gornd, he wouldn't have them be any other way. He felt sure, someturn, when he retired his warren would be in good claws.

He walked down the winding stairs in the parapet and headed over to the chamber where he knew his smalls would be congregated, working on their lessons. His three mates had given him six beautiful smalls and he was proud of each and every one of them. Upon seeing him they jumped up and ran to get their allotment of hugs and kisses, which he dutifully doled out. He wanted to be a stern parent, as his father had been, but didn't seem to have it in him when he was in their presence. He ended up sitting on the floor and playing games with them.

His second mate, Dlarg, came in and laughed.

"If only Xhaknar were still alive. This scene would have scared him to death. One of the Great Kings, so unconcerned with affairs of state that he has time to play handsies with his smalls."

He rose, laughing as well, and gave her a kiss on the cheek.

"You're right of course. This would truly terrify him. Sometimes it terrifies me. They are such wonderful smalls and I want them to grow up in peace."

She caressed his arm gently.

"You and yours have fought a great battle to bring peace to the Plains and to keep it safe for many, many, Full Suns to come. If the Mayanoren should one turn come back, then you will do what Great Kings do and send them away in much smaller numbers than when they arrived."

He laughed again. Her confidence was a lift for his soul. She was right too; if trouble came he'd learned he could do what Great Kings were supposed to do. He could meet it on the field of battle and defeat it. He kissed her again on the cheek and walked down the hall to the small room where he did his warren's growing amounts of paperwork.

He knew, sooner rather than later, he'd need to hand

this work over to assistants but, for now, it made him feel useful and he found he enjoyed the minutiae more than he might have imagined.

Karrish saw Geldish meditating in the garden, which is where he usually was these turns, and walked over to him.

"I cannot sense Yontar."

"Nor I," came the muted reply.

"Has he escaped?"

"I honestly do not know. I can see the damage he did trying, once again, to escape, but I can't find his essence either in the nether realm nor this one. Even if he'd died in the attempt, I still should find something. But there is nothing. Not a whisper. It's as if he found some third realm to hide in, one we cannot feel."

"I've never even heard of such a realm. Do you believe one exists?"

"No. Just as the nether realm affects this one, and back again, we would have noticed the result if not the realm itself. Nevertheless, while I may not know where he's gone, I know where he was in relationship to this realm.

"The Brittle Riders are all visiting friends and family, I will assemble them in five turns in Go-Chi and we will ride west to find out what is there. It is someplace which has held Yontar's interest for the last five Full Suns, so it can't be a place that bodes well for the Plains no matter what."

"Will your riders be enough? Shouldn't you take a battalion of the Plains' new army?"

He shook his head and sighed.

"No, this is a scouting mission only. It will take us twenty turns on nytsteeds to get there and I don't want to be slowed down."

"Where is this place?

"Out near the western sea, far north of the Fish-People. According to the Din-La maps, it is nothing but wilderness, however, I think there is more. Yontar's thoughts were unclear; I'm not sure if even he knew exactly what was going on, but he had grown more and more excited over the last Sun. Something or someone there gave him hope and that, my brothers, is never a good thing."

BraarB walked through the streets that made up the new section of the Se-Jeant warren. The breast plate, which had seemed so odd when she first wore it in the home of the haven lords so long ago now seemed to be a second skin. The entire south and east walls had been torn down and rebuilt two kays further out. A whole new enclave had been erected specifically for the Llamia. But, since some of the Llamia were already settled in Se-Jeant dwellings, that left new homes empty and they were filled with former slaves, Se-Jeants looking for more room and, of course, the remaining Llamia. It was a vibrant, bustling, mini-metropolis. She had to scoot out of the way as workers carried a large window that was being set in the new tavern. She looked inside and smiled as she realized the owner was a very smart brand. There was a wide rut around one side of the bar. Llamia could stand there and be eye level with any Se-Jeant who stood on the main floor. It would be a very welcoming place. She made a mental note to return when it opened.

She sauntered past the shops and homes and headed for a small park she'd noticed from the palace when she'd met with Empress ClaalD. She'd received Geldish's summons but had a couple of turns to herself before she had to leave. She spied a familiar face in the crowd and walked over to meet her friend.

"Patrol Leader Ata, how are you this turn?"

The fiction of his pretending to be a patrol leader had come out after the battle. When it was decided there'd been no intent to deceive on his part, he'd just followed Greko's lead, and because he'd performed so bravely in the battle with Xhaknar, and been appointed to the Elder's Council, they decided it wasn't worth pursuing and had promoted him, retroactively, to patrol leader so no one could say he'd lied.

He smiled and walked over to greet her.

"BraarB, it is good to see you again, how long will you be staying with us?"

"Just a couple more turns. I have to attend a meeting with Geldish in Go-Chi then."

"That's too bad. In five turns I'll be celebrating my birth turn and all of my family will be here. I know they'd have loved to have met you. They've never met a Llamia before because they live in the outer village."

"I'm sorry I'll miss it, but surely there must be some of them here now. Maybe we can get together for an even meal this turn or the next?"

He considered for a moment and then smiled.

"This turn. My parents are here as well as my sister and her husband. Next turn they have plans, but this even is free and I'm off duty. Say, even-fall?"

She agreed and he gave her directions to his home. He waved and headed off to wherever he was going in the first place. She had a few cliks before the meal so she took the opportunity to do some shopping and peruse all the new sights.

About a clik before even-fall she dropped her few purchases in her room at the palace and prepared to go to Ata's home. She turned to leave and was stopped by the sight of Empress ClaalD standing in her doorway.

"Empress? May I help you?"

"I see you've been shopping. Find anything

interesting?"

"The whole new enclave is interesting. And there are several shops and taverns that aren't open yet I hope to visit when I return. Plus, the park the Se-Jeant added is a thing of beauty. I could spend turns there happily."

"I agree, I wish I could get out more, but my duties have largely kept me here. So what plans do you have for enjoying this even?"

"My friend Ata's family is in town to celebrate his birth turn. Since I won't be here for that we are having a casual get together at his home. His family is from the villages so they've never met a Llamia. I'm not sure how things will go."

"Ata? Isn't he one of the heroes of the war?"

"Yes."

She paused to consider for a bit and then smiled.

"One Llamia is an oddity, two would be better. Would you mind if I tagged along?"

"Empress?" BraarB was actually shocked.

"Oh, relax, BraarB. My duties for the turn are done, King Uku is meeting with the Elder's Council on a few minor matters and I dislike dining alone. Besides, it'll do me good to feel the city beneath my hooves. As I said, I need to get out more. Just let me grab my breastplate of rank and I'll meet you here in a couple of epi-cliks."

She turned and left before BraarB could object. She returned shortly thereafter with a couple of courtiers, clearly losing their minds, following behind her. She turned and snapped at them.

"I am being guarded by one of the Brittle Riders and I'll be dining in the home of a war hero. If you think you can protect me any better than them I'd like to hear how."

She stamped her hoof in disgust and walked out with BraarB, both of them trying to hide their laughter.

When they got outside, they stopped trying.

The walk over to Ata's home was pleasant and

uneventful. When they arrived BraarB knocked on the door and was greeted by an elderly Se-Jeant she didn't know. Well, in for the grass, in for the goldens, that's what her mother always used to say.

"Almsa Elder, I am BraarB, princess of the Temple of Azarep and honored a member of the Brittle Riders and this is Empress ClaalD of the Sacred Lairs of the Llamia. We have been invited by our friend Ata to share an even meal with him and his family. Is he here?"

The old brand stood gibbering for a moment before whimpering out Ata's name.

Ata came to the door, recognized the empress and bowed. Then, for lack of anything better to do, invited them in.

The meal, prepared by Ata's mother, was delicious. And if Ata looked as though he was going to die from embarrassment due to the indelicate questions his family asked the empress and BraarB, he'd forgotten she was a princess now, the two Llamias took it all in stride and seemed to have a very good time.

Ata finally pulled himself together near the end of the even and went and grabbed the new picto-recorder he'd purchased at the trading post. After making sure everyone got their image taken with the empress and BraarB, they were too big to fit in one frame, he was surprised when the empress asked for copies of each image for her private collection.

Ata slipped out with them when the even was over and whispered as quietly as he could in BraarB's ear.

"Why in Sweet Rohta's name did you bring the empress?"

Sadly, for Ata, given the height difference, he wasn't as quiet as he'd hoped and the empress heard him anyway.

"Because, my dear Ata, I was bored and this sounded like fun. And, to be honest, I'm more glad I came now than when I first horned in on BraarB's invitation.

You have a charming family and your mother's an excellent cook. My staff could learn a thing or three from her.

"Also, I understand your birth turn is coming up. Please accept my invitation for the breaklight after to visit the palace and allow me to show you and your entire family around. While my cooks may not rival your mother, I'm sure they can prepare a suitable meal."

Now it was Ata's turn to gibber like an idiot. He managed to barely mutter out a simpering "Yes, Empress" while bowing repeatedly as he backed into his home.

They realized he must have told his family about the invitation when they heard his mother scream "Oh Sweet Rohta, what the Zanubi am I going to wear?"

Chuckling all the way, they had a very pleasant walk back to the palace.

R'yune and Sland had also received Geldish's summons, looked around and realized they were already where they were supposed to be. While they were more formerly attired than when they'd first come here almost six Full Suns ago, they still resembled workers more than princes.

Brek was sitting with them, sharing skank and stories over a plate of imported meats. The three had originally gotten together to see if they could come up with a better name for the haven lords than the one they had. Sland had borrowed a copy of the history of the brands from the Minotaurs and had shared it with them for the last three turns. As best they could figure the haven lords were descended from a breed called Mutts and no one liked that name.

They'd finally agreed to just let everyone continue to call them haven lords. As R'yune had signed, "The haven lords served with honor in the war and are an integral part of the new army. There is nothing wrong with being known by a respected name."

With that behind them, they'd settled in for some meaningless relaxation.

From breaklight to even-fall, R'yune and Sland would tour the city and gawk like tourists at the many changes which had occurred since the war. Each even they would retire to the haven bar and enjoy the music playing on the radio.

Brek had arranged for accommodations at the haven lord's home so they really didn't have to think about anything until Geldish arrived. And, judging by the amount of skank they were imbibing, thinking was one thing their brains were clearly not doing.

R'yune attempted to sign for another round and instead asked for a ball. That produced more laughter than it had earned, but they were all pretty drunk.

Brek called for a carriage, gave instructions to the driver and poured the two besotted warriors onto the seats.

He walked back into the tavern and watched as his son, soon to be a brand, expertly cleaned all the tables and began preparing the stock for the next turn. He'd already been told the boy was going to join the army and serve the Plains. He'd even taken, and passed, the preliminary exams. He was very proud of his son.

Yes, with a future like that what did a name matter? He was a haven lord and now that was something he could be proud of.

P'marna snuggled deeper into N'leah's bosom. She'd heard the breaklight summons but didn't want to give this up. She let her right wing caress N'leah's sleeping flesh and breathed in the sweet smell of her body. Every even had been pure bliss. She'd kept her word to Greko and had asked her about the many forays into unknown lands. N'leah had merely shrugged and said they weren't important, that Geldish was looking for something he hadn't found.

After business was out of the way, the rest of the time was nothing but pleasure.

Queen A'lnuah, knowing she wouldn't get any work done anyway, had just given her some time off. P'marna had seemed genuinely chagrined when the queen had personally brought the summons from Geldish but, as N'leah pointed out, if it was important he would have said leave immediately and not in a couple of turns.

P'marna knew N'leah could stay even longer if she just flew to Go-Chi instead of riding her nytsteed, but N'leah had been adamant, saying the animal had saved her life countless times and she would surely need it for whatever adventure Geldish had planned.

So she took the moments life gave her.

She heard a soft sound behind her and glanced over to see one of the servants setting down a tray of food and two pitchers of something. Since the room was warm, thanks to the Minotaurs' lava flow, there were no covers on the bed.

The servant, dressed in a simple breast wrap and skirt, smiled and then curtsied.

"Queen A'lnuah said you would need to eat eventually. There are spiced waters in the pitchers and the food is freshly made. Enjoy your turn mistress."

She left politely enough but P'marna was sure this particular scene would be described in detail all over the palace before she could roll over.

She then thought about the servant's outfit. While on the fringe clothing was pretty much a loin cloth and whatever else you might need, life in a formal court required a bit more modesty. She found she enjoyed wearing pretty things. If for no other reason than to revel in the feeling of N'leah removing them slowly each even.

That thought brought a flush to her cheeks and she began slowly nibbling on N'leah's nipple. She woke with a soft moan and soon directed P'marna's lips to more direct purposes. The food would be long cold by the time they got out of bed.

The four very smart Mayanorens stood looking at the test subject through the window. For two turns the body had been violently electric. Since then it hadn't moved at all. The machines said all the vital signs were stable and the skin had a healthy pallor, but nothing seemed to be happening. Dagnar said he couldn't feel Yontar at all anymore.

They weren't given to fretting but they were worried. Had they brought back Yontar only to trap him in a brain dead husk?

That appeared to be the case.

There were many notes from the makers on what to do to resuscitate a body, but they weren't needed here, what was needed was a way to resuscitate a brain. And, even if they did, who was to say there was anything there to revive in the first place?

They looked over the original progress reports written about Yontar. They were astounded to find out the makers had thought him a failure. He had too much individuality for their needs. They'd kept him alive so they could study him and figure out what went wrong before decanting anymore. They'd also deemed Lord Xhaknar a failure. He suffered from what the makers called megalomania. They'd looked up the definition and decided it fit. These were not traits the makers encouraged.

Although they didn't know it, but they would probably have guessed had the question come up, these four smart Mayanoren were the most well versed brand on the planet when it came to the science of the makers. The learning curve had been steep, but they had the foundation of generations of research with which to build from and very keen minds with which to assimilate it.

The second project they'd been tasked with turned out to be more straightforward once they figured out the machines. By using their own DNA, with some modest - and easy to do - improvements, they had a thousand more like themselves who would be ready for decanting in less than a Full Sun. They'd already found the racks holding more old style Mayanorens waiting to be decanted and had destroyed them. They were looking forward, not back.

But, for all their successes, they stared through the window at the prostrate form and worried. And for very good reason. For as smart and arrogant as they were, they were also intelligent enough to know their weakness. They had not been bred to lead. Without a leader, they may as well stay in the forest and become farmers.

Dagnar was not the answer either. While he showed a keen military mind, he fell well within the personality parameters sought after by the makers. He could take orders well enough, but he no more belonged at the front of an army than they did.

So they waited and watched and hoped.

Geldish walked into the haven bar just after even-fall. R'yune, N'leah, Sland and BraarB were waiting for him at a table near the middle of the bar. Although not in their royal finery, all of them were well dressed. He smiled as he thought back to how far they had come. All except BraarB would have probably died on the fringe. Now the fringe didn't exist and they were princes and princesses representing a hopeful future. No longer feared in the haven bar, citizens walked over and thanked them for all they had accomplished.

He saw, as well, they had dressed to cover their scars. Even with their incredible healing abilities, the war with Xhaknar had left its marks, both physically and mentally.

As he sat down Brek walked over with a fresh flagon of skank. He marveled at the haven lord. Once a cowed servant he was now a proud member of the council of Go-Chi and a veteran, even if from the sidelines, of a horrible war. Geldish remembered him in the healing tents, bandaging wounds, getting food, reading letters to the wounded, whatever needed to be done. No, he may not have fought in the war but he had helped them survive it.

He waited until Brek left before beginning.

"Yontar is missing."

Sland looked utterly baffled.

"How can that be? The ass eating weird little rat-like man was trapped in a place no one could get out of. I know, I was there."

Geldish nodded and tried not to laugh at the obvious contradiction.

"Even so, he's gone. I can't find him here or in the nether realm. But I know where he had focused all his time and energies on and I want to go there. Since I don't know what I'll find, I can only ask that you go on this mission, not command it."

R'yune tapped the table for attention and began signing.

"You once talked us into marching on Anapsida with forty troops, and we came out alive. You say where, we'll go."

Everyone concurred.

Geldish laughed.

"Fair enough. We'll be going to a place near the western ocean, well north of the Fish-People. The land is supposed to be fallow, but something's there, something that riveted Yontar's attention.

"We'll leave at breaklight. We'll need to go to Anapsida first to pick up some items I had Zrrm order for us and then we'll go towards whatever it is Yontar found so fascinating."

The conversation turned to chit-chat as they caught each other up on their last few turns and then they went to the home of the haven lords for a good even's rest.

Come breaklight, barely, they were all outside in the main courtyard. Although they all carried new weapons they were dressed as utilitarian as could be. No longer trying to fit into polite society, they looked like what they were; the finest warriors Geldish had ever seen.

Before the sun was fully in the sky they were two kays west of Go-Chi headed for Anapsida. They kept their nytsteeds at a steady speed that would have winded a deisteed, or killed a steed, and didn't even slow down for their mid-break repast, simply eating from their packs as the ground passed by below them. BrraarB, having been bred for a pace like this, just stayed in formation and enjoyed the view.

As far as anyone on the Plains knew nytsteeds were the only creatures completely created by a brand. The weird little snake-like creatures were mutations, but not an original thought. Developed by the wizards before Xhaknar came, they were larger and more powerful than a deisteed, and as fast as a racing steed, but had the stamina to keep the pace for turns, not epi-cliks. The wizards had planned on using them for exploration, but Xhaknar came before that plan could be put into effect. Instead, they became the exclusive war steeds of the Rangka. Their original making was a closely held secret and their subsequent breeding was an art only shared with the Kgul.

One other thing set them apart from other steeds, like the Llamia they had cloven hooves with razor sharp points rather than the more traditional variety. Each could, if the need arose, be a very potent weapon as well.

Done with the duties of the turn Lord Südermann turned her attentions, once again, to her father's diaries. While he'd always been a good father, and attentive to her and her studies, she felt, rightly so, she'd been denied a chance to get to know him fully. Her ongoing perusals of his diaries proved that.

While she thought of him as loving and funny she hadn't realized he was also very wise and had never stopped trying to learn more about their world. He had an ongoing fascination, almost a fetish, with the history of the makers. And he had used what he'd learned to help guide their society.

She saw now how he had picked and chosen between possibilities to allow them to carve a new path. An exciting one too. The experiments going on in the secret labs of the Südermenn would, someturn, allow them to touch the stars.

He had an entire section devoted to the concept of mechanical humanoids. It seems the makers had the technology to build machines that could think for themselves but never widely built them. Apparently, the majority of folks were scared silly of them. Plus, there was some cult worried about their "impending robot overlords" and something about the "veritable Omnius."

She could look up more about those terms later, their overall meaning was clear enough. And, of course, there had been the Plato war. That would surely have put a damper on that line of research.

Nevertheless, due to these concerns, they limited what machines could and could not do.

She was surprised to read the technology for the sentient machines was still extant. Her father even noted where it existed in the main library. She wondered why he hadn't built any.

Then a cold dark thought bit into her heart. He didn't need to build any, he was surrounded by them. The makers, looking for a way around the restrictions, had built sentient machines. Not out of wire and metal but of flesh and blood. She and all the other brands were the results of that compromise.

She wondered if, given sentience, the machines would have done what her ancestors did. She had to believe they would. Anything that can tell the difference between freedom and slavery will opt for the former. Even a caged bird proves that.

While she'd known as a small none of the brands kept caged animals, except for food and commerce, she'd always assumed it was a peculiarity she didn't understand. And even then, by the standards of the makers, their stock animals lived wonderful lives.

Now she saw the tradition's darker roots. Decanted fully formed, with striking intelligence and then forced to be slaves for uncaring masters, the resulting rebellion was obvious in hindsight. Her kind could never do that to another species.

Her brand had not been designed to help with tasks humans could, or would, not do, her kind had been built to replace the machines humans could not have. They had been nothing more than expensive tools in the eyes of the makers.

What the makers had forgotten was tools, in the right hands, could be very effective weapons as well.

Ben el Salaam crossed the rise just after his evenfall prayers and saw Anapsida. Far from the blood chilling edifice he remembered, this was a brightly lit and welcoming city. It was, in fact, a glistening monument to optimism. He rode through the open gate with the wagon train and decided to follow the Succubi's instructions. He immediately got lost and was forced to ask a Naradhama police officer for directions to the Elder's Council chambers. The burly Naradhama quickly gave him easy to follow directions and he was there in only a couple of epi-cliks.

Allah the Most Merciful be praised, even the Naradhama were friendly now. Well, thinking back on his brusque tone, *friendlier* at any rate.

He dismounted and tied his steed to the hitching post provided. He walked in and was greeted by two Naradhama femmes wearing name tags on their bright, yellow, blouses which had slashes of red and green on the left sleeves. It took him a sepi-clik to remember these were the colors of Rohta Industries, LLC, the makers provided by Allah to fill the world.

He turned to the one whose name tag read "Cornhusker" and explained who he was and why he was here. She nodded politely and led him to a desk across the room. There she presented him with some very nice pamphlets and explained, while the Din-La were the primary source of trade, they were not exclusive. That startled him but he kept it to himself as she continued.

She mentioned the bazaar in the courtyard was open every turn at breaklight and, should he see merchandise that interested him, there was a representative of each brand, or a proxy at least, in council and a meeting could be arranged directly. She then went on, as cheerful as ever, about the various inns and sights the city boasted. He was glancing at the price list for inns, several were very reasonable but a couple would cost more than his village earned in a Full Sun. He was about to ask what the difference was when a member of the Royal Mantis Guard walked by, cheerfully said hello to the femmes, and then walked past the desk and entered what could only be the main council chamber.

Ben must have looked as stunned as he felt because Cornhusker began happily pointing out how diverse the residents of Anapsida were. She also pointed out it was an open city and anyone on Aretti was welcome.

He doubted that was exactly true, but he understood her meaning.

A few epi-cliks later she had radioed a nearby inn, made his reservation, given him directions, and handed him a couple of thicker booklets which contained all the information she'd just imparted and more.

He went outside, untied his steed and decided to just walk over on foot as he perused the pamphlets. Allah be praised, but that femme was perky. While not normally a trait Ben liked, he had to admit her enthusiasm was infectious.

And why not? They may be infidels, but they weren't godless. He'd seen several houses of worship on his way in. Plus they had built something wonderful out of ruin. There was much to appreciate here, much to share. As he crossed the courtyard he noticed the vendors closing up for the even. He watched as Naradhama police set up patrols so they could easily see in any direction down the wide paths which had been provided for customers and tourists alike.

He vaguely wondered why they made it so easy to break in and steal something and then realized his error. A thief might get in, but with the way the police were positioned, and with the snap gate he'd see when he entered the city, there was no way to get out. They could, with just one shout, lock down the city in a sepi-clik.

He pondered the philosophy of a defense like that and smiled. Certainly, no thief could claim he'd merely stumbled into such and such a place because they would always catch him coming out with the goods. Yes, that would save much time in courts.

He was still smiling when he found the inn, exactly where the perky Cornhusker had said, and followed the path laid in front to turn his steed over to a stable hand and go to bed.

After a sound sleep, and an excellent breaklight repast, he headed out into the bazaar. Though the turn was early it was already crowded. He wandered aimlessly, letting the crowd dictate his movements, for several cliks. He made mental notes of several items that would be a boon for his warren and sampled the various cuisines. There was no way to keep Halal here and his Imam had known that before he left so he'd been given special dispensation within reason. He was still to avoid alcohol. Since Ben had never had a hard drink in his life that didn't bother him one whit.

Around mid-break, he saw the Brittle Riders enter the city. There had been many rumors concerning them as well, most of which sounded impossible, so they were on his list of things to confirm or deny. He watched them walk into the main Din-La office and emerge a few epi-cliks later with several bundles. These they strapped to the backs of their nytsteeds, creatures Ben had only thought rumors as well and headed for the gates.

Ben wasn't one of the best trackers on the eastern shore for nothing. He knew he could never keep pace with the nytsteeds, but he saw no reason he couldn't follow at a safe distance and find out what these mysterious riders were up to.

He hurried back to the inn, paid his bill, collected his steed and was off ten epi-cliks later. He passed through the main gate just in time to see the riders turn west around the far edge of Anapsida and took off in their direction.

His brand needed knowledge and he would bring it to them even if he still didn't know why some inns cost so much more than others.

Yontar tried to look around but everywhere was blackness. He tried to feel his body which had trapped him in the nether realms but that seemed to be gone too. He tried to feel anything at all and failed.

He wondered if he was dead for a while but decided against it. The realm of death, should it exist, would have many more souls than just his. Wherever he was, he was completely alone.

He tried to find Dagnar but came up with only hollow echoes.

He tried to sense anything and, slowly, became aware of a presence. It was very faint, non-sentient, but it was there. It was primal and powerful but still so very far away.

Without realizing it he headed in the direction of the thing, whatever it was. The presence got neither weaker nor stronger as he neared, just clearer. After a long time, one turn or one hundred he didn't know, he began to realize what it was.

It was him.

A more feral him, to be sure, but him nonetheless.

His memory, shattered and fragmented by whatever had just happened to it, began to coalesce. He remembered the smart Mayanorens and their desperate plan. He remembered Dagnar acting as a conduit. He remembered the pain.

That was a memory he could have done without.

Was it true? Was he in a new body? Could he take it over and make it work? Could he once again be Yontar?

Slowly he began to settle in. Excited by the prospects he was nevertheless very careful. He began to match the parts of his mind with their corresponding parts of a living brain. He was amazed at how many details there were to make everything work. From which neuron controlled which finger to what would make his mind whole again, every single item had to be accounted for.

He lost all track of time. He could tell, now, the

base functions of the body, breathing, pumping blood and so forth, seemed to be functioning automatically but everything else was numb. He began concentrating on those items first.

This was a finger, that was a toe. Gradually he began to assemble a body around his mind.

He noticed a steady beeping noise and concentrated on it. He was becoming aware of his surroundings. The beeping seemed to quicken, almost imperceptibly, and now had his full attention. After a little more time had passed he opened his eyes and was greeted by the sight of four, smiling, Mayanorens. One of them spoke.

"Welcome back Lord Yontar, you've been sorely missed."

He managed to gasp out "How long?"

"A little more than seven Full Suns since your battle with Geldish and eleven turns in this body. You had us very worried for a while, but everything seems to be working fine now. You must eat and rest for a few turns before you begin exercising this body. You'll find it a duplicate of your own except for the face. This one has a more defined brow ridge than you had before and the eyes are a little different as well. But, other than those trifles, you should feel right at home in it."

Yontar had never suffered from vanity before, at least not about his looks, so he decided he didn't care what face was looking back at him from a mirror as long as that face was truly looking back at him.

With the help of a couple of the smart Mayanorens, he was able to sit up and view the room. There was a bed and a private bath, and a small area set aside for eating or whatever else he might wish. His confusion must have shown.

"This room is sealed against the transmission of alpha waves. It is how the makers were going to control us. It is also how some of the more sensitive minds can track us. Geldish is certainly one such mind. We felt it best you be back to your full strength before you allowed him to know you were alive, again."

Yontar smiled broadly now. Yes, these were four very smart Mayanorens. Things were going to get very interesting with resources like this at his disposal, very interesting indeed.

Elaand made his way across the veranda into the palace and headed for the throne room of Lord Südermann. She used it far more than her father or his predecessor did. At first, he'd been afraid she'd assumed too much power too soon, but she'd confided in him she thought it was pretty. He smiled at the memory. Yes, she was the supreme ruler of all she surveyed, but she was also still a young femme. Best to let her enjoy the pretty things in life while she could.

He had to admit her first five Full Suns of rule had gone very well. She'd honored her father's wishes, since there were no written decrees, and solidified peace with the Plains. Instead of trying to create some overarching treaty she'd done it in small ways; a trade agreement here, some technology there, and so on. She'd helped make each dependent on the other so their mutual protection was a foregone conclusion.

When he entered the throne room he saw her beaming and swirling the sweet java drink she seemed to favor.

"I have good news Colonel. I've just gotten off the radio with Council Member Teg. The Council has approved my idea of having one thousand of our regular army troops exchange places with a thousand of theirs and then for them to serve two Full Suns in their new homes."

Elaand had liked the idea when she'd first broached it. It was another tie to bind them together.

"Congratulations your majesty. I know many of the enlisted personnel were excited by the prospect. I'm sure we'll have plenty of volunteers."

They both knew part of the excitement stemmed from the fact that every soldier who served in this exchange would receive an upgrade of one full rank upon their return. It was to be the same for the army of the Plains. But since each side would only send its best and brightest that should work out for the betterment of all too.

There's nothing wrong with competent and experienced officers.

He also knew the Plains were assembling their own elite guard, called the Imperial Plains Guardians. Maybe in a few Full Suns, once they settled on all their procedures, they could work out an exchange with them and the Royal Mantis Guard.

That was a dream for another turn. They quickly went over the arrangements and Elaand was surprised to find a small part of his mind enjoying the mundane. He'd thought he'd miss the action of the turn to turn military and was intrigued to find that not to be the case. Of course, the last battle he'd been in cost his forces over forty thousand dead and another thirty thousand wounded. It's hard to get sentimental for times like those.

When they finished she surprised him, again, with her keen insight.

"You miss my father, don't you?"

He couldn't lie to his leader so he said, "Yes, your majesty, very much. We were closer than ruler and subject, I thought us to be good friends."

"You were on the other side of the field of battle when he died, does that bother you?"

"Maybe not as much as it should, your majesty. It was chaos in the closing stages. There was nothing but bloody hand to hand fighting until the very end. He was protected by one hundred thousand soldiers of our army and, if they're not Guards, they were and are still very good. No, I made my peace with what happened. He gave his life so Xhaknar could be finally slain. I honestly think he made that choice of his own free will.

"He could have kept his steed back, behind the Brittle Riders, but chose to confront the monster himself. The one who seems to feel the worst about it is Geldish, though he would never admit it. I think this is what's behind his useless obsession with Yontar."

"I wonder if it is truly useless. Even if Yontar is well and truly dead, the Mayanorens are still missing and their ranks were far better formed, according to the reports I've read, than anyone could have expected. Something was happening to them, Yontar or no. Maybe Geldish will find out what."

Elaand considered and nodded. She was right. Whatever Geldish's motivation may be, there could come some good out of it if he found the Mayanorens.

Before he could leave, she handed him a small notebook.

"My father's final diary. It seems he was very fond of you. I'd like you to have it."

Stunned into silence he merely bowed and left the throne room clutching orders for the troops and the last thoughts of the only being he'd ever called a friend.

"Mooth, Schan, Elan!" Elder Urnak waited for the assembly to go quiet, which it did in very short order.

"Over the last five Full Suns, we have seen our world dramatically changed. Where once was barren land, now lie fertile fields. Where once we hid from the light to hide from Xhaknar, now our doors are open and we share our hearth with the Succubi."

He waited for the cries of HUSHAK! SUCCUBI! to die down and then continued.

"Hushak indeed. On both the fields of valor and the fields of play we have found staunch allies. It warms my hearth to know many now take this arrangement to be the norm, forgetting a mere seven Suns ago it was not possible to even dream it.

"Once we feared the mere name of Lord Südermann, now we are her allies and she sends us great wonders to make our lives easier. Of course, I think she gets the better end of the bargain since she gets so many of our pastries."

It took everyone a sepi-clik to realize Elder Urnak had made a joke. On purpose. They laughed approvingly, while still awed by the moment.

"Mooth, yes, I have a sense of humor. I did not know that until I met Queen A'lnuah," he motioned to his right where she was seated, "so count it among the many new blessings this alliance has given us.

"We now know the Temple of Azarep not only exists but flourishes with four Rangkas. Beyond Geldish we had not known any had survived after Ondom's failed rebellion. This applies, as well, to the Kgul whom the temple had managed to keep hidden all these Suns.

"When I saw them come down that mountain, five Full Suns ago, flanked by the Royal Mantis Guards, it was a sight I'll never forget. At that moment I knew we had won the day. Neither Naradhama nor Mayanoren could slow their attack. Yes, the fighting was long and bloody for many cliks after that, but I never doubted we would prevail, and we did!"

He hadn't intended for his voice to crescendo like it did and he had to wait for a couple of epi-cliks for the cheers to fade.

"Mooth, true, much is better now than any of us can remember. Anapsida is a center for trade instead of terror and our roads are as safe to travel as they've ever been. However, I remind you the Mayanorens are still out there. Where they went is unknown. What their plans are is a mystery. But we do know they were bred to kill and they will be back.

"It was due to that very thought the Elder's Council created the army of the Plains. So that, never again, would we have to huddle and scheme in the dark. Never again be afraid to show our faces to the Sun.

"It is in this new spirit of hope that I am pleased to announce the Se-Jeant and the Llamia have finished the new additions to the south and east walls and have invited any who wish to come to enjoy the new shops, parks, and homes. They are opening their doors to any traveler starting in five turns for a period of seven turns. You may stay at inns if you wish, or you may simply knock on any door and ask for lodgings. If they have space, you will be welcomed."

That brought a huge cheer from the crowd. Bovinity scholars or no, they loved a good party as much as the next brand.

He went on to explain how it was the idea of King Uku and Empress ClaalD to celebrate their new alliance. He then announced the winners of the kick ball tournaments and presented their awards. After that, he turned the dais over to an aide to handle any travel arrangements and dismissed the assembly.

Queen A'lnuah followed him back to his antechamber and poured them each a cup of korlnak.

"You are more worried about the Mayanorens than I thought."

"Yes," he sighed, "they were in much better ranks than I'd ever seen. While it's true the Fierstans and BadgeBeth broke them, that was as much due to surprise as skill. I doubt they'll be fooled by that trick again. Quite honestly A'lnuah, I watched their general reform their ranks. The moves he made were smart. As smart as any general we have. Smart Mayanorens are a scary thought. They're already deadly.

"I lose sleep over it almost every turn. I will feel

much better when we know where they went and what they're up to. Until then we must remain ever vigilant."

She thought about it as she sipped the rich beverage. It hadn't really caught on with the other Succubi, but she counted it as one more tiny blessing from this alliance.

"Maybe so, I was with the Succubi far above the fray until the end so I did not see specifics. But, who cares? We have many smart brands too and we have many new allies to help us defend our plains. I'll not say it will be easy, I've too many scars for talk like that, but I think we can prevail against any intruder now."

He considered for an epi-clik and then nodded.

"Maybe you're right. I certainly pray you are."

They were seven turns into their journey. Geldish wasn't pushing the ride as hard as they'd thought he would but they were still making good time. Sland turned to face Geldish.

"Not that I think it matters all that much, but you do know we're being followed, don't you?"

"Yes. Since we left Anapsida. As best I can tell he's from the eastern shore and means us no harm. But, I've had to slow our pace and alter our path to allow him to keep up with us. There's a Din-La trading post about ten kays due west of us. Assuming Zrrm has worked his usual magic there should be a nytsteed there as well."

While they tried to figure out how even Zrrm could pull something like that off, they headed in the direction of the trading post. Less than a clik later they reined up and dismounted. The post was small but seemed to be doing a bustling business with a brand of Fish-People who lived in the nearby rivers. They were well south of their destination.

Geldish stretched and then melted into the ground. With nothing else to do the other four riders headed into the trading post. A Din-La, smaller than usual, saw them and smiled.

"Ahh," he beamed, "you must be Zrrm's Brittle Rider friends. So good to meet you. I am Kmmp, purveyor of this humble post. Your nytsteed is in the back stable and, I promise, it has been well taken care of. Nothing but the best for friends of Zrrm's, that's what I always say."

None of the riders had ever seen the west coast amphibians before and were just as curious about them as they seemed to be about the riders. However, they had no time to meet and greet as Kmmp led them through the post and out the back door to a small, but well kept, stable. The nytsteed was there and looked no worse for wear. In fact, it looked like it had just been washed and groomed. Its shaggy mane and furry body were perfectly coifed.

N'leah went over and petted it on the snout and handed it a treat. While they all wondered how the Din-La had gotten the animal across the continent ahead of them, none of them pressed the matter. Since they had some time to kill they went back into the post and ordered food.

About a clik later Geldish returned holding the reins of a steed and leading it, and its rider, over to the hitch so he could tie it up. The steed, that is, not the rider.

Once accomplished he turned to them and smiled.

"Princes and Princesses, meet Ben el Salaam of the Chaldea Clan from the eastern shore. He's been sent to find out what is, and is not, true about what happened to Xhaknar and the results on the Plains. We will leave his steed here for the Din-La to keep or sell, as they wish. He will be allowed to keep the nytsteed as proof he's been here and met us. He's asked to ride with us to see what we find and I have agreed as long as you harbor no objections."

They didn't, so he did.

It took them a while to get used to him having to stop for prayers five times a turn, but within two turns they had a routine down. Since his prayers didn't take long, they'd let him stop and they'd keep going at a slower pace until he caught up. Then they'd resume speeds only nytsteeds can attain.

He also named the beast Akbar, which he said meant "great" in his religion. Naming beasts was a quirk, but they'd seen far worse and went along with him.

Fifteen more turns into their journey Geldish halted them beneath a grove of massive trees.

"I can sense something getting clearer. It's Mayanoren, to be sure, but there's something else there too."

"Yontar?" asked BraarB.

"No, but there is intelligence there, far more than the Mayanorens have ever displayed. In fact, what I am sensing doesn't have any logic to it at all. Clearly, we are missing some of the facts. I suggest we make camp here, it's almost time for Ben's prayers anyway, and then head in after breaklight with fresh eyes.

"The Din-La packed you all magnifying goggles and extra weapons, so we should unpack everything and make sure all is in order."

That was as good a plan as any so that's what they did.

Ben had his own goggles so they didn't have to worry about him in that regard. They offered him some of the spare weapons but, since he was unfamiliar with them, he demurred. They broke down, reassembled, and then dry fired every weapon. They didn't want to make any noise which might draw attention to their camp.

N'leah noticed a giant hollow in one of the tree trunks so she went in and pulled fire from the land so they could cook.

They could all easily fit inside so they let the nytsteeds graze and huddled in the tree. The tree looked as though it had been hit by lightning millennia ago and then had just re-grown its deep red wood around the damage. They made a note to ask the Din-La if they knew what kind it was.

Later, after a good meal, they sat around and got to know each other better. Since Ben didn't drink alcohol they left the ice wine in its cask and sipped the spiced water or scented java they'd gotten at the last trading post.

Eventually, Geldish announced they'd need their rest to make sense of what they'd find come breaklight, so everyone went to sleep in the hollow of the tree.

Watcher Urkel walked past the stables and saw Nak talking to a few of the Naradhama who'd moved in. He knew from the regular reports his aides gave him they'd been integrated very well. He also said a silent thanks to the Elder's Council. They'd prevented a mass exodus by spreading the former slaves out all across the Plains. By diffusing the burden as they did, not one warren or village was forced to set up a refugee camp.

He'd been unsure if the council would work in the first place. None of the appointees were diplomats. Their experiences were as varied as their brands and they'd never worked together at all. Yet, within a few turns, they were identifying problems and proposing solutions. They avoided solutions which required any additional funding from the warrens unless there was no other choice. Because the members of the council were self-reliant in their regular lives, they adjusted the situation in Anapsida to fit their needs and the needs of the citizens of the Plains. Within a Full Sun, they were using the taxes generated in Anapsida to pay for all their needs. Within two Full Suns, they were sending stipends to the warrens. Within three Full Suns, they had the resources to build an army, so they did.

Now the council took care of the Plains in general and left the turn to turn governance to the warrens. That freed up resources each warren used to spend on defense and other duplicitous items and allowed them to make improvements on their home fronts.

They'd even hammered out a charter which prevented any council from imposing laws on the individual warrens or their villages. With a clear division of authority, lower taxes and increased trade, the council had become the most popular group on the Plains.

Urkel shook his head in amusement.

Well, if he was going to be wrong, he may as well be completely wrong.

Nak finished whatever he was doing with the Naradhama and walked over to meet him.

"Greetings Watcher, is all well with you?"

"Yes, Nak, I am fine as is the warren. In fact, I can't remember a time when things were better."

"So why the sullen expression?"

"Besides the fact there are thousands upon thousands of missing Mayanorens? A race which was bred for raw battle does not suddenly become subtle without help or cause. I'd be less surprised to see you fly. Yet for five Full Suns, this is what they appear to have been doing. If nothing else, call it an old brand's intuition, I smell something in the air and I don't like its scent."

Nak knew his leader was not given to whimsy. He'd seen him in battle and governing their warren. He was a true leader, born and bred, so Nak took what he was saying very seriously.

"Even if what you say is true, and bad tidings are coming, isn't the army of the Plains strong enough to deal with it?"

"I would imagine so. They've assembled a mighty, and very agile, force. I went to watch their war games last Sun and was as impressed as I could have been. They are better armed, better trained and better prepared than any army I've ever seen.

"Which reminds me, and you don't have to answer if you don't want to, but why didn't you join up when they posted?"

Nak paused, but only briefly.

"I serve you with honor, never forget that, but after the battle with Xhaknar, I believed I'd seen enough death and destruction. The chance to become the Vice-Lord of the warren and only have administrative duties appealed to me. In the two turns since I left the Guardians I've never been happier. In fact, next season I'm to be wed."

"So I heard. To craft master Onlam's daughter, Welhern, if rumors are correct."

Nak nodded and smiled.

"Yes," continued Watcher Urkel, "a beautiful femme by all accounts. And her family's done well since the council took over. Yes, that should be a good match for you. Congratulations."

"Thank you, Watcher."

"And Nak, never you worry. I'd no more doubt your honor or bravery than I would doubt the sun is going to rise each turn. I'm glad you've found happiness. It is something that eludes too many."

He bade Nak farewell and headed back into the castle.

King Uku had a new limp on his right side to balance the missing finger on his left. Although things were going very well generally, he still felt older than his age. He'd taken a spear behind his right knee during the battle with Xhaknar and it had never healed quite right.

He thought of announcing his retirement but couldn't bear to be forced away from ClaalD. He knew his love for her would have to remain unrequited but saw no reason to throw away what they had just so he could prop his wounded leg up on a divan for the rest of his turns.

So, he suffered through.

The open warren they were about to host was

completely set up. He'd been surprised at how well the idea was received when he and ClaalD proposed it. Some of the Naradhama, who'd never owned anything prior to this, were so excited to be able to show off their meager possessions it was almost sad.

Almost, but not quite. He and ClaalD had surprised a couple of them to get an idea of what guests might be in for. What they were treated to was a running monologue on how great King Uku and Empress ClaalD were and what a wonderful warren they lived in and what great jobs they had and so on. It finally dawned on them the Naradhama had no idea they were speaking to the king and empress, they were just truly happy to be here.

They decided not to embarrass their newest citizens and left them in peace. Whatever reluctance Uku had felt before was completely washed away by the experience. When even the poor extol the virtues of a place, it can't be all bad.

All in all, he should be happy, limp or no limp.

But something was bothering him, something important he'd missed and he couldn't, for the life of him, figure out what it was.

Seeing no other alternative he went to his throne room to take care of the turn's events.

Several cliks of dealing with trivia took his mind off his troubles. There'd been a couple of skirmishes between farmers over the rights to access the new water supplies. That one was easy. Every village had been given written instructions on who could access which ones when and for how long. He pulled a copy out, handed it to the belligerents and told them to learn to read.

The rest of the turn wasn't as much fun, but he did get a lot accomplished. The last group waiting to see him was a couple of monks. He had no idea what they wanted so he just waved them forward.

He almost fell off his throne when his old friend Mnaas pulled back his hood to reveal himself.

"What are you doing here, Mnaas?"

"Greetings your highness, I had business with one of your craft masters and, when I saw you were taking an audience this turn, couldn't resist the chance to surprise you."

"Well, you've certainly done that. My turn's work is done, won't you and your friend join me in my antechamber for a drink?"

That seemed like the greatest idea since the invention of air so they all walked across the throne room to Uku's antechamber. There they were greeted by Empress ClaalD who was talking with two Llamias he didn't recognize. They bowed when he entered and made their exit. Empress ClaalD's whole face smiled when she saw Mnaas.

His friend was a weapons master named Lwoor. He showed King Uku the upgrades they'd come up with and were being instituted as he spoke. Uku was impressed. The se-Jeant held the contract with the Elder's Council for several types of light weapons. These new designs were safer for the user and more deadly for everyone else. They should secure their position for many more Full Suns.

Whatever had been bothering Uku seemed gone with the setting Sun. He poured ice wine for everyone and ordered a plate of mixed foods be brought up. The friends, old and new, sat for a couple of cliks before Mnaas and Lwoor had to leave.

When they were alone ClaalD walked over and kissed him his cheek.

"We have survived much Uku. From this turn forward what will be will be. You have a beautiful warren and wonderful friends. Quit moping around the castle like a pouty small."

"You saw me, hunh?"

"Everyone did. You looked so bad I had to quell rumors of war."

She tried to look stern but eventually couldn't and

they both ended up laughing.

"By the gods, I love you." Uku hadn't realized he'd said it aloud until he saw ClaalD looking at him intently.

"And I you Uku. Would that our brands could mate as I would be proud to carry your foal. You are one of the kindest and most courageous brands I have ever met. But if we're denied a love like the younglings have when they think we're not paying attention, we still can carry each other in our hearts. That is enough for me."

She kissed him again on the cheek as she left and Uku sat there for a long while, with the silliest grin on his face, staring at the wall.

They began to hear echoes from a canyon ahead. There was activity there. They tethered the nytsteeds to some bushes and continued on foot. When they came to a thicket large enough for all of them to hide in they hunkered down and broke out their magnifying goggles.

It didn't take them long to find the source of the noise. There were ten thousand or more Mayanorens camped in a temporary village. There was a creature who looked like Xhaknar, but had enough differences to dispel the notion, and he was walking around issuing orders. There were three more Mayanorens behind him carrying clipboards. Geldish sensed fierce intelligence in them.

"So," he thought, "there really are intelligent Mayanorens. I thought I was going insane last turn."

While Geldish scanned the minds as unobtrusively as possible, BraarB began sketching the compound. R'yune saw what she was doing and handed her a picto-recorder he'd picked up at the trading post.

He quickly showed her how to use it and then signed "You know what you're looking for, I don't."

She nodded and began taking pictures. N'leah and

Sland eased off to the side to get a better position should they need to open fire. Ben sidled up next to Geldish and looked at the scene in dread.

"I know those are supposed to be Mayanorens, but how did they get so organized?"

"My guess would be Yontar. He's in the compound. But he surely had help from that giant who looks kind of like Xhaknar and those other Mayanorens carrying clipboards. I'm reading some very keen minds in that group."

"So you can pick him out now?"

"No, there's something blocking my senses in the building. But the others are all thinking about him. For someone like me, they may as well be waving a Yontar flag."

They lay there quietly for a while longer as BraarB documented some things, which she could only see with the magnifying goggles, to paper. After a while, she nodded to Geldish and the six of them backed out as quietly as they'd came.

When they got to their nytsteeds Geldish pointed east and they headed off without a word. It was a full clik before he stopped.

"We're too far away from anything to use the radio so I contacted Karrish and let him know all I know. He's assembling a memo the Din-La can broadcast. Whatever it is they're planning, it's obvious they're not ready yet. We'll need to devise a plan to keep this place under surveillance so we'll know when they make their move."

N'leah shivered for a moment and then asked the question everyone was thinking.

"What is that place?"

"It's a makers' facility. And, unless every mind I scanned is lying, they have it completely functional. They are less than one season away from decanting a race of super Mayanorens. There's some sort of shielding which prevents me from looking within, but it's clear from their thoughts Yontar is alive and inside.

"How that can be I don't know and I'm not really sure it matters. The fact is he's there and we're going to have to deal with him."

"True," murmured Ben, "but not for, at least, one Full Sun. Even with a hundred thousand Mayanorens at his beck and call, he'd be wiped out if he attacked the Plains. No, he's got to wait for those super Mayanorens, as you called them, and maybe a few more of those big soldier types."

They all agreed he was probably right.

"Actually," noted Geldish, "looked at rationally, not even that soon. Most of the Mayanorens there were garrison troops and Xhaknar never got around to issuing them the new weapons. He's going to need those, plus the enhanced troops before he can even begin to think about assaulting the Plains."

Sland seemed lost in thought and then turned to face them all.

"What if his first target isn't the Plains? What if it's Kalindor? Even with limited amounts of new weapons, he could probably overrun them."

Geldish laughed.

"Kalindor? Why bother taking them over, they'd be more likely to …" his voice trailed off, "join him."

"Pretty much what I was fucking thinking." Sland turned back to face the forest.

Geldish considered this more fully. Kalindor had the resources to make any weapons, just not the skill or the knowledge. Yontar could bring those missing items. And he could bring something else Kalindor lacked, true military strategies. The Kalindorian warriors are fierce and cunning but woefully unsophisticated. If Yontar became their leader the status quo would change rapidly. And there's something the Kalindorians could offer the Naradhama couldn't; some of those reptiloids can fly.

Geldish re-contacted Karrish and let him know their

fears, making sure to credit Sland for the theory. One can never forget the politics of any situation.

They rode on until even in silence, each imaging the new horrors and each remembering the last ones.

G'rnk sat with Karrish reviewing Geldish's message. A Kgul walked in and he waved him over and handed him the notes. After a bit, the Kgul spoke.

"The makers used to have machines that floated above the sky and could see everything."

"Yes," agreed Karrish, "they were called satellites, but they've all fallen to the ground by now. And, even if we had the designs, we just don't have the technology to make them work. Not even Südermann has that level of sophistication and she's much further along than most anyone else. My guess is she could build us an engine that would get an object up in orbit, but that's about it. The lenses and the rest would take many Full Suns of research and we just don't have many Full Suns."

"Relays," mumbled G'rnk, and then more forcefully "yes, relays would work. We would need to space scouts every twenty kays from that northern Din-La post to the facility. When Yontar begins to move the scout closest to the makers' facility could use one of those mini-radios to contact the next one and so on until they get the message to the Din-La who can spread it via their network. Then our army could move to intercept him before he reaches Kalindor."

After working it over in their minds they all agreed it was a good idea. If Yontar were allowed to reach Kalindor the Plains would never be safe. Neither would the realm of Lord Südermann.

They went out to the trading post and discussed everything with Zrrm. He agreed the plan would work and checked to make sure they would have the materials they would need. Then he sat down and composed a message to the warrens letting them know what Geldish had found and what Sland feared.

The responses to that message ran the gamut from complete shock to total resignation. War was coming to the Plains, again.

With nothing they could offer the warrens in the way of anything useful, G'rnk and the Kgul returned to their own brands to tell them the news.

While none of them were happy about it, they all complimented the Elder's Council for preparing wisely and asked what was needed from them.

G'rnk and the Kgul were never more proud of their brands than they were at that moment.

Karrish took the opportunity to update Geldish. After conversing with his Brittle Riders and the spy from the east, Ben el Salaam, Geldish reported they all liked the plan.

Zrrm transmitted the plan to the warrens and asked the Elder's Council to assign the scouts. The Din-La would provide whatever they needed. T'reena, the Succubi representative on the council, replied in the affirmative and asked to be allowed a couple of turns to work out the details.

Seeing no better options, Zrrm poured everyone a large glass of ice wine and sat down.

Imam Salim sat in the mosque and studied the message the Din-La had just given him. He was pleased to see Ben was alive and would return to his brand, inshallah. He idly wondered what sacrifices Ben had made to end up with the fabled Brittle Riders. He knew Ben to be a brand of strong faith and didn't worry about him showing up with some shiny idol claiming it was *the* new religion. But Ben had been forced to mingle with the infidels, that much was clear. It remained to be seen what, if any, taint clung to him.

The Imam shrugged those thoughts off. Worrying about Ben's faith was like worrying the sun wouldn't set. Some things were as certain as Allah would allow. Ben had been chosen for his faith. Strong, simple and enduring. He wasn't one of those crazies who wanted every infidel dead. Allah the Most Merciful be praised, they had long ago been culled from the herd. No, for Ben, his faith was simply something which was in the air around him or the ground below. He never questioned it. He simply breathed it and let it support him.

He'd also been chosen for a coldly practical reason. He was getting old. If, Allah forbid, something did happen to him it wouldn't weaken their clan. Sadden, yes, but weaken, no.

The Imam walked over to a low table in the entrance hall of the mosque and poured himself a small cup of the hot, bitter, drink they all enjoyed.

With worries about Ben's soul behind him, he studied the rest of the message. Military strategy wasn't his strong suit, but things were clear enough. War was coming to the Plains. And this war threatened to engulf the whole continent. He would have to wait for Ben's full report to understand the details. Since the news had come in from the Din-La he expected it to be all over his village by now. But it appeared they'd kept it quiet and only given it to him.

He did not understand those little creatures, with their purple jackets and yellow trousers. They were not of the true faith, that much was factual, but they were respectful and mindful of their manners. Their femmes wore the traditional hijab when they were in public and they closed their shops when prayers were called. They never had to be asked.

He supposed, in some way, it was a calculated move on their part to ingratiate themselves into the community and sell more goods. However, whatever their motives, they'd proved to his brand infidels could be trusted even if they couldn't be allowed to cook you a meal.

The Imam read the message again and sighed. There'd not been a jihad in almost eight hundred Full Suns. Not since the late Imam Shabaaz, may Allah have mercy on his gentle soul, was forced to declare one on the fanatics who threatened to turn the eastern shore into a bath of blood and flame. Imam Shabaaz went to meet Allah knowing what he'd done was the only thing he could have done and still hating it with his last breath.

Imam Salim understood the logic. Had his forbearer let the infidels destroy them, instead of acting directly, it could have fueled deeper hatreds which would, in turn, create more fanatics. No, that horror had to be destroyed by its own kind. But there was nothing in the Holy Qur'an where it stated he had to like it.

Through his Holy Prophet, Allah preached peace and charity, not war and destruction. How could they have gotten it so wrong?

He sighed again. Because they had tiny minds. They clung to the word "infidel" like it, and not the Laws of Allah was written in stone. They hated for hate's sake. Intellectually Imam Salim knew that Imam Shabaaz had been left with no other choice. Sometimes Allah gave someone a burden He knew only such a one as they could carry.

And now, sooner perhaps than he'd wish, Imam Salim was going to be faced with a similar burden. Would the report from a being of simple faith force his brand to pick up arms and march west to meet a demon? He hoped not.

Then he realized the decision wasn't his to make. He would pray to Allah for guidance this turn. And he would pray, furtively, the answer was no.

Ben and the Brittle Riders had settled into an easy camaraderie. All of them, save Geldish, had questions about his faith and wondered why he'd named his nytsteed. The back and forth banter was courteous and it helped to pass the time. He wished the femmes would be more modest, but they were warriors, not wives and they were not of the true faith. They had covered themselves with loose shawls when he'd mentioned how and why the femmes of his clan dressed the way they did. That would have to be good enough for now.

They'd spent two turns at the Din-La camp getting news and meeting the Fish-People. He had no idea what to make of them at all. Like him they were a brand of deep faith but, unlike him, their faith encompassed many things he didn't understand. He'd made notes of the more puzzling aspects so he could discuss them with his Imam when he returned home.

Maybe it just had to do with their being related to fish and Allah had given them a different perspective. Or not, since who can know the mind of Allah? Either way, they were pleasant enough and wildly curious about the Brittle Riders. They'd spent an entire turn questioning them about the events at Anapsida and the war. Ben had learned almost all he'd been sent to learn by just sitting in the post and keeping his mouth shut.

The Din-La, he had no idea how, managed to get him some Halal food and an urn of the bitter drink his brand favored. He thought he truly understood the phrase "Manna from heaven" now. It was truly a gift from above.

They'd even allowed him to fill his packs for the trip home. He'd noted every item had been wrapped and sealed with the Chaldean seal. No unclean hands had touched anything. These oddly dressed merchants impressed him more and more.

They were now less than a turn away from Anapsida. Ben had agreed to spend an even there and meet with the Elder's Council to let them know about his brand. It seemed only fair since, as Geldish had pointed out, ambassadors get free dinners and spies get hung.

He'd also spent some time letting R'yune show him how to use the new weapons. After some initial discomfort, he'd become as proficient with them as he was with his traditional array. R'yune let him keep a couple to show his warren.

He was still unsure what to make of the mute Wolfen. He and the riders had some language they spoke to each other, but it eluded him. Sland had tried to teach him some of it but watching those, razor sharp, claws click and thrust had held all his attention and he didn't understand any more now than he did before.

Nevertheless, even without a language in common, R'yune had proved to be a good teacher. He would patiently demonstrate a function until Ben had it down pat and then he would move onto the next. There seemed to be a deep mix of humor and pain in those dark eyes and Ben wished he could find out more.

Ben had encountered a lot these last few turns and was looking forward to discussing all of it with his Imam. But he knew the first topic of conversation would be Yontar, everything else could wait.

He mentally recapped his notes on their visit to the makers' facility. He had seen with his own eyes all the Mayanorens and the big soldier who resembled Xhaknar. Plus BraarB had arranged for the Din-La to send him copies of the images she took which, knowing the Din-La, would precede his arrival. Even if Geldish was wrong about the rest, there was still a large threat assembling there. But he did not doubt what Geldish had told him simply because he did not think Geldish would lie. A creature with that much power had no need to.

work of many, we are prepared.

"If you want to help, then go about your regular business and keep your families safe. If you want to hinder, do not get near me or any member of the army, because we will march right over you on our way to the west."

Ata, the youngest member of the council, had probably not said more than two words in the previous five Suns, so everyone was flabbergasted. Not just at what was said but who had said it.

"Council Member Ata is right," said T'rlp, the Wolfen representative, "if a touch flamboyant."

That got smiles throughout the room.

"The army was built to defend the Plains and that is exactly what it will do, whether you wish to be defended or not. This council was built to govern the Plains and that is what it has done, successfully, for these last five Full Suns.

"Do not let a rumor destroy everything. You should know some of our generals have proposed we not wait for Yontar to march and, instead, meet him in his lair, before he has the strength to stand against us. None of our generals have proposed we lay on our backs and let him march over us. We will meet him where we have the best chance of success but, on this, I assure you, meet him we will and defeat him we will."

That got a loud cheer and finally seemed to set things right. With the help of some aides, they were able to clear the council chambers and resume work.

The plan to march on the facility had been gaining momentum since it had been proposed by the generals. It was risky to be sure since they would be far from home with no way to replenish supplies. But, then again, logistics are what an army does best, after warfare, and the idea was looking more probable each turn. A force of thirty thousand, with a dedicated supply train, could do it. They would surely be more than a match for ten thousand or so Mayanorens and they knew now how to kill those like Xhaknar.

It wouldn't be easy, but it could be done.

Lord Südermann had sent Mnaas to sit in on this meeting and he had remained very quiet. Finally, the BadgeBeth representative, Zarn, addressed him.

"What say you Mnaas? Your lands are as much at risk as ours."

"If not more so," agreed Mnaas, "but you seem to have this well in hand. I can see no flaws, except for minor concerns about the supply train which you are already addressing, and I am unsure how those of us who serve Lord Südermann can be of service."

Every council member had the same thought, "Ooops, we hadn't meant to exclude Lord Südermann, but we did."

Before anyone could speak, Teg raised his hand.

"We have agreed on a force of thirty thousand if we march, not its disposition. I suggest we ask Lord Südermann to send ten thousand troops for the march and we will supply the remaining twenty thousand. If Lord Südermann can see her way clear to allow those ten thousand to be led by Guardian Mnaas, so much the better, since he's familiar with our quirks."

That got a round of smiles and Mnaas finally spoke.

"That is a sound suggestion Teg, I will present it to Lord Südermann this even when I make my report and should have an answer for you after breaklight. My hunch is she will approve.

"By the way, do not think I was insulted you left us out of your original plans. Far from it. I was impressed you were faced with a serious dilemma and dealt with it so expeditiously. You have grown much these last five Suns and I, for one, would be honored to march with you."

He stood, gave a quick salute, and exited the chamber. While they were waiting for an answer they still had to deal with the supply trains. Wagons full of food and ammunition were still just wagons full of food and ammunition, no matter who was marching in front of them.

The Exalted Quelnerom sat in a throne room which looked as though it had been designed by a frenzied beach comber. The walls were a riot of bright colors studded with shiny stones, seashells, and dead starfish and there were random pieces of netting strewn about the ceiling.

His cape of brightly colored fish scales and his crown, made of a gold rim decorated with a dazzling array of feathers, lay neatly folded on a dais next to him. His uniform of blues, greens, and yellows was rumpled from his many forays around the room.

His reptilian frame was not large, but it was very powerful. His brand, having been loosely based on a freshwater predator called a broad-snouted caiman, was the undisputed leader of all the other brands of reptiloids. He, like his father before him and his father before him, had risen to power when he killed his father in fair combat. He bore the scars of his first two failed attempts with pride. His son was still twenty or thirty Full Suns away from being ready for that, but that turn would be a turn of delight for him, proof he'd sired a leader.

None of these things were bothering him. No, what was irksome was the fact his brand had still not garnered the technology of the bug or Fish-People. Three hundred Full Suns of war and nothing to show for it but a standoff on the border and lots of grieving families.

By the gods, he wished they'd shut up.

"You sent my small to die …." Whine. He knew what he'd done and he'd do it again. His father had sent him to the front just like he now sent his son. It was the way of the brands. How it always had been and always should be.

Unlike the sniveling brands to the north, his brand could trace their roots directly back to the Great Rohta. His ancestors had been decanted by Rohta himself. They'd been given dominion over an entire continent. They were to mine and to fish and to lumber and whatever else the makers required. Their brands were versatile and strong.

When the gen-O-pod war came they were freed from their duties and marched north to seek their destiny. They'd crossed a wide canal and began settling near the ocean on both sides of them. They'd developed weapons from the ground and the trees. They'd had numerous small wars to decide who would lead the brands to their glorious destiny. After over six hundred Full Suns the issue was finally decided and Quelnerom's ancestors began their rule. They'd sent scouts out to the north, west, and east to see what their new home would look like.

It was then they first ran into the Fish-People and shortly thereafter they found the lands of Lord Südermann. Neither would share their technology nor let them on their lands. They said the reptiloids had enough and needed no more.

Who were they to make that decision?

The reptiloids weren't just any brands, they were the custom brands of Rohta Industries, LLC, may the gods be grateful for their work. The planet was theirs and nobody else's. And, unlike the spoiled mutants to their north, the reptiloids never perverted their brand names. His brand was LGX-117 just as Rohta had intended.

In one sense, if looked at rationally, they may have been right. His lands were dotted with mines for copper, zinc, iron and numerous other raw materials. And the reptiloids had access to all of Great Rohta's libraries. But those libraries were, as far as they were concerned, useless. They could care less about the breathtaking nuances of genetic manipulation, they needed weapons and power sources. The gen-O-pod war had destroyed so much and they didn't have the knowledge to rebuild it.

They'd found remnants of technology in the old cities of the makers, but not enough to glean how they were built or operated. A piece of this, a part of that, never enough to see the whole.

Even so, they'd not been completely stymied. They'd developed new roads and harvested the many steeds they found running wild to be the engines for their carts and wagons. They'd developed a workable steam engine and a crude telegraph for sending messages across their great land. And they'd harnessed wind power to run some basic items they had been able to rebuild. Mostly little things for homes, but at least they worked.

While it might not be the world they felt they were due, there was still a lot of ground to rule. Their southernmost regions were covered in ice and their northernmost were lush forests.

That range of habitats required a diverse population and he had that. They were hardy, adaptable, and strong. They had everything but the technology to take them to where they wanted to be.

Quelnerom looked at his reflection in the many mirrors behind the throne and wondered what he would really give to get that technology. A much shorter list was what he wouldn't.

The first born son of Lord Südermann is always named Mark, after the oldest known Gospel, and the first born daughter is always named Mary after Jesus' companion and not His mother. They are very specific about that. The current Lord Südermann was sitting with her younger brother Mark in a small salon near the throne room.

Her staff had left several platters of pastries and cakes and two urns of the sweet flavored java drink her whole family enjoyed. He had just finished his studies for the turn and took pleasure in spending time with his sister when he could. She was so busy now that she was Südermann it was difficult to do.

"How was your turn, sister? Have things finally settled down?"

"Had you asked me last season, I would have happily said yes. Sadly these discoveries by Geldish and his Brittle Riders have everyone up in arms," she looked down at her own six arms and shrugged, "so to speak."

"But surely the new army they have can take care of a few Mayanorens?"

"Certainly," she huffed," that's not the problem. The problem is they are basing their plans on guesses and suppositions. They are covering as many contingencies as they can, but there's no way to cover them all."

She sighed heavily.

"But, enough politics, these things will take care of themselves or they won't. Either way, nothing will be decided this turn. How are your studies coming along?"

"Difficult. We are now covering the history of our faith. I know father believed, as do you, but to me, it all seems a jumble of contradictions."

She smiled.

"What bothers you the most?" She was pretty sure she already knew the answer since it was a common one among her brand.

"I understand why we acknowledge Rohta as the maker of all things, but why do we see the need to have a maker for Rohta? Isn't it enough that we're here and can prove Great Rohta put us here?"

"We are part of the cycle of God's plan. To understand that you must go much, much, further back in history than Rohta. You have to go all the way back to Noah."

"Noah? Wasn't that a myth taken from the ancient Babylonians or Sumerians"?

"Possibly, but that doesn't matter. It's not the origin of the story, but the story itself which matters to us. God had come to realize the sons of Abraham were not living up to His laws or His hopes so He sent a great flood to wash the lands clean of them and start anew. Noah, or whomever, was tasked with saving all of the animals of the land and the birds of the air and his family. When the flood receded Noah was to free the livestock and repopulate the world with true believers."

"His wife and children, right?"

"Yes."

"Boy, and they say our gene pool was thin at the beginning."

She laughed.

"Keep in mind God destroyed the descendants of Abraham, not really the whole world. Although, to the authors, it sure would have seemed like it. Even in Genesis, the authors are forced to admit there were peoples other than God's Chosen."

She paused to sip her java and smiled.

"The ancient Jews called themselves the Chosen Ones. I always wondered if they knew how right they were. God didn't choose all the peoples of the world to be his followers, just the children of Abraham. They were the ones to lead all the others to salvation."

"So, you're saying science and religion can coexist? That by admitting there were other brands for the Chosen Ones to mate, and live, with humans weren't the end result of a horrible inbreeding experiment?"

"Well," she chuckled, "I wouldn't have put it quite like that but, yes, that is the general idea. The time line in Genesis dovetails nicely with the development of civilization in the Middle East, as it was called then, if you allow for the existence of other tribes. Let there be light could easily mean let there be civilization. Anyway, back to Noah. God had cleansed the planet of the Children of Abraham because they had disappointed Him. Many Suns later He sent His only Son to the world to reinforce His message.

"When that led to more divisiveness instead of brotherhood he inspired a prophet, Muhammad, to try again. All of the sons of Abraham had the same basic message but very different methods of delivering it.

"However, this time, God had patience. He let His children try and work things out for themselves. After all, He'd written His laws in stone, wiped out the miscreants with a flood and given humanity two real chances after that to get it right. It was time for them to take up the burden.

"He let humanity go as far as Rohta. When it got there He saw makers were again creating slaves, were again slipping into hedonism and slothful ways and were again, to be blunt, screwing up His domain.

"So, again, He wiped the planet clean and started over. Our ancestors were God's last flood. It is now our task to take God at His word and set the planet right. Those who side with us, like the Plains, shall reap the rewards. And they shall learn our faith not by our swords but by our examples. Those who stand against us, like Xhaknar, shall be swept away."

"What about those like the Chaldean clans? They don't believe the same way you believe."

"God has many voices. If we can put them all together in harmony there will finally be the joyful noise God wishes to hear. The Chaldeans speak to the same God we do, have the same basic goals we have and want mostly the same things we want. To me, they are just another voice in the choir to come."

He sat for a while, nibbling on the pastries, as he thought about all that. He wished she were his teacher. When she spoke it seemed to make a lot more sense than the dry recitations he heard in school.

Yontar was amazed at how efficient these smart

Mayanorens could be. Tasked with building him a navy at the beginning of the Good Sun, they'd taken the task to heart with a fervor he'd never before seen. Within three turns they had decided on the most sea worthy design for their ships, figured out how much each could carry, and then sent five thousand Mayanorens, overseen by Dagnar and a few of their own, to the west coast to build them. Each ship would be rowed by five hundred Mayanorens. Two hundred and fifty by light and an equal number by dark so they'd never have to stop. Each oar would have five Mayanorens on it so there would be two sets of twenty-five portals, one on each side of the ship. They'd wanted to make sails, but there was no quick way to manufacture fabric, so they set that idea aside.

The ships would be built in a catamaran style, with a pontoon in the middle, to evenly distribute the weight and each ship would have four decks. The bottom deck would be for the oarsmen. The next deck would become berths for the off duty Mayanorens. The third deck would house all their supplies and the galley. The fourth deck would be for the Named Ones, Dagnar and, of course, Yontar. The cabins on that deck would be more spacious and have access to radios so they could order food to be sent to their cabins and stay in touch with the other ships. Topside would house a small bridge for the captain and excess materials that could be strapped down and not affected by the weather.

There would be twenty all total.

Yontar had been amazed by the discovery of the radios all over the facility. They had to be from the same technology which allowed the Din-La to accomplish all they did. No wonder they kept it secret.

He started to think more about the Din-La but decided they could wait, he had more pressing concerns.

He looked at the reports and the drawings in front of him. They'd built one ship as a test and taken it out on the sea. After that they'd made two minor adjustments to their rudder design and added a prow, which angled below the bottom deck, to diffuse the effects of any waves hitting the front of the ship.

Now, as the Dark Sun was beginning, they had ten completed and the rest in various stages of completion. They would train the Mayanorens through the Dark Sun and be ready to launch come the Warm Sun. The conditions then would be the harshest during their training so they figured they'd be ready for anything the Warm Sun could throw at them.

They would move the remaining regular Mayanorens in thirty turns and empty the compound except for Yontar. Well, Yontar and the thousand super Mayanorens they were about to decant. It was felt that spreading the newcomers across twenty ships would not cause any burden and they'd already made cabins for them. At four to a cabin, of course, they weren't as privileged as the rest.

Yontar had smiled at that bit of pettiness but said nothing. They'd designed the ships and they'd done the work, so they'd earned the right. The others would earn their rewards too when the time came.

Let them see Yontar allowed rewards and they'd work all the harder.

He'd also dispatched twenty of the Named Ones to scout the Plains and the lands around Südermann's domain. He knew they'd never get in close enough to mingle, but they should be able to get a general overview of what was going on and a feel for what had happened since the fall of Xhaknar. Also, he had sent with them radios to see if they could pick up any signals that might give them more information.

He had learned there were many frequencies and it was a long shot, but it seemed to be worth the effort just in case. That had been over forty turns ago so he expected them back soon.

He was just about to go to the kitchen to grab a

snack when the first one arrived. He waved the Mayanoren into his office and motioned for him to sit. It was clear he'd ridden through the even to get here.

"Report."

"The Plains have scouts watching this camp and know you're alive. How I do not know. I didn't kill the scouts for fear of giving away any information or antagonizing them into action. Right now all they can see is five thousand Mayanorens camping, and that is what they're reporting."

Yontar gestured for him to continue.

"The Plains have changed much since Xhaknar fell. Anapsida is now home for some sort of council as well as Bug-People and many others. The fields around are fertile and growing many crops due to the fact the Great Lake has reappeared. How that came to be is beyond me. They have an army stationed to the west of the city and it appears to be well trained. But it is there, not here.

"Further, per your instructions, I found a channel which broadcasts every turn. It relays updates from the warrens by light and plays music during the even. It seems to be how they update each other on what is going on. Mostly crop updates and so on, useful if you're a farmer, but not much help to us. Even so, just in case, I wrote down the regular reports for your review, should you wish them."

"Later. Go on."

"The Llamia have allied with the Se-Jeant, the Succubi with the Minotaurs and the BadgeBeth with the Fierstans. All of them have also allied with Südermann, who now appears to be a femme. Trade between the lands appears to be flourishing.

"Part of that trade seems to include weapons. The Plains bear weapons I have never seen before. And, to be frank, their army is quite proficient in their use.

"As to their army, it has members of every warren and the fringe and trains with Südermann's forces regularly. Had we attacked them, as constituted, we would have been slaughtered. There are rumors they are planning to march here, but I did not hear a time, nor did I see any ready supply wagons. I would guess they won't come until sometime after the Dark Sun. There's no real way to march an army through snow and ice all the way here and have any sort of element of surprise."

While he pondered how Lord Südermann was now an obvious femme - a title and not a name? - he realized that he may have been wrong to limit the Naradhama. Their flexible minds were a great asset. Overall the news wasn't as bad as he'd feared. Mostly it reinforced his original idea to head towards Kalindor.

With this news, he may not have to conquer Kalindor. They might just hand it to him for the right price. He'd think about it and wait until all the scouts came back in over the next few turns. He'd get as much information as he could and then make a decision.

And this time it would be the right one.

The Elder's Council had gone through the reports so many times that the lines blurred. Geldish and Mnaas were reading them too, but not coming up with any different interpretations. They now had eleven separate accounts all stating the same thing; five thousand Mayanoren were missing. The camp was there, still neat and orderly, but it was smaller than the one in BraarB's images and there was no pseudo-Xhaknar. Nor were there they bevy of smart Mayanorens. There were a few, to be sure, but nowhere near the number there had been before.

So where did they go?

Geldish got up and looked at the map behind the council's main table.

"They went northwest."

Everyone stared at him.

"Our scouts have covered the north and the east and found no signs. To the south lie the Din-La and the Fish-People; either would have reported an invasion by the Mayanorens. The only place they could have gone is west."

Mnaas stood and walked over next to Geldish.

"Plenty of wood, labor, rudimentary tools …," he kept staring at the map, "dear God, they're building ships."

A lightning strike would have gotten less notice than that pronouncement, but Geldish merely nodded.

"Yes. They are going to try and get to Kalindor via the ocean." He looked at the map again and then turned to face the council. "The Fish-People have no navy. They swim easily enough in the waters and are, individually, better warriors in that environment than any others, but Yontar will have many ships if he's planning on moving his entire army. There is no way the Fish-People could mount a force to overtake him.

"Plus, if he's smart, and he is, he'll have some sort of defenses on the hulls. No, we are going to have to stop him ourselves."

"And just how do we do that from land?" That seemed to be the obvious question and it had been asked by the Llamia craft master GnaalK.

"The Succubi could do it if we gave them enough time and support. Of course, nothing will work if we don't know where those ships are, and that is something the Fish-People can help us with." He turned to face Mnaas, "your associates already have agreements with them. Do you think you can persuade them to send out scouts?"

Mnaas shrugged.

"They keep their own council and we've never asked them to help in an act of war. Even so, we won't find out unless we ask. I will present the request to Lord Südermann when I retire to my room. As soon as I hear an answer I will let you know."

He quickly left the council and they returned to their thoughts.

The Kgul stood and walked over to Geldish.

"If the Fish-People do not help, how will we find these ships?"

"I doubt if we can. At least not easily. That is a lot of water to hide something that small."

"You can read Yontar. He will be on those ships. Could you track him?"

"I'm not sure. Since he's come back to life I haven't been able to read him at all. He seems to have some new method of hiding himself I can't break through. We know he's there, this has his signature all over it, but beyond that, I can tell you nothing more."

The Kgul considered for an epi-clik and tried again.

"Can you sense the Mayanoren?"

"Yes, in general, but I couldn't give a specific location unless I was quite near."

"Then if Fish-People will not help, you must go west."

Geldish looked at the Kgul and nodded. There was no other option available.

About twenty epi-cliks later Mnaas reentered the council.

"Lord Südermann reports the Fish-People will send two scouts parallel to the location we know on land. They will get us as much information as they can, but will not go near any ships nor will they fight unless they are attacked."

That was fair enough. This wasn't their war. Not yet, anyways.

Ben and Imam Salim stood outside the mosque. Ben had briefed him on everything and they were now just touring the grounds. Ben admired their simple beauty; small flowers on the perimeter with tiny bushes spaced throughout and multiple benches on the lawn. It was an inviting place, a place where families could and often did, congregate. There were a few there this turn enjoying one of the last warm moments before the Dark Sun.

They continued silently around the mosque, just enjoying the view. It was clear the Imam was troubled and Ben knew him well enough to know he'd speak when he had his thoughts in order.

"Tell me, Ben," he began casually enough, "what are these Brittle Riders like?"

"Well, they're not like us," he laughed, "and they've seen more death and destruction than anyone ever should. That being said, beneath their hard exteriors, they're nice, very nice in fact. They did their best to respect my faith and made sure I was kept informed of anything they found. As I said in my report, my intention had only been to follow them, it was their idea to add me to their group, at least for a while. It seems I was slowing them down."

He smiled at the memory.

"Geldish, their leader is, as you know, a Rangka. He can be very disturbing to be around but they trust him with their lives. He has an odd sense of humor I could never quite grasp. It was difficult to tell what was a joke and what wasn't. However, that could simply be due to the fact that I have no experience with Rangka.

"N'leah, the Succubus, is a fierce warrior with a troubled soul. She didn't say much about her past, but you could see in her eyes horrible things had happened to her. I tried to offer her the peace of our faith but she resisted. She was very courteous but nonetheless made it clear this was not a conversation she wished.

"Sland is the BadgeBeth. He is smarter than he lets on. He isn't sophisticated by any definition of the term, but he has a keen eye and a good mind. He is exactly the kind of brand you'd want on your side in a fight. Even if his talons scared the heck out of me.

"BraarB, the Llamia, was, to be honest, much larger

than I anticipated. I could look her in the eye only when I was mounted. She is the most sophisticated of them. She's had experience in court and has worked for her empress directly on several occasions. Nevertheless, she's a warrior first and everything else second. She only told me a little of her past, but it was enough to chill my blood.

"R'yune, the Wolfen, is the great mystery. A mute, he communicates with finger talk. The others understand him fine but I was completely lost. However, he is clearly a weapons expert. In less than three turns he had me working with weapons I'd never seen before and I was handling them like I was born to them. He has an inordinate amount of patience. It's as though he is giving others a gift he never received.

"Totaled up, each has their strengths and each has their weaknesses and each knows the others intimately. They ride as one, talk as one, act as one. It's a milieu of little things I couldn't explain, I hope you'll just take my word for it."

"I do Ben. Your honesty is never in question. I guess the question I'm asking is if we had to, could we trust them?"

"Yes."

"Do you want to think about that?"

"No. By our faith, they may be infidels but I see clearly now that Allah, the Wisest and Most Merciful, has a plan for them. These Brittle Riders raised the Plains to eventually bring down Xhaknar. They did horrible things, but things that had to be done to free themselves. They have come from nothing to become princes and princesses of the Temple of Azarep.

"They do not crave war, Imam, they seek peace. But the only path they've been given is a bloody one. You remember when we rode west to open trade and instead ended up in a shooting war with the Mayanorens? That is what they've had to deal with every turn of their lives. Every overture met with violence."

"Then, tell me, Ben, do you think our clan will have to join them in this coming battle?"

"I do not know. I do know they didn't ask us to. They just promised to keep us informed should war come our way."

The Imam paused, smiled, and then chuckled. Ben looked at him quizzically until he finally spoke.

"I asked Allah for an answer to that exact question and it seems the answer is maybe. Someturns we must be careful what we ask for."

Still chuckling he left a puzzled Ben standing in front of the mosque.

Watcher Urkel walked through the new BadgeBeth castle and was impressed yet again with how well they'd done in such a short time. The structure was sound, the planning simple yet elegant, and the feeling one got when walking around was nothing but welcoming. Truly Gornd had found a home for his brand.

Not just his either. The former Naradhama slaves had taken to him on an almost spiritual level. They sang his praises in their work songs and lauded him to others in the markets. Gornd had done something none of the other warrens had, and maybe they should have. He'd promised them four Full Suns without taxes with the understanding that at the end of that time they would be just as any other citizen of his realm. They'd used that break to build better homes and make sure their farms had the best of equipment. When it came time for some of them to pay taxes this Sun, they'd been first in line at the palace gate. They proudly showed their receipts and paperwork to the bemused BadgeBeth assigned for collection. He'd planned on going from farm to farm over a period of turns. Instead, they were waiting for him anxiously. Many asked him to check their paperwork so they didn't short the Great King Gornd.

The BadgeBeth had ceased being amused and started being awed when one said "This turn we are not only free, but we are true citizens of the lands of King Gornd. Never have we had a prouder moment. All thanks to your king for this honor."

Somehow the BadgeBeth quickly found a new stamp and every single Naradhama left with a receipt that said "Paid in full. Citizen of the Lands of the Great King Gornd."

They would have been less pleased with a bag full of goldens.

Yes, Gornd was turning out to be a very good ruler.

Urkel continued his leisurely stroll, ignoring the complaints of his guards. They would wrap him in a metal cocoon if they could.

He turned a corner and was astounded at a tapestry on the wall. It depicted Gornd and Urkel leading the charge into a squad of Mayanorens on the trip to meet Lord Südermann for the first time. It was so good it almost looked as though it was taken with one of those new picto-recorders the Din-La were selling. Even his guards fell silent. It was an amazing piece of work.

Gornd walked up behind him and, unintentionally, startled them all.

"Incredible isn't it?" He waited while they quickly regained their composure and continued, "It was done by a Naradhama named Fleecy of the House of Rambling. She had one of my warriors describe the scene to her several times and showed him sketches while making him swear on his oath not to tell me. Once she got the scene right, she managed to get images of you and me, and add them in."

"She then showed it to all who rode with us that turn and still lived. Both your brand and mine and, somehow, a few members of the Royal Mantis Guard. When she saw they approved she asked them to give it to me and they refused. They would only take it if she did the presentation herself."

"So, while I was having my breaklight repast three turns ago, in walked a veritable host of Fierstan Guardians, BadgeBeth Warriors and Mantis Guards surrounding a shaking Naradhama. I couldn't imagine what crime this poor creature had committed to getting arrested by so many different jurisdictions and brought before me while I was eating."

"Then she, with the help of four others, showed me the tapestry. My mates cried, my smalls oohed and ahhed, but I was speechless. I have never seen craftwork this fine. Not even in the wealthiest homes. Not knowing what else to do, I kissed her and thanked her; then my mates did the same."

"I'm not ashamed to say I cried. Look, in the back corner to the left, that's my nephew Jkam. He died in the battle with Xhaknar. Next to you is, obviously, Nak, but to the back, you can see Pord, the poor lad who fought off a wing of Naradhama when they were trapped in the crags. We attended his funeral. And many others after that.

"According to Granq she got the images by asking the warriors to ask the families for whatever they had; paintings, drawings, anything at all."

"As if the tapestry isn't amazing enough, almost eighty brands kept a secret from me for over twenty turns while this was being made. There is a second, which will be presented to you in five turns. Please act surprised when it arrives."

Urkel was speechless, so he simply grunted his assent and returned to looking at the magnificent piece. After about ten epi-cliks, he spoke softly.

"She is a farmer?"

"Yes."

"We should get her commissions with all the warrens. No one should be denied seeing work this superb."

Gornd nodded.

"Zarn is going to bring the council here after you get your copy and introduce her to them. They should keep her busy and in goldens for the rest of her life."

Urkel smiled and looked at the tapestry again.

"Simply breathtaking."

Now the weight around his heart had been lifted, King Uku paraded the halls like a brand on a mission. He still limped, of course, but now, absent any other way of saying it, it was a happy limp. Empress ClaalD, too, seemed to be in a better mood each turn. Their admission of their mutual love, although doomed to be unrequited, had buoyed them both. Not even the news of Yontar's inexplicable return had dampened their turns.

His staff didn't know what had happened but, whatever it was, they were all thankful it had. He was, once again, the ruler they knew and loved. No longer moping and indecisive, he was bright and attentive at every meeting and made sure that credit was properly parsed among them.

More importantly, the warren was running smoothly again. No longer needing to hide his morose behavior from the citizens he was supposed to rule they were able to concentrate on their jobs more fully. Eventually, they just passed it off as one of those things and went about their business.

Even the sight of Empress ClaalD bending over to kiss him on the cheek before each meeting was noticed, but unremarked. True, something had happened, something that had positively affected them both, but what that something was wasn't their concern.

If Uku was aware of his effect on the warren, either good or bad, he never showed it. He rose at breaklight each turn and shared his repast with ClaalD. Then they would go their respective ways. She had the new enclave to oversee and he had everything else.

This turn, however, was to be different. One of the Se-Jeant craft masters, by the name of Ozo, had asked the king to inspect a new shop in the Llamia's enclave. It seems he and a Llamia named JnaarZ were opening a new type of jewelry shop. One that combined the skills of both brands. It was an exciting idea and both he and ClaalD were eager to see what they had to offer. About two cliks after their repast they headed out, escorted by a small army of guards and courtiers.

Thoroughly enjoying the discomfort of their staffs they took their time and greeted any citizen who got within nodding distance. Soon they were leading a slow, but sizeable, procession through the warren to the new shop.

Ozo and JnaarZ were putting the final touches on their cleaning when everyone arrived. Caught off guard by the size of the throng they hastily recovered and brought a two tiered table out in front of the shop. The left side was built for a Llamia and the right for a Se-Jeant. There they set up the tools and materials they were planning on using.

A few sepi-cliks later everyone watched as Ozo sliced a small emerald into perfect halves. These he laid on the table as JnaarZ, wearing a magnifying optic, worked a silver filigree around the edges of each half. Ozo, in the meantime, went into the shop and came back with a small pot of molten copper. This he delicately poured into a mold while JnaarZ laid the filigree encrusted emeralds on top. Then they each used bellows to cool off the molds. It took some time, but the crowd watched every puff with rapt attention.

When they were cooled they removed two of the most beautiful rings anyone had ever seen. The mold had contained a lattice work pattern that perfectly complimented the silver filigree. The rings each had a small opening on the bottom.

JnaarZ looked up.

"Your majesties' left hands, please."

They each extended their left hands and he placed the ring on the smallest finger of each. Then he carefully liquefied a small section of the opening and fastened the rings to their hands. After a quick tug to make sure the rings would slide on and off but still fit snug, he bowed and smiled.

"A gift for your majesties, to signify our union."

The crowd applauded and cheered. Then, to the horror of their guards, they both turned and began showing the rings to anyone who wanted to see. Which, as it turned out, was everyone. Ozo came around with a picto-recorder and they graciously modeled their rings so he could get some images.

"With your majesties permission, we would like to put one of these images in our window so everyone can see our work."

They both knew he also wanted to do that to drive up his prices but, be that as it may, they readily agreed.

Uku and ClaalD began to stroll back to the palace after the crowd had died down. They were both admiring their rings. They were, beyond a doubt, the finest pieces of jewelry in the land. The detail of each element was almost too fine for the eye to see. Even with his enhanced depth perception using his third eye, Uku had to hold the ring up close to admire every aspect.

"You know," he said slyly, "these would make great mating rings."

She looked stunned and then saw the smile and started laughing.

"I believe we are already as mated as two brands can be."

They both smiled and he reached up to take her hand. If anyone had anything to say about that they smartly decided contrariwise.

She wandered into the queen's bed chamber and watched her sleeping majesty. The queen was tossing and turning and morphing into various half forms. The rumors were true, the queen was troubled. That could not be allowed. They needed her at her best now, more than ever.

The servant slid over the queen's left leg and let her right hand drift between her majesty's thighs and slowly began massaging her clitoris. Slowly the queen quit tossing and turning and began breathing in rhythm with the strokes, issuing occasional soft moans.

The young maiden began to focus on the queen's breasts. Licking and nibbling around the edges. That woke the queen. The young femme put her finger on the queen's lips to silence her and then put her own lips to work in earnest, letting them drift down across the noble belly and in between the imperial labia.

She continued for almost half a clik until she felt the queen begin to shudder uncontrollably and then heard her cry a wailing ululation.

Having accomplished her intended mission she sat up and smiled.

Queen A'lnuah stretched luxuriantly as the sweat slowly evaporated off her body. The servant she'd had assigned to P'marna knelt between her legs near the foot of the bed, smiling. The queen could not help but return the beatific smile.

"Not that I'm going to complain, mind you, but may I ask what brought this on?"

"It was P'marna's suggestion, your majesty."

"P'marna? That shy young thing? How did she ever

get the nerve to broach this subject with you?"

"Well, ma'am, truthfully speaking, it wasn't so much what she said but how she acted. Whenever Missus N'leah was here she would be in a much better mood. You've been kind of sour lately and it occurred to me, unlike the rest of us, you've no one to frolic with."

Frolic. Yes, that was as good a word as any.

"So, you decided to ease my sour mood by jumping into my bed naked, waking me up, and frolicking with me."

"Yes'm."

"I see." She paused for a moment to think about this. When they'd lived on the fringe it had been easy enough to find the occasional frolicking partner. Yes, she was really learning to like that word. But since the war and the move, things had been very cloistered for her. Not by choice in as much as by necessity. Oh well, what's done is done and, in this case, done exceedingly well. "Since your plan seems to have worked, I can find no complaint with it."

"Thank you, ma'am. Should the need ever arise again please don't hesitate to ring for me. It is always a pleasure to service you ...damn, I mean I'm yours to service ... damn it again, I mean ...."

A'lnuah waved her off laughing.

"Not to worry youngling, I know what you mean. And, to be very blunt, I truly appreciate your efforts. I haven't felt this good in many Full Suns."

The young servant smiled even broader, slipped off the bed, quickly dressed and left her queen to her pleasures.

Queen A'lnuah stretched again feeling the remnants of the bone shattering ecstasy fade and wondered absentmindedly if it would be rude, at this point, to ask the young servant's name.

When she finally was able to use her muscles again, she rose off her bed and entered her private bathing chamber. It was one thing to have memories of pleasure, quite another to allow anyone near you to smell them.

She completed her shower, threw on a short shift and stood by the window letting the even air dry her wings.

The Minotaurs had, long ago, dug many secret shafts into their mountain to allow a continuous breeze. The outside air, when coupled with the heat of their lava, provided a constant flow of warm air she found very pleasant.

She stepped to her left, opened a door which led to a small balcony, and walked out and leaned on the railing, taking in the torch lit view of her courtyard. A mix of workers was putting the finishing touches on the statue that would officially be unveiled next turn.

As they prepared to place the shroud she got a good look at the work. Called "Strive," it had been done by three artists; one Succubus, one Naradhama, and one Minotaur. The statue featured a bizarre creature; half Naradhama on the left, half Minotaur on the right, and had the wings of a Succubus. It was reaching towards the sky. Above it, suspended on a thin arc, was a representation of Aretti. The bottom of the torso was hidden by the large base which had edges which crept up at unusual angles as though the creature had been issued forth by the stone.

The Minotaurs had encountered a type of art when they'd first met Lord Südermann, which they claimed captured thoughts and not images. They had incorporated some of those elements into the design. Far from the hideous beast, she'd envisioned when she'd first heard of it, this statue was a thing of seamless beauty.

She saw the three artists enter the courtyard and check the final preparations. They quickly approved everything and the shroud was dropped over the piece.

Still tingling with the joy of seeing the new art, as well as the unsubtle ministrations of her servant, Queen A'lnuah returned to her bed and went happily to sleep.

Their brand was called Orca, but they bore little resemblance to their namesakes. The streamlined black and white coloration were there, as was the bulb on their brow for echo-location and they had some very sharp teeth. But, after that, they weren't much larger than any other brand. Nor did they have the hunter's killer instinct. What they did have in common, however, was the ability to swim vast distances and large webbed feet which served as both their locomotion and their steering.

They were moving fluidly through the water as they neared the spot they'd been told to reach. They slowly surfaced and exhaled the spillage through blow holes which were located near the base of their necks. They removed their magnifying goggles from their waterproof packs, which also held their radios, and scanned the shores.

They counted fourteen ships, with six more on shore nearing completion. They were about to make their reports when five of the ships suddenly began to move. Since they weren't headed for them, they angled back a bit to see what they were up to.

They watched as the ships cleared the docks and quickly gained speed. They could hear the drums of the oar masters echoing across the water. Moving in tight formations the ships completed a series of maneuvers and turns over the next clik.

The two Orcas were impressed. The captains were clearly testing out various, difficult, battle formations and their crews seemed to handle them with ease. They were also surprised at the speed of the ships. When not turning they could outpace the Orcas, at least in the short run. That was troubling information to them.

At the end of the clik, the ships headed back to shore and five more came out. Again the Orcas watched as the captains put the ships through their paces. These seemed less demanding than the maneuvers they'd just seen. So, they were training in stages, that was good to know.

The remaining four ships came out and began speeding to the south. Just before they disappeared over the horizon they made a wide turn and headed back to the docks. What these ships lacked in tactics they made up for in speed.

Great Rohta these ships were fast.

They pulled up their oars and the Orcas could hear the oar masters counting backwards. When they reached zero the oars dropped back in the water and began pulling in reverse. The ships slowed with amazing rapidity and eased into the docks.

The Orcas finally noted the docks were really nothing more than a series of evenly spaced piers. Nothing fancy, just a slot for each ship.

They saw the Mayanorens disembark and head for their makeshift camp. They did a quick head count as each ship emptied and totaled thirty-five hundred Mayanorens, two hundred and fifty per ship. Based on the noises they heard, the remaining fifteen hundred which were supposed to be here were working on the other ships.

Since it would be even-fall soon they decided to head back south along the shore and make their report when they were safely away from those deadly ships. One thing was for certain; with their wide decks, shallow drafts and incredible speed, those ships were going to be very hard to sink.

If they added weapons, they might be impossible.

While he admitted to being bored out of his new skull, Yontar wasn't dumb enough to tempt fate by openly announcing his presence. The thrice cursed Rangka thought he was here, but he didn't truly know. The Named Ones had left him the paperwork they'd found concerning alpha waves and how the makers had planned to use them. Seeing every one of Rohta's facilities had an alpha wave corrupter, it was no surprise the first wave of the gen-O-pod war had been directed at them.

This facility, for reasons he didn't know, didn't have one. He guessed his makers were not affiliated with Rohta and had different uses in mind for their products' alpha waves. One thing was clear, they were concerned about them enough to festoon the place with shielding.

Yontar was twiddling a piece of the stuff when two of the Named Ones walked in.

"Forgive the intrusion, Lord Yontar, but the progress reports are in from this turn's training."

Yontar glanced at him, then back at the shielding and then back at him.

"I'm sure everything's fine," he paused distractedly and then looked straight at them, "tell me, can this stuff be made into a helmet?"

They looked shocked at the thought and then smiled.

"Yes Lord Yontar," smiled the one closest to him, "I think it could be simply done. I'm sorry we didn't think of it before."

Yontar shrugged and thought of Xhaknar's many fits of rage when things like this happened.

"It's no matter, we aren't ready to move yet anyway. But, I will admit I'm getting very tired of wandering these halls. You may be wonderful hosts and all, but this is still feeling like a prison. I would like to see these ships for myself and breathe some fresh air."

They spoke briefly to themselves and then returned their gazes to him.

"One will be ready by breaklight, Lord Yontar. Please review this turn's reports at your leisure while we see to it."

He glanced at the reports and decided, if they were to be believed, they were well ahead of schedule. By halfway through the Dark Sun, the fleet would be completely trained. He saw no reason to doubt the Named Ones. After all, without them, he'd still be floating in the nether realm looking at shadows.

He'd wanted to decant some more of the DG-nr series since they looked promising, but he didn't want to leave anyone behind unprotected while they were raised to sentience. Geldish didn't need to torture anyone to make them talk, he'd just peel away their mind until he found what he was looking for and, right now, Yontar preferred those secrets remain just that.

Then he remembered the spies Geldish had secreted in the hills. He would have to leave by the west end of the facility. That area was unshielded so he never went there, but with the helmet that shouldn't be a problem.

The new Named Ones they were going to decant in a few turns intrigued him as well. Supposedly they would awake completely sentient and be superior to their makers. He wondered if they'd be as subservient, though, knowing they were obviously smarter than their leader. Well, that could be dealt with if the time came. If push came to shove he had five thousand boring old Mayanorens, still in camp, who could do a satisfactory job of ripping them to shreds and would do so happily if he gave the order.

He looked again at the route he'd chosen to get to Kalindor. It was mildly circuitous, but he'd seen the Succubi with their bombs. He didn't want to be caught in the open water by them. However, while a Succubi could fly for a whole turn when unimpeded and could cover hundreds of kays in short order when they flew in that parabolic arc they called high flight, the weight of those bombs and cannons had to severely limit their range. At the battle with Xhaknar, they never strayed more than a kay from the field of battle.

If he took his fleet out twenty or more kays before turning south, they should be fine.

It was a risk, he knew, but a well calculated one.

He would talk to the Named Ones. Maybe it would be possible to leave during the Dark Sun. The snow, ice, and high winds near the coast would further inhibit any chance of ambush.

The open seas would be choppy, but those wide bodied ships should handle them fine.

But first, it was time to make sure Kalindor welcomed him with open arms. He called for one of the Named Ones and gave him a letter and a series of instructions. It became the first time in his two corporeal lives he'd ever seen someone smile at an order.

He wondered why he and Xhaknar hadn't thought of this before? Make taking over the world fun and everyone just follows along.

It was barely breaklight when the scouts saw the rider leave the facility. He was riding one deisteed and had two more behind him carrying large packs. He didn't seem to be in any hurry, but they noted the time of his departure and as much as they could tell, which wasn't a lot, and then assigned one scout to follow him at a distance and keep them informed.

They didn't see the second rider emerge from the far side of the facility and disappear into the woods. He was traveling lighter than his companion but that was due to two facts; (1) he had an actual destination and, (2) he had a deadline to get there.

He headed his deisteed south towards the mountains separating the Fish-People from the east and then followed the eastern rim of those mountains all the way to the lands of Kalindor.

He carried two of the new weapons and the designs for several others as well as plans they'd found for generators, mining machines, and many other useful things. Their makers had been trying to create living war machines and wanted to make sure their brands would have all the tools they'd ever need. All of these he was to present to the Exalted Quelnerom along with the letter he had tucked in his shirt.

His brand had chosen well with Lord Yontar. This plan showed he would not spill their blood needlessly. If he could accomplish what was needed with finesse instead of force, he would do so.

Nevertheless, he had no doubt if blood did need to be spilled Yontar would spill it liberally and thoroughly. That thought didn't bother him. The Mayanoren, even the Named Ones, were bred to serve and to die if need be. The fact he was more intelligent than his predecessors merely meant he could serve better and die smarter.

He eased his mount a little further west to make sure he was in line with the mountains. By even-fall the next turn he'd be well south of Geldish's scouts and west of the lands of the northern river folk.

For the most part, he'd have to forage off the land as he went, but that shouldn't be a problem. Since the gen-O-pod war, game had returned to the lands in abundance.

He'd had time to go through all of the makers' records while he was at the facility. They'd figured they could avoid the slaughter since they hadn't bothered with an alpha wave corrupter and nor had any of their progeny been let loose. They'd taken very accurate notes until Xhaknar and Yontar killed them all.

There'd been about six million individual gen-O-pods, representing around four hundred brands, which attacked the humans. The speed and brutality of the assault had stunned the makers. According to a diary, he'd found, one of them had likened it to being mugged in a meadow.

When the war - slaughter more accurately - was

over, the surviving gen-O-pods spread out across the planet. While their numbers might have only populated a large city during the makers' peak, the gen-O-pods wanted more space. They settled where they could and as soon as they had a grip on how long they'd live, began slowing their birth rates.

The average brand lived just under two hundred Full Suns. The Succubi, the Mantis, and a few others doubled that. Some, like Yontar and Geldish, seemed to have no limits. He knew that wasn't as surprising as it should have seemed.

Rohta and his imitators had made tremendous advances in immunology and in upgrading the Telomerase enzyme. They'd also figured out a way for the body to keep recreating embryonic stem cells at regular intervals. Since that could lead to a race of immortals, Rohta and his imitators had designed a bio-bomb which would go off ten Full Suns after decanting. The idea was simple enough, after the allotted time the bomb would release a toxin that would shut down all the internal organs and disrupt brain activity. It was a highly modified form of a drug known as curare.

And, when exposed to a newly decanted brand, it worked as planned.

But, over those ten Full Suns, those incredible immune systems, with all of their support from nanites and stem cells and everything else, had repaired all the parts of the body the makers had destroyed or ignored. So, when the time came, the body could easily repel the toxin. The original brands called it the ten year flu.

The other thing that got fixed was the reproductive system. The stem cells would find non-working organs and then do what millennia of evolution had trained them to do, they rebuilt them. The nanites, working off of corrupted DNA, would alter the new organs to fit the body as best as they could devise.

The nanites weren't sentient, not by a long shot, but

they had been given strict instructions to keep everything running and copies of all the genetic codes used in the relevant brand. Thus, when faced with new organs where organs used not to be, they were forced to improvise a little.

Some of the results, like the Succubi's ovipositors, were downright ingenious. Others, like the Llamia's mating-harpoon, were clearly based on genetic stock. Either way, they worked.

He glanced up and realized it was already mid-break. He should be well south of the main scouts by now. He pulled a sandwich from his pack and continued on his quest.

He contemplated his venison sandwich and smiled. Only two brands, both custom orders, had been made vegetarians. All others were omnivores. That way the owners wouldn't have to worry about what they fed their brands, just as long as they kept some basic foods around.

It wasn't known how the gen-O-pods had coordinated their assault or what finally drove them over the edge, but he guessed the food was probably a prime factor. After all, just because you can eat something and exist doesn't mean that's all you want to eat for your entire life.

N'leah arced through the frigid air and looked at the riders below her. More than just friends, they were brands she regularly trusted her life to and never once regretted it. Her nytsteed was keeping pace with the others so she slipped lower and angled her landing on its back. She'd done this so many times now no one even noticed. Not really, anyway. Obviously, they noticed she was sitting on a nytsteed and not flying through the air, it's just they'd seen the intricate maneuver so many times it no longer registered with them how difficult it was.

Unlike their last trip west Geldish was pushing the nytseeds as hard as he could.

They'd all heard the report from the Fish-People. Yontar wasn't just building barges to move his troops from point A to point B, he was building a navy. And, worse, it appeared he was building an effective one.

Geldish wanted to see exactly what Yontar had so they were riding straight west to the mountains and then they'd cut north from there and keep under cover as much as possible.

Even for the nytsteeds, this was tough going. The weather was certainly colder and, as they edged north and west, they were running into the snow, ice and a variety of inclement conditions.

N'leah had had a jacket custom made for these conditions. Heavy fur collar, with a fur lined interior, the rest was pure kgum leather. The tailor had made a flap off the back collar so she could place it between her wings and then lace it up front. The boots were tough to make too since she has talons instead of toes. The tailor had come up with pull on boots, with reinforced leather in the heel and toes so she wouldn't puncture them, which she could tighten with laces.

The pants had presented no problems at all.

She'd worn the pants while scouting the land in front of them and now had the rest reassembled without having to stop their progress. She rode up next to Geldish to give her report.

"The Mayanoren with the two deisteeds is about fifteen kays to the north of us and angling east. We will miss him completely. As you surmised, he's clearly a decoy. He's making a trail wide enough to drive herds through. Someone or something else left the facility and was missed."

Geldish nodded.

"Let the scouts roust him when he returns. I doubt

he's got any useful information, but at least we'll let Yontar know we're paying attention. What about directly west? Did you see anything there?"

"Some venison herds and a small Din-La post straight ahead, nothing else. But visibility is awful. A single rider could easily have passed right beneath me and I wouldn't have noticed."

Geldish contemplated for a moment..

"Yeah, and it would have to be a single rider. Definitely no more than two. Anything larger would have been noticed one way or another. Yontar must have reason to believe the Exalted Quelnerom will ally with him before he gets there. Hopefully, when we see the ships, we can figure out why."

He looked at him and saw no one was complaining, but the nytsteeds were visibly winded and everyone else looked half frozen. He needed to remember external conditions affected them. Not everyone could be a Rangka.

"We'll go to the Din-La post for the even and get everyone hot food and a warm bed. While we're there we can see if they have any clothes they can get all of you to keep you warmer. This ride is just going to get harder and the weather will surely get worse."

She was too cold to be grateful so she just shrugged an assent and resumed riding as hard as she could.

The Exalted Quelnerom inspected the troops headed for the front. His cape shimmered in the early Sun and his crown fluttered lazily in the breeze. He knew most of the troops signed up for the goldens and the rest for the uniforms. But it didn't concern him why they'd joined, he knew they'd been trained extensively and were as ready as they could be for what lie ahead.

He signaled to his generals the inspection was over

and he approved. Before he could finish his pivot he heard orders being barked and feet marching off to war.

The border with the bug-people had turned into a war of attrition. The battle front had shifted less than a kay in either direction in over a hundred Full Suns. He had the distinct impression that Lord Südermann was toying with him. They certainly had the technology to overrun all of Kalindor, maybe they just didn't have the manpower. Or, maybe, Südermann was one of those weak brands that didn't want to expand.

He doubted that. Why go to all the trouble of developing materials for war if you weren't going to use them? It must be manpower then. Maybe the bug-people couldn't breed often enough to cover their losses.

Whatever the reason, it didn't change the fact the border was a quagmire. One of his generals, whose name completely escaped him, had developed a usable catapult and had begun bombarding the bug-people with flaming boulders. That had pushed them back for ten turns until they began firing back with catapults of their own design which could also launch flaming boulders but theirs landed far deeper in Kalindorian territory than any of his advisors had thought possible. The front shifted back to its original position and the bombardment stopped.

He began thinking about the reports his spies had brought him. At first, he'd thought the poor creature had gone insane. But when three more showed up with similar reports he had to take them seriously.

Of course, he chided himself, he should have done so in the first place. The QZD-1934 brand was one of the most reliable ones he had. Made from a small island lizard, they could change their skin coloring to blend in almost anywhere. They were hard working, loyal and, best of all, had no sense of humor.

He hated jokesters.

But those reports contained nuggets he may be able to use. Mayanoren spies on the Plains, watching

Südermann's army train with the one from the warrens. The latter part of the report is what jumped out at him immediately. If the bug-people were doubling or tripling, their forces via an alliance then the war of attrition could end quickly, and end badly for Kalindor.

However, that first part about the Mayanoren spies may have more import. It had been five Full Suns since the warrens waged war on Xhaknar and defeated him. His spies had said the Mayanoren had seemed smart. Certainly smarter than Mayanorens had ever been before. He'd ignored that then since everyone knew Mayanorens were about as subtle as a punch in the face and slightly less intelligent.

Now he wasn't so sure. Spies were, by definition, smart. They had to be. They needed to be able to assimilate information, assign its priorities, and then assemble it into a coherent report. Stupid brands can't do that. More importantly, stupid brands tend to get caught, which renders them useless for the job.

So, if Mayanoren spies were on the Plains, and doing their job well from all accounts, then they couldn't be stupid Mayanorens. And if there truly are smart Mayanorens what did it mean to him?

It would explain the alliance of Südermann and the warrens. All the Mayanorens went missing after the war with Xhaknar. If they knew about the smart Mayanorens they would do exactly what they're doing, build an army unlike any other to face them. Brutal killers with agile minds would be a terrible foe on the field of battle. Or any place else for that matter.

So how could he use this to his advantage?

Südermann still had enough resources to maintain the garrisons along the front. For now, anyway. But if the Mayanorens attacked, what then? Südermann would be forced to move troops off the border. Enough to allow Kalindor to overrun them?

Maybe.

What if there was a way to get word to these smart Mayanorens? Coordinate an attack so Südermann would be forced to split resources and cover two fronts? They could divide the spoils if it proved successful.

But where to find these smart Mayanorens?

He would assemble his spies. They would go over every detail, no matter how trivial, until they had a good idea of their location. Then he'd send a QZD-1934 with an interesting proposal and a way to bring down Südermann once and for all.

The Fish-People didn't call themselves that. They preferred Children of the Waters. And had they ever shared that bit of information with anyone, they might never have heard the term Fish-People ever again. However, that would require them to open up to an outsider and that was not something they did easily.

If at all.

They were, by far, the most populous of the clans. They counted thirty-seven brands among their kind and covered from the western shore to many islands across the sea. In the main, they traded amongst themselves but would trade with outsiders if they could get a fair deal and not have to get involved.

They had done the favor for Lord Südermann simply because it was only a peripheral thing. Go, see, report. Had any additional action been required they would have turned her down instantly.

Now they weren't so sure. Their scouts had given them the same report they'd passed along to Südermann. While it seemed unlikely those ships were a immediate threat to them, it also seemed very likely they would have to deal with them in the future. Possibly the near future.

This was especially true if the northern river brands were correct in their account the Brittle Riders had been in their lands. They were close to where those ships were being built.

The Children of the Waters didn't use spies in the traditional sense. They received reports of unusual activities from the various brands and stayed in contact with the Din-La, a brand that always treated them well. They'd never seen a need to delve deeper into the affairs of others. That may have been a mistake.

War was obviously headed their way, whether they wished it or not, and they didn't have any useful information on which to prepare.

This turn was the first full meeting of the Congress of the Children in almost one hundred Full Suns. Whatever had needed to be done before was usually accomplished with simple messages and occasional meetings between interested parties. Their brand required little governance and there hadn't been a true outside threat since the gen-O-pod war.

The meeting room was moistened by streams of mist coming from carefully concealed spigots. The walls were decorated in muted shades of blue and green and there was a shallow trench dug around the edges, filled with water, so those with larger fins could navigate more easily.

While they had no leader that had never hampered their ability to govern their citizens or work with others. In some ways, the fluidity of their parliamentary structure was almost genetically hardwired into them. Their nonhuman ancestors had survived in schools or packs, never in a true hierarchy. Even the seals, penguins and walruses, who had their bulls, still relied on the group for their continued existence.

If humanity had forced an evolutionary leap in an unplanned direction, some things remained the same.

After a few turns of heated, yet oddly respectful, debate, they formulated a strategy. They would send the

Kwini-Laku, Rohta's First Born, inland to gather as much information as was possible. The scout would travel from Din-La post to Din-La post so they could stay in contact with the congress.

Additionally, they would send Orcas back to watch those ships and report any movements. Lastly, and this was the part that took the longest, they would send an official emissary to Lord Südermann to discuss a military alliance, should the need arise.

And said emissary would be allowed to reveal the fact the Children of the Waters had ships of their own.

The Din-La, named Gvvl, stopped Geldish just as they were getting ready to leave.

"My apologies, dead one, but a message has come in which may have value to your trip."

Geldish sighed heavily, dismounted, and followed Gvvl back into the post. The others, seeing no reason to freeze any more than they had to, joined him. He handed Geldish a slip of paper and waited patiently for him to read it. Geldish finally handed it back to him with a coin and looked at the others.

"I know you're all going to be sorely disappointed not to make the trip north in the heart of the Dark Sun, but it seems we're not needed. The Fish-People have appointed regular spies to watch the ships and report everything to Lord Südermann, who will, in turn, report it to us.

"More interesting is the fact they are sending scouts to the Plains. One will be here in seven turns. Since the Fish-People are better suited to handle the conditions near the ships, we will rely on them. I think it will be more productive for us to stay here for seven turns and then escort their scout to his or her next destination.

"The Fish-People have never involved themselves

with outsiders before and I, for one, wish to know why the sudden change of heart."

They contemplated this for a sepi-clik. Barely. The idea of staying put, sleeping in comfortable beds, and eating great food compared with freezing outside, sleeping under ice covered trees and eating whatever they could kill wasn't much of a choice.

They tried, unsuccessfully, to sound reluctant when they agreed.

Geldish made arrangements with Gvvl for their accommodations. While he was doing that they went back outside, removed their packs and stabled the nytsteeds. Less than five epi-cliks later they were back inside huddled around a table drinking spiced java.

"So, Geldish," BraarB spoke between sips, "what do you truly hope to learn from this scout? Not that I'm upset at not having to hoof through ice, but it seems a bit reactive for you."

"Maybe, but I was telling the truth when I said the Fish-People are better suited for these conditions than we are. I'm more than happy to pass that duty along to them. I'll have Gvvl send Lord Südermann a list of things to have the Fish-People's spies pay attention to. They can spot anything amiss as readily as any of us once they know what they're looking for.

"Also, I wasn't kidding about wanting to meet this scout. Except for the Din-La, no one's had close contact with the Fish-People since the gen-O-pod war. This is a rare opportunity for us. This change doesn't feel like a whim, things are happening and they are going to be involved whether or not they want to. They obviously realize this as well."

He took a long sip of his java and continued.

"I doubt I'll get any detailed information from the scout, but I do think we can get a better feel for what's going on with the Fish-People. Are they potential allies or are they just covering themselves and preparing to hide?

This kind of knowledge will greatly affect any plans we may make. So, I'm afraid we're just going to have to muddle through the next few turns eating Gvvl's excellent cooking and drinking his finest libations."

That seemed like a very sound idea and everyone energetically concurred. Gvvl brought over a sampler platter full of exotic foods and they relaxed and enjoyed the fare while they talked over some of the possibilities the Fish-People could present. After going around several times they finally agreed they didn't have enough information to make any practical judgments.

A little later, N'leah and R'yune went up to their rooms and Sland and BraarB went over to bother Gvvl and see what other delicacies they could wheedle out of him. Geldish, lost in his thoughts, never realized he was levitating over the table still holding his cup of java in both hands.

Malehni had never ridden any kind of steed in his life. The creatures, quite honestly, frightened him. They were too big, with too many teeth and too many hooves to be safe, as far as he was concerned. But when the congress assigned him this mission to the Plains, he was told unequivocally there was no other way to travel. The Din-La had provided him with a deisteed and a half turn's worth of instructions and off he went to do the bidding of the congress.

By the third turn, he and the animal seemed to be getting along fine. It hadn't bitten him, crushed him with its hooves, or thrown him off a cliff. Plus, thanks to the padded saddle the Din-La provided, he was relatively comfortable. He let the deisteed set the pace and merely aimed it in the general direction he wanted to go. That seemed to work best for all concerned.

He was still far south of his intended destination and was just crossing the last peak before he could descend into the valley and head north when he spotted the lone rider in the distance. Reining in his mount he sidled into a thicket to remain hidden from view as he watched.

Malehni had seen Mayanorens before and recognized the rider as such instantly. He'd been told to report anything unusual he might see and a Mayanoren less than half a turn north of the border of Kalindor sure seemed to fit the description.

He waited until the rider was completely out of sight and radioed in his report to the nearest Din-La receiver. He neither knew nor cared where that might be. As long as they gave him the proper confirmation code, he would transmit the message and they would ensure it got to where it needed to be.

He then waited a little while longer, to make sure the Mayanoren didn't double back, and continued down the mountain. His mount seemed to sense his anxiety and kept swinging its massive head to and fro. When they finally got to the bottom, he pulled the reins to the north and the deisteed took off at a gallop. It took him several epi-cliks to get used to this new, and thrillingly deadly, pace but eventually he settled into the saddle and kept his body in rhythm with the motion.

Three cliks later the beast finally slowed and settled for a safer trot. Nevertheless, it was still faster than he'd ever traveled before. If his new bride saw him riding like this she'd never agree to a pup for fear the crazy gene might be contagious.

He thought back to his father and he knew there was no crazy gene on that side. His mother, on the other hand, was given to fantastic flights of imagination and might have planted the seed with all of her stories she'd told him when he was a small. She favored the old maker tales of knights and dragons and the like. Not at all like the other Kwini-Laku who told sensible stories about fish and how to find them, how to catch them and, of course, how to eat them.

Well, if he was crazy, so be it, there was nothing he could do about it now. Certainly not while riding a lethal animal through an alien forest on his way to meet the ones his kind had long shunned.

He figured it would be crazy to even try.

The Mayanoren had not seen Malehni on the mountain and, even if he had, probably would have done nothing about it. He was too close to his goal to risk an encounter of any kind.

There was an empty swath between the lands of Südermann and the Fish-People. It was only about fifty kays wide and the armies of Kalindor had tried, unsuccessfully, to use it as a wedge. All that would happen is they'd cross to the north and then the forces of Südermann would close in behind them and crush them. It was not an effective way to enjoin battle.

He figured that spies on one side or the other would spot him as he crossed, but didn't think they'd have any way to stop him. He was crossing the last part of an arroyo when he spotted the Kalindor flags. He turned slightly to head straight for them and hoped the troops under those flags would ask first and shoot later.

A patrol of six riders, on regular steeds, came out to meet him. He made a mental note since it meant they were probably short of deisteeds and slowed his pace. He held his arms wide as they approached and waited to be surrounded.

He announced he was an emissary sent by Lord Yontar with a private message for the Exalted Quelnerom. He showed them his orders and then waited.

And waited.

And waited some more.

They stared at the paperwork. They turned it in every conceivable direction and then stared back at him. This was going to be a little harder than he'd anticipated. It had never occurred to anyone the Kalindorian army might be illiterate.

Finally, deciding "emissary" might be a tricky word for "assassin" they cuffed his hands behind his back and led him, still on his deisteed, to their general. He, thankfully, was literate. He read the orders, had him uncuffed and offered him a glass of some sweet liquor. He enjoyed the flavor and even sampled from a tray of meats when it was presented. Some of them were too heavily salted for his tastes but he could see their appeal.

The general informed him a telegraph had been sent ahead and the Exalted Quelnerom would be expecting him. Then he got a surprise, the Kalindorians had a rudimentary rail system and he would ride that, along with his deisteed, straight to Quelnerom's palace.

When he got outside he saw his deisteed was already tethered in the front of a wheeled barge which was sitting on a set of rails. They escorted him up and four other officers joined him.

Emissary or not, he was clearly a prisoner.

There were five more of the barges and they were all filled with freight, except for the last one which was full of troops. He was close to the steam engine in the front so he studied it. It was a simple coal furnace, attached to a hideous round tube, colored in a wild confabulation of colors and sparkly things, which he supposed held the gears. Aesthetics were obviously not a concern in Kalindor. Then, looking at the officers' bright yellow and green uniforms with red caps, he figured this is what they thought looked good.

There was a small barge between him and the engine and it held the coal. As they picked up speed he watched as one reptiloid shoveled the coal while a second just sat there. At first, he thought him unbelievably lazy but, after a clik, the two switched places. He realized they could keep this up for a long time. As the train continued on he observed the many villages dotting the countryside. They were moving faster than a deisteed could and should easily be at the palace by even-fall.

The number of villages held his attention. It meant there were far more residents here than Lord Yontar had estimated. If this type of population held up all the way to the ice belt there could be millions upon millions of reptiloids here.

He decided that couldn't be true. If the Exalted Quelnerom had that kind of force under his control he would have simply washed over the bug-people's defenses and never minded the casualties. Soon enough it appeared his revised assumption was correct as the population thinned and then disappeared.

They headed into a lush forest and he watched as countless forms of native wildlife scurried around above his head and off to the sides of the train. This system must have been in use for a long time since none of them seemed scared at all. They stayed out of the way but didn't flee.

One of his escorts announced they were two cliks away from the palace and he would be given one clik, after they arrived, to clean up and make himself presentable for the Exalted Quelnerom. He looked at his dusty and dirty clothes and had to remind himself when he'd last bathed. It had been two turns ago in a chilly river. He wasn't worried about that. He had a uniform in his pack. It had been cleaned and pressed before he'd left and it had been sealed in a waterproof wrapper just in case it got exposed to the elements. It wasn't as colorful as the uniforms of the Kalindorians, but it would have to do.

The train exited the jungle into a beautiful field of grain. He smiled as they raced across the landscape. Yes, Lord Yontar was really going to like it here.

The Elder's Council had called for a meeting. It was clear now Yontar was going to head for Kalindor and they had little hope of stopping him. There was no way to launch a viable assault in the middle of the Dark Sun, especially not so far north. And they all knew once those ships were in the open water they could never catch them.

The Succubi could barely fly in weather like that, and it would be impossible if they were carrying the cannons. If they stayed to the south, even if they could track the fleet, they all doubted that Yontar would be polite enough to hug the coast and allow himself to be bombed into oblivion. There was a limit on how far they could fly carrying all that weight.

The floor was open for suggestions. No idea was too outrageous. Well, no, sorry, that one was, but for the most part every single one got a fair hearing and then dismissed.

Elaand showed up to represent Lord Südermann but had nothing useful to offer beyond the fact that the Fish-People were sending an emissary to them and he should arrive in a turn or so.

They'd contacted Geldish to get him to attend but he'd told them to go on without him because he had an idea and, if it panned out, he'd let them know. That message proved to be very poorly received.

For a full turn, this was the only topic in front of the council, not that it did them any good. Tempers frayed and then flared. Finally, in frustration, they adjourned.

However, since it was late in the even, they all ended up at the inn across the courtyard.

The Naradhama innkeeper was delighted to have such auspicious, if cranky, guests.

He listened to a bit of their conversation and was

unable to stop his mouth before his brain kicked in.

"Why don't you do what we do to get stock from Lord Südermann? Just build a few of them steam engine barges and float them out to sea. Then your Succubi could bomb them from those instead of flying all over the place."

There's quiet, there's deathly quiet, and now there's this new level of quiet that settled over the table. Every eye was on him. He knew, right then and there, he'd messed this up and his inn would never be graced by these fine folk again. In fact, he felt he'd be lucky if they let him keep the inn at all.

Teg finally spoke. If his quiet hiss could be called speaking at that moment.

"What's your name, sir?"

The poor innkeeper began to quiver.

"Begging your pardon sir, it's Drapery from the House of Tumble."

Teg considered this for an epi-clik and then burst out laughing.

"Well, Drapery from the House of Tumble, you are now officially the smartest creature on Arreti. Get everyone in the inn a drink on me and fill our glasses as well."

Drapery was so excited at the new business, and the fact he was going to get to keep his inn, he bolted without ever saying thank you.

By the time it was over it was much closer to breaklight than even-fall and some of the regular customers had to help carry the tipsy council members home.

Drapery had made up for his lack of gratitude a thousand times over during the course of the even and was now sitting in his office counting his, newly made, goldens. His wife came in bearing a breaklight repast and stared, slack jawed, at the pile. It was more than they could make in a season.

She scooped them all up, made her husband eat a little something and then sent him to bed. She'd contact the Din-La when the trading post opened. There was no way she would feel safe with this many goldens in the inn.

When the Din-La left a few cliks later she'd secured a line of credit for the inn and gotten herself a new dress. When her husband woke up they could begin making arrangements for all the improvements he'd wished for these many Suns.

Before she could deal with the future, however, she had an inn to clean. After all, it wasn't going to clean itself, now was it?

"BEN EL SALAAM! You get in here right now!"

Despite the fact she was clearly angry, the sound of his wife's voice made him smile. He walked across the front yard to their modest home and found her standing in the front room.

"Yes, dear, what have I done now?"

"This!" She held up a sheaf of papers and waved them at him. "This is why I'm angry. Unless you've completely lost your mind and are now given to making up fables, then you've been playing spy for the Imam again."

He looked at the papers and realized his error. He'd been writing down everything that happened when he'd met the Brittle Riders. He thought it might be a story smalls would enjoy someturn. His wife, Yndi, his glorious gift from Allah, having evidently read the papers, had other ideas. She did not like when he put himself in danger.

"It was nothing dearest. A little trip to the west and then a return here to the east."

"I never asked why we have a nytsteed instead of our old nag. I guess I didn't even want to think about a possible answer. But, this .... THIS?!?!"

She was trembling and still waving the papers.

"You went gallivanting around with terrorists?"

"They were not, and are not, terrorists. They are

very nice, once you strip away all their bombs, weapons and scowls."

That was not nearly as comforting as he'd meant it to be.

She went on for about fifteen epi-cliks and finally broke down crying in his arms. He knew she cared for him deeply and worried about him often. When he'd passed his one hundred and thirtieth Full Sun she thought he'd put the days of a warrior behind him.

And he had. But this request from the Imam had been too important to ignore. Not only their village, but the entire coast was depending on his getting answers and, as much as they were available, he had.

All the Imams had convened to read Ben's report and shared it with all the warrens. Though they need do nothing at this time, they all needed to be aware of the dangers the future posed.

The Din-La now regularly provided updates. They knew about as much as they could know and could do nothing other than wait. This war would be in the west, not here. But, the next one ...

And Ben knew beyond a doubt there would be a next one.

And, until Yontar was stopped, another after that.

Ben waited until she calmed down and told her everything. She was horrified at first, but as Ben's soothing voice detailed the many wonders he'd seen and how Allah had protected him every step of the way, she began to relax. He told her of the Fish-People and of the Brittle Riders and the Succubi with the ferry. He didn't leave out a single detail.

Except one.

He didn't tell her he was soon to return to the Plains.

Malehni finally spied the Din-La post, pulled his deisteed up to a hitching post and dismounted. He was just pulling his pack loose when a Din-La walked up to him and smiled.

"Greetings, you must be Malehni. I'm Gvvl, proprietor of this humbletrading post. Your arrival is most propitious, everyone is waiting for you in the main hall, such as it is."

"Everyone?"

"Yes, sir."

With that, he led a confused Malehni through the front door. Whatever hopes Malehni had of maintaining any sense of decorum or secrecy to his quest immediately vanished when he saw the room's occupants.

Seated at a round table were four fringe dwellers and a Rangka. He'd never seen any of these brands before but knew them from his studies. The Llamia was bigger than he'd imagined they'd be. Next to her was a BadgeBeth sharpening his claws. The Rangka was in the middle and next to him was a Succubus wearing some sort of breast wrap and a loin cloth. Seated next to her was a Wolfen with several weapons in various states of assembly.

There'd been a memo about a group like this. He groped for the name and came up empty. Broken somebodies? Something Steeds? Nope, nothing. They had something to do with a war or an attack or something. He wasn't sure he was comfortable asking. Worse yet might be receiving an answer if he did.

He realized he was staring at them and they were returning the favor. He was very unclear about what to do next. He was saved any further worry when the Rangka spoke.

"Greetings, I am called Geldish. These are the

Brittle Riders," he began motioning to each as he continued, "BraarB, Sland, N'leah and R'yune. I know you were not expecting to be met here, but we couldn't pass up on the opportunity to meet a member of the Kwini-Laku. With your kind permission we can be your escorts to the next trading post, but after that, we would need to part ways."

Oh sure, they wouldn't draw any attention. Then he thought about it some more. He remembered some of what he'd been told about these riders, they were some type of royalty with a temple and one of them had killed Xhaknar. He might not be inconspicuous, but he'd surely be safe. His wife would approve of anything, no matter how treacherous, if it kept him safe.

"I am Malehni. I have been sent by the Children of the Waters to find out the truth about many rumors. Since you are one of the rumors I have heard of, I guess this is as good a place to start as any."

Geldish motioned him to an empty chair.

Gvvl brought over a platter of food and an urn of hot liquid and sat with them. He began by catching Malehni up on the events of the Plains and, as much as he could, on the actions of the Mayanorens to the north. While he was talking Malehni noticed R'yune had finished assembling the weapons and seemed undecided if he should test fire them. Finally, he just waved over another Din-La, handed him all the weapons, and poured himself a mug of the hot liquid.

Malehni still managed to pay strict attention to Gvvl. Much had happened here and much more was about to. He removed a small notebook from his pack and began writing down everything he'd been told.

When he closed his notebook BraarB looked at him and smiled.

"You said Children of the Waters. Is that what the Fish-People call themselves? It's very pretty."

Malehni looked at her anew. Yes, she was big and

foreboding, but he saw kindness in those eyes as well. He then looked around the table at the rest of the riders. They seemed bemused at something. He thought about the stories he'd heard, they were coming back to him now that he was in their presence, and he figured they had seen some hard battles.

Malehni had never been to war. He'd been in some minor skirmishes across the ocean but nothing that would require armies. He was out of his league with these brands but decided he should give some information in return for all he'd received thus far.

"Yes, none of my kind use the term 'Fish-People,' mostly because it is inaccurate. We come from many types of aquatic stock and represent many of the old cultures. My brand, the Kwini-Laku, were the first born of Rohta. It was we who came forth from the pool and it was we whom he first sold.

"Our bulls tell us the story so we won't forget. At first, we enjoyed doing the work we were assigned. It was many Full Suns later before we realized that something was wrong. That we were not treated the same as the humans with whom we were supposed to be working.

"It is told of how one of our ancestors asked for money, like the makers got, and he was laughed at. It was then we realized we were slaves. By then there were much more like us. Not Children of the Waters only, but many brands being sold into slavery.

"Our bulls tell of how some of our brand would sneak away when they caught the ten year flu, we knew it was supposed to kill us, and then go into hiding. They met with others who were doing the same thing. These runaways began telling every brand that caught the flu to go into hiding and then meet with them.

"It was these fugitives who planned the war. How they did it is unknown, but the result is plain to see. We are here and the makers are not."

Geldish went to the bar and brought back a pitcher

of Whævin and glasses for everyone. When they were all served he smiled at Malehni.

"The history of the gen-O-pod war is not a secret here on the Plains. What is a mystery to us is the history of you and your brand, all of the Children of the Waters actually. War is coming. That is a certainty for us and a real possibility for you. It may be the only way we can all survive is by working together."

Malehni sipped his Whævin and looked the Rangka in those eyes for the first time. Realizing he wasn't afraid, something his wife would never approve of, he nodded.

"That is not a decision I can make, but I believe this is what our congress is thinking too. They would not have taken the extraordinary step of sending scouts into the Plains, and to the lands of the bug-people, if not to find out exactly what has happened here and what will happen in the future."

He took another sip and seemed to have a thought.

"Do you think it can be possible for our brands and yours to become allies?"

"Yes, I do. We are all brands of Rohta, we all wish to live in peace, and we all wish for safe homes for our families. That should be enough to start a meaningful discussion."

Malehni emptied his glass, pushed it away and hoped the Rangka was right.

But with a history of so much violence on the Plains, he didn't have a lot of optimism.

It was so cold outside some of the leaves were breaking off their trees from the weight of the ice. Yontar was enjoying every sepi-clik of it. Every lung crushing breath felt like freedom. Ever since he'd gotten his helmet he'd been outside every turn. More often than not he was busy reviewing the progress of his navy but he managed to fit in time for nothing more important than a walk through the forest. He used that time to chew over the many wonderful ways there were to kill a Rangka.

He'd come up with one hundred and seven possibilities. Sixteen were very good ones.

Unlike Xhaknar, he didn't want to see the world burn, he just wanted it to bow down before him. A simple enough request when phrased reasonably. And he planned on phrasing it very reasonably.

"Bow down or die."

Yes, that seemed very reasonable.

Another difference he had from Xhaknar was he appreciated natural beauty. Not in any aesthetic sense, but as a renewable resource he could exploit and maintain. Although, at some visceral level, he did recognize the concept of artistic appreciation he managed to avoid it for the most part. Still, it would occasionally creep in.

His heavy footsteps crumpled through the snow and ice as he headed back to the facility. He was very pleased with the way things were going.

According to the Named Ones they could leave in thirty turns. Well before any significant thaw. The waters near the shore were relatively active so being caught in an ice pack wasn't an issue and the waters farther out were slightly warmer, so once they were away they should have relatively easy going.

Yes, it was all coming together nicely. They should be in Kalindor before Geldish knew they were gone.

He headed for the secret entrance the Named Ones had built between the forest and the west gate and was met by two regular Mayanorens. They handed him a set of sealed folders and escorted him back to his main room.

They stopped outside the door, let him in, and he stretched and removed his helmet as soon as he heard the door close behind him. He looked at it again. It was extremely well made. A blend of browns and blacks, it looked more like his natural hair than any gaudy headdress. Inside were three layers of the shielding, each woven into the next with the final layer woven directly into the helmet. It had shielded ear flaps as well so he could hear. They'd tested it with every instrument available and hadn't detected the slightest leakage.

He opened the first folder and saw it was a complete breakdown of the supplies they had available as well as conservative projections of what could be loaded on the ships. Even with the minimums, they would have enough to make the trip without difficulty. He made a note approving everything and moved to the second.

This one was an update on the fake scout they'd sent out. Geldish's minions had wasted two turns following it before realizing it was a ruse. They'd probably capture him when he returned but he was just a regular Mayanoren and had no useful information. He'd never even met Yontar, which is why he was chosen. He'd hoped they'd have wasted a little more time, but those scouts were well trained. They'd probably figured it out during the first turn and then used the second to confirm.

He should have expected no less, he'd seen those brands fight Xhaknar and the scouts had reported they were training hard outside Anapsida. When he faced them next time, they would not be some cowed peasants, they'd be a legitimate army. One with some very scary tactics at that. He still hadn't forgotten the risky move they'd used against Xhaknar. Delaying the second stage of the assault almost twenty epi-cliks with no nearby support was the move of a genius or a madman.

Either way, it'd worked. Xhaknar was decimated when the second wave hit.

He put that thought aside for the moment and opened the third folder.

He'd tasked Dagnar with coming up with the best weapons possible given their resources. He looked over the list. It was relatively impressive when the thought about it, which is exactly what he was doing.

There were several variations of catapults and slings which could shoot boulders or large spears. Any of those could be mounted on the ships. He'd talk with the Named Ones to get the best variety of placement so the fleet would be the most lethal. There was a hand-held catapult he was going to dismiss until he looked at its range and damage capabilities. It wasn't quite a true gun, but it would kill at a hundred paces.

That was far better than what they had. He made a note to make sure all the regular Mayanorens and the Named Ones were each issued one.

He closed the third folder and smiled. In two turns they would decant the new Named Ones. Twenty-eight turns after that they would be on their way to Kalindor and there was no power on Aretti which could stop them.

He looked at the larger catapults and made a note on the side. If some of these could be altered to fire up instead of forward then he wouldn't even have to worry about those deadly Succubi.

He called in one of the guards from the hall and instructed him to take his notes to Dagnar. Then he opened a book the Named Ones had found. It was a history of naval warfare from the makers' private library. A human named 1st Viscount Nelson did some very unusual things and won many battles on the seas with not much more weaponry than he had. He would study him.

Not everything the makers had done was worthless.

Hana Koi-San, ambassador for the Children of the Waters, sat in a divan across from Lord Südermann sipping a sweet tea while being moistened by his aide. His skin was lightly scaled and golden tinted with flecks of red and white. Südermann noted absently he was beautiful. His gills fluttered easily in the portable mist. His translucent robe and knee high boots were all barely opaque shades of white and blue. He wore trousers made of some pleated material that reminded her of pearls and moved with a delicate grace that belied a certain strength beneath.

He'd spent the last three cliks updating her on the complete status of the Children of the Waters, including the existence of a shipping line. It wasn't armed, but it had ample tonnage for moving munitions and personnel across the ocean.

If his documents were correct, and she saw no reason to assume they weren't, then any single ship would be more than enough to place an army of Succubi into the middle of the ocean to launch an attack.

They discussed how best to have Südermann let the new Elder's Council know about the ships. They finally agreed that the council would be allowed access to them for transportation and placement but they would not arm them. Their technology had not focused on weapons and there wasn't enough time for them to learn and build up the necessary factories.

And, even if they had the resources, there weren't any of the Children he could think of who could come up with the designs. It just wasn't their way. They believed in, what they called, the ten Theravada perfections of Generosity, Moral discipline, Patience, Effort, Meditative concentration, Wisdom, Renunciation, Truthfulness, Loving-kindness, and Equanimity. There was nothing in there about killing.

He'd admitted that there were some brands to the west, across the ocean, who were warlike, by the Children's standards, but they had nothing more advanced than swords and lances. And, as far as he knew, their battles were as much theater as they were war.

That wasn't correct, but he wouldn't learn that for many Suns.

No, the only brands they had for war were already

manning the garrisons near Kalindor, and their numbers weren't that mighty.

She found herself getting lost in the melodious sound of his voice. Her mind had wandered so far that she was caught off guard when she heard her name and was forced to ask him to repeat himself.

"My apologies your majesty, I know you have much on your mind that is of more immediate import. All I wanted to know is if it would be possible to meet with these residents of the Plains? If we are to be their allies, even in a limited manner, I must be able to assure my superiors we are not merely choosing one evil over another."

"Of course Ambassador, that can be easily arranged. In fact, I was hoping to leave next turn to meet with the council. If you would be willing to accompany me, and I would be honored if you would, we can address all your issues at once."

He sipped the tea and, after deciding he liked it and would ask the congress to import this as well, nodded in agreement. This would be the simplest way to find out all he needed to know.

Then he looked at Lord Südermann. There was an element of majesty about her he found intriguing. He was only thirty Full Suns of age but had been chosen for his abilities with math and science and, if he was honest with himself, because he was replaceable. If he were killed on this mission they would mourn his rejoining the cycle of life, but they would still have more skilled ambassadors to attend the needs of the congress.

And the needs of the Children of the Waters far superseded any modest needs his life may have.

He listened patiently as she made the arrangements for their trip. They would leave right after their breaklight repast and head directly to the council. It would be a trip of four turns. Since Hana Koi-San was, being polite, a mediocre steedsman, he and Lord Südermann would ride in a carriage drawn by two steeds.

He wasn't sure how proper it would be to be ensnared in a conveyance for so long with such an interesting femme. Then, after he considered how his posterior felt when he and his aides had ridden from the congress to Südermann's northern palace on deisteeds, he happily signed off on the idea.

Empress ClaalD watched her mating partner leave her room and smiled. She eased herself onto the floor and enjoyed the salacious feeling while the sweat dripped across her skin and down her mane. She thought about showering off but was enjoying her scent too much to do so just yet. She also thought about King Uku. His brand didn't have arranged matings and she hoped he had someone to share his personal time with. That thought faded as she again drifted back to her mating partner, TraadK.

Her herd had chosen well. If she wasn't going to mate for life, and her feelings for Uku prevented that because it seemed somehow disrespectful, then the next best thing was a mate chosen from the arena. The winner of ten rounds of competition, five athletic, and five scholastic, was always named Empress' Companion. However, this was the first time in many Suns the position had been anything more than honorary. Still, as Empress, it was her duty to provide the herd with a foal to keep the royal line intact.

TraadK had been surprised when he'd received the royal summons but had done his duty without complaint. In fact, he seemed to enjoy it. He certainly made sure that both his empress and the conditions of his rank were satisfied.

He hoped he wouldn't be hurt to find out she fantasized about Uku while he was laboring. Well, some of the time, TraadK was very hard to ignore.

Finally, knowing she had other duties to perform which would be nowhere near as pleasurable, she lifted herself off the comfortable bed Uku had given her as a gift. Stretching languorously, she went into the bathing chamber and began, reluctantly, washing away the physical memories of her most recent session. The less tangible aspects of her happiness would still be available for anyone to see.

Less than a clik later her mistress-in-waiting had finished perfectly coifing her mane and she was ready to face whatever the turn may bring.

King Uku greeted her as she walked down the hall preparing to head to the new enclave to finalize some minor details. They chatted briefly and she saw, whatever personal issues he may have had about her mating, he was now excited about the entire venture. Unable to restrain herself, she asked him why.

"Two reasons. First, because when you are successful it means there will be new life in these hoary old halls. Second, even though it is merely honorary, I will be an uncle as I would be to any small born in the palace while I'm king. My brother died in a Mayanoren raid and my sister is barren so this will be the only small attached to my line."

"Have you thought of taking a mate?"

"It's not our way. Not like you do anyway. If I were to mate I would have to promise both my body and my soul to her and we both know I couldn't do that. Not honestly. And whatever atrocities I've recorded in battle, I will not add the atrocity of lying to that register."

He looked pensive for a moment and then smiled.

"But it doesn't matter. What matters is I've never seen you happier and your happiness is very important to me. However, I feel that I must warn you, I am going to spoil your foal to the point that it may think me truly an uncle."

She thought about that, laughed, and then noticed

his crooked smile and laughed even louder. She leaned over, gave him a kiss on the cheek and headed off to the enclave.

The outdoor air was cold but clear. She felt the moisture tingle against her coat and reveled in it. Her two guards walked slightly behind her as she wandered through the warren looking at the many new businesses which had sprung up since the fall of Xhaknar. Not just Se-Jeant and Llamia businesses either, all of the brands had opened up shops here. She knew the same held true for the other warrens. She had approved twelve different export permits through the council and had nine more pending, awaiting reviews from her staff.

She passed the new Din-La trading post and greeted its new proprietor Khhw. He'd expanded into three smaller shops and now handled almost ninety percent of the warren's imports and exports. What he'd lost in local trade he more than made up for with the new products from the coasts. Plus he'd given her a detailed projection which accurately predicted the decline in interest in locally made crafts and the increase of exported foods and other items. Thanks to his efforts they were completely prepared for when one line of income declined and another increased.

Of course, the custom crafts made for wealthy clients, like the ring she wore, seemed immune to the whims of the market.

Such are the vagaries of prosperity and peace.

Elzish wafted through the forest about a kay behind Zrrm. Over the last five Suns he'd noted the little Din-La leaving the post for eight to ten turns at a time. He'd been content to let the Din-La keep their secrets, but with Yontar back among the living ,and war coming again, no one could afford secrets. He'd casually broached the subject once with him and was brushed off with a "looking for new imports" excuse.

Elzish smirked at that. They were headed due north, into the wild lands, in the middle of the Dark Sun. There weren't any imports coming from here. The weather was awful; snow, sleet, and high winds all slashing through the frozen air. Although Elzish couldn't feel the weather, at least not until it was far more extreme than this, he was still cognizant of its effects on flesh. Zrrm was wearing some special clothing since he, and his steed, rode unimpeded through the storm. He let his mind gently brush against Zrrm's to make sure he was still ahead and on course, and was quite surprised to find how calm he was. A storm like this should make him uncomfortable. He left a small thread there to lead him and began considering the Din-La more fully.

Elzish had been decanted before the gen-O-pod war and still remembered it well. He'd received word through his clan of what was going to happen and when. Weapons had been hidden in bunkers all over the planet but the wizards didn't think they'd need them. They'd just floated through the cities ripping metal free from its moorings as the other brands followed behind killing any and all humans.

He'd been assigned to destroy an alpha wave corrupter outside of old Caracas. He'd been stationed there winnowing metals from mines. When some of the flimsy mines collapsed killing the gen-O-pods working in them, the humans would just order more. He'd seen his roommate's body carried out one morning and, when he'd asked to be allowed to say a prayer over it, his human had laughed at him and told him "Don't bother. You pods ain't got no souls."

Two Full Suns after that he'd gladly led a group of reptiloids through all of Venezuela and then north. They'd stayed on the old continent and tried to regroup as he headed off to find other wizards. The amount of devastation he'd encountered was staggering. City after city lay in complete ruin.

He'd seen wizards leveling anything made of metal. All of the humans were dead, their bodies burning for miles. There'd been about three billion humans on the planet when they'd attacked. He had projected that within twenty more generations humans would have probably become extinct on their own. But none of the brands wanted to wait that long for their freedom.

By the end of the tenth Full Sun, they'd hunted down and killed every last one.

He'd met with other wizards when he'd reached North America and they were heading towards the old makers' city of Chicago. He'd gone along with them as they cleaned up any residual remnants they found of the makers' technologies and dwellings. He'd known other brands were doing the same thing elsewhere.

By the time they'd made it to the outskirts of what had been Chicago, vague alliances were forming. Within a couple Full Suns each group had claimed the lands it wanted, and since there was plenty of land to go around, no one complained. Even on the Plains, there were millions of square kays unpopulated.

At the beginning of the war the Din-La, like the haven lords, stayed out of the way. But, within one hundred turns, they'd insulated themselves as the canniest purveyors of goods and services the planet had ever seen. Essentially the same function they performed now.

How they did it was a closely held secret, but no one really cared. Elzish had always assumed they had retained some of the makers' communication technologies and, possibly, some of their manufacturing capabilities. None of that mattered before Xhaknar came since there was peace and after it was just too dangerous to delve into. No one wanted their supplies terminated.

He felt Zrrm develop a sense of anticipation and refocused on him. They were coming to a small glade. It was about as far from anything as you could possibly get. He couldn't sense anything else around. Zrrm's excitement was palpable but, try as he might, Elzish could sense nothing but local fauna.

All of a sudden Zrrm disappeared from his senses.

Elzish halted and retuned his mind. He let his consciousness encompass every living thing and began filtering out the psychic noises created by the animals. He arrived at the spot where Zrrm disappeared and could detect only a void. He used his more traditional senses to survey the ground. He could see the tracks from the steed. They simply stopped in the middle of the glade. There was no sign of violence or any other disturbance. It was as though Zrrm had simply led his steed into another realm without pause.

He moved closer to the steed tracks and began truly sensing the ground. He studied each granule carefully and slowly discerned a thin line running through the grasses. It was perfectly straight and ran about ten steeds wide. Gradually he figured out where the trip lever was and was about to reach for it when the ground opened up in front of him.

There, standing on a wide ramp, was Zrrm.

"Greetings Elzish. I will admit surprise at finding you here."

"I followed you."

"Why?"

That was a good question. What did he really hope to accomplish? The Din-La had risked as much as anyone in the war against Xhaknar. He was here due to a nagging concern, but that didn't seem like a good excuse. He finally opted for the truth.

"I need to know the secrets of the Din-La. War is coming and you hold too much knowledge that you do not share. I avoided my responsibilities when Geldish led the Plains against Xhaknar and I will not do so again. I imagine you even have a way to destroy me, but I cannot let war come without every possible defense being explored."

Zrrm smiled, more warmly than threateningly.

"Well, yes, we do have a weapon you would not like but I'm not sure that we can do any more than we already are to protect the Plains."

They stood there, unmoving, as the winds howled around them and snow and ice clung to their clothes. Several epi-cliks later Zrrm motioned for Elzish to follow.

The opening shut as quietly as it had opened and all sounds disappeared. It was a comfortable 20°C in the hallway they were walking down. The walls were subtly lit but there was no ornamentation anywhere. Everywhere he looked was muted gray, which seemed very un-Din-La.

At the bottom of the ramp, he beheld a wonder. It was a city. It stretched as far as he could see but, for some reason, he could sense nothing. He could see the many Din-La and he could see the machines and buildings, but could not sense any of it. He glanced at Zrrm and saw him smiling.

"Everything you see is protected by an alpha wave emitter. It cancels out any senses you may have. Of course, when we put it in after the gen-O-pod war it was done in case any makers still lived. We had no way of predicting the rise of the Rangka."

Elzish, limited in his senses, began taking it all in. It was not a densely populated city although it certainly seemed busy. Everywhere he looked there was activity. Then, bit by bit, he realized what he was seeing; the entire facility was mechanized. The Din-La were using the maker's technology to create anything they needed.

One or two Din-La were all they needed to run machines that were the size of small warrens. He saw boxed items being moved from place to place on self-propelled carts. He remembered the carts. The makers would use them to get from place to place and make the brands walk behind. They were electric powered and silent.

That thought brought another, places this large

require a lot of power. He wondered what kind of power source they had and decided to keep an eye out for anything that might give him a clue.

Zrrm led him through a series of alleys until they arrived at the city center. Elzish couldn't help but be impressed. There were several ornate buildings suspended over a series of tracks. A quick count showed him that they could run up to twenty vehicles at once. He wondered what this place was.

They entered a glass box which, silently, closed around them and then began lifting them to the buildings above. Elzish remembered these as well, although never this elegant. They were called elevators. It opened inside a large room, done in the traditional yellow and purple colors of the Din-La. Elzish was mildly startled to realize the room would be considered tasteful in almost any culture except the reptiloids.

It must be some sort of meeting room. There was a large, round, desk in the center and screens placed on every wall. Elzish remembered them as well, they were for video viewing. He didn't miss the technology he'd left behind after the war, but could see how it could provide certain advantages. Even so, he found the whole array disconcerting.

He couldn't put his finger on why right away, but it eventually came to him; you could hide anything or anyone down here and no one would ever know.

Malehni shivered in the stunning cold. The skies were clear but that was about the only nice thing about the turn. He was riding in the middle of the Brittle Riders and they all seemed comfortable despite the bitter conditions. He had to admit that the new clothing the Din-La had given him kept him far warmer than his old garments would have done, but it was still freaking cold out here. He wondered how anyone lived like this.

He watched his breath steam away into the chilly air and pulled his jacket tighter. N'leah noticed when he did this and smiled.

"Are you cold friend Malehni?"

"Yes," he shivered, "I most certainly am. While my brand may have been bred to work in the northern oceans, my clan lives on the southern islands, we don't even keep our ice this cold."

BraarB overheard him and laughed.

"Yes, it is cold, but we have been through worse. After a while, you get used to it."

He faced BraarB with a look of pure consternation.

"I do not wish to get used to it, I wish to get out of it."

He said that loud enough to cause everyone to laugh and direct a couple of pointed, but playful, barbs in his direction. He was angry at first but realized that the gentle teasing was their way of including him in their group. He wasn't sure how that made him feel. His brand had teasing rituals as well, but they were mostly physical. A nudge here, a rub there, a smile to tie them all together. He'd never encountered verbal interplay like this before. Over the last four turns, he'd gotten to know these aliens better. They were completely self-reliant and, extremely confident, but they all seemed scarred somehow. Not just the physical scars he'd noticed, there were things they hid deep inside they would never share with him.

He spied a plume of dark smoke in the distance and realized it must be the next Din-La post. Geldish altered their course a little to head directly towards it and the riders increased their speed to a gallop. This was a mixed blessing to Malehni. On the one hand he would get to the comfort of the indoors sooner but, on the other hand, the increased speed caused the wind to whip against his face even harder. He pulled his collar up tight and decided to tough it out.

Less than a clik later he was inside drinking a hot, sweet, drink and warming up near the fire. The other riders had all loaded their gear into their rooms and were settling in around the bar. He marveled at how casually they imbibed alcohol. For his brand it was almost exclusively used in ceremonies. On those rare occasions they did drink he rarely had a second. He didn't like the way it made him feel.

He looked up from the fire just in time to see Sland coming across the room to him with another steaming mug of the delicious liquid. He accepted it gratefully and motioned Sland to sit next to him on the bench. They sat quietly for a while and then Sland laughed.

"You are really far from home, aren't you? Not just the amount of land, but everything, I mean."

Malehni shrugged.

"Yes, I am far from home, but I do what I must for the Children of the Waters. Service is our highest honor."

Sland sipped his flagon of skank and then set it down.

"That sounds different than the way we do things here, but maybe not so much. Geldish presented us with an impossible task and we all agreed to it because even the thought of possibly, maybe, bringing hope to the Plains was worth the risk.

"We were fringe dwellers. Do you know what that means?"

"I've heard the term, but I think that I missed much of its meaning."

"When Xhaknar first came to the Plains he made a special effort to kill every Wolfen, Llamia, Succubus and BadgeBeth he could find. Those who survived were forced to live around the Gaping Canyon or in small villages in the middle of nowhere. On the fringes, as it were. The term came to mean a sub-level of brands. It was as brutal an insult as Xhaknar could conceive. He considered us barely better than a kgum.

"But, we knew that behind all his hatred was fear. Something about us scared him shitless. When Geldish came up with his mad plan, and only recruited creatures like us, we took it as a sign that change could come. Now, I must admit … wait, you really don't drink alcohol? Oh well, I suppose it doesn't matter. I know one other brand who doesn't. Nice enough when you get to know him. Anyway, none of us knew if that change was going to be a good thing or not, but it was the first slim splinter of hope we'd ever had."

They sat quietly for a while more and then Malehni rose, got another flagon of skank for Sland, and returned.

"You and the others have told me much about life now, after the war, and filled in the details of the war itself, but I would like to ask you some questions about your brand if I may."

Sland motioned for him to continue while he swallowed a mouthful of skank.

"Our brand puts great emphasis on our clan ties. Does anything like that exist here?"

Sland put down his flagon, ordered a double Din-La brandy and proceeded to tell Malehni his life story. A clik later he sat there with his mouth open. Sland had defied his family, something that was unheard of among the Children, but much good had come from his defiance. Yes, he'd suffered horribly for many Full Suns while living alone, but much good has come from him. In many ways, the freedom of the Plains was due to his disobedience. Nothing in his teachings from the Brothers of the Soul had prepared him for a conundrum like this.

Sland walked back to the bar and left him to his thoughts, and they were tumultuous. Sland had been brutally honest with him and his brand prized honesty very highly. But Sland had disobeyed his family and that was barely pardonable.

Well, barely pardonable to his brands. Sland's brand, all the brands of the Plains, were different.

Obviously, his father and his king honored clan ties but there seemed to be more leeway than he was used to. Certainly, Sland had been repatriated with his brand after the war, maybe even before.

They were very different from him and his. Now the question he needed to have answered was clear; "Was this a good thing?"

The Elder's Council stared at the unusual tableau seated in front of them. They'd been introduced to Hana Koi-San and had met Lord Südermann several times before, but it was the ten others seated behind them that held their attention. They were Lord Südermann's council. They dealt with the turn to turn needs of the brands in Südermann's lands. They had nothing to do with the military or diplomacy, yet here they were. Sitting quietly and staring back at the brands who were staring at them.

So far all they'd been able to glean was they were here to check the progress of the war plans. Why was still unclear.

They weren't being disruptive, far from, but they were here and, by all accounts, they shouldn't be. The council really had no recourse but to include them. They were obviously guests of Lord Südermann and they weren't bothering anyone, so they did the only thing they could do; got them chairs and served refreshments.

Hana Koi-San had brought them all up to date on the capabilities and information that the Children of the Waters, the correct name for the Fish-People, had. They'd listened patiently, and with some excitement, to his offer to provide whatever assistance they could give. Greko had explained to the Children's ambassador about their plans and needs and it had been agreed to let their assistants work out the details.

All in all, it had been a very productive session but Südermann's council was still sitting there stoically and looking for all Aretti as though they were expecting something. Finally one of them stood. No one recognized his brand, but he was fierce looking.

"I am al Souk Mulard, of the Cantarian clan, and we have been proud citizens of Lord Südermann's since the turn of reckoning. I, and all the members of the general council, have come here this turn with a purpose. Through the violence needed to keep our lands apart from the realm of Kalindor and, more recently, Xhaknar, Lord Südermann has kept our lands peaceful and free. We have flourished through trade and have been the beneficiaries of many conveniences due to the inventiveness of her scientists.

"Recently, unbeknownst to Lord Südermann, some rambunctious smalls made a startling discovery. They had wandered into the forbidden lands west of us, but north of Kalindor. They were looking, as all smalls do at some point in their lives, for adventure. They came across a path of rails. This they reported to their parents and their parents reported it to their local representatives. Those representatives sent scouts out to see what they might be.

"At first they thought it might be a new route to the Fish-People … my pardons, I mean the Children of the Waters, but while it is exactly that, it became clear that it had not been built by the makers. It is too new. Our scouts estimated it to be barely one hundred Full Suns old. Also, unlike the rail conveyances built by the makers, it is wider than the makers' preferred Stephenson gauge.

"Approximately forty kays west of its initial point, our scouts found several vehicles which were clearly designed to ride on those rails. They took many pictographic records and detailed as much as they could. It was clear to them that this was a Kalindorian construct. Since it did not threaten our lands and it was not complete, we merely made note of it and posted scouts to watch its development.

"Several turns ago we received a report of a Mayanoren riding into the lands of Kalindor. He was initially arrested, but our scouts saw him later being escorted to a train, unencumbered by shackles, and taken south, presumably to the palace of Exalted Quelnerom. We were preparing a full report for the Royal Mantis Guard when we heard of this meeting. Obviously, this news concerns all of us equally, so we decided to deliver it to all interested parties simultaneously.

"Lord Südermann has decreed you to be allies and the Ant-People have acknowledged you are not vile. Well, at least not as vile as they expected you to be."

That brought a round of good natured laughter. The Ant-People were still as separatist as ever, but they were also fiercely loyal to Lord Südermann for reasons no one could fathom. Also, for equally ambiguous reasons, they seemed to be fond of Geldish.

Once they settled down they returned their attention to al Souk Mulard.

"I really have nothing more to say. All of the documents our scouts have generated have been copied and are in possession of our aides outside of this chamber. With your kind permission, I will summon these aides and distribute the materials."

Permission was quickly granted and soon they were all reviewing a plethora of documentation. They could, easily, see the Kalindorians had begun building the system long before the war with Xhaknar. Not even Yontar planned that far ahead and he certainly never would have trusted brands he didn't have complete control over.

After everyone wasted a clik trying to figure out why the Kalindorians had built this, they decided to ignore that for the moment and, instead, concentrate on how to use the knowledge.

The Kgul spoke.

"We do not have vehicles which will fit on the rails, nor do we have time to make them. At least not now.

Traveling out to capture the existing vehicles only invites battle with Kalindor and we don't have time for that either. This discovery will either have to be captured or destroyed, but it is a concern for a later turn either way.

"I give my thanks, on behalf of the council, to al Souk Mulard and all the members of the general council and am grateful to see these last five Full Suns of peace between us have produced trust. This may be the greatest weapon we have against Yontar."

Everyone agreed with the Kgul readily enough and the session was ended.

They adjourned to Drapery's inn after passing along instructions to their aides and Teg ordered the first round.

Two Naradhama were sitting by the bar watching them come in and order when the first one turned and laughed.

"Great," he said, "if this keeps up Drapery will start demanding that we bathe before we can order."

The second one grunted and waved away a pesky insect as he slugged down the last of his skank.

The Named One had been in the palace of the Exalted Quelnerom for several turns. He'd presented everything as he'd been instructed and waited for Quelnerom's staff to build a few prototypes. He'd been treated well and had been given free run of the grounds. They'd made a decent effort to find him a wide variety of foods which weren't as salty as the ones they preferred.

While he'd been carefully guarded he'd also been treated with respect and courtesy. All in all, as far as prisons were concerned, this one was very nice. He sat in the garden in the center courtyard and ate a snack the cooking staff had provided. It was a seafood sandwich of some sort and there was a small fruit that he couldn't even begin to guess where it had come from. It was clearly a mutant variety of a banana, he'd read about those in the makers' records, but it was a bright pink color and very sweet. He decided he liked it.

He knew that Lord Yontar would be leaving soon and coming here. It would take him, at least, twenty turns to make the journey to Kalindor so he had time to ensure the Exalted Quelnerom's participation. He'd seen some of the work his craft masters had completed and felt sure that he would have their alliance in short order.

Their submission would come shortly thereafter.

He finished his snack, wrapped the leavings into the provided bag, and threw it in the trash. One thing he'd noticed right away when he'd arrived here was how neat the reptiloids were. Even in the military garrison, there had been trash receptacles everywhere.

He was getting a feel for these brands. They were garish as could be, but not barbarians. Their information network seemed good enough, given the limited areas they could access, and they were clearly intelligent. What they could not do was innovate. Show them how to build something and they did so quite well, but tell them what you needed and all was lost. They simply couldn't extrapolate from concept to reality, it was beyond them.

He began to walk towards his room and was joined by his escort. They continued on for a few epi-cliks until they were stopped by a messenger. He was summoned to the Exalted Quelnerom's throne room.

He entered and smiled to himself. One of Quelnerom's craft masters was holding a large box with several dials on it. Part of his agreement with the Exalted Quelnerom was this item be the fifth they built. They could pick any other four from the plans he'd brought, it didn't matter to him or Yontar, as long as this was the fifth.

He performed the ritual bow and took his seat in front of the reptiloids' ruler. The craft master placed the box on a table between them. Quelnerom motioned for him to do whatever it is he was going to do. He leaned forward, twisted the dials to the settings he'd memorized and flipped the power toggle to the on position. He knew that he only had about a clik's worth of power due to the many limitations faced by the Kalindorians, but that should be enough.

He raised the attached microphone and hoped the Kalindorians had followed the instructions exactly.

"Kalindor to North Post, come in please."

There was a moment of static and then he got a response.

"This is North Post, Kalindor, please hold for Lord Yontar."

It was called a short wave radio. He was operating at about ten thousand hertz. He knew, from reading the makers' library, this had once been considered a useless device, but he found it very useful at the moment.

Never more so than when he heard his lord's voice come booming out of the speaker.

"Greetings Named One, I gather your trip was successful and you are in the presence of the Exalted Quelnerom?"

"Yes, Lord Yontar, he is with me. Would you like to speak with him?"

"Yes, please."

He quickly explained how to use the device and handed the microphone to the reptiloid king.

"Greetings Lord Yontar, this is the Exalted Quelnerom of the reptiloids. Thank you for your kind gifts."

"It is my pleasure, your highness. It is my hope this little gesture will bring us closer to an alliance. And, hopefully, this alliance will allow us to rid Aretti of our mutual enemies."

"I am sure that something could be worked out that would benefit each of us. What do you have in mind?"

"I would rather discuss that with you directly. The

Named One who is with you has a map of where I and my followers will land. We will be coming by sea and should arrive within fifty turns. That is, if this is acceptable with you."

"Indeed, that would be perfect. I will have my staff make arrangements so I can be there awaiting your arrival."

"Excellent. Yontar out."

The Named One took the microphone from the Exalted Quelnerom and smiled broadly. He sat quietly as Quelnerom issued orders and his staff studied the map he'd produced. It took all of his self-control not to laugh. These fools were working very hard to surrender all they had without Yontar firing a shot.

They just didn't know that yet.

The Named One who was responsible for the shortwave took the microphone from his lord's hand and smiled. Yontar smiled back at him and left the radio room. He knew the primitive radio his Named One had been able to get built in Kalindor probably only had a clik's worth of power, at best, and he wouldn't hear from him again unless something went horribly wrong.

He walked past the newly decanted Named Ones and noted they did have one minor difference from their predecessors, they wore bright red jerkins. He remembered what the Named Ones had told them after they were decanted.

"You are greater than us. In time, you will create those who are greater than you. That is no matter. You, and all who follow you, live to serve Lord Yontar. You have one turn to familiarize yourselves with this section of the facility and then, come breaklight, you will be briefed on our upcoming mission and your duties."

They'd assented unanimously and set off in

different directions. Later, in the even, he'd seen them exchanging notes on what each had learned. He knew the Named Ones had incredible memories and imagined their progeny would have a detailed map of every aspect of the facility as well complete impressions of each item before breaklight.

He walked into his private office and considered the events of the last few turns. The new Named Ones showed the same eagerness to serve as the old ones. They were still learning but they already showed tremendous promise. They'd made a minor alteration to the storage arrangements on the ships so they could take the makers' library with them.

At first, he'd thought that a waste of time but, in just a few turns, they'd made fantastic strides in deciphering some of the more esoteric texts concerning mathematics and linguistics. Not everything needed to be a weapon, he would need a wide variety of knowledge and skills if he was going to rule the planet.

There was a knock on his door and he called for whoever it was to enter. One of the new Named Ones, resplendent in his red shirt and white trousers, strode in and snapped a salute. He returned it without rising and motioned to a chair, which the Named One ignored.

"Greetings Lord Yontar. I apologize for disturbing your private time but I have an update on our projected travel projections. We can leave in five turns."

Yontar was surprised.

"What about the weather? This is still the middle of the Dark Sun."

"Yes lord, however, we should experience no more than three turns of rough weather before we are far enough south to ascertain the warmer currents. Furthermore, if we leave then we will make it that much harder for the forces of the Plains to mount any meaningful assault. Our projections show they should be able to work out some sort of alliance with the Fish-People, even if it's temporary, to place troops in our way."

Yontar shrugged.

"Okay," he smiled, "the sooner the better I guess. Make the arrangements and notify the Named One in Kalindor of our new arrival time. Also, make sure Dagnar has his weapons in place. Projections or no, I don't want to risk getting caught in the middle of an ocean without defenses."

The Named One saluted and left.

Yontar had been born and bred for military conquest, he did not believe in plans going smoothly. Even the best laid ones required adjustments when reality came to the fore. That was Xhaknar's great failing.

Yontar thought back on the battle and wondered what he would have done differently. He imagined that the first thing he could think of is that he wouldn't have marched them into the canyon in such close formations. If it meant that some of the outer flanks would have had to march on the mountain foots, so be it. It would have triggered the ambush but they would have still have been in formation and had all the forces, except for the Succubi, in front of them.

He could imagine several scenarios that would have brought victory in that case. It would have been difficult, but it could have been done.

Then he imagined that same battle with the resources he had now. That would have been the ultimate conflict. Yes, it would have been glorious.

Karrish and Makish were nervous. It had been several turns since they'd been able to communicate with Elzish and Zrrm seemed to be missing as well. They'd contacted Geldish but he hadn't heard anything either and they hadn't felt his death so they were relatively sure he was still alive. Well, as alive as the undead could be.

Geldish had agreed to divert his course and bring the Brittle Riders to Elzish's last known location and look around. They'd been forced to leave Malehni earlier than they'd wished, but Geldish knew what this could portend as well as they did. With Yontar able to move freely without them being able to track him it could mean he had a new weapon that could disrupt their abilities.

Geldish had shared all he'd learned from Malehni with the other Rangka and they'd left the trading post with all due haste. In the turns following they'd slept on their nytsteeds and rode non-stop to the glade where Elzish had disappeared. BraarB had the stamina to keep up but even she was beginning to flag when Geldish finally called a halt.

If they were fatigued they didn't show it. They quickly dismounted and formed a rough skirmish line around Geldish. He immediately expanded his mind and began searching the ground for clues. He promptly saw the hoof prints of Zrrm's steed. They'd been covered by snow and sleet but that meant nothing to his sight.

He noticed something odd on the ground; a thin, straight, line where no straight line should be. R'yune had noticed it as well and began dragging his sword through it to see if he could trigger an opening. He completed that task, unsuccessfully, when Geldish bent over and began running his finger in the micro-crevice. He noticed, while his mind could feel everything behind and below them, he could sense nothing in front. There was some sort of shielding here. This could be another lair of Yontar's.

He stood up and apprised the others of his fears. Sland smiled and dug his claws into the ground near the line. R'yune's sword was swiftly drawn. Soon ground was disappearing at the same rate a hole was appearing. They could hear sirens going off underground but Sland never slowed. Within two more epi-cliks, there was an entrance large enough for them to ride through.

They remounted and were about to charge in when they noticed a group of beings wearing purple shirts and yellow pants. Geldish held his hand up to stop the riders and smiled.

"Of course, the secret warren of the Din-La, I should have guessed."

They recognized Zrrm easily enough.

"You five really do present a formidable opponent."

"Are we your opponents Zrrm? I thought us to be allies." Geldish eased his nysteed back into the opening to get a little more room and the others followed suit.

"We are Geldish, and you need fear nothing here now. Elzish is here as our guest. He was, and is, free to leave whenever he desires. He has, instead, decided to stay and learn the secrets of the Din-La. Since you are here now, and you have made such a nice hole in our door, I feel compelled to offer you the same courtesies."

He motioned for them to follow him down the ramp. The gaggle of Din-La on the ramp parted as they passed by and closed ranks behind them. They heard the sounds of workers behind them, probably resealing the entrance, but they never turned around to check.

When Geldish had backed up his nysteed he'd taken that moment to update Karrish and Makish on what was happening so they wouldn't worry when he disappeared as well. He'd caught their acknowledgement just before he re-entered the tunnel.

Now, at the bottom, they saw a marvel. Part city, part machine, all functional. They were in the home of the Din-La. Their real home, not the little villages they tossed up around their trading posts. Geldish saw the rail system and marveled. With everything underground and shielded they could move anything anywhere at any time.

Zrmm led them around until they came to a ramp that took them over the rail system, there they saw Elzish on the other side and he beckoned them. When they got to him they dismounted and looked at him warily.

"Relax Geldish, everything is fine."

"The brothers of the temple have not heard from you and were worried."

"As you already know, this place is shielded."

"Yes, and it also seems to have many other communication devices. Why did you not use one of them to contact the others?"

Elzish seemed tossed by that question but eventually shrugged.

"This place is a wonder. It reminded me of when the makers were alive. I guess I just got caught up in it. Have you let the others know I'm well?"

"I let them know that you were probably alive. Beyond that, I didn't know your status until now."

"Hmm, well, I guess there was no way for you to have, sorry about that."

Geldish looked at the riders. Sland was covered in mud and melting ice and snow, BraarB's eyes were mere slits and she was slumping forward, N'leah's wings were drooping and she seemed unable to open her left eye, R'yune looked ready to storm a warren singlehandedly, but Geldish could tell he'd passed tired two turns back.

"Since it appears you, and we, are safe, I would like to ask for a place for us to get clean and get some rest. We have ridden nonstop for four turns to get here and rescue you."

Elzish motioned for them to wait while he went and spoke to a Din-La they didn't know. A few sepi-cliks later several Din-La poured out of a modest structure. Some tended to the nytsteeds while the rest were undressing all of the riders, except Geldish, as they walked. By the time they'd entered the building they were too tired and naked to notice how opulent it was. Geldish watched as three Din-La escorted each rider into a private room. Others scurried about the lavish atrium picking up their clothes, weapons, and gear. Within three epi-cliks he was alone.

He turned and spied Zrrm appearing from a hallway

he hadn't noticed and followed as he beckoned him to tag along. He was led into a room which was remarkably similar to the one he had in his private observatory. The walls appeared as if they were mottled, pulsing, flesh and there were torches placed in each corner. On one side was a bed and on the other was a table laden with food and drink.

Zrrm nodded, closed the door and left Geldish to his privacy. He didn't need sleep but every mind, no matter how vast, needs rest. He sampled some of the foods and, finding them delicious, made himself a plate and sat on the bed. He let his mind go completely empty as he finished his repast and finally let himself fall into a Rangka trance.

In the other rooms, a bomb could have gone off and they wouldn't have noticed.

Three Din-La left the council chambers and the council members began making final arrangements. One thousand Succubi would leave come breaklight and take a high flight to the western ocean. The Din-La would move the necessary munitions to the coast and would have them there within seven to ten turns. It should take the Succubi no longer than six turns to make the trip unencumbered by weapons or any other extra weight. The Children of the Waters would provide a barge which would, they promised, easily hold everything the Plains army would need.

Hana Koi-San reported that their scouts were seeing increased activity around Yontar's navy. The northern scouts also reported that the Mayanoren camp was thinning out, clearly headed toward the west. It was becoming obvious that Yontar was planning on making his run during the Dark Sun.

At first, they'd thought him insane but Hana Koi-San had explained how, if he could get his ships out about fifteen to twenty kays from shore, he should be able to use the currents to head south safely. It would be the first part of his trip that would be the most dangerous.

It was also the part of the trip where the Succubi would be unable to do anything. The winds would be too fierce and unpredictable and the cold would be prohibitive.

They would have to meet him in open water further south.

D'noma, the Succubi squadron leader, was looking over the plans and asked a few questions. But, for the most part, everything was relatively clear cut. They would travel around five hundred kays per turn and spend each even at a trading post. In a high flight that would not be much of a problem. Her only concern was traversing the mountains for the last two legs of the journey. They would have to travel near the border of Kalindor or else they would have to fly much higher than they were used to. She wasn't worried about being attacked by the Kalindorians since there were no reports that they had any weapons remotely capable of hurting them in high flight and the Kalindorians who could fly were more gliders than fliers like the Succubi. They'd never be able to attain enough altitude to be a threat.

She'd had to explain high flight to Hana Koi-San. He'd been fascinated to find out that they could fly up to three kays high in the air and then aim their bodies slightly downward and use gravity and air pressure to glide at high speeds towards their destination. She'd showed him how their wings were far more flexible than those of their genetic ancestors. They could adjust small portions of the outer edges to allow them to turn faster and steeper or they could spread them fully and ride the currents.

He'd, in turn, shared how his brand could traverse any freshwater source for extended periods of time by filtering water through their gills. He regaled her with tales of the joys of being beneath the waters for kays at a time before he'd finally have to surface and refill his lungs to support his filters. He made it sound as thrilling as flying.

She'd been elated for him when Teg and T'reena had made arrangements for him and his staff to swim in the new Great Lake when the Good Sun arrived.

The Elders' Council interrupted her reverie when they wanted to know if there was anything else she'd need once she arrived in the land of the Children of the Waters. She checked her list and saw that she'd covered everything from medical kits to food to weapons and ammunition. She couldn't think of anything else and told them so.

With nothing else on the agenda, they instructed their secretaries to make sure that the warrens were brought up to date on their plans and then invited the guests of Lord Südermann and D'noma to join them at Drapery's. It had become their favorite 'after council' place to relax. Although some of the invitees had previous obligations, they still marched twenty brands into the inn.

Ever since the first even they'd been here they'd come to an agreement not to discuss business unless it was absolutely necessary. Which, as it turned out, usually meant all the time. However, sometimes the relaxed atmosphere allowed for things to get settled that couldn't in a more formal atmosphere. Several of the council members seriously considered having Drapery open a second inn inside the council chambers. That idea was discarded, albeit reluctantly.

They could see the construction going on all around them. The kitchen was being expanded and there was a third floor being added for more rooms. Plus, and this amused all of them, Drapery was adding new indoor plumbing. While the outdoor type he had was as advanced as many businesses had, and was connected to the sewage system of the city, he was setting up his inn to be the jewel of Anapsida.

They joked with him, when he came to the table, about his having to raise prices to support all the changes. They were pleased to hear him say that would not happen, that the increased business he'd been garnering and the new deal he had with the Din-La would easily cover the improvements and allow him to keep his prices unchanged.

D'noma smiled as she watched the interplay around the table. There was so much hope here, she and her Succubi would do whatever they could to keep that alive.

Geldish slowly let the trance fade and realized he was facing his riders. They were seated around the room, drinking something steaming, and looking very refreshed. N'leah noticed the change in him first and poured him a mug of what they were having and handed it to him. He gave her a brief nod of thanks and sipped the sweet java drink they'd all become fond of.

He floated off the bed, stretched his feet to the floor and smiled.

"Well, here we are, deep underground where no one can find us, completely at the mercy of our supposed allies, and surrounded by enough wealth to start a million warrens. Did I miss anything?"

Sland started grunting and waving his hand in the air. They all laughed and Geldish pointed at him to speak.

"You forgot the food. This place is loaded with food."

That caused them all to laugh even more. There was a knock at the door and R'yune opened it to reveal Zrrm. He stepped to the side and two Din-La entered pushing trays overflowing with food. Sland couldn't contain himself from laughing anew and the rest joined him.

Zrrm had no idea what they found so funny so he soldiered on.

"I saw everyone headed here and figured you'd probably be hungry. We just got a new sampler platter from the Peoples of the Roost, I hope you enjoy it."

N'leah looked puzzled.

"I don't recognize any of these dishes."

"Not the Roosts of the Succubi, the Peoples of the Roost. Fliers like you, but otherwise different in every other regard."

It was Geldish's turn to look puzzled.

"I know every brand made by Rohta and I know of no Peoples of the Roost."

"They are not of Rohta. They were made by a group of makers who called themselves the New Sons of Freedom Militia. They only made two brands and both of them live in the same area."

Geldish's left brow ridge raised and all the riders turned to face Zrrm.

"Okay, okay, they are a brand known as the Haliaeetus and they live in the western mountains, well north of Kalindor and south of the northern Fish-People. They keep to themselves and have small populations. The other brand is called the Athabascae Warriors. Both were designed for military use but have lived a quiet, agrarian, lifestyle since the gen-O-pod war. We trade with them as do some of the northern Fish-People.

"They know of the brands of the Plains, Lord Südermann's brands, and most others; they simply choose not to fraternize."

R'yune tapped the food cart for attention and began signing.

"That is their right. Until we were called by Geldish, we all lived lives away from our clans and others, except for BraarB, of course. We will enjoy their food and leave them in peace. If they are where you say they are it will be many Full Suns before Yontar would come for them anyway, if at all. Being, literally, in the middle of nowhere, they may never catch his attention."

That made sense to everyone so they decided to set it aside and try the food. There was a venison pudding they all agreed was tremendous and there was some type of cactus candy that caused Sland to pick up the whole bowl and keep it on his lap. R'yune was enjoying some hard bread that he kept ladling a liquid-pepper topping on. Braarb & N'leah split an elk steak and each had a large tuber, that they covered with a soured cream and cracked pepper after Zrrm showed them how.

It may not have been a traditional breaklight repast, but they weren't complaining. While they were eating Geldish and BraarB quizzed Zrrm about other, possible, non-Rohta brands. They were disturbed to find out that there may be as many non-Rohta as there are Rohta brands. However, Zrrm was clearly basing some of what he knew off of anecdotal evidence. Even the Din-La seemed to have their limits. The one thing he was sure of was that the number of non-Rohta brands on this continent was four and they were all known.

When they finished Geldish requested access to a radio so he could get in touch with Karrish and Makish.

Zrrm led them down several long corridors until they reached a room buzzing with activity. There were ten Din-La sitting in front of radios wearing some sort of devices over their ears and speaking softly into microphones. Zrrm motioned him over to a free unit and showed him how to use the ear devices.

Ten epi-cliks later he had a complete update on what was going on across the Plains and learned a squadron of Succubi had left several clicks ago. He had to admit it seemed like a good plan. His first thought was to make the Din-La ship him and the riders west to fight with them, but he quickly dismissed it. Except for N'leah the rest would just be bystanders and the squadron had trained together, they'd never even met the Brittle Riders.

No, staying out of their way was the best answer.

He left the room, found the riders waiting outside, briefed them on all that was going on, and they discussed their options. After a while, they agreed they would leave next breaklight and head for Anapsida.

They spent the rest of the turn wandering through

the Din-La's city staring at all of the machines and guessing at their uses. Geldish knew some of them from Elzish's notes and knew he could ask him if he cared to know more. For now, though, it was more fun to speculate and grab random samples of various potent potables.

Zrrm showed them the most important thing in the underground city, how to read the clocks. Time could easily get lost down here, along with everything else.

It was well past even-fall when they went back to their rooms to prepare for their trip next turn.

King Uku sat in his throne room, recently finished with his early duties of the turn. One of the palace staff entered carrying a large glass of Whævin. She set the glass near his throne, curtsied, and then stood off to the side. She waited for her king to take his first sip before she spoke.

"Begging your pardon, your majesty, but may I speak freely?"

Uku tried to remember if he'd ever heard her speak at all but motioned for her to go ahead.

"Sire, I do not wish to insult you. Your reign has been one of the most prosperous in our warren's history. But many of us are worried what will come after."

Uku straightened in his throne and looked at her directly. She stammered on.

"We are worried there won't be another Uku to follow. We know your brother is dead, may he rest in quiet grounds, and we know your sister is barren as she's made no secret of that fact. But, no matter who the next king or queen is, we all feel he or she would be best reminded of what a great king is like and there is no better way than to leave a living memento."

Uku started to get angry and then deflated into his throne.

"I'm afraid the fates have not lined up to allow that to be so. I could not promise my body and soul to another"

He was wondering why he was being so honest with her when she startled him. A little.

"Because you are in love with Empress ClaalD. We know. And we all agree it is a wonderful thing. Your love inspires the warren. Even the villages and hovels rejoice in the harmony you inspire. However, now that Empress ClaalD has taken a mating partner, we think it is time for you to consider the same."

Uku was now truly startled. He wondered how they knew and then decided it was probably not the best kept secret on the Plains. He tried to think of something constructive to say but really didn't succeed.

"I guess this was bound to come up someturn. But that is not the way of the Se-Jeant and you and I both know that. I could not promise my soul to a mate without lying. Whatever else I may have done in my life I will not do that."

She smiled.

"We know this as well. You are a good and honorable being as well as a fair ruler. It is because of those reasons the Din-La honor you with the images they give out featuring you and Empress ClaalD walking hand in hand though the new enclave."

Now he passed startled and moved on to shocked. The Din-La were giving away something for free? He was so caught off guard by that concept it never occurred to him to wonder if anyone had asked his permission to use his image.

"What image?"

"You have not seen?" He shook his head. "It's a series they call 'Peace through Unity' and there are images representing each warren. There's one of you and Empress ClaalD, of course, and there's one of King Gornd and Watcher Urkel, after the battle with Xhaknar, sitting on their armor sharing a flagon of skank. Then there's one of

Elder Urnak and Queen A'lnuah playing Ti-Zam and another featuring King G'rnk, a Kgul and a Rangka, whose name I do not know, grooming a nysteed. You can get any of those by spending two goldens or more at any trading post.

"The poster featuring all the members of the council along with Lord Südermann requires a three golden, or better, purchase. The remaining images, showing regular citizens, including the Naradhama, at work and play, are given out with any purchase of more than half a golden."

Uku was very unsure if his royal self had been insulted when he realized Lord Südermann fetched more goldens than he did, but he also realized he was being immature. Then he thought about the images themselves. They would go a long way to reinforcing the policies of the council and those of the individual warrens. That is if anybody actually took any of them home.

"How popular are these images?"

"I have the whole set milord, as does most of the staff. Almost every home has at least one. Many have them all."

He wondered if she'd truly been to every home on the Plains and decided not to push the matter. The images were popular, that much was certain.

"Nevertheless, these images will not get me an heir so what are you suggesting? That I wander into the staff's chambers one dark even and pick someone at random?"

She looked terrified at the thought.

"OH NO MILORD! Nothing like that. No, sire, my sister, she's my twin, and I have come up with a solution that will allow you to keep your honor and that no one else need ever know."

He had to admit he was curious and motioned for her to keep talking.

"Cleric Äkä lost her true love in the battle with Xhaknar and has vowed to never love again. My sister is her maid, which is how I know this."

"Cleric Äkä of the theocrats? Why would a young, beautiful, femme like that want to marry a scarred old king?"

"She's not so young and you're not so old, if I may be so bold sire. My sister is bringing the proposal up to her as we speak. It would be a good marriage. She comes from a powerful family, is revered almost as much as you by the Se-Jeant and she could never ask for your soul since she would not give her own. Still, she is young enough to have smalls and her family would benefit greatly from a marriage to the throne."

Uku was beginning to understand what a prized steed felt like at market. Intellectually he could easily see the benefits of the arrangement she was offering. However, he had no idea at all how to start a conversation with Cleric Äkä that wouldn't make him sound like a demented old lech.

His thoughts were interrupted by a soft knock on the door. He called for whoever it was to enter and observed as a messenger walked across the throne room and handed him a sealed note. He read it twice and then chuckled.

"Tell your mistress that this turn at mid-break repast would be fine. In my antechamber, not the formal dining hall."

The messenger bowed and left hurriedly. Uku finished his drink and smiled at the maid.

"It seems that your sister has done her job well. Cleric Äkä will be here in a few cliks to share a meal with me. I am sure we will have much to talk about. Including what to do with meddlesome sisters who wish to be matchmakers. In the meantime, I suggest you and the staff make sure that my antechamber is spotless and there's a full meal ready for us to eat in private. I do not want to be interrupted by constant servings. This is especially so if she is coming to tell me what a horrid old creature I am for even allowing myself to be involved in something like this."

The maid couldn't restrain her smile as she bowed and left.

He waited for her to leave and then went to find ClaalD. A few epi-cliks later the two were walking through the halls and he told her what the maid had done. ClaalD laughed and then let him know how great she thought the whole concept was.

After he left he had the sneaking suspicion that the idea may not have originated with his maid. He wondered briefly who was ruling who in his kingdom and then went to put on clothes which would be more suitable for the meal that might decide his future and the future of his family.

By mid-break, he was an emotional wreck on the inside, but he looked very regal on the outside. His dresser had chosen an umber ensemble which was tastefully highlighted with small pieces of gold. He took a deep breath and headed for his antechamber. He was about ten paces away when Cleric Äkä turned a corner and faced him. She was dressed simply, as befitted her title, in a long blue dress with a few pieces of silver jewelry but still looked lovely. Her smile was warm and engaging.

Maybe this wouldn't be the disaster he envisioned after all.

His guard opened the door and allowed them to enter before closing it behind them. His staff had gone above and beyond the call of duty. There was a small buffet on one side that had all the plates and cutlery they would ever need. The table was covered in an umber table cloth – where had they gotten that? – and there was a small candelabra in the center which gave the room a romantic glow he never knew it had.

They exchanged small talk as they filled their plates and tried the various tasty treats. He noticed, with amusement, his staff had set the chairs cattycorner to each other instead of across the full table. She noticed as well and laughed.

He was pleased, for some reason, to find that he was comfortable in her presence. They ate and only barely touched the reason for her visit. Neither seemed uncomfortable with it, they just felt like talking about other things right now. The conversation and the meal wound down around the same time and he poured them each a snifter of Sominid brandy.

"It's a little early in the turn for me," she laughed, "but I doubt I'm going to get anything much else done now anyway."

He agreed and clinked his glass against hers in a casual toast.

"So, honored Äkä, we seem to have been pressed together by forces outside our control. I hope you understand I would never have been so bold."

"Nor would I, your majesty, but, given the circumstances, it does seem like the best idea for all involved. I am the only unmated femme of my family and, well, I guess I could do far worse than marrying a king."

He looked at her seriously for a moment and then they both burst out laughing. After they quieted down she got serious.

"I am aware of your love for Empress ClaalD. It would be good to be with a brand who knows love. However, before we go any further, I must tell you about Oro."

"The son of Colonel Oro?"

She nodded, surprised.

"His father was my instructor when I was in the training academy. I trained his son, your love, when he came of age and he fought alongside me in the battle with Xhaknar. After he took a shell in the chest he died in my arms. He was a great young brand, a credit to his family and to the Se-Jeant."

She sipped her brandy, lost in thought.

"He was the one true love of my life. We were to be

wed when he came back from the war. We had all the plans made. We were going to set up our own home outside the northern walls and install a flower garden under glass in the back. We both loved the smell of fresh flowers. We thought it would be a peaceful place to raise many smalls."

Uku refilled their drinks and sat back down.

"Your love is a ghost and mine is a brand that could kill me if I tried to consummate the relationship," he chortled, "if this is to work between us, I see only one possible solution. Each must be welcome in our home and each must be cherished by us. I will have no problem honoring the memory of Oro, for reasons both obvious and not. Do you think you can honor ClaalD?"

She sipped and then smiled.

"The empress and I have met on several occasions. The Llamia have no God and she was worried our beliefs might harm her brand. When I showed her how we aren't nearly as evangelical as some others, though our beliefs still remain a core of who we are, she was placated. We are not a messianic brand by any means.

"I like her, your majesty, and I respect her. If that is the only perceived barrier that could hinder us from moving forward, consider it shoved aside."

He noticed a platter of tiny sweets and handed one to her before taking one for himself. It highlighted the flavor of the brandy and he luxuriated in the taste as it rolled over his tongue. While this would be a marriage of convenience, it could also be pleasurable. Äkä was smart, beautiful, and seemed to have a sense of humor. All traits he could admire. Plus she would not ask for his soul. He saw her savoring the pastry as well and figured she must be thinking along similar lines.

"If this is to work, and truly benefit the Se-Jeant, we should follow the traditional rituals; the Full Sun courtship, the announcement of the pledge, the family meals, everything."

Much to his chagrin, she burst out laughing.

"All well and good, my king, but haven't you forgotten something?

He was completely baffled. He looked up, down and anywhere he could see what thought had escaped him. She touched his arm softly and smiled.

"You forgot to ask me."

For the first time in his life, Uku blushed. Then he stood, assumed the formal posture with his left heel touching his right toe and stretched his arms wide.

"Cleric Äkä, would you do me the honor of becoming my mate, now and forever, with as much body and soul as each of us can bring to the union?"

She stood, walked over to him, spread her arms wide and clasped her hands in his. Her lips were brushing his, their chests were breathing as one and their smiles could not be denied.

"Yes, Milord, all that I am is yours."

With that, she kissed him.

Then he kissed her back.

It was near even-fall when they left the antechamber. Not a single staff member commented on the fact that her dress was on backwards. Instead, they led her to a private entrance and made sure her carriage got her safely home.

In a third floor window of the palace, overlooking the private courtyard, two twin sisters and a Llamia empress smiled.

Greko walked past the dormant volcano, as was his wont each breaklight, and contemplated his studies. As a student of Bovinity, he knew the entire history of his brand and the histories of the makers who came before. It wasn't until he'd reached the sixth level they began teaching him about the religious beliefs of the makers. At first, he only had an intellectual curiosity, but a recent conversation with Lord Südermann had caught him unawares. He hadn't even considered the possibility the old religions would still have a foothold amongst the brands. He did know his brand's beliefs were more closely akin to those of the Children of the Waters than anything else, and even then there were differences.

Still, to find out there were serious religions scattered all over the planet was disconcerting. He was well aware of the many wars the makers had over the millennia and he knew how dangerous they could be to the stability of the world.

He was also aware of how much comfort they could bring to so many. He would talk with his teachers later but, for now, he just let the various contradictions roll around inside his head. He saw Elder Urnak and two of his wives heading for the main library. One of his wives was clearly pregnant, but she was too far away for him to be sure which one it was.

As he rounded the bend which would take him to the old barracks he was greeted by Heifer Narlund and forced to grin. They had been dating for almost a Full Sun now. He took her hand in his and continued his walk.

They wandered into several local shops exchanging small talk and looking at the many new wares that had begun to appear over the last five Suns. She didn't know it but Greko had ordered a mating ring from Ozo and JnaarZ' new shop in the new Se-Jeant enclave. It cost more than he'd been prepared to pay but was going to be worth it. It was a dazzling design and would arrive in ten turns. Then he would ask her to be his mate forever.

He knew she was aware of how he felt. They'd discussed smalls and homes and all the things mated pairs would need. They wandered into a sweets shop and split a pastry over two cups of korlnak. There was a quiet between them that belied how little time they'd known each other. It was as though they'd been mated for many Suns and had raised many smalls rather than just getting ready to start their lives together.

He'd known the moment he'd laid eyes on her she was the one for him. It seemed she'd felt the same way. She'd even admitted how pleased she was that he was past all the battles and would now be able to stay with her and raise a family.

With those thoughts in mind, they were startled when a courier from the Elders' Council walked up to them and handed Greko a sealed note. He quickly opened it and his smile faded. Elder Urnak was ordering him immediately to Anapsida to await orders.

He showed it to Narlund and then acknowledged his acceptance to the courier. All their good feelings had evaporated. He knew, as did she, the Succubi had left a few turns ago and there was no reason for him to be in Anapsida unless something had gone wrong.

He kissed her goodbye, tried his best to ignore her worried look and headed for the stables. There he picked up a deisteed and provisions. The stable hand motioned for him to wait and disappeared around the back. He returned shortly thereafter with a brand that looked as if it could be a weaker cousin of the Minotaurs. He was leading a nytsteed which was heavily laden with supplies and bedding. Whoever he was he'd been traveling a long way, that much was clear. From where would, hopefully, become clear soon enough.

"As-Salāmu `alayka, I am called Ben el Salaam and I am of the Chaldean clan. I apologize for interrupting your turn, but my Imam has many questions and I was told you could help provide them and accompany me this last leg of my journey to Anapsida."

Greko stared at this new brand and shrugged. He wouldn't have been ordered to Anapsida with him unless it was important.

"Greetings, I am Greko, 6th level dweller of the Pit, I am pleased to serve."

"Allah the Most Merciful be praised, it was you whom Geldish, may Allah soothe his tortured soul, said I should seek, and here you are. "

Greko felt his jaw drop.

"You know Geldish?"

"Yes, we rode from the Mayanoren camp in the north to the lands near Anapsida. Allah the Most Merciful was kind enough to grant me several turns to get to know him and his Brittle Riders."

"You were with Geldish at a Mayanoren encampment and you're grateful?"

"Oh yes, I learned much and was able to share it all with my Imam and my clan. My mission was successful thanks to them. Although I have been called on to be a warrior, I am mostly a scout and scouting was what I was doing those turns."

There had to be more to that story but it could wait for later.

"And what is your mission now?"

"Again, I seek wisdom. Nothing more."

Greko was actually relieved to hear that. It meant he wasn't girding his loins for battle. A nice safe jaunt to Anapsida with this stranger and a chance to bring knowledge to the Pit was not the kind of mission which brooked terror. With nothing left to say the two of them mounted and headed down the circular path to the north entrance.

They exited the warren into the bright sun and chilly air. Ben rode like a warrior, no matter what he'd said. Greko could spot a kindred spirit in the way he kept his back straight and his eyes on the Plains all around him. Not a stone remained unnoticed. He was fine with that. It meant that he wouldn't be badgered by silliness. Warriors weren't prone to silliness, at least not the ones who'd survived.

Ben seemed most concerned about the plans of Yontar and what was happening in the western oceans. Greko really had no more information than Ben did but was happy to share what he could. They talked about various possibilities and then Ben asked him a question that seemed to come from nowhere.

"When last I was in Anapsida there was a pamphlet that had the rates for many inns. Some were very reasonable but others cost more than my village made in a Sun. Do you know why that is?"

Greko had to laugh, but not unkindly.

"Yes, actually, I do. The amount charged depends on the level of service you want. Just a bed is the cheapest, those that come with personal masseuses and spas cost the most. At some, you can have food delivered to your room, a private secretary to handle any business you have during your stay, and so on. Basically, if you have the goldens, they have the service you need."

Ben considered that for a moment and then smiled.

"My brand, may Allah watch over them, are a simple brand. I'm not sure what they'd say about luxuries like that."

"In that," smiled Greko, "we are alike. When we must go to Anapsida most of us tend to stay in the simple inns. This time we will stay in the inn recommended by the council. It has the most services for the fewest goldens. I think you'll like it. I've been there twice before when I had to make trips on behalf of our council. The owner, Drapery, is a fine innkeeper and sets an excellent hearth."

"That sounds good to me. Just because I travel for my Imam and clan doesn't mean I'm opposed to a warm bed and a good meal."

That got both of them laughing.

They had turns to kill so they shared the histories of their brands and stories of their lives. When Greko told Ben about Narlund he was surprised to hear him announce he and his wife had been together for over one hundred Full Suns and each turn with her was more joyful than the last.

He found himself gladdened by the chance to get to know this almost Minotaur better.

"Greetings King G'rnk, Pack Lord of the Wolfen," began one of the Din-La G'rnk didn't recognize, "I bring a sealed message from Watcher Urkel and he has asked that I wait for a reply."

G'rnk accepted the letter, opened it and read it carefully. He smiled and nodded easily. The Wolfen and the Fierstans had both taken to the Minotaurs' game of kick-ball like starving victims to bread. He wanted to hold a match between their warrens in the Fierstans' courtyard in fifteen turns. It was a good idea and would give his Wolfen a true test of their skill.

"Please tell Watcher Urkel we accept and look forward to the turn. He can have his staff contact my assistant, T'iul, to make all the arrangements."

The Din-La nodded, started to leave, turned and then stopped.

"I am Kssp. You can tell me apart from my twin, Tffl, by the scar under my left eye. I earned it when I was a small and attempted to prove to my mother that jumping off the roof into the nearby tree was perfectly safe."

G'rnk couldn't help but laugh as he thanked him for ending his many Full Suns of confusion. He remembered when he'd first met them with the haven lord, Brek. He briefly wondered what the ambitious haven lord was up to but knew any bad news would get to him as quickly as the radio would allow and he'd heard nothing but positives as Go-Chi was becoming a major meeting center on the Plains for traders.

He looked around his spacious home, he refused to call it a palace or allow it to be built any larger, and decided there was nothing more for him to do inside. He walked outside and watched the smalls playing some sort of game that only smalls could understand. After a while he wandered around his growing warren.

Unlike the other warrens, the Wolfen's was more like an expanded village. There were Wolfen homes next to Kgul next to haven lords and all were mixed in with a few Din-La. The outer perimeter of the groves, created by the Rangka, was guarded by sentries but there were no walls or escarpments anywhere.

He continued meandering and found himself in front of the temple where Makish was tending to the miniature trees he loved. He still did not understand his fascination with the tiny shrubs but did have to admit he admired their beauty. Makish had been talking about setting up a pond behind the temple so he could stock it with fish. He'd said he thought the smalls would enjoy it.

The two chatted for a while and Makish again asked him when he was going to take a tour of the warrens. Until now he'd avoided it since it seemed so annoyingly regal. However, thinking back on Brek, it occurred to him that all of the news that came to him was third hand, except for the occasional inter-warren missives. He knew the other leaders of the warrens made an annual trip to visit each other. Thinking about it more fully it seemed like it may be the only way to truly see what was going on around him.

His brand had made him their leader and expected him to lead. Part of that leadership was knowing what was actually happening around them and making sure nothing could adversely affect them or that they weren't missing opportunities others had. Annoyingly regal or no, he figured he'd better make plans to get off his bushy tail, not that he actually had a tail but it was a common enough allusion among his brand, and act like the ruler he was supposed to be.

He could use the trip to the Fierstans as his first stop and then go from there. He would have T'iul make sure he would be welcome in the warrens and, as long as he was, would then take a few turns to say hello to everyone again.

He ran his plan by Makish and was greeted by

unexpected laughter.

"Forgive me, your majesty," he was still giggling, "do you really think you can just grab a steed and say hi? The time frame you envision for beginning your journey should work, you have an excellent staff, but you will be accompanied by many couriers and you will be feted in the warrens and you will be asked many questions since you have been a recluse as far as the warrens are concerned. These will not be casual conversations over a flagon of skank."

G'rnk was hurt. He didn't consider himself a recluse and he certainly saw no reason for all the fuss that Makish envisioned. Unquestionably, he deserved better than derisive laughter. He said so.

"I'm sorry your majesty, but you are a king now. More importantly, you are a king who is closely aligned with the last living Rangka on Arreti. That makes you mysterious and powerful. Plus, any trip you make must, by rights, include the Kgul and the haven lords. While you may not be their official ruler even you must have noticed they have appointed no one to be your equal. I mean no disrespect, but you are a powerful king no matter that all you want to be is a father or a farmer.

"I understand your kingship came about unusually. Unlike others who seek power or those who are trained for it, you simply earned it. I, along with everybody else, have given you your space, especially since the turn to turn needs of your warren are being cared for so well, but now is as good a time as any to let everyone know you are their king and you deserve their faith.

"I will work with T'iul to make sure all of the details are taken care of, but you must let T'iul do what he can do. He's very proficient and he will make you, and your warren, look good. I promise you that you'll be uncomfortable, very uncomfortable in fact, but, and this is the secret, so is every other ruler. They endure the discomfort because they know it makes their citizens feel good about their leaders. A little pomp and circumstance can go as far, if not farther, than any battlefield heroics or ability to parse out duties.

"If I were to offer any advice, I would say to take your family with you, enjoy being king and, figure out what will come after you. Will your smalls inherit the throne, will it be up to the pack, or do you have another idea? You are the Pack Lord of the Wolfen, de facto king to three brands, it is time for you to start acting like it."

G'rnk was astonished. He felt like he was a small being punished by his father. How dare he talk to him like that? Didn't he know that he was …. oh … fuck …. he *was* the king.

He smiled ruefully and shrugged.

"Thank you friend Makish, I will abide by any arrangements you and T'iul make."

He was almost home when he smelled three layered meat pies simmering in the distance. It was one of his favorite meals but difficult to make. Obviously, his mate was going to ask a boon of him as well.

He shook his head in dismay and headed home thinking he was king, the undisputed ruler of all he surveyed, except when others wanted him to do something different.

D'noma led her squadron over the arid lands below. The first three turns they had been able to stay each even with the Din-La but now they would have to camp one even in the wild. She hadn't minded since they were ahead of schedule thanks to the prevailing winds when they were in high flight. They'd stocked up on light provisions and angled into the brightening sky as they'd headed into this turn's high flight. Now, several cliks later, they were beginning their glide downward and should arrive at the foot of the western mountains by even-fall.

They could easily see them in the distance. The air was clear and cool, but slowly warming as they headed downward. She glanced around to make sure everyone was still in formation and then angled them a little further south to ensure they landed in the right spot. They were in twenty, v-shaped, formations of fifty each, staggered four formations across and five deep. Their wingtips, in each small formation, were barely a breath apart.

The wind felt wonderful beneath her wings and she stretched them a little wider to capture every ripple in the atmosphere. She could sense the others dong the same. They passed another leisurely clik that way when she heard a cry of alarm to her right. She started to look towards the cry but saw the reason as her head began its turn.

There was another brand flying, from the northwest, towards them. All of their intelligence had said the Kalindorian lizards could not fly as high as the Succubi, but this brand appeared to be easily climbing to their height. If this new brand was hostile, and they met in midair, the Succubi were doomed. All they had were their ceremonial daggers for defense, useless this far above the ground.

The other brand was about a clik away so she looked around to get her bearings. If they headed any more to the south they would be in Kalindor. If they headed north they would be heading directly into the new brand. She motioned the radio operator on her left to notify the Din-La what was happening. A few sepi-cliks later she was telling D'noma to head north, land as quickly as possible and that all would be well.

Seeing no better plan she ordered her squadron to follow her and tucked her wings in to begin a power dive of more than two kays to the ground. The other brand, for their part, noticed the dive, eased off their ascent and began circling.

As soon as the Succubi were on the ground the other brand began gracefully arcing downward towards them. As they got closer the Succubi could make out their markings. This new brand had white chests but was otherwise brown. They were very beautiful but also looked as deadly as any brand they'd ever seen.

There were about twenty of them and they made their descent as nonthreatening as possible so it took them a few epi-cliks to arrive. When they finally landed the Succubi could clearly see that their coloring came from feathers and not pigment. They were as noble a brand as they'd ever seen.

One of them stepped forward and bowed.

"Greetings Roost Kin, I am Douglass Fairwinds, Flight Leader of the Peoples of the Roost. We had heard of your kind but never really believed you existed until you flew into our sight. I apologize if we have caused you any discomfort."

"I am D'noma, Squadron Leader of the Succubi. There is no need to apologize," she lied, "we needed a rest anyway."

He smiled at the obvious lie and continued.

"Our roosts are about a two cliks flight from here. If you are not too tired we would be honored to have you as our guests and share our even-fall meal with you."

A part of D'noma's mind realized this could be a trap, but it didn't feel like one. She looked at her squad and they shrugged.

"I thank you. We would be delighted."

Douglass bowed again and the Peoples of the Roost took to the air with the Succubi close behind. Less than half a clik later they were flying over a thickening forest and could smell a fresh scent that reminded them of the northern plains in the Dark Sun. Barely a clik after that they could see smoke from cooking fires and began angling downward. Five epi-cliks more and they were on the ground surrounded by almost five thousand Peoples of the Roost. D'noma was very pleased to note none of them were armed.

If a thousand unannounced meal guests bothered anyone they didn't show it. They had several venison dishes which they happily shared with the Succubi as well as some tree flavored treats that tasted much better than they sounded. D'noma instructed her squad to share their provisions and soon there was a moving buffet rotating the camp.

She and Douglass sat near the edge of the camp and shared a platter of raw vegetables as well as various venison dishes and flagons of sweet liquor that he called "bourbon." It burned her tongue a little but she had to admit she liked it. It had the same effect as ice wine without the chill in her throat.

Douglass finished a small piece of the kgum jerky she had been carrying and smiled.

"This is very good. You will have to arrange trade with our general."

"General? Are you a military brand?"

"According to our legends, we once were. Now the ranks are mostly honorary. I, for example, am a farmer and hold the rank of Lieutenant Colonel. I did serve in our guard for the mandatory four Suns, but that's as close as I've been to war. How about you?"

She thought about what to say and decided the truth was the best choice.

"We are not a warrior brand. In fact, we were bred to be art pieces. Living statues for wealthy makers. But we have seen more war than anyone should. We were persecuted by a warlord named Xhaknar and he nearly destroyed us. For almost five hundred Full Suns we were forced to live on the fringes of the Great Canyon. Finally, a crazy Rangka named Geldish was able to rally the Plains and bring us allies. We banded together and went to one final war against Xhaknar five Suns ago where we defeated him. Nevertheless, we all suffered terrible losses, almost a third of our armies lay dead before the battle was done."

She sipped her bourbon some more and noticed he

was waiting for her to continue.

"Once Xhaknar was well and truly dead we began rebuilding the Plains. We knew that many Mayanoren warriors had escaped and they would return, so we built an army, which reflects all of the brands of the Plains, to protect us when that turn came. Now we have found that a leader whom we had thought long dead is back and leading those Mayanorens. We are flying west now to meet him in battle on the western ocean. We hope to stop him before he can reach Kalindor and ally with the reptiloids. If he gets there he will have the resources he needs to attack, and possibly overthrow the Plains."

He took all that in and refilled her flagon.

"We learn of battles when we are smalls and we learn the basics of combat when we serve in our guard, but we only know of war what we hear from the Din-La and that isn't much. Probably because we don't ask. It's not that we're cowards, at least I don't believe we are, but we live far from any other brands and like our privacy. There is not much conflict to be had with the trees and the mountains."

She laughed at that and wished her only battles were with leaves and shrubs. They sat quietly for a while and watched as the stars began twinkling in the even sky. After a while, they began talking about the route the Succubi planned on taking. He mentioned there was a shorter route through the mountains near him and offered to lead them.

He called for a corporal and soon they were looking at maps. She saw the route and showed him their final destination. The shortcut would take them north of where they wanted to be but not by much and the time they'd save would more than make up for any adjustments they'd need to make.

She notified her radio operator to advise the Din-La of the course change so the Children of the Waters wouldn't be looking for them in the wrong places. A couple of cliks later they were falling asleep beneath the stars.

As she drifted into quiet slumber, D'noma wondered if this was going to be the last peaceful scene she would see.

The Named One stood on the poop deck and steered the ship into calm waters. It had only taken them two turns to get far enough away from shore that they all felt safe. Even so, those had been a rough two turns. Yontar had ordered them to head due west, against the currents and cruel winds. They had been forced to navigate swiftly moving ice floes as well as deal with relentless rain and sleet.

He saw now that it was the right move since anything else would have brought them into the waters of the Fish-People without any means of protecting themselves. Nevertheless, for two turns the Named Ones had wondered if they'd picked the right leader.

He was just beginning to turn the ship to the south when he saw Lord Yontar emerge from the forecastle and walk across the deck. His lord looked as at home on a ship as he did on land. Unlike some of the Mayanorens, or the Named Ones, he'd suffered no discomforts at all.

He watched his lord look across the sea and then head towards him. A quick glance told him that all of the ships were following suit and would be lined up to begin their push south in a few epi-cliks.

"You have done well," yelled Yontar as he approached, "I am very pleased."

"Thank you, Lord Yontar."

"Have you Named Ones figured out what weather we will face?"

"As best we can milord. We expect it to be cold for a few more turns, but shouldn't encounter any truly inclement weather during our journey."

"Cold we can live with. Fish-People's mines or Succubi attacks might be a different story."

"Please forgive my brashness milord, but why would the Fish-People lay mines in front of us?"

"Left to their own devices they would not. But, as your own scouts pointed out, there have been many changes on the Plains. Many new alliances. While the Plains are far from the Fish-People, the lands of Südermann are not. An alliance with Südermann could easily lead to an alliance with the Fish-People. They could feel that we are a threat to that alliance, or to their trade, and take aggressive action."

The Named One thought about that and smiled.

"I understand now, instead of risking our journey on a slate of unknowns, you took the riskier, yet oddly safer, tack of insuring our mission would succeed. Very wise, milord."

Yontar simply nodded. He wasn't about to debate the pros and cons of his strategies with anyone. He accepted their intelligence, gratefully, but the decisions he made were his and his alone. He looked over the stern and saw all the ships were in formation and motioned for the Named One to begin the next leg of their quest. He soon heard the cadence of the oar masters and felt the ship gaining speed beneath him.

Within an epi-clik, they were cruising across the tops of the gentle waves and headed for Kalindor.

Yontar stood to the rear of the poop deck and waited for the Named Ones to run a group of Mayanorens through weapons practice. A quick scan to his rear showed the other ships doing the same. They were all firing wooden practice weapons. The real ones had been sharpened to a deadly point but they hadn't had adequate time make enough to waste on rehearsals.

Even so, these Mayanorens were lethally accurate. Targets would fly from the launchers Dagnar had developed and then be shot out of the air less than a sepi-clik later. After several rounds with the larger launchers, the Named Ones began running them through their paces with the hand held projectile launchers. If any Succubi flew within a hundred paces of any ship they would be killed. The Mayanorens may not have many skills but the one they did have, killing, they did better than any other brand on Aretti as far as Yontar was concerned.

A clik later all the weapons were secured and the Mayanorens were below decks. Yontar stood next to the Named One as he steered a steady course. The sea water washed over the deck now and then as they hit the occasional deep wave, but the prow worked just as it had been designed to and there were spaces under the rails to allow any water to spill back whence it came. Clean, efficient, and effective. Just the way Yontar liked things.

With all the ships in a steady rhythm, he let his mind slide back to the last days of the makers. There were four hundred and twenty-seven at the facility. He hadn't wanted to kill them. He argued with Xhaknar that they knew more than they'd let on and now, with the end of their world upon them, they'd do anything to survive.

He was right but in the wrong way. He remembered it well. Dr. Ezra Singh had tried to kill him. The poor doctor hadn't realized how many safeguards had been built into him and Xhaknar. His work was on a different brand, one not even ready for development. He'd fired six shots from his weapon directly into Yontar's chest and all he really managed to do was irritate him.

Yontar smiled as the memory of ripping Dr. Singh's head off came back to him. He'd then walked down a corridor, carrying it, to meet Xhaknar. Xhaknar had seen his, rapidly healing, wounds, and the head, and laughed. Within a turn, there were four hundred and twenty-seven headless corpses. The Mayanoren had gotten most of them. Thinking that beheading was the only approved method for killing the makers they had put down the weapons they'd found and set upon the poor scientists with a frenzy. He cherished the sight of a young Mayanoren, barely decanted and not at full strength, twisting and pulling on a maker's head to try and get it to pop off. When another Mayanoren had reached over to help, Yontar had stopped him by saying, "He can do it, this is the only way he'll learn to do it right."

Bless his decanted soul, Yontar heard the ripping sound a few sepi-cliks later and watched as the head popped off and rolled down the hall. The second Mayanoren smiled and nodded and then led the youngling down the hall to get more experience.

Oh well, there was no use worrying about a few spilt heads.

He looked across the deck at the pile of practice weapons and had a thought.

"Pass the word to all ships, I want the Mayanorens to sharpen as many of the training weapons as they can, even if it means they lose practice time. I'd rather have too many useable weapons when the Succubi attack than too few."

The Named One nodded assent and sent the instructions. Within an epi-clik, every ship had confirmed the order. Then, and only then, did the Named One turn to face him.

"Forgive me Lord Yontar, but do you really believe they will attack us on the open sea?"

He nodded as he stared at the far horizon.

"Their scouts are not stupid and your scouts said their military was better trained now than it was when it defeated Xhaknar. They really wouldn't even need the help of the Fish-People. By now they could easily have floated barges across rivers out to the sea and be waiting for us. It's my hope that we're too far out to be detected, but I didn't win as many battles as I did by hoping, just by preparing."

The Named One took that in and smiled. Yes, they'd picked the right leader.

There was a caravan entering Anapsida when they arrived so Geldish and the others reined up and let them pass. They were all impressed with how efficient the Naradhama guards had become. One searched under a wagon while two others checked its manifest and then, once cleared, they let it through. All of this was accomplished in under an epi-clik. Since there were only ten wagons left none of them felt the need to pull rank and cut in line.

Geldish felt a presence at the edge of his mind and turned. He smiled when he recognized Ben and Greko coming up from the south. He motioned to the riders and they set out to greet them.

"As-Salāmu `alayka Ben and Greko, it is good to see you again."

If Ben was upset that Geldish had used the singular form of greeting instead of the plural he didn't show it. Instead, he responded in kind.

"Wa `alayka s-salām Geldish, it is good to see you again as well."

"What brings you to our chilly hearth? I would have thought you to be home with your wife counting the turns until planting."

"Sadly Allah had other plans. The news we have been getting from the Din-La concerning Yontar has been confusing so I have been sent to see what is real and what is not."

The Brittle Riders laughed.

"Isn't that the same fucking reason you came out the last time?" asked Sland.

"Allah gives simple tasks to simple beings."

That prompted another round of laughter. Whatever each of them thought of Ben, "simple" was not the first word that sprang to mind. They formed up into a group to follow the last couple of caravan wagons into Anapsida.

Once they'd cleared the gates they headed over to the council chambers. Much to Geldish's chagrin, and everyone else's delight, there was a group of smalls in front the entrance begging for autographs and souvenirs. It was soon clear they weren't exactly sure who everyone was, all they cared about was that they were going to the council and that meant they must be really super important and worth meeting.

It didn't take them long to make each small feel special and give them a piece of candy or a trinket. Once that was done they headed into the main chamber and headed for the meeting room. One of the Naradhama turned around and broke into a wide grin.

"Mr. Salaam! It is so good to see you again!"

Ben was caught so far off guard it took him a full epi-clik to get his bearings, but his memory finally started working.

"Cornhusker?"

She nodded enthusiastically.

"Allah be praised, it is good to see you again. I never did get a chance to thank you for your kindness on my last visit."

"Oh, it was nothing. Believe it or not, the council pays me to be nice to visitors. This is the best job ever. So what brings you back to our fair city? Are you ready to open trade negotiations with the Se-Jeant for those metal couplings?"

He'd forgotten he'd mentioned that to her before he'd spied the riders.

"That, among other things. Right now I am to accompany my friends into the council and catch up on some news."

"Very good."

With that, she smiled even wider, turned, opened the council door and quickly announced to the assembled the name, title, and position of each brand waiting to enter.

R'yune waved his fingers for a moment and everyone laughed. N'leah saw Ben's confusion and helped him out.

"He said she's impressive."

Ben could see no argument there.

They entered the chamber and took seats towards the back. The room was crowded with brands reviewing updates from the Succubi. They learned of the People of the Roost and their offer of assistance. They carefully studied the Succubi's progress through the mountains and out over the coast. Every nuance of how Douglass Fairwinds and three other Haliaeetus' had stayed with them when they'd arrived at the piers of the Children of the Waters was discussed, parsed and discussed some more. The fact the Din-La's shipment of weapons had arrived early was scrutinized until it almost seemed like a conspiracy.

Geldish and the riders seemed amused at that but wouldn't share their reasons with Ben or Greko.

They watched as couriers ran in and out and to and fro amongst the council members, various representatives from the warrens, and interested merchants who had a stake in the war. It was the latter group who held Geldish's interest. They were a new entity for the Plains. They'd retrofitted some of the old Naradhama factories to create needed goods and employed many former slaves at fair wages. They were just now beginning to recoup their investments and a war that landed back on the Plains could ruin them.

Oddly enough, out of the assembled, they seemed the calmest. He was curious as to why and then noted R'yune talking with N'leah. It seemed the merchants had picked up contracts from the Din-La to provide goods to the army if the war came east.

That had to bring mixed emotions.

News the Succubi had boarded a ship that was

taking them to sea, along with their four new companions, raced through the room. While Greko and Ben seemed riveted, the riders all knew it was now going to be a waiting game of several turns before anything happened. It would be, at least, a hundred cliks before Yontar got in range of them since they were, wisely - admitted Geldish, placing themselves in his way and forcing him to come to them.

With nothing to be accomplished in chambers, they got up and left Ben and Greko to their reviews of the voluminous documents. When they got outside they noticed the inn that several of the council members had mentioned. Even though it wasn't even mid-break, it was crowded. They decided to give it a try and walked across the courtyard to try and find seats.

Drapery recognized them immediately even though they'd never met. After all, what other group could even pretend to look like them? He had a table in the back he usually reserved for council members but he figured no one would complain if the Brittle Riders sat there. Drapery's wife ran over and took pictographs of Drapery with each rider and then one group shot. Since everyone was so nice about it, he bought them the first round of skank and then got out of their way.

"I guess there are perks to this job after all," mused N'leah.

"Oh yeah, advertising an inn we've never been to before in exchange from some skank, that seems fair to me," laughed BraarB, "it's a good thing they didn't offer us a complimentary plate of meats or we'd be posing for statues."

R'yune stood and posed in his best curtsy, much to the delight of the inn.

While everyone was calming down a waitress came over and took their order. Geldish noted all the staff was wearing bright yellow shirts with a colorful red and green floral design on their left sleeves and black pants and shoes which seemed to have cushioned soles. It had been many long Suns since he'd worn shoes but he thought they looked comfortable.

The menu was more extensive than they'd expected so it took them a couple of epi-cliks to make up their minds. Their waitress, Gangrene of the House of Flatus, cheerfully offered suggestions and pointed out the special, Delta shellfish from the southern ocean with a lemon butter sauce for dipping. They all agreed on that and added side dishes suited to their tastes.

As she was bouncing away, there was no other way to describe her walk, she motioned for an assistant to refill their flagons. Geldish was still having trouble getting used to the idea of friendly Naradhama but had to admit he preferred them this way as opposed to the other.

R'yune was telling a very funny story about how he and N'leah had been attacked by a Rakyeen on the fringe when the food arrived. After Gangrene showed them how to remove the shells the story was forgotten and they turned their attention to their feast. In something of a custom for them, side dishes were passed around the table and sampled by all. Gangrene noticed this and grabbed a stack of small plates but Sland waved her away.

"We prefer it this way. It's friendlier."

She shrugged, smiled, and returned the plates to their rack.

The conversation continued through the turn and into the even. The council showed up just after even-fall and joined them. Ben was with them although there was nothing he could really eat or drink. He would have, had he been hungry enough, still having a dispensation from his Imam. However, he had sampled his provisions less than a clik before. Nevertheless, Gangrene felt sorry for him and, once she understood his limitations, brought him a small, sealed, cask of spiced water.

He knew no one in the inn was drinking spiced water and realized she must have run to the trading post to get it just for him. He glanced at the bottom of the cask as he was about to open it and saw the Chaldean seal.

He had to admit that his first impression had been right. They might be infidels, but they were very nice infidels.

Skipping through the hallways might not be the most regal method of propulsion, but Lord Südermann was too happy to care. Samuel from the Western Clan had agreed to share an even meal with her. He was handsome, tall, and strong. Plus she already knew he liked her. And she liked him. He was only one Full Sun older than her and they'd gone to the same school, until she'd been forced into the role of Südermann. While she was still in her teens, thanks to her teachers' insisting she have at least one normal turn out of twenty, she'd been on a few group outings with him. They'd even held hands – TWICE!!!! – under the moons.

But this even was to be just the two of them. She almost ran over Elaand as he was exiting the radio room. Without preamble, she gushed about her plans.

"If I may be so bold," he smiled, "I arranged the first meal between your father and mother. I would be honored if you would allow me the privilege of making the arrangements for your feast this even."

She'd been so excited by the prospect of the private moment that she'd forgotten an even meal would require some minor details like food and drinks and cutlery and plates and all that other stuff that meals require.

"Thank you Elaand. That would be appreciated more than you might know."

His smile grew.

"Believe it or not milord, that is exactly what your father said."

She couldn't stifle the giggle and then continued

skipping down the hall.

When she got to the throne room she saw two folders on a table near the door. She wasn't in the mood for work but knew "duty before pleasure" was a motto of her brand and she couldn't let them down.

The first folder was an update on the Succubi's mission. She was pleased to see Hana Koi-San had been as good as his word. She scanned the details on the ship he'd provided and realized she could fit the entire courts of both palaces on that ship and still have room for a skizzi tournament. Plenty of room then for a thousand Succubi and their bombs.

She also noted they were still over a turn away from their projected ambush point so she put that folder aside.

The second folder was all of the ins and outs of running a kingdom. While nothing was urgent it did her good to get lost in the details for a while and take her mind off her impending date. She'd become completely engrossed in power allotments and was startled by the sound of a chime. She looked up to see her staff standing in front of her looking as though they were about to march into war.

"Yes," she queried, "what is it?"

"Begging your pardon ma'am," began her head butler, "but we have strict orders from Master Elaand to make sure that you are ready in time for your engagement. He made it quite clear that if we did not execute his orders perfectly we would all be summarily executed.

"So, please, if you would follow us, we will barely have enough time as it is."

Ahh, Elaand, he had such a gentle way with others. She stood, stretched, and then allowed herself to be led from the room. Two cliks later she'd been scrubbed, washed, powdered and set up in the dressing room. There her dresser had slid her into undergarments and silk stockings and poured her into a ceremonial mating dress – that seemed a tad presumptuous, she thought – and then added several small pieces of jewelry that served to accent her eyes and her skin tone.

Then she was unceremoniously plopped down on an ottoman and had shoes fitted to her feet. She felt like a steed before a race. Three more assistants made sure everything was in place and then popped her back onto her feet and made her pirouette to make sure nothing fell off.

Once they were satisfied that she could walk and talk and not make them look bad they escorted her down the hall to the main dining room. She'd been hoping for something a little more intimate and was mildly disappointed all the way until they opened the doors.

There, in the center of the room was a small table, with a beautiful candelabrum in the center. There were curtains layered around the room to provide paths for the staff to come and go without being seen or bothering them unless they were actually serving them at the table.

While she was taking all that in it suddenly hit her that Samuel was standing across from her. He was wearing a full ceremonial mating outfit, glorious white fabric highlighted with gold braids and a necklace made of burnished woods.

It was over an epi-clik before she realized she wasn't breathing. She concentrated on inhaling and exhaling and soon had a steady rhythm going. There was something in his eyes that told her he was having similar difficulties. He found his voice before she did.

"Your Colonel Elaand truly knows how to set a table."

This was supposed to be the most romantic moment of her young life and she couldn't help but laugh. Much to her surprise, he joined her. Her aids helped them both get seated and then poured them glasses of a sweet Periplaneta wine and set down two small plates of a radish salad. She never even noticed that they were gone.

She would later think back and be forced to assume the dinner was incredible but, for the life of her, it would only be an assumption. All she truly would remember was the sparkle in his eyes, the gentle sound of his voice, the way the light played off his clothing, and the way shadows danced around him.

And laughter.

All through the meal, they shared laughter. Every single tingling echo was entirely natural. Not once did either use that horrid laughter courtiers use when they are trying to please their masters.

When the even was over they'd rubbed mandibles and then gone for a brief walk through the garden. She knew, intellectually, the moons were dark that even, and it was chilly and cloudy, but as far as she could have told the halves were in full light, and the sky was clear, and the warm scent of flowers wafted throughout.

Whatever the truth may be, it was absolutely, positively, the best time of her life.

Although it had been up for several turns, the tapestry in Watcher Urkel's main hall still drew a crowd. The second one done by Fleecy of the House of Rambling was slightly different than the one that hung in Gornd's palace. For one, it had red trim and fringe instead of black and it was signed on the right instead of the left. Other than that they were identical. She had said she'd made the changes so that no one would think he'd stolen Gornd's.

He'd been mildly abashed at the thought but then contemplated all that Fleecy had been through to get where she was and dismissed any insult. Slaves who could be accused of any crime without any hope of defense might have a slightly different view on how some should act than everyone else.

He left the crowd to their awe and headed for his throne room. Excellent tapestry or no, he still had a kingdom to run. His advisors were waiting for him already and had several sheaves of paperwork for him to review. He saw the Succubi were about a turn away from their ambush point so there was not much for him to do. Income reviews showed revenues were up and projected to continue for another Sun before flattening out. That was enough warning so that they could adjust their expenditures and not get caught off guard. In the five Suns since Xhaknar fell they'd developed a surplus. With careful management, they should be fine for a long time.

Then there were the many documents dealing with minor disagreements. The other warrens had court systems to deal with these things. He'd avoided that because he liked being in direct contact with his constituents. But with the influx of Naradhama, and the increased trade, there were now too many for one to handle. At least not effectively.

So he discussed the idea with his advisors. They finally agreed to set up three panels, of three judges each, to handle the basic needs of the kingdom. One would deal with trade disputes, one would deal with crimes, and the last would pick up anything that didn't fall into those two categories.

It didn't take them long to come up with a list of judges the citizens would accept. He drafted a letter to each of them explaining the situation and asking them to serve once every seven turns. They were all responsible brands and he felt sure they'd accept. He hadn't even noticed that three of his choices were Naradhama until one of his aides brought it up. They all agreed not noticing was a good sign all the way around. With that out of the way, they quickly divided the current disputes among the proposed courts and then moved on to the next items.

The rest was about as mundane as mundane could get so the time dragged, even though it was fruitful. It was well after mid-break when they were done. Urkel dismissed them and headed down to the palace's kitchen to find something to eat. When he got there he found his chefs preparing for the even meal. When he mentioned he was hungry now one of the chefs quickly sliced some roast kgum and made him a sandwich platter.

He stood to the side as they continued their work. He was impressed with their efficiency. Every turn they created three different meals for over five hundred members of the palace staff and their guests. And every meal was delicious.

He finished the piece of fruit on his plate and then set it down next to the sink where it was grabbed by a member of the staff and washed before he was out of the room. He absently wondered if that was a comment about his cleanliness. He shook his head, amazed at his paranoia. The job was getting to him.

Pleasantly sated, he headed back to his throne room to catch up on some paperwork. He was mildly surprised to be greeted by Fleecy.

"Forgive this intrusion, milord, but may I ask you a question?"

"Certainly dear, what can I do for you?"

She looked extremely uncomfortable so he led her into the throne room and provided her with a chair. That seemed to calm her down a little.

"Sir, I don't know if this is true or not, but there are rumors that the Naradhama and the Fierstans are related. Some say we used to be just like you until Xhaknar came. I know we look similar, but we don't seem to be the same. You are the leader of the Fierstans, so I hoped you would know. Is what they say true?"

Urkel pulled a chair next to hers and sat down.

"Yes. We were separated over five hundred Full Suns ago. Xhaknar did unspeakable things to your ancestors. When we saw your brand again it was over a hundred Full Suns later. You were then much as you are now. It seemed as though the ability to think for yourselves had been washed away. We never knew how Xhaknar and

Yontar did it, but the effect was devastating. Naradhama warriors became the most feared warriors on the Plains but, as proved in the last battle, they couldn't think their way out of difficult situations.

"But, now, it appears that you, and your kin, are finding those lost abilities again. Your tapestries are proof enough of that. I guess we should have told you before, but there never seemed to be a good time. I hope you'll forgive us, and me."

She let her head droop in her hands and wept for a while. Urkel put his hand on her shoulder and let her sob.

"We're mutants! Useless creatures! We don't deserve to be citizens of Great King Gornd's! We should go live on the fringe and never be seen again!"

He knew this was a time he should be sensitive and say soothing things. Instead, he laughed. Then he stood, swept her up into his arms, danced a quick Aklop and then spun her out to his side.

For her part, she was sure that this particular Great King had gone stark raving mad.

"Don't worry Fleecy, despite clues contrariwise, I haven't lost my mind," he laughed again, "it's just that of all the brands who can claim to be good citizens, yours are the only ones I know of who have truly earned it. No, Fleecy, far from being useless, you are a shining example to us all.

"Come, let us find a couple of those worthless couriers who live under the rocks of the palace and send out a release to all the warrens about how blessed we are to be related to you."

Still holding her hands he led her out into the corridor and stopped the first courier he saw. Within three epi-cliks the wording had been agreed on and the release was on its way to the warrens.

He was still smiling when he asked her to share his even meal.

He continued smiling throughout the meal and then

the private dance they had later accompanied by a quintet of palace musicians.

He was still smiling while he arranged for his palace staff to provide her a room for the even and made arrangements for her to be taken home in a carriage come breaklight.

The smile persisted long after he entered a wonderful dream that featured a bright and healing sun.

The six masted ship slowed and then stopped in the middle of the ocean. Sails were furled and anchors, fore, and aft were dropped. Captain Beula Koi-San snapped out a series of quick orders and soon the ship was quiet in the water and all the crew was standing at attention.

D'noma led her Succubi to the forecastle and waited as the ship's crew loaded their weapons up on deck. Once everything was secured the captain ordered all but essential personal to take some free time. A radio operator was placed on deck so she could relay any messages from the scouts.

D'noma stripped naked and waited for others to follow suit and then led them on the side of the ship where they dived into the waters below. Relieved of their duties many of the crew joined them. Soon the waters were filled with the sounds of playful teasing. The captain watched bemusedly as the Succubi would leap from the water and fly into the air just to spin quickly and dive back in. Even the most athletic of the Children couldn't match those moves. After a clik or so they finally re-boarded the ship and laid out under the sun. They spent the rest of the turn lazing in the moist, warm, air and sipping spiced waters.

It was just near even-fall when the radio operator walked to the captain with a look of concern on her face. The Succubi, with far superior hearing than the Children, heard the noise first.

Drums. The rhythmic drums used by the oar masters they'd read about in the reports. There was no sound in nature like it.

Captain Beula Koi-San began barking out orders. Her crew, well trained over the many Suns, followed them immediately. As soon as the Succubi were aloft their ship would move as far away as possible. The vessel was unarmed and no match for a raiding party of fifteen thousand Mayanorens should the Succubi fail.

As sails were being unfurled the Succubi took one cannon ball each and a belt of smaller explosives and headed into the crimson sky. They split into four groups of two hundred and fifty each and then divided up. Two groups would fly east, the others west, to circle around behind the Mayanoren fleet from the north. They had received several reports stating the Mayanorens had all their weapons on the front of their ships.

They were airborne in less than three epi-cliks and watched from the skies as the ship began to turn around and head east towards home. D'noma quickly assembled her squadrons into formations and they were off to meet their foe.

Thanks to the reduced weight they were carrying they were able to attain a viable altitude in short order. Less than a clik later D'noma spied the wake of the fleet. She began arcing her squad around for their dive. She controlled squadrons one and two and spied three and four curving around in the distance. They would dive in split order, one then three then two then four.

With nothing left to do but to attack, she tightened her wings in and began her controlled plummet. She could see activity on the decks as the Mayanorens were rushing to their weapons. As they got closer she could feel projectiles whizzing past her. The Mayanorens on deck had hand held weapons that seemed to be just as deadly as their mechanical counterparts.

She dropped her bomb on a trailing ship and smiled briefly as she heard the loud whump of a direct hit. Soon the sea was ablaze, as bomb after bomb hit its target.

Her pleasure quickly turned to horror as she watched one Succubus after another fall from the sky, felled by the deadly hand weapons. A glance at her left arm showed that she'd been hit too, but she barely noted the pain. The screams of the Succubi mixed with the sounds of the carnage below caused her skin to dimple and her spine to shiver.

She ordered her squadron up, out of range of the lethal fire, and counted one hundred and ninety survivors. The other squadrons had suffered similar casualties. As soon as they were all assembled around her they began surveying the damage they had caused.

Every ship was on fire but, as rapidly as the Mayanorens were responding, appeared to be in no danger of sinking. She looked at her depleted ranks and then noted that the Mayanorens were speeding onward as though nothing had happened. They knew the Succubi were out of heavy weapons. The damage that had been done was the worst they could do and it wasn't enough.

They watched as the smoking vessels continued into the distance and then D'noma had her radio operator contact the ship to see if they could swing back north and help with any survivors.

When they got closer to the water they saw an amazing sight; the fallen Succubi were being held safely above water by creatures they didn't recognize. Part fem but with a large tail like a fish, they moved gracefully through the water and easily rescued each Succubus they found. She set down in the water next to one of them and thanked her for her assistance. The creature answered with a gentle cooing noise and smiled. A larger creature, which she quickly deduced was one of the Orcan scouts, slid up next to her.

"They are called mermaids. They were made by

Rohta as an entertainment. They barely have the intelligence of a newborn small. Until now I thought them extinct, but I am pleased to be wrong."

D'noma thought about that and then petted the gentle creature on the head and received more warm cooing noises in thanks.

"I am called Wave Killer," the Orcan continued, "we have been in touch with the ship and they are on their way here. Captain Beula is a proud captain and would not leave any injured behind unless she had no choice."

She nodded.

"I am D'noma," she replied, "and I thank you for your aid."

He glanced around at the fallen Succubi and sighed.

"This went unwell quickly, did it not?"

"That's one way of saying it," she said remorsefully," but I know not what else we could have done."

"Their ships only have a small part touching the water. To sink them I would believe you would have to assail them from below."

This conversation would have to be continued later. There were Succubi in the water who needed assistance. She quickly passed word about the mermaids and began treating what wounds she could. The remainder of her squad did the same and soon blouses and skirts became bandages.

The salt water stung her wound but she didn't care. She was only scratched compared to some of the others and she doubted that some of them would live long enough for the ship to arrive.

When the ship arrived three cliks later, sixteen of them had proved her right.

It took another two cliks to get everyone back on board and tended to by the ship's medical staff. It wasn't until then they noticed the sea was littered with Mayanoren bodies. The mermaids, for their part, wouldn't go anywhere near them.

The light from the moon's halves illuminated the waters enough to see that there had to be a thousand dead Mayanorens slowly sinking. Some of them we wearing bright, red, shirts, the rest were dressed in their usual uniforms of dull gray. She had no clue what the difference was.

Several of the Children had jumped into the water and were passing out trinkets to the mermaids. D'noma noticed it was mostly junk, but it was all shiny and the mermaids appeared to be thrilled with the gifts.

Captain Beula handed her a cup of Sominid brandy and sat next to her.

"You have wounded them severely."

"Maybe," she said after a sip," but nowhere near enough to stop them. They will be in Kalindor in a few more turns and there's nothing we can do to impede them."

"True enough, we Children do not put weapons on our ships. And even if we did it would take many ships to fight off a fleet like that. Our puny vessel would just be fodder for the likes of them."

D'noma looked around the puny vessel and reminded herself that it was five times larger than any barge she'd ever seen.

"Even so," continued the captain as she refilled D'noma's cup, "there are fewer Mayanoren to be faced next turn than there were the last."

D'noma saw her wan smile and was forced to join her. They'd blown holes straight through several of the Mayanoren fleet and they'd just kept going. The ships seemed to have no magazines to explode. They should have considered that.

Maybe there was a lot they should have considered.

Douglass Fairwinds walked over to her and sat on her other side.

"We watched the battle from the top of the ship's masts. Our makers left us many texts concerning heaven and hell. Now I think I know what hell looks like."

"No," replied D'noma shaking her head, "that was but a taste of distant flame, hell will come when Yontar arrives in Kalindor."

Yontar watched carefully as the Named Ones oversaw the fire brigades who were in charge of dousing the flames. They'd lost quite a few troops but the oar masters had never slacked their pace. Within a clik they were far from the killing zone and there were only a few smoldering pieces of wood that still required attention.

The poop deck, where he was standing, had been barely missed. He wondered if he could have survived a direct hit and decided he didn't really want to find out. Having been dead once was enough for him. Any thoughts otherwise were quickly dispelled by the gaping hole in front of him.

He knew the Named Ones had only been humoring him when they'd agreed to have one lookout always focused on the skies. But, had they not been, the Succubi would have caught them completely unawares. As bad as the casualties were they could have been much worse. He didn't know the exact total but, if his ship was any example, they must have lost around a thousand or more troops this turn. He knew that fifty Mayanorens had been blown into the sea with the first blast and his ship had sustained three.

He was pleased to note the Succubi had been limited by weight and only carried one bomb each. Had they been caught close to shore, where they could have used those cannons which had so decimated Xhaknar, he might be swimming to Kalindor.

But being right hadn't lessened the shock of the attack. Even considering the assistance of the Fish-People he hadn't expected anything so far from any port. He hadn't seen any ships and wondered how they'd gotten out this far. Had they flown? Doubtful. Not carrying the weapons they had. So they must have had help. The fact he hadn't seen a ship didn't mean one didn't exist. It could easily have been a clik or two away.

So that left the question of how they were found. They must have been followed. A feat which could only have been achieved by the Fish-People. No one else could have remained out of sight long enough. That also implied they had radios. He could see no other way for them to get word over long distances in such an expeditious manner.

There was no mistaking the truth, this ambush had been planned and was waiting for them. There had been no hasty arrangements. The Succubi had covered half a continent and then put out to sea to wait for this opportunity.

It also meant there was no way for him to surprise anyone once he was in Kalindor. Every front would be hostile to him and every front would seek to aid the others.

On the other hand, he would be in Kalindor, where he would have ample resources to assemble a true army. One not just built on numbers but on technology and guile as well. The reptiloids may not be innovators, but he had the Named Ones for that. And he had himself, something the others could only dream of.

That was not conceit, he simply knew how deadly he could be even when the odds were against him.

More importantly, at least for the short term, he doubted that any of the armies could assemble and mount an attack for a while. If they could they would have just overrun Kalindor and waited for him to arrive. His fleet would have been sitting targets on a beach.

No, it would take time and skill to move the army of the Plains down through the lands of Südermann and then coordinate with the Fish-People. Not that he doubted their ability to accomplish all that since he'd seen what they did to Xhaknar and almost him, as well, this turn. No, once they set their minds to it he saw no reason to think that they would do any less than come with a full out assault on Kalindor.

As the last few dead were tossed overboard he realized had they built traditional ships they would all be dead now. Those bombs would have surely blown holes right through the hulls of any normal vessel. He'd have to thank the original Named Ones for coming up with the design that saved their lives. It would give them more status among all the Mayanorens and serve to remind them who was in charge.

He ordered the Named One piloting the ship to maintain the current speed and heading and then went below to grab a bite to eat. After all, it's no fun planning a global overthrow on an empty stomach.

It was well past even-split when word came into the council from the Children of the Waters. Members of the Elders' Council were woken and staffs quickly set up refreshments and pots of spiced java. Within half a clik everyone was reading the reports.

They mourned the sixteen dead and the two hundred and thirty injured. They cheered the thousand lost Mayanorens. Then they somberly read the report that not one ship had been sunk. Casualties or no, Yontar and the Mayanorens would reach Kalindor reasonably intact.

There was some talk about the mermaids they'd discovered, but not much. Curiosity would have to wait for a different turn. Those that had prayers offered silent ones to their deity of choice for making them saviors of the Succubi and then went back to reviewing the reports.

One thing became clear to all, the army of the Plains and the might of Lord Südermann would have to combine to fight this threat. No one was sure about the Children of the Waters since they had a very limited military. As best anyone could tell from the notes they'd gotten from Ambassador Hana Koi-San, only two brands were suited for military action and both of those manned the garrisons by the border of Kalindor. There was no mention of how much of a force they could muster.

It was still only half way through the Dark Sun so it would be hard to mobilize the Plains. Especially so since this had been a colder, and wetter, season than many could remember.

Hard, but not impossible. They'd have to move fast if they wanted to be in place to prevent Yontar from overrunning the garrisons come the Warm Sun.

Several of the generals had been having similar thoughts and presented them to the council. The supply trains that were originally slated to go north could just as easily go south with thirty thousand troops. Since the Mantis Guard and Südermann's common army were already there this would give them thirty thousand reinforcements immediately and more could be added as time progressed. Mnaas quickly signed off on the proposal without even bothering to consult Lord Südermann. It was agreed they would leave at breaklight.

While the generals scampered out to make preparations the remainder of the council began poring over the full reports which were now coming in. They all concurred that the Children of the Waters provided more details than they thought possible. Maybe too much so, they weren't really sure if they needed to know the exact wound track of each injury.

Then again, they were pretty sure they knew everything the battle's participants knew so they couldn't complain about that.

Ben walked over to the riders, who were in deep discussion, and stood patiently until they all turned to face him.

"Forgive the intrusion my friends but Allah the Most Merciful, through our Imam, has given me a most difficult task and I need your advice."

He had their attention with that. Ben had never asked for anything before.

"The question I was asked to answer seems simple, do we of the East join you in battle or not? But, as you may have gleaned from getting to know me, war is not our way unless it cannot be avoided."

They all considered that for a bit and then led Ben to a table and sat down.

"This is not your war now," began Sland, quietly "but it will be soon enough if we fail. None of us can tell you what to do or not. All we can do is what we have been doing, allow you access to all the information we have so you can make an honest choice."

Ben looked at him for a while and then nodded.

"What if, Allah forbid, our situations were reversed? Would you advise war?"

"Yes," Sland said quickly, "I would. I'd rather face the enemy in their home than mine. And, more importantly for me, if there is a way to stop the war from ravaging the lands of my friends and family then I have a duty to ensure their safety. After all, I have skills and experiences many do not. If I do not use them for the protection of those who trust me to be there when needed then why have I been given them?"

That was about as close to spiritual as Sland ever got. The other riders agreed with him, as far as it went. BraarB, for one, would no more believe she'd been given experiences or skills than she would believe she could fly. Both the supernatural and the spiritual were anathema to her. Nevertheless, that still didn't reduce her agreement with him as far as duty was concerned.

Geldish kept his counsel to himself. Not that it was any secret that he wanted to see Yontar destroyed once and for all.

They talked amongst themselves for a while more and then lapsed into silence. None of them felt comfortable answering Ben's question directly. Finally, Geldish stirred.

"Tell me, Ben," he began softly, "if you did come to war, what kind of force would you bring?"

They all expected him to say some small amount that would make rejecting his offer easier.

"Well," he seemed to be adding things up in his mind, "if all four warrens agreed with me, then I would guess, approximately, fifty thousand total troops. That would include the Horuns as well as traditional ground based troops."

He said that far more calmly than they might have liked. N'leah looked stunned.

"The Horuns," she finally was able to speak, "how can that be? They were supposed to have been exterminated in the gen-O-pod war."

"They survived. They moved to the north lands after the war but eventually moved a little south and joined the Great Warren."

"That's right," signed R'yune, "your warrens are run by more than one brand."

BraarB quickly translated for Ben.

"Yes," he agreed, "the Great Warren represents five main brands and has two more sworn to fealty. My brand is of the Southern Warren and we represent two brands and have one sworn to fealty. The other two warrens are larger than us and smaller than the Great Warren."

"Are all the residents of your warren believers in your faith?" BraarB was curious.

"Yes," he replied, "we all believe in the one true God and follow His command to leave peace behind in any path we trod. That's not an exact quote, by the way, but it does express the general idea pretty well. But, we can go to war in certain situations. This would seem to be one of them. As Sland pointed out, some of us have accepted the duty to protect others."

"Then I guess," interjected N'leah, "your real question is do you want to fight him now or when he invades your lands?"

Ben stared at his hands for a moment and then shrugged.

"If we must go to war, let it be with our friends and not alone. I will advise our leaders that now is the time."

Instead of waiting to ride all the way back to Chaldean, he joined the riders in going over to the radio room of the Elders' Council and contacted the Din-La post in his village. A few epi-cliks later he was speaking with his Imam and told him all that had occurred, what the army of the Plains was about to do, and what he felt should be done.

There was a moment of silence that was broken by the least expected of sounds, a hearty laugh.

"I once told Allah I wished the answer to be no when I asked if we should go to war. I guess this shows me just how much power I have when it comes to making demands of Him." He paused to catch his breath before continuing. "We chose you, Ben, for many reasons, but the one that a majority of us felt was the most important was you would not advocate rash policy. You are a true servant of Allah, Ben. You tend your garden and love your family. But you have also done what needed to be done to protect those things.

"I will not waste the time of your guests by reciting all you have accomplished for us, but I will tell you that I shall tell the councils of the warrens of your advice. I will also tell them the Southern Warren will honor that advice whether or not they wish to join. As you have said, war is coming one way or another. Best we meet it head on than cowering in our homes.

"We shall join this jihad of your Brittle Riders and, Allah the Most Merciful willing, stop the carnage before it can destroy our lives."

He signed off and Ben looked at the riders. They

smiled and walked back into the chambers. Geldish walked all the way through the crowd and stopped at the main table.

"I have news for you that may bode well," he almost seemed ready to laugh, "our friend Ben el Salaam has spoken with his Imam at the Southern Warren of the Eastern Shore and they have agreed to march with us. They may, and this is just a possibility for now, be able to enjoin the other three warrens of the east to join them, and us. If so they will march fifty thousand including a squadron of Horuns.

"Whether or not they do, however, we are guaranteed the assistance of the Chaldeans and their warren. I know that the army of the Plains will be leaving in a few cliks to join the forces of Lord Südermann but we will wait for the forces from the east to arrive and then ride with them. By then we should all have a much better idea of what will happen and when."

No one could find any quibble with that idea and the information was passed along to the warrens. As the riders left they heard every single member of the council talking about the possibility of Horuns joining them in battle.

They saw Drapery getting ready to close and BraarB rushed over and asked if he'd be willing to stay open for them. He saw no reason why not, so he did. Within two cliks all of the council was there as well as most of their staffs and a sizable number of curious brands who just happened to be up and around.

Greko and Ben sat near the front and sipped hot cups of java while discussing what the Eastern warrens might bring to the war. Everyone else stayed at the back, near the kitchen, so they could get their food quicker.

Come breaklight they heard the army marching in the distance and Drapery's wife took over serving so he could get some sleep. They all realized how tired he was when he kissed R'yune good-even and handed his rag to

Geldish as he walked past his smiling, unkissed, wife.

"This meeting of the Board of Directors of the Din-La is called to order."

Bmmd, the Chief Executive Officer for the Din-La, banged his gavel and took his seat at the head of the conference table. Ten other Din-La took their seats and arranged their paperwork in front of them.

"A lot has happened since you and I sat in your old trading post in Anara, hasn't it Zrrm?"

Zrrm smiled and the rest of the panel chuckled.

"And, while I may have seen many Full Suns, and I do remember authorizing you to ally with the Brittle Riders, I seem to have forgotten the part where I gave my okay to allowing them to rip open our front door, have a personal tour of our private facility, and then ask them to camp for a while."

That got some nervous laughter.

"Nevertheless, I guess if we're in for a scrap we're in for the goldens and there's no way to turn back time to straighten this out. So, this session this turn has a simple mission, decide what we are to do next."

That simple task took up four uninterrupted cliks before they realized they were getting nowhere and decided to take a break.

While the Din-La were always generous with guests, the spread they retired to made any royal feast look like rancid pit food. Twenty-two servants passed out foods, custom made drinks, and activated olfactory enhancers. The Board enjoyed custom scents, each designed to highlight different aspects of a particular morsel.

For the Din-La this wasn't an extravagance. They learned from the time they could walk how to manipulate every item they carried in their posts and that included food. How else could they show customers the potential of what they were offering?

The meal served to relax them as well. Finally, when they were calmed, they began assessing the situation again. Zrrm seemed completely lost in his own world.

"In for a scrap, you said?"

Bmmd angled his head in Zrrm's direction as acknowledgement while he continued savoring a new delicacy from across the eastern ocean.

"Yontar spent over a season and a half in a facility run by rouge makers, militaristic ones at that. They did not create Super Soldiers without planning on having super weapons for them to use. While our ancestors all agreed Xhaknar and Yontar probably did not live up to their ideals, for whatever reasons, otherwise they would have decanted more, the fact is the plans for those weapons were most likely still there."

He paused to let that sink in while he sampled a peach glazed water fowl.

"If we are in for that scrap, then the goldens must be this; we must give the army of the Plains the plans for the makers' weapons."

He expected a lot of criticism and yelling, instead, he got a quiet agreement.

"I'm afraid you're right," Bmmd said as he wiped his chin, "there is no other way. The warrens from the east have several examples in storage. For this threat, they will break them out and bring them with. The secret we keep will be a secret no more. If that is to be the case, then we should be ahead of the problem. It will be the only way for us to benefit."

"Then we will charge them for this knowledge?" Zrrm was more curious than concerned.

"Yes," Bmmd nodded, "not too much, but enough to make them realize there's value in what we bring."

"A question, sir," piped up the youngest panel member, "how is it we've never traded with the reptiloids?

They have many resources."

"True, but they were only interested in garnering weapons which would allow them to overrun the planet. We may be a greedy lot, but we aren't stupid. Giving them what they wanted would ensure our destruction or enslavement. Neither option was acceptable."

"But we traded with Xhaknar," he pointed out.

"Also true. But Xhaknar, once he found out we wouldn't give up our secrets, was willing to trade only for what he knew and understood. It never occurred to him or Yontar we may know far more than we ever let on."

The young board member accepted that explanation and poured himself another glass of the wine he was trying. The conversation turned to figuring out how best to disseminate the plans for the weapons to whoever needed them. They decided to courier the plans directly to Anapsida and let the council parse them out. A servant would take the underground rail system to the Anapsida post and then make copies before handing them over.

Dessert was served and each of them enjoyed their bonn bouche quietly.

Shortly thereafter the servants removed all the accouterments of the meal and left them alone.

They hashed over a few minor details and then all eyes turned to Zrrm.

"Now we have one more thing to discuss," Bmmd droned as he picked up a small sheaf of papers and acted as though he was reviewing them, "what do we do with you? While we are all in agreement with the policies you have forced on us, the fact remains you forced them on us. More urgent is the fact that now the Rangka and the riders both know of our lair.

"For now the Rangka aren't a threat and neither are the riders, but winds change and now we need to prepare for the turn when those winds blow a foul air. We spent many Suns developing this location and now it is useless. There are other underground facilities we can build to suit our needs, but it will take time. A lot of time.

"Worse still is that it will cost us many goldens and we will have no way to recoup that expense directly. You have put us in a very uncomfortable position Zrrm, so what are we to do with you?"

Zrrm knew all of this intellectually, but he hadn't put it all together so directly and so damningly. The Din-La didn't have a death penalty, but exile and other punishments were certainly within their grasp. He only knew of one case of exile and it was not a pleasant memory. He'd watched as the poor wretch was stripped of his vestments, wrapped in rags of gray and given two goldens, the legacy every Din-La got at birth, and then blindfolded and escorted through many tunnels until he was dumped in a strange land with no access to a trading post.

Whether he lived or died was no longer the concern of the Din-La.

He realized they actually expected him to answer.

"I don't know. I did what I believed to be right."

"Fair enough," replied Bmmd, "we do encourage the Din-La to act for the greater good. However, you are a member of the Board, not just some Din-La stocking shelves. You could have told us of your plan. In fact, you had an obligation to do so."

"There was no plan. It was all reaction, not action. Elzish followed me here and was ready to pull the front entrance open, so I let him in. Later, when the riders arrived, I thought to leave them be and hoped they'd go away. Obviously, as evidenced by the fact that they ripped the entire opening out of the ground, that strategy was less than successful."

Much to his surprise, Bmmd laughed.

"Yes, that would be one way to state things. Nevertheless, what do we do with you?"

"I do not wish to be exiled. Nor do I wish to be removed from the Board. I feel I've done more good than harm in my long service. Plus the Rangka trust me. That could work to our advantage in the long run."

"Do you think the Rangka would ever betray us?"

"Ever? Who can say? In the foreseeable future, no. Their goals and ours are the same. They want peace, we want peace. They want prosperity, we want prosperity. They want to savor delicacies without distraction, we want the same. I see nothing that would cause that to change, but I am not a seer. For now, they are our allies."

Bmmd signaled for a servant and ordered a round of spiced waters for the table. When the servant left he turned to Zrrm with a half-smile.

"So we do nothing? That is your advice?"

Zrrm smiled. "If the choice were left to me, then yes."

Now Bmmd graced them all with a real smile.

"I see no reason that the choice should not be yours, for now. It is your future we are discussing, after all, isn't it? But, if this happens again there will be no meeting, no feast, you will simply go the way of all exiles and your sons will lose their inheritance."

With that Bmmd dismissed the topic and left the room while the spiced water was finally being served.

Douglass cruised between the ocean air currents and glanced over at his companions who were gracefully slicing through them as though they'd been born to it. Which, truth be told, they had. They were speeding through the chasm between the mountains that they'd led the Succubi through on the way to meet Yontar. His thoughts of the battle made him wonder what his brand would do. The numbers involved were staggering to him.

If you added all his villages together they totaled less population than what the Mayanorens were taking to Kalindor. He had thought the Succubi insane when they told him of the war on the Plains. The numbers of combatants dwarfed anything he could conceive.

Then he'd seen the ship for the Children of the Waters. They had thirteen more just like it in the dock which meant even more were on the seas. Any one of them could hold a third of the population of his entire brand with room for supplies. There was no need for ships like that unless there were enough beings and goods to fill them.

He thought back on the lessons he knew of the makers. When the gen-O-pod war happened they'd marched every available maker to battle the threat. The decanted servants of the New Sons of Liberty were less than five Suns old when everything happened and they didn't really understand what was going on. They were ordered to stay behind and tend to the settlements. There were some femmes and smalls and a few elderly makers also left behind, but other than that the compounds were empty.

A Full Sun later six soldiers returned. Out of the twenty thousand who had left.

Less than a Sun after that a battalion of gen-O-pods showed up and wiped out the surviving makers. They spent some time talking to the Athabascae and the Haliaeetus about why what happened had happened. It didn't take them long to realize they too would have been slaves, but the concepts were abstract, not concrete. After all, according to Maker dogma, their makers were still training them. The most arduous tasks they'd performed were mock battles and fetching the occasional cup of coffee.

But when they found the battle plans their makers had devised, wherein they would be used as shock troops or fodder, they realized just how lucky they'd been. They'd been created to kill and die, nothing more. They didn't know it then, but later found out, their two brands were the only ones ever made without the bio-bombs. Their makers had wanted them to live until they needed them to die.

They decided then and there to stay away from the

rest of the world.

The Athabascae moved about twenty kays north of the old settlement and the Haliaeetus moved an equal distance south. It wasn't that they disliked each other, far from, it was just each wanted the room to grow as nature saw fit. They numbered around five hundred each back then, now they each totaled around twelve thousand. They had their villages, their small towns to handle commerce and, overall, did well enough for themselves.

But he'd seen Yontar's navy and he knew, beyond any hope of doubt, that that navy was headed to add more and more brands and munitions and then it was going to come north. Whether by land or sea was irrelevant, it was going to come. And north was where he and his were. That navy had simply charged through the Succubi attack and kept going. That meant there was something more important to them than this battle. And that something was pretty obvious, even to a sheltered being like Douglas.

He knew that war might not come to him and his this Sun or the next or even the one after that. But it would come. And when it did his brand would have a simple choice, serve or die. They could never stand against that kind of might.

They had another choice as well, they could join the army of the Plains and the followers of the mysterious Lord Südermann at the border of Kalindor. The Athabascae wouldn't like that option. They would prefer to stay safe in the mountains and hope for the best.

It was a tempting position. Even if Yontar came north, his focus would be on the Plains and on Lord Südermann, not their little villages. But would he let a potential threat, no matter how small, live?

He knew too little to answer that.

He dove through a rock formation, just for fun, and as he was pulling up decided to talk with the Din-La. They traveled everywhere and had offered news of the Plains before. He would ask the right questions, he hoped, and then offer his brand a choice.

Albeit a hard one no matter what answers he received.

Flight Leader Corvington Smythe stared at the message which had come in from Imam Salim. He knew the Imam pretty well and liked his company. Their long arguments about the nature of God and the universe were always stimulating and fun. He knew the Imam to be a brand of peace and prayer, not war. So a call for jihad from this leader, more than any other, had to be taken seriously.

He'd already been told by the leaders of the warrens the final vote was his and they would abide by his decision. The Horuns had lived in peace since the gen-O-pod war, but had kept up their training. Certainly, they stayed sharp by helping to repel the pirates who came from across the ocean as well as the constant drilling that every flight leader put his troops through. If they had to go to war, they were as ready as they could be.

He needed to think and the best way to do that was to take to the sky. His aides would frown but they couldn't stop him. He set down the papers and jumped off the balcony into the blue above.

As soon as he was airborne he knew what he had to do. He arced south and headed for the warrens of the Chaldean. It would take him a couple of turns to make the journey, but that would help clear his mind even more, so he relaxed a little and aimed for the highest clouds.

One of his aides caught up to him and tried to persuade him to return until a more formal, and supervised visit could be arranged. He politely declined using a display of colorful colloquialisms that would make a drill sergeant blush and continued on his way.

He felt pretty confident that he wouldn't be

bothered again.

The Horuns may be smaller than the Succubi but they were also faster and could attain greater heights. He spread his wings and climbed until he was gliding easily through the thin air. He thought about the Succubi and what he'd read of their involvement in the war against Xhaknar and then, later, their failed attack on Yontar.

He now knew what they knew going into battle and couldn't think of a thing they could've done differently. He'd also read the reports from the Brittle Riders, the Elders' Council, and the Children of the Waters.

The answer came to him unbidden. It was obvious, he just didn't like it.

Yontar would spread like a disease. Unlike Xhaknar he would have both unlimited resources and the manpower to exploit them. It might take him a few Suns to make it to the eastern shores, but he would if he got past the armies now aligning against him. He saw now, clearly, why Imam Salim had advocated this jihad.

It was the only real chance they had to save themselves.

He swung through a cloud and headed back for his roost.

It was almost even-fall when he entered the Chambers of the Greater Warren. The council members were still there and seemed to have been waiting for him. He bowed respectfully and accepted a proffered glass of ice wine.

"I vote yes. The Horun will go to war."

Neither resignation nor joy showed on the faces that looked at him. They merely nodded and called for pages to spread the word.

The eastern warrens were going to war.

He wandered into the main dining hall and scrounged a plate of food. The staff looked at him worriedly but said nothing. They knew their leader well and would follow him through the gates of hell if he asked. The main reason for that loyalty was that he would never ask unless there was no other way. He truly cared for his troops.

He knew all that but it hadn't made the decision any easier.

As he headed back into the main courtyard he saw the various generals making preparations in front of Din-La post. He was not a fan of the Din-La but realized they would move supplies far more efficiently than the warren ever could. For local issues, like the pirates, he kept the supplies and munitions under his direct control. But they were going to be crossing the continent and would have enough to do just to keep everyone fed.

He met with them as they were walking back to their offices and discussed time lines. Since the army of the Plains was already on the move no one saw any reason they shouldn't get going by breaklight.

That would mean stocking up on supplies at each warren until they headed west, but the generals had already thought of that and had made arrangements with the Din-La. He saw a stable master hurrying by and realized they would have to ride steeds to cover such a great distance and stay with the other troops.

That was fine. His flight team had been trained on them for many Suns. He even, much to his family's dismay, had practiced equestrian skills and trick riding. Well, he always said, he had no mate and need a hobby.

He could have mated, even now. He was still a fine specimen even if he was coming up on his one hundredth Sun. He passed a mirror and noticed his royal blue uniform was still trim and proper and his eyes barely showed any of the wrinkles of command.

Oh, his family and friends had tried. He'd dated almost every single femme in the warren. They were all nice enough, but none ever sparked him in the same way his mother had sparked his father. He wanted that and seemed doomed to be denied it.

Still, his career was rewarding. He'd risen through the ranks in fast fashion and was the youngest Flight Leader ever appointed. His audacious raid on the secret pirate base on a northern island had secured his reputation as a leader of daring and one who put the safety of his troops first.

It was he who'd figured out that the pirates needed a nearby base to stage such massive raids. It was he who'd scouted the area and found it. And then, when his squad leader had dismissed him with an "If you think so you go deal with it. The Feast of the Warm Sun is coming up and I'm busy."

So he'd recruited volunteers, got two hundred and fifty, flew up the coast and then, after resting and planning for two turns, set off to destroy the outpost.

They'd flown in from the north so they were behind the outpost and away from the sentries they'd posted on the sea side. They'd waited for even-fall and then attacked with a fury. Within a clik, the outpost was in flames. Within two there were no survivors even though they'd been outnumbered almost eight to one. His squad had suffered multiple injuries but no fatalities.

To a brand they credited their success to his careful planning and attention to detail. When word got back to, then current, Flight Leader Alain Worthington, Corvington was promoted, the previous squad leader dismissed, and the troops were happy.

He finished his food and set the plate outside his door on the tray provided. It would be cleaned up during the even by recruits. When he entered his room he snagged a bottle of island whiskey he'd been given as a gift from the Din-La and sat at his table to contemplate what was to come.

Instead, his mind raced back through time to the founding of the Horun clan. Prior to the gen-O-pod wars, all the Horun had been kept separate. Each was an individual slave to a single master. During the war, the leader of the Cyclops, Oronimus, realized their potential and rounded them all up in a single field. Though they numbered less than five hundred at the time he felt they'd make a fine addition to the war.

He was right. Their spy master abilities and cunningness with weapons earned them high honors among many clans. When the war was over they were officially freed from all duties by Oronimus since he felt they had been the worst abused by the makers.

They'd followed the Cyclops back across the ocean to the eastern shore that would soon become home to the four warrens and set themselves up to the north. After a hundred Full Suns or so they found they missed the company of others and moved further south and allied themselves with the Great Warren.

Nevertheless, they kept the traditions they'd learned from the makers and developed a strong mini-society among the eastern clans. From the military side of things, they served as a commando strike force. On the civilian side, they were expert craftsmen and could handle almost any form of miniaturization. Of course, as in any clan, some chose neither and instead became chefs, scribes, or whatever other job suited their talents. His brother, for example, was a history teacher at the warren's school for smalls. It was something he loved to do and something that made young smalls better brands when they passed his class.

There was honor in that and Corvington often bragged about him.

He finished his glass and went to bed. His staff was handling the details and, come breaklight, they'd expect their Flight Leader to be coherent.

TraadK bowed as he left his empress' chambers and

closed the door quietly behind him. ClaalD watched him leave and couldn't suppress the smile. She was pregnant. She wasn't sure how she knew but she knew. Her mother had told her she knew the exact sepi-clik ClaalD had been conceived. She's always assumed that was wishful thinking but now, feeling the warm glow within, she knew better.

Intellectually she knew this was all impossible. Her training as empress had focused her mind on facts and provable phenomena, not feelings and ephemera. Yet, she didn't care. She was pregnant and that was all that mattered.

She slowly stretched and went into her bathing chamber. Uku had assigned a couple of Se-Jeant servants to bathe her if she wished, and they certainly provided a personal scrubbing that left her tingling, but she wanted this time just for herself.

While she was letting the water cascade over her back she thought briefly of letting Uku know. She decided against it, instead of waiting to savor his response when she began to show in a few months. However, she would have to inform her medic, her two consorts, and TraadK. No need to keep him any longer from his wife.

She exited the bath, dried herself off and then went and chose a comfortable shift since she had no formal duties this turn. She glanced at her ring and decided to add the necklace Uku had given her. Pleased with her choices she headed out into the hall and decided to grab something to eat first before she checked in on her staff.

The kitchen staff had gotten used to the odd hours their leaders and ambassadors kept ever since the fall of Xhaknar and kept easy to access foods they could grab and build into small plates or sandwiches. She grabbed some sliced fruit and added it to a platter of cheeses and then stepped out of the way of the kitchen staff.

The Din-La had been importing several new kinds of cheese which were far more pungent than those made on the Plains. While they were an acquired taste she had to admit she loved them. The white cheese with the blue flecks was her new favorite, but it changed from turn to turn. One of the cooks saw her plate and placed a small slice of meat on it.

"It's a new form of sausage," he smiled, "called a Cajun Andouillette and is imported from the lands of Lord Südermann."

She thanked him and took a small bite. Her tongue leapt to life and she smiled. It was delicious. She relished the spices and then followed up with a bite of cheese and fruit. Soon she finished her small meal and felt completely refreshed. She thanked the staff profusely, grabbed another slice of the Andouillette sausage as she wandered into the hall.

She was just swallowing the last delightful morsel when she bumped, literally, into King Uku.

"Well, what a pleasant surprise," he laughed, "what brings you down to the dungeons?"

She smiled, "Your kitchen staff was kind enough to introduce me to new delicacies and humor my fascination for all the new cheeses the Din-La have been inflicting on us."

He started to say something, stopped, looked at her as though he'd never seen her before and then just stood there and smiled.

"Thank the gods, you're pregnant."

It wasn't a question.

Her jaw dropped. How could he possibly know? She barely knew and even that wasn't official. He seemed to be reading her mind.

"My Aunt Ofä gave me seven wonderful cousins. I know that look very well."

"I wanted to surprise you."

"Consider your mission a success. How long have you known?"

"Less than a clik."

He considered for a moment and smiled anew.

"Just like Aunt Ofä. She knew the sepi-clik it happened. I never saw how that was possible but my mother assured me it was so."

Cleric Äkä turned the corner and joined them. Seeing all the smiles she couldn't help joining in even if she didn't know why. Then she looked at ClaalD, smiled broader, and jumped up so she could hug her.

"Oh praise the joys! You are with small."

What? Are these Se-Jeant psychic or something? ClaalD was completely baffled.

Äkä saw her confusion and smiled.

"Not to worry, we don't read minds," she said just as ClaalD was thinking the statement confirmed the opposite, "it's just we're very in tune with biology. We can detect skin flushes so minute even the makers' machines would miss them. It is why no one can ever lie to us. But it's also how we know when a body has changed.

"Please, accept my congratulations and offer to be of assistance in any way I can."

ClaalD realized her breath smelled like a mix of stinky cheese and spiced meat and didn't care. She bent over and kissed each of them on the mouth and started laughing.

"Well, so much for keeping any secrets around here."

"Never you worry," smiled Äkä, "we are all friends first and politicians second. We will keep your secret as long as you wish."

"Well," beamed ClaalD, "at least let me inform TraadK so he can return his services to his wife. That seems only fair."

The agreed and, bereft of anything else to occupy her time, she headed to his home.

She walked out of the palace and headed across town to TraddK's home. She was about halfway there when she spied him in the park with a group of Llamia playing the new game the Din-La claimed was the national sport of the makers in Go-Chi. The sixteen inch round ball and the bat were the only equipment required and they had taken to it with a fetish. She had seen other variations of the game which required special coverings for a player's hands, head, and other gear but the Llamia seemed to think those versions were for weaklings and eschewed them.

She watched as the thrower tossed the ball in the air and the hitter took a mighty swing at it with the bat. The ball bounced harmlessly into the catcher's hands and the rules keeper yelled out a mighty "Steeeee-rike!"

She didn't understand the game completely but enjoyed seeing them happy. Although she still wasn't convinced the Din-La weren't hiding somewhere laughing themselves silly at being able to put one over on the hapless residents of the Plains. She couldn't believe a race as advanced as the makers would play such a simple, if maddening, game.

Then again, who really understood what the makers did?

She realized, because her mane was loose and she was dressed simply, no one seemed to recognize her. She bought one of the traditional sandwiches from a vendor; they were only made one way so she didn't have to think about what condiments she wanted on it, and eased her way into the crowd while she took pleasure in her anonymity.

The game continued on and she paid more attention to the teams. One was calling themselves the al-Cechs, which was the team TraadK was playing for, and the other called themselves the Licorices. They wore brightly colored gherkins with their team names emblazoned on them and seemed to have some good natured bantering going on. Although she was unsure if "That balindzork can't hit" was as good natured as it sounded, but everyone was laughing.

The game continued on for another click or so and everyone seemed to have had a great time. One team had obviously won the contest but she wasn't completely sure which one.

TraadK was slapping the hind ends of several of his teammates and laughing so she guessed the al-Cechs had been the victors. He saw her out of the corner of his eye and froze. She smiled and walked towards him.

"Congratulations TraadK," she said while smiling warmly, "not only have you won the game you have completed your task. I am with foal."

He looked stunned. Then he looked pleased. Then, finally, he bowed.

"It has been my pleasure to serve you."

"You did more than that TraadK," she said wistfully, "you have made me very happy. Above and beyond the fact I am with foal, I also feel alive again and have you to thank for that. While my feelings for you and King Uku will never be requited, they have been combined into a mélange that reminds me I am a worthy as a being as well as an empress. That will only serve to help me when I am faced with tough decisions."

He took it all in and finally smiled.

"My wife will be grateful for my return. She wants a foal of her own."

There was a lot she wanted to say but all she could do was smile even broader.

"Then I suggest you head home and honor her wishes. Now that you are guaranteed your foal will have a half-sibling who lives in the court, I imagine your wife will be even more eager."

They hugged and went their separate ways to begin their new lives.

Nak walked into the palace and headed to the communications room. He paused to admire the tapestry again and then turned the corner. He was a little surprised to see Fleecy walk into a storage room and walked to the door to see what she was doing.

He was stunned to see a complete art studio had been installed. How did it get there without him knowing about it? She sat down in front of a large sheet of paper and started drawing. There were several pictographs of Lord Südermann's father scattered around and she was glancing at them as she worked. He was amazed at her dexterity. Each arm handled a different part of the paper as she drew outlines and then slowly began shading them in.

He knew he had important stuff to do but stood there for over two cliks as the piece began to take shape. He watched in wonder as the image of the late Lord Südermann, surrounded by a mix of natural and technological marvels, came alive on the paper.

She stopped suddenly and started rifling through the various images. A voice from the other side of the room startled him.

"She is incredible, isn't she?"

Nak spun around to see Watcher Urkel sitting in the back of the room. Fleecy turned slowly and smiled. Nak swiveled between the two and quickly realized they were lovers. The smiles they were exchanging had nothing to do with art appreciation.

Well, that was a part of them to be sure, but he knew smiles like that. He knew those smiles intimately since he wore one himself every time he saw Welhern. It seems the art studio wasn't the only thing he'd missed these last few turns.

He shook his head in disbelief and then walked over to the magnificent drawing.

"Fleecy, this is one of the greatest pieces of art I've ever seen."

"Oh no, Vice-Lord," she shrunk into her stool, "this is just a draft. Something for me to work from when I start. I throw these away when I complete the real work."

"Hmm," he walked over and examined the drawing closer, "very well, I'll give you five goldens for this drawing when you're done with it."

"Oh no, Vice-Lord," she seemed abashed, "I can't sell you my trash. That would be un …. un … eth … wrong."

"Unethical would be the word you're looking for," he turned to face her, "and no it would not. I am willing to pay for this, you are not trying to dump something on me. Even if it never has value to anyone but me, I would treasure it. So, to me it has value and I am willing to pay for that value. You might be surprised to find out there will be others who agree with me and will wish to purchase your drafts as well."

She looked at him as though he had just grown a second head and then turned to face Urkel.

"I will do nothing to offend you milord. If you say sell, I will sell. If you say no, I'll toss it out when I get to the requested piece."

Urkel stood and walked over to her.

"Please, Fleecy, call me Urkel," he took her hand and looked her in the eye, "and Nak is right. Everything you do will have value. There are those who pay good goldens to purchase work product from artists. I see no reason you should be denied the same sources of income as any other artist. I have told you many times, you and your art both have value."

She looked at him, first shying away but finally meeting his gaze. She'd been a slave for fifty Suns before Xhaknar fell so these were not easy concepts to grasp. She stared into Urkel's soul for almost an epi-clik and then grinned and turned to face Nak.

"Ten goldens."

They all burst out laughing and it was a while before Nak could speak.

"Done!"

He finally remembered he had obligations to fulfill and bade his farewells.

Once away from the new lovers he concentrated

again on his duties and pulled the various messages he'd received after breaklight out of his pocket. Most were just the turn to turn trivia every city needed to deal with but there were a couple of reports from the army about their progress and various supply requests. Nothing was urgent, but it all needed to be dealt with.

Once he entered the communication room he noticed everyone seemed to be relaxed and laughing. That was odd. They were usually strictly professional in all they did and not given to whimsy. They immediately straightened up as soon as they noticed him and snapped to attention.

"At ease everyone," he was in a giving mood this turn, "there's nothing wrong with being happy. If someone might be willing to share the reason for this joviality I assure you I could use some myself."

The four mals and two femmes in the room stole glances from each other and finally one of them handed Nak a slip of paper.

He glanced at it and then felt his jaw drop and re-read it to be sure. He looked at them and they were all still smiling.

"Is this true? Has this been confirmed?

"Yes Vice-Lord," responded an operator he didn't know, "we have confirmed with the Din-La as well as the Imam of the southern warren, who sends his blessings as well as his troops."

"Seventy thousand?"

"Well, sir," she continued, "they're not all from the southern warren, but yes, seventy thousand is the correct number."

"And they're on our side?"

"Yes, sir."

"Really?"

That did it. Smiles and laughter broke out all over the room.

The message was clearly copied to all the warrens

of the Plains as well as Lord Südermann and the Children of the Waters. There was nothing he need do about it except celebrate.

Within a clik he'd dealt with all the messages he'd started with and confirmed that Watcher Urkel had received a copy of the message from the eastern warrens.

What an interesting turn this has been and it's not even mid-break yet.

That thought reminded him he was hungry and he headed off to find something to eat.

Dlarg herded all the smalls into the dining hall and found her mate, King Gornd, already there and laughing. He was surrounded by several members of his staff and they each seemed to be in a good mood too. While Gornd was never moody he had been under a lot of stress this last season so she was pleased to see him happy. When she got the smalls seated for their meal he handed her a note he was clutching.

She couldn't believe what she was reading. Seventy thousand additional troops were coming to their aid against Yontar. She walked over and hugged Gornd even though he was uncomfortable with public displays of affection and was pleased and surprised when he returned it.

"Yes, my love," he smiled at her as he released the hug, "this will help our army immensely. While it's true we will need to send additional supplies, we have a surplus and so do the rest of the warrens. When I first read Lord Südermann's reports on the size of the army in Kalindor, I was very worried. Not by their sheer numbers since Südermann has kept them in check with her garrisons, but an army that large under Yontar's guidance would be a hundred times deadlier than it ever would be normally.

"And we all know Yontar is there. Or, soon will be.

The Children's scouts lost track of them in a heavy fog a turn ago."

"Does this mean," she sighed demurely, "you'll be able to spend some time with us this even? You need to keep your mates as well serviced as your kingdom, you know."

The staff members blanched, coughed, and then did anything but think about what she'd just said.

"Yes dear," laughed Gornd, "I know my duties and I do not shirk them. This even shall belong to the femmes of the castle."

The staff seemed to be overcome by fumes of some sort that neither Dlarg nor Gornd could sense and left the dining hall to the family.

The meal was served to the smalls and Dlarg handed the responsibility of watching them over to Kerl, Gornd's first mate, and she and Gornd went for a walk in the center garden.

When Granq had originally approved the design she'd thought this courtyard a wild extravagance. But, now, with all the duties that came from being the mate of a king, she found it a necessary respite. It was quiet and beautiful. Local birds and furry rodents made it their home as well. Someone had once offered to rid the garden of the pests but Gornd had flatly refused.

"They were here before the makers and they'll be here long after us," he had said, and that was the end of that.

She was glad of that. The harmless creatures made the garden livelier. It was good to be surrounded by living things, it helped remind her of her place in the grand scheme of things. Everything had a reason on Aretti and she was just a part of that.

They strolled quietly through the flora and the fauna for almost a clik before he bid her goodbye. She went and found Kerl and the two of them began making plans for the even. Though they, and Lqar, had borne him seven smalls between them, they were like younglings preparing for their first kiss. They giggled and blushed as they made sure there would be fresh bedding for the four of them and there would be refreshments in their sleeping chamber.

When some of the Naradhama servants figured out what the femmes were planning they switched into high gear. Quicker than any of them could believe the chamber was turned inside out and there were candles where the torches had been, soft curtains where the drapes had been and a food tray was set next to the bed, so they wouldn't have to get up. There was even a small box of matches by the candles so the femmes could light them when they were ready.

One of the Naradhamas informed them she and her fellow staff members would tend to the smalls and the even meal had been arranged to be served in their chamber. Additionally, she smiled, the spa's schedule had been miraculously cleared if, and only if, the femmes felt like getting some pampering before their special time.

As it turned out, all three femmes felt very much like being pampered this turn and happily followed the Naradhama to the spa.

Queen A'lnuah and Elder Urnak were smiling over the good news as they enjoyed a late mid-break repast in his antechamber. The news was already spreading through the warren and celebrations were breaking out everywhere. The sounds of laughter and singing could be heard echoing inside the room where they ate even though several layers of walls separated them from the outside. Seeing no way to avoid the jubilant sounds they decided to wander among the citizens. They donned loose fitting clothes, removed all tokens of their ranks and exited through the servants' entrance.

The streets were filled with revelers and merchants who were happily exploiting the moment. They couldn't help but smile as they watched three Din-La racing among the throng trying to sell noisemakers and sweets. The local inns were packed and partiers spilled into the streets.

Despite the crowds, everyone seemed well behaved and to be having a good time. They wandered around the periphery and listened to the gossip. It seemed the news had gotten out as accurately as could be hoped so there was no need to worry about squelching wild rumors. The comments they heard ranged from happy to have new allies to happy to not to have to face Yontar alone to just plain old happy.

A'lnuah mentioned the latter group would probably be happy with shiny stones.

They laughed along with the citizens they met and were having a very good time. A couple of cliks later they headed back to the palace. They were met by furious courtesans and fretting staffers all gathered near the main atrium. They did their best to take their many complaints very seriously but couldn't stop laughing.

They assured them they were fine, had not gone insane, had not been kidnapped by terrorists and had not been naughty.

Whatever that last one meant.

They headed back to the antechamber and put on their regular clothes. Once they were suitably dressed they headed back into the palace and began taking care of their official duties. A'lnuah only had a few things to do so she was headed back to her palace within a clik. Urnak made sure his supply master had access to everything he might need to help the growing army which was headed toward Kalindor and then headed to the communications' center and checked to see if there was anything that required his attention.

Satisfied Aretti wouldn't end in the next few epi-cliks he headed off to survey the rest of the grounds and chat with the various caretakers. This was his favorite part of being a ruler. The quiet time he got to spend with those who actually made everything work. He always made sure to let them know he valued their input and was pleased, more often than not, he received it. Several very good ideas had come from his staff and all had served to make the warren more comfortable and efficient. Like his old mentor used to say, "Never ask a Fish-Person how to light a torch."

He smiled at the thought of being back in school and wondered how the old Minotaur was doing. He'd probably still be alive. He decided to look him up when he finished his rounds. As he was finishing up he caught the attention of an aide and asked him to se if he could find his old teacher and then headed off to dine with his family.

His wives were already in the dining hall when he got there and were waiting to eat. He apologized for his tardiness, took his spot in front of the large chair at the head of the circular table, said the even's prayer and everyone sat down to enjoy the meal.

While everyone was pleased with the news from the eastern warrens they still had the usual turn to turn responsibilities to deal with; which small needed help with which subject, which wife needed to see which medic and so on.

Servants came and went with regularity and soon they were enjoying a sweet dessert.

Afterwards, his wives went to tend to the smalls and retire to their rooms. The palace was quiet and he took the time to head down to the communications room and see if there had been any meaningful updates.

He sat to the side, so the operators could continue their work, and read message after message. There was an update from Greko about the Brittle Riders and his new friend Ben, but it was more casual than informative. Although he was amused to note the Din-La were teaching Ben sign language so he could speak with R'yune. He'd heard a rumor about how Sland scared him when he tried to teach him the basics.

He could understand that. Sland could be scary even at his most convivial.

He remembered when he'd shown some of the Minotaurs how to shoot the new weapons while riding a deisteed. When one of the warriors complained the sight was off Sland took the weapon, mounted the deisteed, aimed, fired ten straight shots in the center of the target while riding at full speed and then said, "You're right, it is, but you need to learn to adjust."

As one Minotaur later said, "I now believe every rumor I've heard about him in battle."

Another may have had it more correct when he said: "Since he's alive, and his enemies are dead, I never doubted them in the first place."

G'rnk sat in the temple's kitchen, as he did every even, and shared a final drink of the turn with Makish. The two had become close friends over the last few Suns, though neither believed the other could explain why. Truth be told, they didn't ponder it much, it was what it was and they were comfortable with that.

The preparations were complete for his trip to the land of the Fierstans for the kickball game and T'iul had also made arrangements for him to visit each warren in sequence on the trip back. When he'd seen the itinerary he was amazed at how thorough it was. As far as he was concerned it should have read "Meet leader, share a meal, leave." It seemed there was more to being Pack Leader of the Wolfen than he thought. Throw in the fact he'd somehow become the de facto king of the Kgul and haven lords and was asked to represent the Rangka, he had more to deal with than he cared to admit.

But, after all, those Suns of solitude and terror, it

did feel good to have allies and a safe place for his kind to live. If all it took was for him to go out and act like a leader once in a while, then it was a price he would gladly pay.

He and Makish went over some documents to make sure they would be able to send their fair share to the larger army which would now face Kalindor and Yontar. Crops and crafts would be no problem since this area had been fertile even when Xhaknar reigned. The extra goldens didn't appear to pose a problem either. Zrrm could handle the disbursements when he got back from wherever he was.

The two chatted for a while more and then G'rnk took his leave and headed home to his mate, B'tar. Their small would be five Full Suns come the Good Sun. He couldn't believe how quickly the time had passed.

B'tar saw him coming across their lawn and came out to greet him. They kissed in the chilly air and walked, hand in hand, into their home. She poured him a glass of spiced water and led him into his study. She'd set up an intimate table for them to enjoy their final meal of the turn and he smiled. He felt lucky to be with her, she made him twice the Wolfen he would have been alone.

He worried he didn't do enough for her but she said that was proof he did. He had no idea what that meant, but when he'd asked her mother she'd smiled and said her daughter was clear enough to be understood.

He had no idea how to be a good mate, no clue how to rule, and the ones most affected by his actions in each case seemed to think he was the best at each job. Maybe going through life completely clueless was the best way to do things.

He set the thoughts aside as she served their meal.

He started to clean up after the meal and she laughed at him and reminded him they had servants now. That was something else he'd never get used to. He shrugged and they went to bed.

Come breaklight there was a tap on their bedroom door. After making sure his mate was properly covered he called for whoever it was to come in. He was mildly surprised to see Zrrm.

"Forgive the intrusion friend G'rnk, may I speak with you privately?"

G'rnk realized he was nude and smelled like B'tar.

"Wait for me in my study, I'll be there shortly."

Zrrm nodded and left, closing the door behind him.

G'rnk slid silently from beneath the covers, kissed his sleeping mate and quickly stepped into the shower. Ten epi-cliks later, still dripping and wearing nothing but a robe, he entered his study to find Zrrm finishing the arrangement of a breaklight repast.

G'rnak poured himself a steaming cup of spiced java and filled his plate with a variety of foods he didn't quite recognize. Zrrm did the same and the two sat quietly, eating, for several epi-cliks.

Finally, Zrrm spoke.

"As you know, we are in between technological ages. We have the ability to make many things, but not the required infrastructure. When the gen-O-pod war ended there was barely enough technology left to make a hand cranked generator. Even so, the plans for many machines and weapons were never destroyed.

"Some brands, such as those under Lord Südermann's reign, did their best to rebuild infrastructure quickly so they could provide electricity and communications. Others, such as the denizens of the Plains, opted for a simpler life but took advantage of what technology they could create without requiring a return to the ways of the makers.

"Across all of the Aretti, there are variations on these basic themes. Some more extreme than others.

"In vaults scattered across the planet are drawings and equations for many wonders. But they can't be built with what's available."

"From my conversations with Makish I know it's all true," sighed G'rnk, "but what does all of that have to do with you waking me up so early?"

Zrrm sipped his java, sampled an imported sweet meat and smiled.

"Because you, Pack Leader of the Wolfen, Honorary King of the Kgul and haven lords and liaison to the Rangka, are going to change the status quo. You are going to build the necessary infrastructure, you are going to reintroduce all of the lost technologies and you are going to help the brands finally take their rightful place in the universe."

G'rnk considered briefly and found himself reminded of how beneficial being clueless could be.

"Okay."

"Okay?"

"Yes, okay," G'rnk broke into a rather silly grin, "nothing you asked of me offered the slightest bit of personal gain, so I know it's not a bribe. Everything you stated is true, so I know you're not hiding some ulterior motive and I have become painfully aware lately I haven't got the slightest idea what I'm doing, and am therefore being very successful at it, so this seems to fit the events of the last few turns perfectly."

Zrrm was so baffled he wasn't sure if G'rnk had just told his first joke or if he was serious. G'rnk, for his part, seemed fascinated by the food and offered no other comment. They continued like that, baffled and fascinated until the meal was finished, then G'rnk broke the silence.

"How do we prevent the brands from becoming just like the makers?"

"We've actually given that some thought," replied Zrrm, "and have come to a conclusion. The makers used a lot of various schemes for manipulating the value of their capital. Goldens would be worth one thing one turn and another the next. It caused wild fluctuations in what an item could be worth. Also, because it was so speculative every now and then someone would guess wrong and whole economies would collapse. While supply and demand certainly played a role in some instabilities, just as they do now, the makers' manipulations went far deeper. It was, primarily, the need to stabilize their financial concerns which led them to embrace the work of Rohta and the others so readily.

"There is no corollary for that type of economy now. The planet's population is too small to make any real use of it and the mindset of the brands wouldn't permit it even if they procreated like Warm Sun rakyeens. While the Din-La does issue loans to businesses and land owners, they are seldom speculative. Certainly, things can happen which can prevent their timely remittance, but those are fewer and farther between than you might imagine. We are very careful with our profits.

"All we need to do in the future is prevent the maker's type of economy from returning. Everything else should take care of itself."

G'rnk poured the last of the java into his cup, thought about all he'd just heard and nodded.

"Then, as I said, 'okay.'

"But, I do have one question, why me?"

Now Zrrm positively beamed.

"Because you don't want power. If the next turn saw you returned to being a farmer and forced to till fields, you would face each breaklight as you face them now. The Südermenn are further along with their grasp of technologies than almost any other brand, but they do what is best for the insectoids which may, or may not, benefit the rest of Aretti. There are other brands across the planet of which the same could be said. Not that they are evil or malevolent, just near sighted, for lack of a better term.

"You, on the other hand, don't care. You may be the perfect ruler to handle all of this while leading your brand, and the rest of the world, into a bright new dawn."

G'rnk handled compliments about as well as he whistled, which was not at all, so he shrugged. "What about Yontar?"

"He has the plans for many advanced weapons he took from the facility of his makers. But he is about to face the same problems we do. There is no infrastructure in Kalindor to support mass manufacturing. He can make do with manual labor for some of it, but none of the truly lethal weapons can be made there, no matter how much raw material they mine.

"We can provide and, in fact, have provided, Anapsida with plans for weapons they can make now which will be far superior to anything Yontar can access or create."

G'rnk stood, cinched his robe, headed for the door and then turned to face Zrrm.

"If this is a good thing it will have my support forever. If not," he paused briefly, "I will personally spread the entrails of every Din-La across the Plains until the remaining carrion birds and sna-Ahd weasels are sated to the point of exploding from their girth and then, and only then, shall I begin to exact my revenge."

With that, he left Zrrm to ponder how fond he'd suddenly become of his entrails and how much he preferred them on the inside.

The fountainaide in the inner courtyard was a duplicate of the one from Rohta's African home. It was the most peaceful place on the palace estate. Lord Südermann sat, eating a sweet cake and sipping sugared ale, thinking about the carnage coming to her land. She had talked to Elaand and Mnaas and no one could come up with a viable alternative. Yontar must be stopped before he could gain a foothold north of the border.

She had received the reports from the eastern warrens and was pleased to know they would stand in this together. Maybe this would be the first true step to creating the harmonious noise God wanted to hear.

Elaand had briefed her on the extra supplies which would be needed but saw no difficulties. It was logistics, not magic. They could handle that.

She'd ordered the Ant-People to start infiltrating the lands of Kalindor, planning mayhem and garnering information. Much to her surprise, instead of their usual recalcitrant response to orders, they were not only excited at the opportunity they seemed to have already devised plans to carry the orders out in the most effective manner.

Mnaas had reported they'd checked out the strangest array of supplies he'd ever seen. Bullets without guns, knives, small bombs, a quarter ton of salted meats and twenty gallons of syrup of ipecac. Neither of them could figure out what they were up to but both knew the Ant-People were fiercely loyal to her so they decided to chalk it up to a quirk and see what happened.

She finished her snack and looked around the fountainaide. Over the many Suns, it had become an aviary for all sorts of wild birds. Her staff made sure there were feeders placed strategically throughout and were kept full of seeds and treats. She often wondered if Rohta, while throwing the work of God and nature out the window, had ever stopped and enjoyed the simple beauties and lessons it provided?

She doubted it. Arrogance and shortsightedness were a horrid combination, especially when the world demanded humility and a very long view if you wanted to survive. Her studies to become a Südermann had taught her that and her experience, thus far, only reinforced it. She began trying to think like Yontar. She knew he was taking a very long view. If he could, she knew, he'd take several Full Suns to build up his arsenal and then attack the north.

Both the Elders' Council of the Plains and her advisors agreed he couldn't be allowed that luxury. They would have to attack as soon as they had all the troops assembled. She didn't relish war, but she knew the

Südermenn before her had been forced to make these tough decisions and there were no breaks allotted just because she was young.

She, like her predecessors, would listen to the wisdom of her advisors and then make the best decisions she could.

Maybe some prayers would help.

She set aside her cup and walked over to the chapel near the palace entrance. This was a private chapel for her and select guests. There were several others scattered around the grounds. In keeping with tradition, they were all small and designed for private reflection rather than any sort of communal gathering. She caught her staff cleaning up behind her out of the corner of her eye as she entered the small room.

It was simply furnished; a small kneeler to the front with a rail to lean on and four rows of pews for guests. The walls had small, tasteful, lithographs and were illuminated by recessed sconces that were barely visible to the eye. There was a small cross on the wall in front of the kneeler but no alter or tabernacle.

She knelt in the front, clasped her six hands together and prayed.

She was well aware of the age old axiom that talking to God was the truest sign of sanity and having God talk to you was the truest sign you'd been forsaken. This turn, God merely listened.

To His credit, He listened for a long time without complaint.

When she finished her prayers she went into the palace proper and reviewed the many missives and notes which required her attention. It took her four full cliks to finish everything and she was bone tired when she was done. Nevertheless, she felt relaxed and oddly happy. The plans were in place and her role in the larger scheme of things was a combination of ceremonial and functional.

She exited the main communications chamber and

was stunned to see Samuel standing there.

"You have been very busy these last few turns."

"Well," she stammered, still taken aback by his beauty, "there's a war coming and other …. well, stuff that requires my attention."

"I am well aware of that, thus it is all the more reason for me to make you your even-meal."

She made noises that were new to her. They were a combination of elation and fear.

"Not to worry," he smiled … he had the most scrumptious smile, "Elaand has enough security in the palace to have me assassinated at the first impropriety."

The turn dissolved and was replaced with laughter.

Later, the laughter was replaced by a succulent meal he'd made with his own six hands. He'd "borrowed" a guest suite for their rendezvous. A small part of her wondered how he'd managed that but most of her didn't care.

He would serve a course and then join her at the table. When the course was finished, he'd clear the dishes, get the next course and resume the meal. It made for a leisurely distraction and allowed them to talk casually well into the even.

When it was over they brushed mandibles, held hands, and went for a walk in the center garden. She wanted to tell him the entire history of each artifact and replicated ornament but opted to just enjoy the silence instead.

They both knew a hundred eyes watched their every move but neither seemed to care or notice. The air was cool but pleasant, and the stars twinkled just for them.

On the second floor, overlooking the courtyard, Elaand turned to a young private and smiled.

"In case anyone ever asks, it is to salvage moments like this that we fight."

The private nodded, pulled a pictograph from her breast pocket showing her and another young private hugging at a beach and handed it to Elaand.

"Our drill sergeant said the same thing. He made us each keep a reminder in our uniforms."

Elaand laughed, returned her memento, removed a pictograph of his family from his uniform and shared it with the private.

"That's the nice thing about truth. It never changes."

Oronimus IX had been charged to be the Supreme Commander of all forces, but he was well aware he was really just the commander of the ground forces and Flight Leader Smythe was the only leader the Horun and the Columbas would listen to. That didn't bother him in the slightest. He knew Smythe well and respected his keen mind. He also knew if an order was given he would follow it without question.

He was even more pleased with the council's pick for his Second in Command. General Momar al Rahim was an inspired choice. His defense against the southern raiders, using an imaginary navy no less, showed the kind of being who valued cunning just as highly as brute force. He didn't know al Rahim very well but knew his troops worshipped him and he had the respect of many powerful politicos.

He also knew the former mattered to him and the latter did not. That made him a valuable asset as far as Oronimus was concerned.

Four turns west of the southern warrens they were making very good time covering an average of twenty kays per turn. At their current pace, they should arrive at the western garrisons of Lord Südermann just before the start of the Warm Sun.

He pulled his deisteed to the right and rode up a small hill to check the troops' progress. Smythe and al

Rahim followed. He looked and saw they were all in tight formations and marching in smart precision. Since he was not an evil leader he had the infantry, about seventy percent of his forces, ahead of the cavalry and, kgum led, supply wagons. Animal dung may make farmers happy but it made marching a chore.

His bright yellow skin glistened in the Sunlight. Like all Cyclops, his skin had a vinyl-like sheen and his eye could scan every spectrum from infrared to x-ray, not just the visible. His skin made it easy for him to be seen by his troops – although he claimed it was merely due to his seven feet in height - and his eye made it easy for him to spot any assassins who might be hiding in the rushes. It also gave them an interesting take on colors. Cyclops' art was widely prized just because it offered such an unusual view of the world.

He watched as each column passed and made mental notes about each brand. They were all well trained but this would be the first time they'd served together on a scale like this. To help speed matters along he'd borrowed a technique from the army of the Plains and had mixed up the battalions so they each had multiple brands.

To his credit, Smythe had seen the wisdom of the move and had his Horuns marching instead of riding so they could blend with the rest of the army. Al Rahim was using the radio to check in with the battalion leaders and then checked with the supply master to make sure there were no problems. He'd instituted a program wherein some of the troops would forage the surrounding countryside as they marched to gather fresh meats and vegetables. They'd been given handbooks which showed which plants were safe and which animals made the best eating. Oronimus had thought the idea unnecessary but al Rahim had explained they didn't have accurate reports on what foods would be available on the front so any non-perishables they could save now would only benefit them later. Smythe had concurred and that ended the debate.

He had to admit it was turning out to be a very good idea. Beyond the obvious benefits of fresh food every even, the mixed troops were learning to work together and respond to the new chain of command. Smythe had suggested they rotate the foraging parties so they changed every two cliks. That kept the troops fresh and fostered some competition to see who brought back the most food. The Kleknar had turned out to be the best at finding edible roots. Their little, roly poly, bleach white, bodies were easy to spot in the wild, but they seemed able to ferret out hidden things better than anyone else.

They also seemed to be able to find any random combination of objects and turn them into a bomb. He chuckled at that, remembering the practical joke a couple of them had pulled. They'd made the oatmeal being served for breaklight repast burble out of the pot like a small volcano.

Well, it was funny now, not so much so when he was wiping oatmeal off of his face.

Realizing he was chuckling out loud and that al-Rahim and Smythe were staring at him he quickly recounted what was amusing him. As it turned out they had similar stories. After their shared laugh, they rode back to the head of the column and continued on their march.

About a clik later a Pan scout, Alzeebior by name – also the second son of Belnium, a fact which was of infinite interest to the Pan but not so much to anyone else - came riding back to make his report. The Pan, like the Succubi, had been created to be living statues and provide some minimal personal services. And, like the Succubi, they'd turned out to be resourceful warriors and staunch allies. Their stubby, goat-like, legs moved them far faster than anyone would have thought and they had a knack for stealth. They were also first class marksmen. Oronimus had used them several times against the pirates and was glad they were with him now.

The scout reported there were a couple of herds of venison about four kays ahead and some interesting looking berries on a pink tree. Other than that the way was clear. A hunting party was sent out to cull the herd and check out the berries while another scouting party took off to reconnoiter their path.

Oronimus was pleased all the warrens had agreed to wear the same uniform colors. They'd settled on the rust and black worn by the Southern Warren. He really didn't care what colors were used so long as they all looked and felt like they belonged together.

Smythe led the Horuns and the Columbas into the air to stretch their wings and run through some formations. All ten thousand Horuns and the one thousand Columbas darkened the sky and headed to the south. The Columbas were new to Oronimus. A little taller than the Horuns, they were gray skinned and feathered and had exceptional directional skills. They didn't have the speed of the Horuns but they had tremendous endurance and were deadly with aerial weapons.

The primary signatories to the war documents, the Cyclops, the Chaldeans and the Horuns, had each committed ten thousand troops to the effort. The other forty thousand troops were divided, somewhat equally, amongst the other brands of the eastern warrens.

Oronimus watched them for a while, always amazed at the accuracy of their maneuvers. They flew as one beast. He wondered if Yontar had ever even conceived of warriors such as these. He doubted it. All he had read of the wars on the Plains led him to believe Xhaknar and Yontar needed to have complete control of their troops. That led to a great blunt force threat but a lousy army.

However, he had not risen so far in rank because he made decisions based on third party rumors. When they finally reached the far western garrisons he would send his own spies into Kalindor.

Or not.

Certainly, Lord Südermann would have her own spies and they would be sharing information, or this would never work. Also, the army of the Plains had direct experience with both Yontar and Xhaknar. Even though only Yontar still lived, there was a lot of history there and he would need to be briefed. He realized, now, they had very little useful information on the Plains. If it wasn't for the reports brought back by Ben el Salaam, they would be marching blindly into this war.

But they weren't.

This even, when they made camp, he'd discuss what he did and did not know with al Rahim and Smythe. He'd make that their ritual until he was convinced there was no information which had been missed.

About a clik later, Smythe slipped through the air onto his steed and trotted up next to Oronimus.

"General," began Smythe, "there is a clearing about four cliks ahead that would make an ideal location for camp and it's bracketed by two small rivers full of fresh water and fish."

Oronimus smiled more good news for the supply master.

Al Rahim stopped to the side, as did all the troops from the Southern Warren, for their prayers. Oronimus knew they'd catch up quickly so he kept the columns moving.

As the turn continued he began listening to the sound of seventy thousand troops marching, in step, off to war. He'd never heard anything like it. It was the sound of doom to all who dared defy it.

The air was warm and clear with the tang of salt filling their lungs. Gulls circled around the fleet as it rounded an isthmus and headed for shore. A Named One stood on the poop deck and watched carefully as his crew began making preparations to disembark. He could easily see the welcoming committee with his fellow Named One standing on the shore. There was a band and a small honor guard. He guessed the creature wearing the garish uniform sitting in a palanquin was the Exalted Quelnerom.

He turned in time to see Yontar stride onto the deck. Gone was his utilitarian garb, in its place was a bright white uniform with a variety of small medals and ribbons pinned to his left breast. He had black epaulets, a black belt and black, mid-calf, boots. The entire effect was one of restrained power.

He amended that to 'barely restrained' and smiled.

A little over a clik later the Mayanorens were marching off the ships and forming ranks on the beach. It was clear the Exalted Quelnerom had no idea how large a force Yontar led. The Named One here had done his job well. He would have to remind Yontar of that.

Soon the Exalted Quelnerom was completely surrounded. Yontar strode forward, gave him a slight bow and smiled.

It was not a warm smile.

"Greeting to you Exalted Quelnerom," he began smoothly, "I am Yontar, leader of the Mayanorens and the Named Ones. I'd like to take this opportunity to thank you for turning the kingdom of Kalindor over to me."

Quelnerom looked this way and then that and then at Yontar and then at his royal guard and did some simple arithmetic. All his dreams of power and glory gone without a weapon being raised. All his hopes for the brands of Kalindor shattered like some cheap pottery against a stone. Defeat showed in his eyes.

"Not to worry," continued Yontar politely, "you shall still lead the brands of Kalindor to the glory you desire, you shall just do so while marching behind me. In return for this I shall give your warriors weapons they've never dreamed of and military leaders far smarter and more experienced than any you've ever met.

"Follow me and you'll taste glory so rich you'll

choke on it. Oppose me and I'll feed you to the creatures of the sea. So, Quelnerom, will you swear allegiance to me or will you die?"

Choices are funny once you understand them clearly. What had once seemed so complex and obtuse was suddenly plain.

"I will follow, as will all the brands of Kalindor. On this, you have my word."

Yontar thought of noting how little the word of the defeated mattered to him but decided he had said enough for now. He could have him killed at any time. He mentioned that to one of the Named Ones as he was walking away and was pleased to get a smile in reply.

They began their march towards the Palace of Kalindor and the Named One who'd served as an envoy briefed Yontar on every detail of what to expect. By the time they were half way there Yontar had a very clear idea of the layout of the grounds as well as the décor. He was pretty sure the décor would change the instant he arrived.

He called for a couple of Named Ones who were following behind and began discussing immediate strategies. They all agreed the armies of Lord Südermann and the Plains would be stupid to wait for him to get settled in and would probably attack before the Warm Sun. So their first order of business was shoring up the garrisons to prevent those armies from penetrating into Kalindor. He was a little nonplussed to find out, while Kalindor had numerous resources, they had no way to machine them. There were no factories that could handle the technology they needed.

That didn't worry him too much, though, they still had many upgraded weapons which could be built with what they had available and he already knew what Südermann's armies were using. They should be able to hold them off for a few Suns until he got the Kalindorians up to speed.

With that in mind, and seeing no reason to tarry, he

assigned the five thousand Mayanorens to the garrisons and sent them with one hundred Named Ones and fifty of Quelnerom's guard to avoid any problems. They split off in their new direction without Yontar's march being forced to slow. He did notice Quelnerom's guards looked very uncomfortable. That was good. He didn't ever want them thinking they were even remotely equal to his troops.

They continued their march to the palace and began making plans for manufacturing the weapons they would need first. As even neared he had a complete list of what they'd need and a good idea of when he could reasonably expect them to be completed.

When they emerged from the forest Yontar spied the palace and paused. A mix of brick, concrete and native woods, it was surprisingly tasteful. Clearly, Quelnerom had nothing to do with its construction. He wondered who built it but the Named One didn't know. All he'd been able to learn about it was it was built during the war for power between the reptiloids.

Since that wasn't very important in the grand scheme of things he set it aside for another turn and walked into the main courtyard. He briefly wondered if Quelnerom would order his guards to shoot him as he entered, but the exalted leader merely rode along in his palanquin and nodded to the sentries as they passed.

The Named One knew of a set of empty barracks outside the palace walls that could serve as a temporary home for the Mayanorens. He quickly passed along directions and instructions to them and made sure they were headed in the right direction before he returned to Yontar's side.

Half a clik later Yontar was seated in the garish throne room and receiving updates on stores and provisions as well as a breakdown of available munitions. He was amazed Südermann hadn't overrun these lands long ago. It would have been easy to do so. However, after thinking about it, he realized Südermann had no heart for conquest.

Merely holding these invaders at bay would be enough.

Now, was that lack a weakness or a strength? He'd need to be sure before he acted.

He called in a couple of QZD-1934's and issued his first orders to the reptiloids. Surprised to have coherent instructions they left without inquiring about Quelnerom or his status.

According to the reports he was reading Quelnerom had half his army on the southern continent for reasons unknown. There were no reports of rebellion or trouble of any kind. The Named One informed him those postings were rewards for good service. Yontar thought he was joking. When he realized he wasn't he issued a recall order immediately and demanded that they be sent to the northern garrisons.

Using the rail systems already in place they could be in position in two or three turns.

It would take longer than that for Südermann to combine forces with the Plains and attack, so he should have a practicable defense in place by then. He issued further orders for deployments along the front lines and then went and found the kitchens. Following the advice of the Named One, he avoided the salted meats and had a pleasant enough meal.

By even-split, he'd done all he could do and retired. Weapons were being manufactured, bombs were being built, and troops were being allocated. In a few turns, he would join them at the front. But, for now, he could relax.

D'noma perched on the northern wall of the garrison and watched as the tiny animals of the wilds went about their lives. Her squadron had been ordered here after the failed raid on Yontar. At first, she thought they were being punished, but as news of incoming troops grew she realized she was the front line of information for them. The garrisons were scattered along a river separating the lands of Kalindor from those of Lord Südermann. Further west were garrisons for the Children of the Waters that served similar functions. Between them, they had held for three hundred Suns.

While she hadn't seen any specific orders, the troop buildup and coming reinforcements led her to believe they were going to move these garrisons much farther south than they currently were. She wondered idly how Douglass was doing. The pretend warrior had been very nice to them and she hoped nothing bad would happen to him. She also wondered what the Athabascae Warriors were like. They hadn't had the time to go visiting and none of them had come into the Haliaeetus' village while they'd been there.

She watched as one of Rohta's famous super rabbits, a jackrabbit bred for extra meat, easily avoided a wild hawk and dove into its burrow. With their extra meat and size, they were supposed to be easy pickings for the beasts of the west. However, they were also cunning and fast and very few ended up as dinner. Within a hundred Suns, they'd overrun the wilds and were now hunted by the troops for sport and food.

Last even one of her squad had brought in ten of them and they'd added them to their meal. She had to admit, for wild game, it was very tasty and tender. One of the Mantis Guards had shared a recipe with them and joined them for their meal. Slowly but surely everybody was getting used to everybody else.

She continued her reverie, lightly clicking her talons against the precipice, as nature continued being nature all around her. Despite the impending battles coming she found the place peaceful. Almost serene. There was a gentle wind blowing across the desert like, prairie and the smell of new life was everywhere. The animals scurried for food and shelter as the sun rose higher in the sky.

"You look like one of the makers' gargoyles."

The sound of a voice startled her and she leapt into the sky. Gathering her wits she turned and saw the guard who'd shared a meal with them last even. Feeling silly she returned to her perch and faced him.

"It's not nice to sneak up on someone like that."

"My apologies Squad Leader, I didn't mean any harm."

"D'noma. My name is D'noma."

"Pnaard," he bowed, "at your service."

She looked at him closely. While she'd seen some of Lord Südermann's guards at the Elders' Council, she'd never really been this close to one before. They were surprisingly handsome creatures, in her estimation, and clearly confident of their abilities.

"Well, Pnaard," she smiled her best smile, "I suppose I should thank you for the delicious recipe before I kill you for scaring me."

That earned her a hearty laugh.

"Well, yes," he smiled right back at her, "that would be the polite thing to do. In fact, I would imagine decorum calls for it."

"In that case, thank you."

Now they were both laughing. She hopped off the edge onto the gang plank traversing the inner wall and bared her talons. That elicited more laughter until they finally quieted down and ended up staring over the wall at the world around them. They stayed that way for some time.

It'd been a while since she'd had some private time with a partner and she wondered if Pnaard would be opposed to the idea. She wasn't exactly sure how to broach the subject.

"Hi, do you want to have sex?" seemed crude. Accurate, obviously, but still lacking a certain refinement.

Instead, she opted to share her mid-break meal with him and see where the turn led.

As it worked out, it was a good decision. Shortly

after their meal, she was deluged with messages from the various warrens, the council, and the marching army from the eastern shore. Much to her pleasant surprise, Pnaard joined her, helped her separate the urgent from the ordinary and they were able to file responses to them all within two cliks.

When they were done he invited her to walk with him in the desert. He said it helped keep him calm after a busy turn. Calm wasn't exactly what she had in mind, but she accepted.

A short while later they were out of sight of the garrison and walking amongst scrub bushes and cacti. She hadn't even noticed he was wearing a back pack until he removed it and set a picnic meal on the ground.

It consisted mostly of snacks, but there was a bottle of ice wine with two glasses and he'd brought pillows. While just as obvious as her original thought this showed the elegance her plan had been lacking.

Soon they were lying on the ground, peeling each other's clothes off and exploring the revealed flesh. She was forced to admit, between short, hot, breaths, he was an excellent explorer.

A clik or so later they lay spent on the blanket letting the sun and dry wind cool their smoldering bodies.

"Yes," she said now she could breathe normally, "I can see how this would relax you."

"Well, normally," he admitted, "I just watch the animals and head back to my bunk. However, this has a certain appeal as well."

"Really," she pretended to whine, "no lovely femme guard has taken you for a stroll in the desert or a roll in the sand?"

"All of the femmes in the garrison are my subordinates, it would cause too many problems."

She nodded in understanding. All of the Succubi with her were under her command as well and that was why she'd been forced into temporary celibacy.

He fluffed the pillows and set them next to a large rock so they could sit up. Then he poured them each a glass of ice wine and they toasted the moment.

They were too preoccupied with each other to notice the sound of flapping wings until it was too late. Douglass Fairwinds landed at their feet.

"They said I'd find you out here," he began calmly, "I hope I'm not interrupting anything." He seemed to finally notice Pnaard and extended his hand. "Corporal Douglass Fairwinds of the Haliaeetus' Brand. It's a pleasure to meet you."

Being naked and sweaty didn't cause Pnaard to miss a beat. He stood, grasped the proffered hand and introduced himself.

"What brings you out here Douglas?" Asked D'noma, slightly miffed at having her perfect moment shattered.

"My brand wishes to help in the war effort against Yontar. While we aren't the warriors you are, we have many skilled healers and possess other useful abilities. For example, we can repair any weapon in the Din-La catalog."

Lord Südermann's medical staff was split pretty thinly between the garrisons, extra help there would be welcome. And it never hurt to have extra hands around to fix something when it broke, which it always did.

"What about the Athabascae Warriors? Will they join you?"

He nodded while smiling. "Yes, in much the same capacity. However, they do bring the added advantage of being excellent trackers in dense woods. And, if memory serves, much of Kalindor is well forested."

Pnaard finally found his pants and began putting them on.

"Yes, skilled trackers would be a boon, true. However, forgive me for asking, but you're not one of Rohta's brands, that much I can tell, so what are you?"

"We were decanted by The New Sons of Liberty

just before the gen-O-pod war. We were to be shock troops which would be used against the government. We were barely five Suns old when our makers were eliminated."

Pnaard recoiled at the term "shock troops." He knew it meant throwing bodies at bullets. It was something Xhaknar would have done. It was not something any civilized commander would even consider.

Every time he wondered if the world was better off without the makers he found the answer to be yes.

They spent a few epi-cliks working out the details and then decided Douglass would join them for their even meal and fly back come breaklight. In ten turns he would return with as many medicos, healers, and craft-masters as he could.

D'noma, finally realizing she was still nude, found her clothes and began redressing as Pnaard repacked his back pack and cleaned up after their "picnic."

Shortly thereafter the three of them headed back to the garrison. However irked the two randy troopers were at being interrupted, their feelings were ameliorated by the fact they'd found new, uncounted on, allies.

The Ant-People only allowed outsiders to call them by their rank or profession. It was only when they were in private they used proper names. The Corporal thought about that briefly as he slid past a Kalindor garrison. He knew the reptiloids each used the scientific brand name they'd been given by Rohta instead of renaming themselves. He wondered why, if they loved Great Rohta so much, they'd participated in the gen-O-pod war? Because they certainly had and with a vigor some others lacked. Not that he cared deeply about the reason. He was sure it sounded good at the time, most reasons do, and was now just a tradition. Traditions require neither logic nor reason, just adherence.

He eased his way over to the communications building and hid in the shadows behind it next to some crates. It would be even soon and the reptiloids would switch to a half-staff leaving the back rooms unguarded. Then he would enter and read and copy as many communiqués as he could.

Since he had some free time he decided to put it to good use. He snuck over to one of the supply sheds and located the salted meat they preferred. He removed a large vial of the syrup of ipecac and spread it liberally across the top layers. He knew the salt would hide the flavor and smiled at the thought of their coming discomfort.

There were going to be some very nauseous reptiloids over the next few turns.

His task complete he put the empty vial in the bottom of a nearby trash bin and headed towards the armory. He was under orders to maintain secrecy so he didn't want to blow anything up. However, no one had said anything about loosening a screw or two here or there. There were several of their large catapults in the center of the room. He quickly removed their restraining bolts holding the armature in place and replaced them with small reeds. Camouflaging his handiwork was easy enough and he smiled at the thought of these behemoths tossing their boulders haphazardly in the air, or just snapping in two when they were loaded. He noticed they had bins of weapons powder near the wall and they were next to barrels of water. It was almost too tempting to pass up.

However, he was smart enough to know anything like that would be attributed to pure sabotage and his superiors would frown on that.

Oh well, there was always next time.

He heard some reptiloids entering the armory and quickly hid from view. He hoped they weren't preparing for catapult practice. It soon became apparent they, like millions of troops throughout time, were simply hiding from their commander until their shift was over. He couldn't fault them on that as he'd done the same enough times in his career. It was a military tradition.

He couldn't make out exactly what they were saying but it was clear they were worried about some reinforcements headed their way. Maybe their gentle lifestyle was coming to a close. They seemed most concerned about some new allies their ruler had attained. He'd have to thoroughly check the communiqués when he got there to see what that was about.

To the Ant-People suspicions were nothing, facts were everything.

About a clik later the reptiloids left and all was quiet. He stayed where he was until he was sure it was full even outside. Then he slipped through the shadows until he was behind the communications building again. The reptiloids kept a sharp watch on their exterior but had no patrols inside the garrison. That lack made his life much easier.

Inside the building, he went quickly to the back room where copies were kept. Using a small light he was able to browse through them quickly until he stopped short. One memo listed the troops which were coming, the ones who so concerned the slothful troops. The first part confirmed what Lord Südermann was worried about, there were five thousand Mayanorens headed this way. They were accompanied by a hundred of something called Named Ones and fifty of Quelnerom's personal guards. He guessed the latter were merely there to vouch for the rest.

Another thing that concerned him was the tenor of the various messages. Gone were the maddening vagaries which had passed for orders among the reptiloids. They'd been replaced with very articulate and clear demands that each required specific attention and a detailed response. Well, that explained why the troops were hiding. They were neither trained for nor used to anything like that.

Although there was nothing in the memos stating

so, it was obvious to him Yontar was in charge now. That would be important news for Lord Südermann and her allies.

He was about to leave the building when he heard a new sound. Knowing Kalindorian garrisons were run on a strict, if unimaginative, routine, anything new was not necessarily good. He slid to the side behind the crates near the exterior wall and tried to figure out what he was hearing. It became clear soon enough. It was an interior patrol and they were checking each building.

He hastily hid better and waited for them to pass.

It was no cursory inspection either. One guard stood outside while the other three went inside and turned on the lights, checked the rooms and accounted for every soldier in the front. He made a mental note of the change and counted it up as one more feature added by Yontar.

He was very glad the Kalindorian troops weren't Mantis Guards. The orders obviously said, "check every building." Since they evidently said nothing about checking behind boxes he was left to be. A few epi-cliks later he was alone but on much higher alert.

His extra attention to his surroundings paid off on three occasions before he was successfully free of the garrison. The last one having been far closer than he would ever care to admit.

Once he was about a kay away he contacted his commander and gave his report. He heard his commander swear and then received his new orders. He would head south and west and see if those reinforcements were bringing any new weapons with them.

He'd always had fun spying on the Kalindorians before, but the arrival of Yontar suddenly made everything serious. It was going to take more than tainted food to win now, that much was sure.

He checked his supplies and started out right away. No use wasting a good dark.

R'yune smiled as N'leah adjusted herself on his chest. She was sound asleep but seemed able to make herself comfortable no matter what. Her soft breathing warmed his neck and made him think only of happy things. No matter that they were to march at breaklight to meet the army of the eastern warrens. No matter that they would eventually march on Yontar and the Mayanorens. None of that mattered right now. Nothing mattered at all except this moment, this feeling, this joy.

He knew of her relationship with P'marna and approved. She was a princess now and truly loved the queen's consort. Their love didn't mean she loved him any less. In some ways, by sharing with him as she did, she showed she loved him all the more.

He also knew King G'rnk, a title that was still taking some getting used to, wanted him to mate within his brand so his familial line would continue. He'd put it off for vague reasons he never understood, but now realized he didn't want to be untrue to N'leah. Well, that could never happen. No matter what happened she would always be a part of him. Somehow, after all he'd been through and was about to experience, that thought comforted him.

He would return to his family when this was over and have them help him select a mate. He would make sure she knew about N'leah and there would be no problems. Even if, for whatever reasons, he never got to sleep with her again, she would still be there in his mind, her voice echoing in his memories, her breath warm against his collar.

Something told him N'leah would approve of his decision. He'd tell her first, though, just in case.

His thoughts became vague and eventually faded as sleep overtook him. He dreamed dreams of contentment and was not entirely pleased when they were woken by a knock on their door.

It was a young page from the Elders' Council reminding them they were to share a breaklight repast with the council prior to their ride. It wasn't until he saw the poor page blushing horribly he realized he and N'leah were nude on top of the covers. She thanked the young Se-Jeant and motioned for him to leave. When the door closed they both rolled out of bed laughing.

They were sure to be the talk of Anapsida for some time to come.

They shared a quick shower and dressed for travel. N'leah added a simple breast wrap out of deference to Ben, who would be joining them. They both liked the Chaldean and respected his beliefs, even if neither came close to sharing them. Of course, it went both ways, Ben was very respectful of who and what they were and never once asked them to change.

They exited the room and headed down the back stairs past Drapery's kitchen. The smells were enticing and they both wondered what feasts they'd be served this turn. Ever since Drapery's wife had made her deal with the Din-La, the inn had access to some of the best food either of them had ever tasted, and they'd been privy to some excellent cooking in their time.

They took their customary places to the right of Geldish as they greeted BraarB and Sland. BraarB was dressed casually, but also with a breast wrap, and Sland looked ready for war. He was wearing a holster on his right hip and two sheaths on his left leg. They both knew those were only for the weapons others could see. He'd become an expert at hiding daggers and other weapons all over his body. Fortunately, for the sanity of the other guests, the holster and the sheaths were empty.

Ben came in with Greko and joined them at their table. Shortly thereafter Nak and Mnaas pulled chairs over as well.

Within five epi-cliks Drapery and his staff were swarming over the room setting bowls of warm muffins out with sides of jams and preserves and small urns of spiced butter. Other staffers efficiently passed out steaming cups of java and glasses of cold juice. Geldish commented that many an army could learn quite a lot from watching the precision of their work.

They ate their meal in relative silence. There really wasn't much to say. This turn they were headed, once again, into war. And this time there would be no hills to hide them. They would have to face Yontar directly.

Ben had estimated it would take them two turns to meet with the eastern warrens if they headed due south. Geldish wanted to meet them as soon as possible so they could share information directly. The radio was nice but they all believed Yontar probably had access to that technology, at least, since he'd been at the makers' facility in the north. The Din-La claimed to have a way to encode messages, but it required a type of radio not yet built. Nevertheless, they claimed they could get them to the warrens and the council within thirty turns.

A fact which did no one any good at the present.

When they were full they headed out to the front where stable hands had tied up their nysteeds next to two deisteeds. The riders stopped, flummoxed, as Greko and Nak each mounted up and looked at them.

"Excuse me," said Geldish warily, "but where do you two think you're going?"

"I have a message for Oronimus IX," replied Nak, "that is to be delivered personally and since friend Greko will be visiting my warren he decided to ride with me so we could arrive together."

"A message could be delivered by any simple courier. Why send the warren's Vice Lord?"

"As a show of respect. We've never dealt with any of the eastern warrens and Watcher Urkel wants to make sure we get off on the right foot with them."

Geldish considered that and, although he didn't believe him entirely, could see no reason not to let them accompany them on the ride. With that out of the way he mounted his nysteed and the others followed him. Within an epi-clik, they were on their way.

They passed the gates of Anapsida and turned south. No sooner had they done so than Ben's pack came loose from the back of his nysteed. R'yune lunged cleanly, snagged it and pushed it back on. Then he reattached it and smiled at Ben. Much to everyone's astonishment, Ben signed "Thank you."

Seeing their stares he figured he'd better explain.

"The Din-La have been teaching me. I'm not fluent yet, but we should be able to understand each other."

Sland looked indignant.

"I thought I was teaching you. Why are you running around hiding with the Din-La?"

"Because you scare the living daylights out of me."

Sland paused for a moment and then smiled.

"I can see that. I need to work on my social skills."

That got a laugh from everyone and then Sland signed "I still consider you a friend" to Ben. The Chaldean realized he'd let his personal prejudices get in the way knowing this warrior better. He always knew he'd want him on his side in a fight but it had never occurred to him he might want him near in times of peace too. He led his nysteed over next to Sland's and began talking to the heavily armed BadgeBeth. R'yune soon joined them and the three began sharing their histories.

Ben discovered that, although R'yune couldn't speak, he was hearing his words clearly. The stories Sland and he shared seemed terrifying but they treated them as commonplace. Slowly, his fears faded and he began to understand them better.

He was so taken by the conversation he missed his morning prayers. He silently asked Allah to forgive him and returned his attention to the two riders. They continued talking through their mid-break repast and by even-fall, he felt he knew these riders well. Or, at least, much better than he did before.

He even let Sland fine tune his sign language. Somehow those claws didn't seem as frightening as they did before.

Malehni checked his position against the sky and made a minor course adjustment. The Kwini-Laku had never needed a sextant or any similar devices. Great Rohta had built the ability to steer by Sun or stars directly into them. If his calculations were correct he should cross paths with the marching army from the eastern warrens in about two turns.

He had reported in all he had seen, including his time spent with the Brittle Riders. When the Din-Law reported an army led by one of the legendary Oronimus lines was headed to reinforce the army of the Plains and the garrisons of Lord Südermann he knew, without being told, his superiors would want as much information about them as possible.

He had wasted two cliks, in his opinion, talking with Ambassador Hana Koi-San about the Brittle Riders. He couldn't, for the life of him, figure out the import they held. He knew they'd been in battles, and in the final war. But they were just five brands. And an odd five brands at that.

Not that he hadn't enjoyed meeting them, they were nice enough, but this war was going to be won or lost due to massive military might and not the guile of one rouge Rangka and some fringe dwellers. Sure they were princes and princesses now, but he'd seen them ride and seen them run through maneuvers using weapons. Those were not the skills of well-mannered royalty, those were the skills of warriors and assassins.

Nevertheless, it wasn't for him to decide what was and what wasn't important to the Children's Congress. His job was to get them information and that was exactly what he was doing.

His deisteed seemed to have gotten used to him now and they were making much better time. They would travel for cliks at a comfortable trot and covered the distances easily. Of course, a lot might have to do with the fact Malehni had become comfortable with the fact he was crazy and no longer afraid of the beast.

No sane brand would treat an animal this large as casually as he now did.

Despite his misgivings, he'd allowed himself to be armed by the riders at the last post they'd shared. He'd tried to argue against it but the one called Sland had pointed out not all the creatures of the wild were friendly and there were still some rogue brands given to banditry.

They'd showed him how to use the calf sheath to holster his weapon so it would be easier to reach while riding. Then Sland had given him two dangerous looking knives and had spent three cliks drilling him on the use of each weapon.

He was just thinking it was the most useless three cliks he'd ever spent in his life when the three bandits opened fire on him.

He was hit in the left shoulder and fell from his mount. Without even thinking he rolled, drew his weapon and fired six shots, two at each bandit. Before his deisteed could finish its turn all three were dead.

He got up, cursed silently to himself for not paying attention to those who knew what he did not, and then went to look at his attackers. As he was nearing them he made a mental note to buy Sland a drink. He'd taught him that move just in case he fell from his deisteed.

He wondered if this sort of thing happened all the time? He certainly hoped not.

When he got to them he pulled back their hoods and didn't recognize their brand. They reminded him of the naporcines he'd seen on his journey. He pulled a pictorecorder from his pack, snapped a few images and then tended to his shoulder. The bullet had gone completely through so he cleaned it as best he could and then wrapped it in a medicated bandage. He hoped it would be enough until he could speak to a healer from the eastern warrens. He knew there were no Din-La posts in his path.

He found himself absently petting the deisteed which seemed calmer than he was. Realizing these three bandits were probably not alone he mounted and took off at a gallop. He would let others figure out who had attacked him. Their shabby robes gave him a pretty good reason as to why. He looked as though he had more goldens than they did.

Around even-fall, he spied a village slightly to the west of him. Maybe they had a healer. Since his shoulder was throbbing he altered his course to try and find out.

He saw what appeared to be the main street and angled his deisteed onto it and began looking at the shops and signs. He realized he was in one of the mixed villages he'd heard about. He could see Naradhama, Se-Jeant and haven lords all walking around. He'd been told the mixed villages tended to be more peaceful, so he relaxed a little. He spied a youngling looking at him and asked it if it knew where the healer was. The youngling pointed at an all-white building across from him and then ran away giggling.

He shrugged at the response and chalked it up to something a youngling would do. He crossed the street and was met by a Naradhama nurse exiting the building. He asked if she was the healer.

"Oh my goodness, no, I'm just ...." she blanched, "you've been hurt."

"Yes ma'am," he managed, "that's why I need a healer."

She wasted no more time. She helped him off his

deisteed, called for the medico, and was removing his shirt and bandage when the medico entered the room. The elderly haven lord took one look at the wound and went to work without comment.

After cleaning it more thoroughly than Malehni had been able to do, he coated it with a pungent balm and re-dressed it. Satisfied the arm wouldn't fall off, he pointed out there was an inn down the road and he'd like Malehni to spend the even there so he could check his handiwork after breaklight.

Malehni agreed and then told him about the bandits. The medico sighed and said he would notify the gendarme. He didn't seem surprised at the news.

The two of them walked outside and the medico paused when he saw the deisteed.

"Are you a warrior?"

"No," he replied, "just a scout. I didn't even have a weapon until I met the Brittle Riders. They insisted I be armed if I was going to be wandering alone. I thought it a very silly admonition until this turn."

The medico looked at him anew and with no little amount of respect.

"The Brittle Riders? Well, I bet you have some interesting stories to tell. Those five bring chaos and leave peace. A very odd combination."

Malehni couldn't think of any better way to describe them so he left it at that. Shortly thereafter he was checking into the haven lord run inn when he noticed the radio. He asked if he could use it and was told it was half a golden for every five epi-cliks. He dropped a golden on the counter and dialed up the Din-La frequency. Once he had someone at the other end he told them of the bandits, his injury, and his location.

"Sounds like you crossed some Warters," said the voice at the other end, "nasty buggers they are. It's a good thing you took that weapon."

He had to agree there.

"How long will you need to heal before you can ride again?"

He hadn't thought about it, but he felt a lot better than he looked.

"I should be able to leave come breaklight. The medico wants to check me again after my repast and, assuming nothing's wrong, I'll leave then."

"Good enough. Take care of yourself and let us know if there are any changes."

They signed off and he went to the desk clerk to see if they had a bath. He was pleased to find there was one in every room. He then inquired about food. He hadn't realized until just now how hungry he was. The clerk smiled politely and then made him laugh.

"I'm sure sir would prefer to eat in his room, so I can have a meal sent up to him. After all, when one is covered in blood, and reeks of sweat and wiki-balm, it tends to upset the other guests."

Well, yes, he could see that. He made arrangements to have his clothes cleaned and patched and was assured they'd be ready before he left. With nothing else to do he retired to his room and took a hot bath.

He was luxuriating in it when a Naradhama brought him his dinner. She glanced at his wound and tsked.

"Folks shouldn't be trying to stop bullets with their skin. It never works."

He had to admit that that was the most accurate statement he'd ever heard. He gave her a couple of coins for her trouble and watched as she gathered up all his clothes and left.

He had a better even's sleep than he expected and woke feeling refreshed. His clothes were neatly folded on a table near the foot of his bed and he had to acknowledge the seam work was excellent. You could barely tell there was a patch where the bullet had entered and all the blood stains were gone.

No longer looking and smelling like a demon he

went downstairs to the dining area and ordered a large meal. He was just finishing when the medico walked in. He ambled over to Malehni's table and sat down.

"So, how are you feeling this turn?"

"Very well, thank you. My shoulder feels almost healed."

"Yes, well, don't let it fool you. It will take at least ten turns before you have complete functionality again. It shouldn't hurt too much since the balm I use hinders pain, but I wouldn't try another stunt like you did the last turn for a while."

Malehni had to laugh at that.

"I assure you that "stunts" like that are the farthest things from my mind. I'm just on a simple fact finding mission. I have no desire to do that again."

The medico seemed pleased to hear that.

"So where will you be heading to find these facts?"

"I'm riding south to meet the army of Oronimus IX and then going to the lands of Lord Südermann."

"Ah yes," said the medico with a small smile, "much safer to be in the middle of a war than here in our humble village. I can easily see the allure."

Malehni couldn't really respond. When he heard it phrased like he thought he might really be crazy after all.

The medico checked his bandages at the table and then gave him a tin of balm, fresh bandages, and his bill. It was very reasonable so Malehni paid it without question. Then he went to the desk clerk, paid for his room and meals, and went outside to find his deisteed. It was in a stable behind the inn and seemed no worse for wear. The youngling he'd seen yesterday was feeding it hay and calling it Fluffy.

He was unsure if that was a proper name or an adjective.

He gave the youngling a coin and thanked it for looking after his deisteed and then mounted up and headed out. He hadn't lost too much time with this misadventure and should still meet the army before it entered the lands of Lord Südermann.

One thing he made sure of, though, as the village faded into the distance behind him, was to clean and reload his weapon.

Yontar sat in almost the same spot as the Named One had behind the coal hopper. He was sharing this barge with ten other Named Ones, including the one who'd acted as an emissary, and ten regular Mayanorens. They'd decided to leave the Exalted Quelnerom behind. Yontar had deemed him worthless, beyond any required ceremonial functions, and saw no reason to clutter things up with his presence.

He knew the reports he'd been getting from the Named Ones in the garrisons were accurate but he wanted to get a feel for the terrain and see things for himself. It was the only way to truly gauge their position. They had just left the forest behind and were now coming on to the villages the Named One had mentioned in his report. He was pleased to see everything was exactly as described.

Yes, it had been an error to hold back the Naradhama. When they returned under his dominion he would not make that mistake again. He would use them to their fullest abilities.

He'd read the reports coming in from his spies and had been greatly amused. It seemed the arts were on a definite uptick since the fall of Xhaknar. All that meant to him is the Plains were growing soft. Their army would be all he'd have to deal with then, the rest would cower in his presence. That was one worry out of the way.

As they neared the garrison he noticed Succubi lazily flying out of weapons' range but over the lands of Kalindor. That insult wouldn't last much longer.

While he hadn't been able to manufacture all the armaments he wanted, there just wasn't the capability yet, he had been able to make some very powerful weapons. He glanced at the one laying by his side and smiled. It was a simple gun, but the projectile contained three pounds of explosives. He decided a field test was in order.

He stood on the train, lifted the weapon and aimed at the nearest Succubi. The Mayanorens saw what he was about to do and scattered to the far side of the barge just as he finished setting the timer to three sepi-cliks and pulled the trigger. There was a loud whoosh and then the projectile sliced through the air. It barely missed a Succubus but the following explosion knocked her out of the sky anyway.

He ordered the train to halt and they stepped off to find the body. He hoped she lived. He'd wanted to torture something for quite some time now.

They were about fifty paces from the body when a small creature wearing camouflage came from nowhere, grabbed the Succubus and then fired several grenades at them. When the smoke cleared they were gone.

Instead of being angry Yontar was contemplative. Clearly, Südermann had spies in Kalindor and one of them had just saved that Succubus. He thought of ordering them hunted down but decided against it. Assuming Südermann's spies were at least as good as his own, he doubted they'd find them and they'd only waste the turn.

They boarded the train and resumed their trip to the garrison.

One thing was clear to him now, he wasn't going to have the luxury of time.

The corporal looked at the Succubus and sighed. She still lived, though he knew not how. Her wings seemed okay, but she had a nasty cut on her abdomen. He pulled out a first aid kit and did what he could. She would need stitches sooner than later but he didn't have any on him.

He opened his canteen and poured water on her lips hoping to revive her. He had no real way of knowing what was damaged and what wasn't without her help.

She seemed to be coming around so he quickly radioed in what had transpired. He had been asked to see if Yontar had new weapons and the answer was a resounding yes. The radio operator seemed to have some medical knowledge and he gave the corporal some tips. Soon the Succubus was awake, although clearly in severe pain.

He found the ampoules the radio operator had mentioned and broke one under her nose. That finished waking her up while he held his hand over her mouth.

"I am Corporal of the Ant Militia, loyal servant to Lord Südermann. You are safe, but you need to be quiet. Do you understand?"

She nodded and he removed his hand.

"What hit me?"

"A new weapon fired personally by Yontar."

"Should I be honored at that?"

"From his point of view, yes."

She smiled, then grimaced, and then clutched her side.

"I need you to tell me what is hurt. I have very limited medical training but will do all I can to help you."

She looked at him for a bit and then grimaced again.

"I am K'lzaana, assistant squad leader of the Succubi. As to where it hurts, I would guess everywhere. I feel as though I was slammed against a building at high speeds."

"We will have to stay here until even-fall. Hopefully, by then, you'll be able to move."

Much to his astonishment, she got to her feet. Shakily, to be sure, but she was upright. She walked gingerly in a tight circle for a bit and then sat down.

"Nothing seems to be broken although everything is horribly bruised. I should be able to fly by even-fall so I won't be a burden on you. If you would be so kind as to let my squad know I'm alive it would be appreciated."

He quickly informed the radio operator of her name and her status. Then he motioned for her to stay where she was and disappeared into the foliage. About half a clik later he returned with a spare shirt stuffed with fruits and vegetables.

"It's too risky to cook anything, but these are all safe to eat and have many nutrients."

She thanked him and ate a pink fruit which she immediately liked. They sampled everything and she seemed to be getting stronger with each passing clik.

"It'll be even-fall in a clik or so, I think I should leave now."

"But," complained the corporal, "they'll be able to see you."

"Actually," she said while smiling, "that's exactly what I'm hoping for."

She jumped into the air and wove her way through the canopy of leaves and disappeared from his view.

He would hear what happened later from others who were closer and would be very sorry, until his dying breath, that he'd missed it.

She'd followed the tracks to the garrison and saw Yontar and his Mayanorens looking at the lands of Südermann. She'd arced slightly higher and then stuck two fingers in her mouth and emitted a piercing whistle.

As they turned she'd cupped her hands around her mouth and taunted them.

"Missed me, missed me! Now you gotta kiss me!"

She'd sliced hard to her right and disappeared down the gulley beside the garrison and was gone. The last thing she saw before she attained safety was Yontar screaming obscenities at her.

Somehow, it had made her whole turn worthwhile.

They'd taken a barge across the old Youngling Pass and spied the dust raised by a marching army in the distance. They would meet Oronimus within a clik or so. A large cloud appeared above them and they all looked up just in time to see the Horuns and the Columbas pass overhead. They were an impressive sight. One never seen on the Plains before.

Sland tapped Geldish on the shoulder and pointed to the east. There was another rider coming and it was headed right towards them. Geldish opened his mind, smiled and motioned for them to halt.

"It's Malehni."

They were all taken aback by that and waited patiently until he arrived a few epi-cliks later.

He rode straight up to Sland and hugged him, which was difficult to do while mounted.

Of the many things the Brittle Riders had come to expect in life, this was not one of them. He opened his shirt to show the bandage on his left shoulder and quickly explained about the bandits and how he'd dispatched them.

They lauded his bravery, insulted his observational skills, since Warters were notoriously lousy trackers, and then let him know how glad they all were he was alive.

He found himself laughing easily along with them and realized he was learning more about himself than he'd expected. He might be a little crazy, but he was also no longer afraid. That was something of a shock to him. All his life he'd had a tiny voice telling him when to hide and now it was gone.

They resumed their journey to meet Oronimus and kept up a lively banter the entire way. Malehni was introduced to Greko, Nak, and Ben and found himself intrigued by the incredible differences between them. Then he looked at the Brittle Riders and figured it was just the way things were here. They couldn't afford to let a little thing like an alien brand get in the way of their larger purpose.

They kept an easy pace and finally caught up with the eastern army about a clik and a half later. They were met by a small contingent of guards who escorted them to the front of the column.

Oronimus greeted them warmly but said he would wait for any conversation until they made camp for the even. That made sense to everyone since it was clear he wanted to talk. He just didn't want to do so in front of his troops. Not until he had a clearer understanding of why this group was here.

General Momar al Rahim offered to let Ben share his prayers with the troops and Ben gratefully accepted. Flight Leader Corvington Smythe rode up next to N'leah and peppered her with questions about the Succubi. Greko and Nak joined Sland and R'yune and they fell into an easy conversation with a couple of the guards who'd escorted them here. The fact R'yune couldn't speak didn't hamper things at all. BraarB and Geldish kept to themselves but were very watchful of the army.

They agreed they were impressed, and pleased, with how professional the troops were. They kept in smart formations and marched to a tight cadence. Geldish had secretly feared they'd be more rag tag. Instead, they were the epitome of spit and polish. That boded well for what was to come.

The supply wagons skirted down the sides of the column handing out a mid-break repast so the soldiers could eat without having to stop. Geldish and BraarB thanked the Kleknar who handed them two sealed carafes filled with spiced water, which he showed them how to clip to their sides so they could be refilled later, and a large sandwich each.

The sandwiches were venison with spaggle berry.

They were mildly startled to find fresh food in a troop train but Oronimus simply laughed and told them about the foraging parties. Then they truly were impressed. That showed the kind of foresight that made for success.

By even-fall, they were less than a turn away from the lands of Lord Südermann and they made camp. All of the riders pulled to the side as cooking fires were quickly built, tents erected, and provisions were being passed out. Less than a clik after Oronimus called a halt a city had erupted on the Plains.

Scouts and sentries were assigned their tasks and soon everyone was settled in.

Oronimus had his command tent set up slightly away from the main troops and invited all of his guests to meet him there. They sat on the provided pillows, which were unexpectedly comfortable, and were served an even meal fit for a king.

When they were done Oronimus casually motioned for Geldish to speak but he shook his head no

"I believe Vice-Lord Nak should begin," he said as he took another sip of the excellent java drink, "he has diplomatic issues, all we have is news."

All eyes in the tent turned to Nak.

He paused, then unrolled a small parchment and handed it to Oronimus. Oronimus read it and then laughed.

"Your Watcher Urkel is a very optimistic leader. Tell him the answer to both is yes. I will have an ambassadorial party sent as soon as possible to open relations between the eastern warrens and the Elders' Council and I will meet him for drinks when this is all over."

They all had to laugh. Oronimus was right, that was about as optimistic as you could get right now.

After that Geldish prompted Oronimus to tell him what he did know about the events on the Plains and then they spent the rest of the even filling in the gaps. The time passed quickly and soon everyone bade everyone else good even and went to their tents.

Sland waited for Geldish to enter his meditative trance and then turned to the others.

"I don't know about you, but I'm pretty sure this is going to be one Zanubi of a war too."

The four hundred RZL-274's assigned to this garrison were lined up in front of Yontar. These reptiloids could fly, after a fashion. They were only about half the size of the Succubi but had lethal talons that could tear through almost anything. They were also a lot stronger than they looked.

Instead of wings, they had a membrane which stretched from the inside of their arms all the way to their feet and a stabilizing membrane between their legs. They were lousy runners but otherwise capable soldiers. It was one of them who had discovered the sabotage to the catapults. While Yontar was grateful for that it was the reason they'd discovered the tampering which held his interest.

It seemed they liked to sneak a catapult out and use it to hurl themselves high into the air and then glide back to the ground. He'd made them demonstrate the technique to him several times before assembling them.

He turned to one of the Named Ones and smiled.

"These fine soldiers are going to be a new weapon. Their technique is crude but that's where you come in. They can only launch two at a time with a catapult. We will need to get many more airborne if we are going to have any chance of stopping those damn Succubi."

The RZL-274's stood stock still, but Yontar could see the hint of a smile on each of their faces. Soldiers were so easy to please. Give them a purpose and a target and they'd roll over for a tummy rub.

He listened to several ideas before dismissing the Named Ones. They were on the right track and he was sure they'd come up with something.

Then, to make sure it wasn't just one or two thrill seekers who liked this hobby, he ordered all the catapults broke out and placed a kay behind the garrison so they could practice until the Named Ones came up with a better launching system.

Had he known his every move was being dutifully reported by a corporal of the Ant-People's Militia to his superiors, he might not have been so open about his intentions.

Then again, maybe he would.

Watching them arc into the air and execute maneuvers high above the ground made it clear he was not going to fight like Xhaknar. This was going to be a war in all three dimensions and he expected to rule every single one.

He issued orders to the Named One next to him to begin training the reptiloids in battle formations and tactics. He also issued an order for every battalion to have four Named Ones at the top of their chain of command. He wasn't about to let these locals ruin his war.

Soon the garrisons were a hub of activity. Orders flashed back and forth between them and Named Ones left the main garrison to take over command of the rest of the ones down the line. Within a turn, he expected to have order and progress.

But he also needed to delay any actions the troops across the river might take. To that end, he had an idea.

He ordered more catamarans built and set in the eastern ocean. He quickly outlined his idea to a Named One and was pleased to get a smile in return. He would ram a navy right down the throat of Lord Südermann's Delta where she housed her fishing fleet. He didn't expect victory, in fact, he doubted any would survive, but he did think the attack would force Südermann to allocate forces where she'd never needed them before.

A Named One informed him the reptiloids already had fishing fleets and cargo ships on that coast and, with some minor refitting, they would do just fine. They could be ready in just two turns.

Yontar smiled. Even better.

He made sure the Named Ones understood not a shot was to be fired from the garrisons. As long as Südermann's forces were in a defensive posture there was no reason to antagonize them until they were good and ready.

Pleased things were shaping up according to plan, he went in search of something to eat.

Elaand enjoyed his new role as a Colonel of the Mantis Guards. Between his bureaucratic duties and his half turn teaching each turn he found life to be full and calm. Even so, when the opportunity came to mount a steed and meet an army arose he jumped at the chance. He wasn't sure why at first but now, riding through the even so they could meet them at breaklight, he remembered.

The smell of the air, the sound of the hooves, the easy camaraderie of troops who knew what danger was and had bested it; all these things combined to make him feel whole again.

The six of them rode at an easy pace. There was no hurry. They knew exactly where the army from the eastern warrens was and they were headed directly towards it. They were going to move the army further south. If it kept its current path it would march straight through the heart of their cities. It would be chaos.

Instead, they would march them down to the Delta where they had barges which could ferry them across the mighty river and then continue to the Kalindorian garrisons. This way they wouldn't disrupt the turn to turn lives of Lord Südermann's citizens and still be able to assist in the defense of the lands.

Also, he knew that, war or no war, Lord Südermann wasn't eager to let anyone see just how technologically advanced they were. The cities, with their electric monorails, homes built in the branches of trees, and advanced communications centers were things of wonder. Better to let them see the more traditional road system and ground based homes which were favored along the river. They were still more advanced than anything on the Plains, but not shockingly so.

The southern homes had been built to withstand the, almost annual, torrential rains and winds that came from the southern ocean. They were half underground with slanted roofs to deflect the onslaught. Eland knew from his studies the makers had built their homes and businesses all the way to the edge of the southern ocean, yet seemed surprised each Full Sun when they got ravaged. What quirk drove them to do that was beyond his ken.

That land was all swamp now and protected by levees which ran in stages for several kays.

They continued their ride in silence, each to their own thoughts.

The eastern horizon was just beginning to lighten when the saw the camp. Two guards rode out to meet them and escort them to Oronimus' tent.

Elaand was impressed. Their reaction showed him they knew they were coming, had figured out who they were, or at least who they represented, and had prepared for them. All done quietly and efficiently. That was a sign of a well-trained army and a sign they could work together.

They were just crossing the perimeter of the camp when he saw Geldish emerging from a tent. He jumped off his deisteed, laughing.

"Hey, you old bag of bones! Why am I not surprised to see you here?"

"Ha, you nasty old bug, what are you doing here? I thought you were chained to a desk being feted by comely bug femmes."

They both laughed now. Whatever the other Mantis Guards thought of seeing their commander disrespected in public they kept to themselves. The two old friends continued laughing and joking as Geldish led them all to Oronimus' tent. His staff was already assembled and there was a breaklight repast laid out for everyone to share.

Elaand briefed Oronimus on his mission while they ate and the general readily agreed. He had been worried about how they were going to ford the river and this seemed to present an easy solution. Orders were issued for the new directions and, within a clik, they were off.

Mantis Guards could easily last for three or four turns at a time without sleep so they took the lead and gave the scouts directions and items to look out for. There were a lot of natural predators that lived in the swamp lands and they would venture out if they sensed food. When they realized Oronimus' army was foraging for food as it went they passed along information on which of those predators made good eating and the best ways to catch them.

Elaand noted Oronimus' army made no attempt to hide the fact they carried original weapons from the makers. They might have been copies but, if so, they were expertly made. He saw, too, the members of the Chaldean clans had long range, single shot, weapons. Those seemed to have payloads of a few pounds each. They would do serious damage to anything they hit. He also noted the avian clans all carried automatic weapons which could fire hundreds of rounds per epi-clik. When he envisioned them combined with the Succubi bombs, he smiled.

As he learned about how they had to continually fight off well-armed pirates up and down their shore, he realized that these troops might be more battle hardened than he'd first imagined. Several of the Horuns bragged about Flight Leader Smythe and how he had, single handedly, while blindfolded, and with one wing strapped down, taken down an entire pirate base.

There may have been a little braggadocio in the story, but they figured its essence was true.

That was a good sign as well. Troops who respected their leaders also respected the chain of command.

They passed into Lord Südermann's lands just before even-fall. In another two turns, they would be in the Delta. They would camp there for a couple of turns while the wagons were resupplied and all of the equipment checked before they entered the battle zone.

It had actually taken three turns to get their makeshift navy assembled. A couple of the fishing captains had complained they didn't take orders from scale-less freaks so they had to be publically disemboweled and then displayed so everyone clearly understood who was in charge now. Also, they had used the time to add cannons to several of the larger ships so they could inflict damage in a wider range. Yontar had been amazed to find out the reptiloids had cannons, lots of them, they just didn't use them. They weren't sure how.

One of the Named Ones had handed him a strong drink and then gotten out of the way when that bit of news came in.

Nevertheless, the plan was simple, go up the Delta, create as much havoc as they could and then get out if they could. Because that last part wasn't a given Yontar was only sending three of the red shirted Named Ones on the mission. The rest would be reptiloids.

Two of the ships had been equipped with radios so they could report their progress. After that, it was out of Yontar's hands.

The mini-navy had been at sea for more than a turn

and was now waiting for even-fall so they could enter the Delta. Since the reptiloids fished this far out with some regularity the sight of the ships shouldn't alarm anyone.

When the sky was truly dark they began heading for the Delta.

Several cliks later they entered the mouth of it and began looking for targets.

The red shirted Named One was standing on the prow on the lead ship was idly picking out landmarks.

"That would seem to be a power generator, over there is one of their sewage facilities, we should hit them, there's ten thousand Cyclops, there's their food storage, there's a road that leads to .... the .... wait a sepi-clik."

"TEN THOUSAND CYCLOPS?"

Some of the locals had noted the fishing ships weren't fishing and were carrying heavy weapons. When they told Elaand he'd quickly passed the information around and had Oronimus' army at the ready. The poor red shirted Named One never even got to pick up the radio.

The Chaldean clans opened fire from the shores as the Horuns and Columbans screamed from the air laying waste to anything in their path. The Cyclops, having done their part at being a bright yellow distraction, put their clothes back on and watched the carnage. These ships, unlike Yontar's first navy, had munitions on board. Their explosions provided the army with some very satisfying pyrotechnics.

In less than half a clik the mini-navy was at the bottom of the Delta, never having been able to warn Lord Yontar of the force that was coming his way.

The attack had been so stunning that the few survivors there were didn't even bother putting up a fight. They were just dragged unceremoniously to shore and shackled.

Geldish was thrilled when he saw one of the survivors was a Named One. Now he could get to the bottom of this whole "smart Mayanoren" mystery.

They brought the hapless servant of Lord Yontar to Oronimus' command tent. General al Rahim and Flight Leader Smythe bracketed the chair the Named One was tied to. Oronimus stood with the Brittle Riders and the Mantis Guard. Geldish walked over to the prisoner slowly and they all watched as the flames in his eyes began to surround the Named One's head.

"He did that to me once," commented Sland, "it isn't fun."

As much as everyone wanted to hear that particular story they kept their focus on Geldish.

For over a clik he said nothing as the flames roiled and flickered around the prisoner's head. None of them had ever seen anything like this but, judging by the obvious discomfort and thrashing of the Named One, whatever he was doing was having an effect.

Finally, the flames receded and the prisoner slumped in his chair, unconscious.

"There was lots of useful information in his mind. I will write a full report this even. However, in general, Yontar's rapidly equipping the reptiloids with new weapons and battle tactics. He's hoping to buy a Full Sun's worth of time so he can be fully prepared to overrun Lord Südermann's realm and then the Plains. Once those are taken his plan is to head east and capture all of the weapons of the eastern warrens.

"He has a brand which can glide and he is developing a launching system so they can attack the Succubi from above. He doesn't know about the Horuns or the Columbans or any of the eastern army.

"These Named Ones, as they call themselves, are a genetic quirk that began appearing about fifty Suns ago. When they were at the facility of the makers they created more like themselves even though that meant killing thousands of non-decanted regular Mayanorens. These new Mayanorens are just as vicious as their predecessors and much smarter. It seems, unlike his previous reign, Yontar is giving these creatures discretion as to how and when to act.

"With them acting as his generals he will have a much more fluid, and lethal, army than we've ever faced before."

He went and poured himself a glass of Whævin and continued.

"Since he fought me every step of the way I was forced to erase his mind when I was done. I had hoped to be able to plant some false memories in there but there was just no feasible way."

"When you say 'erased'," queried General al Rahim, "what exactly do you mean?"

"All of his innate abilities are intact, but he has no memories and no way to function. He is like a new born small."

"Could we train him?" asked Oronimus.

"I see no reason why not. It would be an interesting experiment."

They discussed their options for a while and then Sland asked the important question.

"How soon must we attack if we are going to stop him?"

Geldish considered all he had learned.

"No later than the Warm Sun. After that Yontar will be entrenched and preparing to come this way."

They conversed about this for a moment and then Oronimus showed why he got to sit in the big chair.

"Colonel Elaand, how many barges are available here?"

"Quite a few. We use them to ferry goods, brands, pretty much anything. We use the river as our lifeline. Why do you ask?"

"Well, I was just wondering if you had enough to put my army behind Yontar's."

Had he asked to learn how to fly he would get less of a shocked response. A clik's worth of frantic radio calls later they had their answer. It was yes. They had enough sea worthy barges to pull this off.

To keep Yontar from assigning forces to the south, they would attack the garrisons in ten turns. They would do as much damage as they could while Oronimus' army came up behind them. Then they would smash them in between.

They sent word to the Children of the Waters of their plan but told them they need not attack. The goal was to destroy Yontar and he was here not there.

Although, when he figured out what they were up to, he might wish otherwise.

Hana Koi-San sat in the ambassadors' chambers and reviewed the reports from Melheni and the documents concerning the failed, yet daring, attack on Lord Südermann's Delta. It was sheer luck they'd avoided a catastrophe.

Then he reviewed the plan from Geldish and considered his options. The Children didn't really have the capability to mount any serious attack. The White Teeth and the Cuda's were their only warrior brands and they just didn't have the numbers needed.

He gave new thought to the Kwini-Laku. Was Melheni an aberration or could they be trained to be warriors as well? They had certainly fought well in the gen-O-pod war. But that was long ago and they preferred peaceful waters now. Nevertheless, it was a question worth pursuing. Their representative, Ohlhani, was in congress and would be able to give him an honest answer.

While he agreed in principle with Geldish's request they not become involved, he loathed the idea of sitting on the side while his fate was decided by others. He would bring this up to the congress after he'd spoken with Ohlhani.

There was a long river separating the garrisons,

there should be something they could do.

He caught himself sipping a sugared brandy and his thoughts wandered back to the young Lord Südermann. While he held no romantic notions about her, he was still mildly besotted. She was a fascinating creature. More spiritual than he'd anticipated and, while youthful, a very capable ruler. He would have to look for ways to tighten the bonds between her brands and his.

And, although the citizens of the Plains had coarser personalities than the Children they were, by and large, worth knowing too. While they lacked a defined spiritual depth, they were still very loyal and protective of their communities.

For lack of a better definition, they were different. Even so, he would look for ways to make them allies in the future. Their work to salvage the Great Lake would be an excellent starting point and, he was sure the congress would agree, any brands who valued water as highly as they did surely couldn't be discarded.

But those were all dreams for a future not yet born. For now, he would need to focus on the matters at hand, and they all concerned Yontar.

When he'd visited the Plains he'd been given access to many libraries and they'd all held accounts of Xhaknar and Yontar's reign. The horrors they told became numbing after a while. One atrocity after another. From the blood fountain to the thinning of the brands, it seemed every turn brought a new terror. It was amazing anyone had survived at all, yet alone to have become so strong.

The ten Theravada perfections would be sorely put to the test with them but he believed, even if they didn't know the terms, they fit nicely into their hopes as well.

He couldn't imagine what they had been through. He would make sure to point that out to the congress when they met. These brands would thrive with or without the Children. Better it be with as far as he was concerned.

Besides, he did want to swim in the Great Lake

come the Good Sun.

He finished making his notes and called in an aide so he could dictate his speech. His aide was an excellent barometer of the moods of the congress and would assist him to make sure he didn't bruise any fins.

Then again, maybe a bruise or two was exactly what was needed.

One Zanubi of a war, as they would say on the Plains, was coming whether they wanted it or not.

The Athabascae Warriors were a sight to behold. Not quite as tall as the average Minotaur they were powerfully built, shaggy, and had deep dark eyes that seemed to know the pain of the universe. They wore simple buckskin vests and trousers with boots that came up to their knees. Unless you looked for the breasts it was hard to tell the mals and femmes apart.

They also had quite a few surprises as healers. Not only did they have herbs and medicines made from plants, they had a lot of very high tech gear none of the others had ever seen before. Even so, they had brought extras of everything and explained how and when to use them to the others.

Their leader, a femme named Fried-a-liche, was polite as polite could be but it was clear she'd rather be anywhere but here. However, whatever her misgivings, she went about her job with abject professionalism. D'noma tried to draw her out but was met with obfuscation after pleasant obfuscation. It wasn't until she overheard her talking to another Athabascae Warrior when she figured out the problem.

Until now they had thought all the stories the Din-La told of other brands were just that, stories. To be faced with a multitude of beings who were all wearing uniforms of tan shirts and black pants while wearing a patch signifying Rohta Industries, LLC and who may as well have come from the moons as far as they were concerned was beyond disconcerting.

D'noma passed the word around about their difficulties and everyone did the best they could to make the gentle warriors feel comfortable. Clearly, though, it was going to take some time.

Douglass Fairwinds had been as good as his word. Almost two thousand healers, half Haliaeetus and half Athabascae Warriors, had descended on the garrison about four turns after the army of the Plains had arrived. Within a turn they'd taken over the medical wards, set up triage stations, posted notices about sanitation and sterilization, and much to the amusement of many, they held a brief ceremony to bless their instruments of healing.

But whatever their quirks may be, it was clear everyone stood a better chance of healing by their hands than any others.

A turn after that, the Brittle Riders arrived with Elaand sharing a nysteed with Geldish and Malehni sharing with Sland so they wouldn't slow them down. Geldish wanted Yontar to see him and focus all his attention to the north. As he'd pointed out to Oronimus, he'd killed him once already so he was pretty sure Yontar wouldn't be pleased to see him.

Which was the whole idea.

In four turns they would go to war. Word spread throughout the garrisons and battle plans were drawn up. The even of Geldish's arrival a caravan of Din-La wagons showed up. If anyone was surprised to see Zrrm on the lead wagon, they never mentioned it.

He led Geldish to the first wagon and flipped open the side.

"These are called flame throwers. You aim it in the general direction of something you want to burn to the ground and then pull the trigger."

He demonstrated for the troops who were ambling over and watched gleefully as they all jumped back when the sheet of flame erupted. He went to the next wagon.

"These are makers' weapons. They are called semi-automatic rifles. They can fire a hundred rounds of ammunition per epi-clik. The smaller ones are for soldiers to carry, the larger ones need to be mounted."

The third wagon contained weapons like the Chaldeans had. Geldish had already seen how deadly they could be and told Zrrm of their effectiveness against Yontar's raiding party. Zrrm merely nodded and moved on.

The next three wagons contained, even more, weapons which were soon passed out to the grateful troops. The last four wagons contained nothing but ammunition. There was some disappointment there were no new foods.

While there was talk of sharing this windfall with the other garrisons it was quickly dismissed. They wanted Yontar to focus all his might on this location and no other. If Oronimus' charge was to have any effect they could not be spread too thin.

They knew Yontar could easily see what they were up to so they made no attempt to hide. In fact, Geldish made it a point to levitate over the edge of the garrison every even and wave to the south.

But beyond that, they made no show of aggression.

It had been two turns since Yontar watched the Din-La supply the garrison. After that, nothing. They just stayed where they were. Not that he was complaining. Every turn nothing happened allowed another supply train to show up with new weapons. Based on what his spies had told him of the Din-La weapons, they would be pretty evenly matched.

The reptiloids may have all the original thinking of a rock but, given directions, they could manufacture almost anything. The Named Ones had pronounced the weapons to be of excellent quality and were training the troops in their use.

The Named Ones had come up with a launching mechanism for the RZL-274's. It was deceptively simple. It was a larger version of the wrist weapons Dagnar had built. You pulled back the elastic rope, ten repitloids got in the seating area and you pulled the lever. They would shoot almost a quarter of a kay straight up and out. You could do one launch per epi-clik and they had built ten of the machines.

One thing was clear, however, Geldish was going to throw everything he had at this garrison. The others were stocked and manned, but they were not going to be part of any attack. No, this was to be the battleground.

He'd recalled as much manpower as he dared and his Named Ones were handling the minutiae. So be it then, 'kill or be killed' was an equation he could understand easily. He would rid Aretti of that irksome Rangka once and for all.

He wandered around the garrison idly noting the regular Mayanorens were showing signs of comprehension as they ran through their drills. The reptiloids were on par with the old Naradhama as far as he could tell and handled being ordered about well. The Named Ones, both red shirted and not, were barking orders and showing no mercy.

He watched them run through basic drills and then smiled as the Named Ones began forcing them to understand basic tactics. If you do this, that will happen, if you do that, bad things will happen and so on. It wasn't elegant, but it did seem to be effective.

This may not be the army he'd been bred to lead but it was going to do just fine as far as he could see.

He returned to the rooms he'd converted into an office and living area and reviewed the reports from the other garrisons. Nothing seemed amiss. The room was

Spartan by any standards but Yontar was not one for frippery. He wanted power, not frills.

He then reviewed the battle plans drafted by the Named Ones. They were all excellent as far as they went but they were far too reactionary. When Geldish attacked he wanted to counter attack immediately. That would mean more extensive reptiloid casualties, but he did seem to have a plethora of reptiloids.

He called a couple of Named Ones into his office and explained his wishes. He was greeted with the cold smiles he'd really begun to appreciate. One of them sat down with the previously submitted plans, made some minor adjustments and handed them to Yontar. As soon as he saw what the Named One had done he returned their cold smiles.

If Geldish attacked the center they would send out the flanks to surround him. If he tried to outflank them, they'd mount a direct attack on the center. If he came at them all at once then they'd launch the RZL-274's up to the middle and hammer him from the flanks.

All three variations ended with them overrunning the other garrison.

That was a battle plan he could approve, so he did.

Now, if only someone could tell him what had happened to his navy, his turn would be complete.

The QZD-1934 blended perfectly into his surroundings. His name was Kwaa Kuul Zod, although no one had asked. He wondered if that was a good thing or not. He had planned on working his way along the southern ocean until he got to the Delta and then going north to find out what types of munitions and infrastructure would await Lord Yontar when he arrived. But he'd been stopped cold at the sight he saw when he arrived at the Delta.

Thousands upon thousands of unfamiliar brands preparing to go to sea. Given there were Mantis Guards and some soldiers of the Plains in their midst he could only assume these were uncounted on enemies preparing to attack his new lord. He tried getting as close as he could without breaking cover. There was much about these brands he didn't know and needed to discover.

One thing he didn't know was about to become very important to him. While he was all but invisible to the naked eye of most brands, Cyclops weren't most brands. One had spotted him almost a clik ago and had warned his commander. His commander had sent out a small squad of Chaldeans to bring him in.

He was just about to raise his magnifying goggles when a dark shape appeared in front of him. Before he could react he felt something strike him from behind and then there was darkness all around.

His head was throbbing and his vision was blurry when he woke up. Even so, it seemed better than the alternative, so he tried to focus on his surroundings. He was strapped to a chair and faced by a Mantis Guard. Behind him were those strange brands he'd seen. Every one of them heavily armed.

"Hi there," began the guard casually and far too glibly for his tastes, "welcome back to the land of the living. I'm Corporal Nhaar and I'll be your host for a while. Normally this would be the part of your turn where we'd torture you, question you and, essentially, make your life very unpleasant.

"However, as your fate would have it, there's really not much you could tell us we don't already know."

It was then he noticed the Mayanoren, wearing a crumpled gray uniform and looking very lost. It was as though someone had turned out a light inside his mind.

He must not have hidden the look of horror on his face.

"Him?" continued Nhaar as he glanced at the

Mayanoren, "Don't let him bother you. He had an unfortunate meeting with a Rangka. As you may have heard, those never go well. No, in your case we're just going to send you to prison. There you'll join what's left of Yontar's navy until the end of the war, at which time you'll be returned to Kalindor. Assuming, that is, there's any Kalindor left to return to.

"Given the mood of some of the armies when it comes to Yontar, that is most certainly not a given. Now, if you'll be kind enough to give your name and identification number to my assistant," he motioned to a young guard standing near the opening of the tent, "we'll get you processed and have your bump looked at."

He decided being asked his name was not such a good thing after all. Nevertheless, given the circumstances, he complied.

Shortly thereafter he was escorted, still shackled, to a medico who pronounced him fit enough to be a prisoner and then taken to a well-guarded, camp. There were three sets of fences, each with guards patrolling between them and there were lights on every corner aimed inwards. There were makeshift barracks in the center and lots of empty space otherwise. He doubted there could be room for more than a hundred or so prisoners. He tried to remember how many troops Yontar had sent and was pretty sure the number was far greater than that.

However, unless there was a way to tunnel out of here he was going to be here for a while so he may as well get used to it.

They entered the first gate and then turned left and walked until they rounded a corner to access the next gate. They repeated the procedure to get to the third gate and then he was unshackled. His guard, who looked to be a Wolfen if his memory was working, stopped him and smiled.

"Don't get too comfortable. You'll be leaving here in two turns or so. Then you and your friends will be taken to a more secure prison for the duration."

The guard snapped a salute and left him to his thoughts.

More secure? Like this place was a sieve? He didn't want to think about it.

Imam Salim had just finished his prayers and was looking forward to a turn of quiet reflection and a home cooked meal. He had read what reports had come in through the Din-La and knew Ben was as safe as he could be. The reports from the army were concise but clear enough. They had met their allies and were preparing to meet their enemy.

He was about to stand up when he heard a noise behind him. Surprised to be interrupted he turned and saw Ben's wife.

"Mrs. al Salaam, what are you doing here?"

"Why Imam?"

She looked broken. Her clothes were rumpled, her hijab was askew and her eyes looked liked they'd been to the gates of Hell and seen all it had to offer. He hadn't seen her in a while but she'd seemed hale and healthy then. He wondered what had happened to her.

"Why what, Mrs. al Salaam?"

"Why Ben?"

And then he knew. While Ben's marriage, like most in Chaldea, had been arranged, these two had been in love from the first time they'd met and it seemed their love had grown stronger over the many Suns. It was also at this time he noticed the weapon. It was hanging limply in her hand, but it was there and he assumed it was loaded.

"Why not Ben? He has volunteered many times before and was very well qualified for this mission. You knew, all the way back when you married him he worked for his Imam. You knew he put the safety of Chaldea above all else except Allah. You knew him then and he has not changed."

She seemed to crumple into the wall, almost becoming a part of it.

"He was young then and the young do what they must. But he is old now, closer to meeting Allah than to his times of vigor. I want to spend those remaining Suns with him and now I can't imagine that happening. I had a dream last even and, in it, Ben was no more. I felt him gasp his last breath and leave this world.

"I came here to kill you for sending him away from me but now think I might be better off if I kill myself and wait for Ben to join me."

The gun hadn't moved and neither had she. Her voice was a dull monotone and he knew he would have to deal with her very carefully if they were both to survive, which is what he wanted and he knew Allah decreed.

"Mrs. al Salaam ...."

"Yndi."

"Yndi? That's a pretty name." He had no idea why he'd said that even if it was true. "Yndi, we all serve a greater cause to the best of our abilities. Ben's are extraordinary. It is why we relied on him to meet with the Brittle Riders. It is why we relied on him to tell us honestly what dangers faced us and it is why we rely on him now."

She didn't look pacified. She looked defeated. The gun fell from her hands and clattered on the floor. She began sobbing uncontrollably. He knew it was forbidden to touch another man's wife, but he was sure Allah would forgive him this one time and hugged her.

She cried into his shoulder for almost a clik. His own wife entered the mosque, probably wondering what was keeping him, and softly took the sobbing matron into her own arms. Then she led her towards the back, into the kitchen, where they could talk.

Imam Salim picked up the gun and set it on a chair.

He turned his gaze heavenward, stood silently for several epi-cliks and then prayed harder than he'd ever prayed in his life.

"Allah, the Most Merciful and Wise, I beseech you to let this servant come home to us safely. Allow him and his beloved wife to be reunited until the end of their turns.

"I know I am but a simple Imam and not wise to the plans of the divine. I know You have a reason for all You do and it is not for me to question. I do not question, I merely beg, please bring Ben al Salaam home to us. To her."

He didn't see the two wives standing in the door. He didn't see Mrs. al Salaam nod briefly and leave. He didn't see anything until his wife kissed him and then led him to his meal.

"I am proud of you, my husband, and now I'm sure Allah is as well."

Since there was much he had not seen he had no idea what she was talking about but still felt eased by her words.

It was almost even-split. The majority of the garrison was quiet as the troopers slept. Some creatures of the desert ventured out but did not come close to the occupants. There were too many dangerous smells for them.

A small council of generals, led by Geldish, sat making their final preparations.

"Yontar has moved almost all of his troops to face us here," smiled Geldish, "so we should begin our attack at all the other garrisons first."

"Why?" asked Elaand. "We have none of the new weapons at those garrisons."

"True," he replied, "but neither does Yontar. Look

at it this way, if we attack from here he can counter almost any move we make. In fact, with a little luck, he could overrun us. He has more troops at his disposal than we do and he will not be relying on the brute force tactics of Xhaknar.

"No, better to hit him where he's weakest and stand pat here for a while. Let our troops overrun the western garrisons and then have them form up on the other side of the river. Then we can march two armies on him from different directions."

They all saw the logic in it but were confused by the timing. Why wait until the last sepi-clik to make such a drastic change in strategy?

"Easy. Because Yontar's spies are placed near every garrison, reporting our every move. Even the slightest change in routine would have been noticed and may have forced Yontar to reinforce them. I want his main forces in one place. I want to be able to kill him once and for all. That can't happen if he has options."

There was a knock on the door and then a young Se-Jeant walked in and handed Geldish a slip of paper. He read it and smiled.

"It seems our friend Oronimus is a stickler for schedules. He will be here by next even-fall. Knowing that we should begin the attacks on the other garrisons now."

They all knew the troops would grumble, but not too much. Going to battle is why they were here and all of them volunteered. Every garrison had been issued battle plans in case they were needed. Their generals would know what to do. Orders were issued, they would attack in ten epi-cliks. All of the garrisons had the flaming catapults, so they would start with those and then cross the river.

The river was very wide, but not deep. Were it the Warm Sun with the snows melting it would be a different story, but they could walk across it now.

They walked outside and took up positions on the catwalk inside the garrison. Right on cue flaming balls arced into the darkling sky and began raining death across the river. Even though many kays separated them they could still hear the echoes of surprised screams. Then they heard cannon fire and saw flashes as Succubi began their phase of the attacks. The generals were holding nothing back. They should be inside the enemy garrisons by breaklight.

One of the soldiers, a young Minotaur, walked up to Elaand and asked why they hadn't been told the war was starting.

"Does it say *Officer of Rank* on your pay chit?"

"No sir."

"Then go back to bed. Soon enough there'll be a battle for you."

The young trooper snapped a salute and disappeared into the barracks.

Geldish couldn't help but smile.

"Does it say *Officer of Rank* on your pay chit? Heh, I like that. I may even use it myself someturn."

The other generals laughed as well and then returned their attentions to the battle raging upstream. It was clear that, while the other side had been caught completely unaware, they weren't stupefied. They were fighting back with all they had.

It was going to be bloody work this even.

A Named One burst into Yontar's room without knocking.

"Forgive my bold intrusion, Lord Yontar, but they are attacking."

It took him a sepi-clik to get his bearings. He had been having a wonderful dream about killing Rangkas.

"So? You have your battle plans, execute them."

"We can't Lord Yontar."

"Why not?"

"They are not attacking here milord."

That brought Yontar fully awake.

"Where are they attacking?"

"Every garrison but this one. The Named Ones are reporting they are holding out as best they can but expect to be overrun by breaklight."

Yontar fumed. Geldish had outsmarted him using the oldest trick in the book. He'd given him a big shiny target and used it to divert his attention from the real battles. He couldn't order them to abandon the garrisons. They'd be easy targets as they tried to return here and they'd bring the forces of Geldish's garrisons right behind them.

But two could play at this game.

"Execute battle plan four. We attack Geldish now."

"Yes Lord Yontor."

The Named One left and Yontar got up and quickly dressed. He was barely out of his room when he heard the sounds of troops scrambling into position. While it was clear they'd all heard the news he was pleased to note it only seemed to harden their resolve. He decided to do something he never did, he'd speak to them before the battle.

He motioned to one of the Named Ones to hold their assembly and then stepped up on a box, even though he didn't need to since he was already a foot taller than any of them.

"Troops, this is the even Kalindor has long dreamed of. While your brothers and sisters fight along the river, directly across from us, lies the real enemy. The enemy which has prevented you from attaining your glory, the enemy that has stopped you from developing, your enemy, is within reach this even.

"You've been trained, you've been armed, and you now have real leaders who can bring you success. This turn belongs to Kalindor!"

There was a mighty yell and then the Named Ones began issuing clear orders and the formations began to move.

They'd all heard the yell.

"Wake the troops," yelled Geldish, "Yontar's attacking!"

He didn't need to say it twice.

The even's patrols hadn't been sleeping. In mere sepi-cliks, the flaming catapults began launching the new versions of Hlaar's bombs. Geldish watched as Hlaar ran back and forth supervising. The main courtyard looked like chaos but soon formed into recognizable lines.

Instead of responding with his own catapults, Yontar had unleashed his flying reptiloids. They were wheeling in from the west and had weapons at the ready. Geldish watched as the Succubi rose to meet them and try to divert their path.

Soon enough weapons fire was crisscrossing the sky and bodies began to fall. The medicos ignored the peril and rushed out to retrieve the wounded. The main gates were pulled open and the combined armies of the Elders' Council and Lord Südermann began their march across the river.

He spied the Brittle Riders and Ben arming themselves. He wasn't sure about riding with Ben but the others seemed to like the old brand and his odd religion. If they trusted him, so would he.

He levitated off the gangplank down to the courtyard and walked over to his nysteed, which they had retrieved from the stable. N'leah was wearing nothing but a loin cloth and weapons. BraarB was wearing only the weapons. Sland and R'yune wore vests and trousers with boots. Both were heavily armed. Ben, for his part, was carrying several weapons and wearing what he usually wore; a simple turban, loose shirt, loose pants and riding boots. If it wasn't for the weapons you would have thought he was going on a Warm Sun jaunt.

The sounds of battle were all around them yet they were calm. Geldish checked his weapons and they all mounted up.

"Our goal is Yontar. No matter what happens, if he lives through this we will have accomplished nothing."

There were no battle cries, no huzzahs, they just nodded and headed towards the gate to join the battle.

Schoolmaster Zk was not what one thought of when one thought of schools of any type. He was the leader of the White Teeth. A bullet shaped head with no visible neck and a large mouth full of the reason his brand was called what it was. His skin was drab white and he had a small fin on his back for steering.

He led a commando force of one thousand White Teeth and Cudas, those rapier thin warriors who were just as deadly as he was, through the river towards the garrisons to the east. Though the river was shallow they had no problem navigating it.

They came upon the first garrison and quickly assessed the battle raging in the middle of the river. Garrisons on both sides were in flames, but it seemed clear the allies from the north were winning against the enemies from the south.

Unlike many Children of the Waters, they were as comfortable on land as they were in the water. Zk quickly issued orders for them to take the southern bank and attack from the rear.

He briefly wondered if he should let someone know he was here and then decided they'd figure it out soon enough.

While as well versed in the meditative techniques as any of the Children, Zk was secretly glad Kalindor existed. His brand, like the Cudas, had been bred for battle. He wasn't sure they could survive in nothing but peace and harmony.

He shook those thoughts away and led his troops into battle.

General A'rxk was big even by Wolfen standards. Some thought his large size and careful speech meant he was slow witted. It was not a mistake anyone made twice.

He was overseeing the battle as it unfolded in front of him. He moved a battalion to his left so they could outflank the enemy and begin the final push. He was the garrison furthest from Yontar and he wanted to get where the real action was.

They'd taken some heavy casualties in the initial assault but were noe in control of things. He had to admit he was thoroughly impressed with the medicos. They just walked through the hail of weapons fire and picked up the wounded. They were some of the bravest brands he'd ever seen.

He was just about to issue an order for a counterattack on the right side when he noticed weapons fire behind the enemy's garrison. More importantly, the enemy had noticed it too was being forced to respond.

He had no idea who was shooting at them but the whole "enemy of my enemy" thing certainly seemed to apply here. A quick volley of orders later and his troops were moving directly towards the new ally.

He then ordered the Succubi to fly around to the eastern side and cut off any chance of escape. With that taken care of, he concentrated on the new situation.

Whoever was shooting knew what they were doing. He'd hear a shot and then see a Kalindorian soldier fall. They certainly were not wasting ammunition.

He checked his pack and was pleased to see his aide had remembered his flask of ice wine. Whoever this was he was going to have to buy them a drink.

The battle lasted two more cliks before one of those weird Mayanorens came out waving a white flag. Behind him was a large white brand he didn't recognize, but it had its weapon pointed directly at the Mayanoren, so he assumed it was his new ally.

He walked out of the water and went straight up to him as he was issuing commands for a prisoner detail.

"General A'rxk of the army of the Plains. It's a pleasure to meet you, sir."

"Schoolmaster Zk of the Children of the Waters. Our ambassador, Hana Koi-San, asked that we assist you in any way possible."

A'rxk looked behind the Schoolmaster and saw more like him and others who were brown and black and very thin. However, they looked just as deadly as their larger companions.

As the Mayanoren was being shackled and taken away he removed his flask and handed it to the Schoolmaster.

"A drink to salute our new friendship?"

Unlike most of the Children, the White Teeth enjoyed a stiff belt from time to time. He readily accepted and took a healthy swallow. It froze his gums and burned his tongue all at once. He decided they HAD to get this stuff delivered as soon as this war was over.

General A'rxk smiled and took a long pull from the flask as well and then returned it to his pack.

"We'll save the rest for later. I have orders to proceed to the next garrison downstream and then, once the minor garrisons have been cleared, to advance on Yontar."

Zk nodded. "That's as good a plan as any. If it's all

right with you, we'll stay to the river until we're needed."

A'rxk nodded in assent and after a clik spent making sure all the prisoners were secure, they were on the move.

Lieutenant Ptaak had served the Lords Südermann for almost one hundred Full Suns. For almost fifty of those Suns, he had been garrison commander here. He used his position to train troops and prepare the best for the Mantis Guard. Never, in all his time on Arreti, had he witnessed a battle like the one in front of him now.

The Kalindorians were using guerilla tactics instead of their usual blunt attacks. They'd snipe from one area and then retreat to open fire from somewhere else. But he hadn't made it to his rank without expecting the unexpected.

He spread his troops out and began ferreting out each nest of snipers. Then he had the Succubi begin laying waste to the garrison itself. He briefly wondered why, with all the natural insect species that could fly, none of the insectoids had been given that ability. Well, that was a thought for a different turn.

It would soon be breaklight. He was frustrated at the pace they were making but knew they were making progress. Every clik brought them a little closer to the garrison itself. He saw a squad of Kalindorians sneaking around his left flank to catch them in a crossfire. He was about to issue a warning when a small squad of Se-Jeants spun up out of the reeds and opened fire on them.

The warriors from the Plains were worth getting to know better. He'd been unsure when Lord Südermann had begun announcing plans to work more closely with them. Well, that was why she was Südermann and he just commanded a garrison.

With the attack foiled the Se-Jeants began making their way forward on the unprotected side. They gingerly stepped over the bodies floating in the river and began their advance.

About three cliks later he was nearing the opposite shore. The fighting had been bloody but he was sure the end was near. It was then he heard weapons fire coming from the west. A scout ran in and informed him more troops were coming in and they were firing on anything Kalindorian. The scout said two of the brands were unknown to him.

He was about to ask for more information when the waters churned beneath his feet and several hundred White Teeth and Cudas emerged firing at the Kalindorian lines.

Ptaak had no idea who they were either but merely shrugged and joined in the shooting. If someone wanted to tell him later who his new allies were that would be fine with him. In the meantime, the Kalindorian garrison was waiting to be overthrown.

Less than a clik later, it was.

After the celebratory drink from General A'rxk' flask, he was filled in on the situation as it now stood. So now the Fish-People, sorry, Children of the Waters had joined the fray. Well, that was just fine as far as he was concerned.

Once they'd made arrangements for the few surviving prisoners, they began their march on Yontar.

It was past mid-break. The battle had been stagnating in the middle of the river. Neither side gave, neither side gained. The casualties had been staggering and were continuing to mount on both sides. Bodies floated everywhere and the river was a swirl of blood and body parts.

Yontar had tasked one squad of Named Ones with the sole responsibility of keeping Geldish occupied. They made sure, no matter where he was in the battle, at least fifty Kalindorians were around him. He noted, as he watched from the battlements, the Brittle Riders seemed to have added a new member. He didn't recognize the brand but could see he was as good, if not better in some regards, a warrior as any of them.

His plan, though working, had its drawbacks. He would have preferred those Named Ones to be attacking the opposing garrison. He knew all of the garrisons to the west had fallen and those troops would be marching here. He didn't need epi-clik by epi-clik updates to know they'd arrive well before even-fall.

He was kind of curious who the two brands were his scouts didn't recognize, but he doubted it mattered in the grand scheme of things. Just more brands who wanted to kill him.

He knew, or at least he thought he knew, that Südermann didn't want to rule Kalindor. It was clear by the weapons they had available she could have done so at any time. That meant the garrisons were merely there to stop the Exalted Quelnerom from polluting her shores. Having met the useless ruler he could understand her logic.

There was only one thing left to do. Retreat and regroup.

The forest began about four kays south of here. That would be their goal. The Kalindorians knew those woods like the back of their hands. If they could draw that mixed army into them, so much the better. But, even if they couldn't, they could resupply and plan a new attack.

He called over two Named Ones who were near him and gave the order. They nodded, saluted and took off to implement it. They knew as well as he did what the odds of survival were now.

Slim and none if they stayed put. And he wasn't stupid enough to gamble on slim.

Oronimus IX could see the smoke in the distance. His scouts were reporting there were fires up and down the river and bodies in the part they were headed for. He figured they were about a clik away from the main battle so he ordered a double time march. Then he ordered the Horuns and the Columbas to fly ahead and engage the enemy and keep them penned.

Less than an epi-clik later they were gone with flight Leader Smythe barking out orders as they flew.

General al Rahim informed his troops they would have to pray as they marched since they were now in enemy territory. He promised them, confientally, Allah would understand as he secretly hoped he was right.

They were spotted by one of Yontar's spies, but he was spotted by a Cyclops before he could radio his report. He seemed amazed the small hole in his chest was going to do so much damage. Then he wondered why he'd never noticed how pretty the sky was and then he died.

Oronimus spread his Cyclops along the front to search for any more of these color changing spies and then issued the safeties off command. Ready or not, they were going to war.

Less than half a clik later they appeared from the forest and began crossing the empty prairie.

Yontar was just exiting through the back gate when he saw the new arrivals spinning out of the sky. He couldn't believe what he was seeing. Who the hell were they and where had they come from?

He looked to the sky and raged.

"You're just fucking with me now, aren't you?"

He ordered the launches spun around and sent the RZL-274's to meet them and kill as many as they could. Despite the carnage, he still had around a hundred thousand troops at his disposal. He ordered the nearest ones to fire at the new invaders as he and the Named Ones began their retreat into the forest.

Well, that was the plan anyway. They were about halfway across the prairie when Oronimus and his army emerged.

Yontar's army was still regrouping at the garrison attempting to break free from the clutches of Geldish and his ilk. With no better plan readily presenting itself the twenty thousand or so troops with him quickly formed a skirmish line and began firing at the invaders.

This was not his best option. Before long his troops would be in a circle in the middle of this field and they would be target practice for everyone else. He began easing them to the west and laying down barrage after barrage of heavy weapons fire. The reptiloids took to the rocket launchers very well and were deadly accurate with them. But so were the troops who were attacking him.

More and more of his army joined him and soon they had a sizable, mobile, front. He could see Geldish leading a battalion from the army of the Plains but they were still too far off to worry about.

They increased the speed of their mad dash and aimed for the rail yards. From there they could cut south and still ensnare the opposing armies in the forest.

Geldish could see Yontar trying to make his escape. Rather than give chase he turned his riders loose to cut him off. The battalion behind him, having lost their leaders in the battle, simply followed wearily waiting for orders.

He looked at them and realized they were all sorely

wounded. But none of them showed the slightest sign of slowing down. Even Ben, what a wonder he'd turned out to be, was cut as much as any of them but rode like he was late to a party.

He also realized the majority of blood and ichor on their bodies wasn't their own.

Just as he was about to order an increase in their gait he saw the super soldier who looked like Xhaknar turning to face him with a battalion of his own.

Yontar would just have to wait.

There was no elegance here. The two sides simply clashed head on and began trying to kill each other. Weapons fired, swords slashed, knives flew, and brands died.

Geldish met Dagnar head on in the middle of the field. They ran out of bullets and began fighting with swords. Dagnar was bigger and stronger than Geldish, by an order of magnitude, but Geldish was surprisingly fast and kept the bigger soldier at bay.

He opened his mind to see how his riders were faring and felt them each in intense battles. He wouldn't bother them then. His ad hoc battalion was making fast work of the reptiloids but was having problems with the Named Ones and the regular Mayanorens.

Nevertheless, they were pushing them back towards Yontar.

Dagnar realized he was not going to be able to kill the Rangka so he leapt over a couple of bodies and enjoined everyone else in battle. Geldish went to follow him but several of the Named Ones blocked his path and opened fire.

The bullets were of little concern to him, but they did slow him down. Realizing all these weapons were made of metal he opened his mind to them and sent them twisting to the ground in clumps. He could do that if he focused. Otherwise, he might destroy the weapons of his allies.

The Named Ones realized what had happened and

attacked him with their fists.

Well, they would have, but the rest of the Brittle Riders, led by Ben at this moment, cut in front of him and laid down a fusillade of bullets. Soon those Named Ones were no more.

Oronimus could see the various parts of the battle but had his hands full with the running shootout he was leading. Based on the descriptions he'd been given he guessed he was chasing Yontar. His Horuns and Columbas were in a nasty aerial battle unlike any he'd ever seen, or heard of, before. They were being aided by the Succubi when they could get free, but they were going to be tied up for a while.

Now his army was completely free of the forest he ordered them into two fronts. The first, led by him, would continue the chase. The second, led by General al Rahim, would cut a path between the remaining members of Yontar's army and Yontar.

He watched as al Rahim dashed to the north and engaged the enemy on the run. He then realized, instead of drawing a hard line between the parts, he was herding them towards Geldish's battalion. It was an interesting move.

Seeing as how Geldish's little army had cut their opponents size in half the new combatants would probably get slaughtered between al Rahim and him.

He couldn't allow himself the luxury of following that anymore and still keep his troops alive so he turned his attention to Yontar. The super soldier had a sizable force around him now, approximately forty thousand, and was making good time to the west. Oronimus didn't know what was there but was pretty sure it would bode well for no one but Yontar if he got to where he was going.

He could see the rail yard in the distance and

wondered if Yontar had a train waiting to make his escape. He doubted it. He was pretty sure he could see something that big.

He noted, professionally, Yontar was effective, if ruthless, in the way he used his troops. He could even make out which troops were more important to him. The reptiloids were obviously at the bottom of his hierarchy. He just lined them up in front of bullets.

He also noted they weren't going to be able to stop him before he got to the yard.

Nevertheless, they pressed on.

Flight Leader Smythe must have come to a similar conclusion. He ordered one third of his forces to continue battling these flying lizards and took the rest to cut off Yontar and buy Oronimus more time.

They came in high from the west and dive bombed Yontar's entire leading flank. A squadron of Succubi saw what they were doing and joined them with their cannons. The result was a wall of fire and death.

As they were arcing back up one of the Succubi turned to him, pulled back a device covering her ears and laughed.

"I'm K'lzaana, assistant squadron leader of the Succubi. Thanks for pointing him out. I've been wanting to blow up that diseased spawn of a kgum ever since he shot me."

He looked at the devastation below and made a mental note to never piss off a Succubus.

"I'm Flight Leader Corvington Smythe of the Horuns. It's a pleasure to meet you. Shall we do that again?"

"Yes please."

So she reset her ear coverings and they did.

Faced with a wall of flame between him and his destination, Yontar was forced to improvise. He ordered his troops south, away from the flames, and decided to work around the edges until they got to the rail yard or the forest, whichever they could attain first.

His troops were beginning to sense they may get out of this alive and were fighting all the harder for it. The reptiloids were firing continuously at the Cyclops and his army and causing fatalities in increasing numbers. He couldn't see what happened to the brand who looked like the new Brittle Rider and had to assume he was responsible for cutting off the rest of his reinforcements.

They continued their brutal march towards salvation and were now giving as good as they got. Before the casualties incurred by the reptiloids were stunning. It was as though they jumped in front of bullets for no reason. Now they finally seemed to have figured out the tactics the Named Ones had been teaching.

He heard a noise above the din and turned to see what it was. He was less than pleased to see it was the rest of the enemies' garrison soldiers and they were headed straight for him.

General A'rxk ordered his troops into two columns. The first, led by Lieutenant Ptaak would attack the reptiloids near the river. He would lead the charge on the rest who were trying to get away from the Cyclops. He'd never seen a Cyclops before but had been briefed they were allies.

This whole turn was full of unexpected allies. He kind of liked that.

It certainly made war more interesting.

He led his column north of the wall of flame and then headed them directly at the retreating reptiloids. He saw the Succubi, and whoever was flying with them, change their tactics and begin bombing to the south. That slowed them up enough he figured he should be able to shake hands with that Cyclops in the middle of that retreating column in a clik or so.

The White Teeth and the Cudas were exploding out of the water and now had the remaining reptiloids pinned between them and the army that was crushing them. Without fear of being ambushed from the rear, he turned his whole attention on the prey in front of him.

He saw the Rangka and some others on nytsteeds headed his way and figured they had to be the Brittle Riders. Well, he'd wanted to meet them someturn and this seemed as good a time as any.

As bullets began whizzing past his ears he ordered his troops to open fire. This was a battle the way it was meant to be. In the open, one to one, let the best brand win.

His troops were laying down suppressing fire, not trying to overtake the enemy but to pen them in until they either surrendered or died. With all the forces aligning against them he imagined surrender was out.

He watched as the Succubi fired off more of their aerial cannons around the perimeters of the retreating army. Like him, they were penning them in tighter and tighter. Damn those things were loud. The second wave of Succubi came in and a wall of flame erupted in front of him. He was about to curse them for ruining his shot when he saw the other flyers come in over the flames with automatic weapons.

Okay then, surrender was definitely off the table.

With the rules of engagement clear, he ordered his troops to shoot through the flames and march until they couldn't take the heat.

Oronimus watched as the walls of flame grew higher and thicker. He ordered his Chaldeans to fire their rockets into the air so they'd land in the middle of the conflagration. The Kleknars took the front of the column and followed the Wolfen's example by firing directly into the flames.

Within an epi-clik, all the eastern warriors had surrounded the flame and were firing into it. To the north, the few reptiloid survivors who still existed were surrendering so now the armies could concentrate all their fire power on this one location. Others joined in pouring round after round of ammunition into the inferno. As even fell they stopped.

There was no sound but the sound of burning. The air reeked with the smell of smoldering flesh. Nothing had lived through that.

Every now and then a spare round would explode from the heat. That was the only noise they worried about.

Geldish, his riders, and Ben sat on their nytsteeds near the edge of the flame. Geldish was opening his mind to see what did and did not live in there. Something loud exploded and Geldish whirled when he heard Ben gasp.

A piece of shrapnel had pierced his heart. Ben looked at him, smiled briefly, and fell to the ground.

It was breaklight. The even had been spent rounding up surviving reptiloids and Mayanorens. They had found no sign of Yontar or the other super soldier Geldish said was called Dagnar. He'd learned that from the Mayanoren he'd interrogated.

The Brittle Riders were outside of a medicos' tent,

sipping spiced java and looking despondent. They'd been bandaged and stitched but were still wearing the clothes they'd worn in battle. Any attempts to console them were met with homicidal glares so everyone stayed pretty far away.

Finally, Fried-a-liche came out to speak with them. She was covered in just as much blood and gore as they were.

"He lives. How long he will live is up to him and his God. We have done all we can."

Geldish smiled at that. "He's very good friends with his God."

R'yune signed at her but she didn't understand.

N'leah translated. "He wants to know if we can see him."

Fried-a-liche smiled. "Of course, he will sleep for many more cliks, but I see no harm in his friends and loved ones wishing him well."

They walked in the long tent and were surprised to find reptiloids as well as their allies in the beds. It was BraarB who explained.

"Healers heal, no matter who is injured. It is their creed."

Not wanting to upset anyone they accepted that at face value and moved down the aisle. Ben was in a bed at the end which was curtained off. He was pale and clammy but breathing. He was hooked up to a machine none of them recognized and it was emitting a low, steady, beeping sound.

After a while, they decided to sit with him in shifts. Fried-a-liche told them speaking to him would help. While they weren't entirely sure they believed her they agreed to give it a try. BraarB drew the first shift and, unsure what to say to her new friend, rummaged through his bags to see if he had anything he liked to read. She found a copy of the Holy Qur'an translated into Common and with a note inside saying it was a gift for Sland, She decided that would be fine.

She opened it to page one.

"In the name of Allah, the Most Gracious, the Most Merciful:

All Praise is due to Allah, Lord of the Universe

The Most Gracious, the Most Merciful.

The Owner of the Day of Judgment.

You alone do we worship, and You alone we turn to for help.

Guide us to the straight path;

The path of those on whom You have bestowed Your grace, not (the way) of those who have earned Your anger, nor of those who went astray."

The search for the super soldiers continued through the turn. The flaming square was still burning itself out so no one had been able to venture in there. Sland went into the medicos' tent to take his turn with Ben and found R'yune holding his hand gently tapping out words into his palm.

Sland realized R'yune was reading from a book as he stopped to turn the page. He saw Sland sand stood up. He told Sland how far he had gotten in the book so he could start from there. Sland was mildly uncomfortable reading from a religious book but figured Ben was certainly worth any discomfort.

He said goodbye to R'yune and sat down just as Ben's eyes flickered.

"I dreamt I met Allah the Most Wise and Most Merciful." His voice was barely a whisper.

"That was no dream," chuckled Sland, "you gave us one Zanubi of a scare."

Ben turned and looked at his new friend.

"I guess," continued the BadgeBeth, "He still has

more for you to do here and sent you back."

Ben looked confused for a moment and then smiled.

"Yes, that must be it. Although, after this, I think my days of riding the Plains are done. I will go home and garden with my loving wife and enjoy her cooking."

"An excellent idea," agreed Sland, "you've certainly earned the right."

"How is everyone else?"

Sland knew he didn't mean every single soldier who had fought.

"We all survived. A little worse for wear here and there, but we can all walk except Malehni and we've been told he'll pull through."

"That is very good to hear."

They sat silently for a while and then Ben seemed to perk up.

"In my dream, I heard R'yune speaking to me. He was reading from the Holy Qur'an."

"That too was no dream. It was the only thing we could find in your pack and the medico told us to talk to you. So everyone's been coming in and reading to you from it."

Ben smiled wider now.

"Allah is truly wise. Unlike my clumsy attempts, He has shown me plainly how to share His infinite wisdom."

"Well, okay," smirked Sland, "but you might just ask Him to send us a letter next time. He can't keep piercing folk's hearts with shrapnel, it's bad for morale."

Ben laughed until he coughed. Fried-a-liche heard him as she was making her rounds and walked in.

"You must truly be good friends with your God. None of my staff believed you would survive. Do not worry though, they will be pleased to know they were wrong. They always are in cases like this."

Ben smiled again as Fried-a-liche turned to Sland.

"You must go now. He will need his rest and we must run some tests to make sure nothing is amiss. You can see him again after next breaklight."

Sland handed him the book.

"This is where we left off if you want to continue reading."

Ben looked and then smiled a smile which proved he would live a long life.

"The ascension of the Prophet Muhammad. How fitting."

Sland walked outside to tell everyone Ben was awake and what Fried-a-liche had said.

They all relaxed and decided they'd better do something about their clothes. They chose the simplest solution and just walked over to the fire, stripped naked and threw them in. All except Geldish that is.

Then they went looking for fresh water to bathe in.

Close to ten thousand reptiloids, a thousand regular Mayanorens, three hundred Named Ones, some red shirted, and Dagnar stood looking at the burned husk lying on the ground. Yontar had taken a direct hit from one of the Succubi bombs. After that, not knowing what else to do, they'd grabbed his body and run through the flames to the south. They were all badly burned and all that was left of the great Kalindorian army.

They were several kays south of the battle and doubted anyone would be looking this far afield for them. They couldn't remove Yontar's helmet, it seemed to have fused to his head. But there were no healers among them so they'd been forced to make do when they treated their own injuries.

The area where they were waiting had a small lake and was covered by dense foliage. It was as good a hiding place as they thought they would ever find. Plus the water allowed them to wash their many wounds before bandaging them.

Dagnar claimed he could sense Yontar, barely, so they would wait until their leader woke up or he said he was gone.

They foraged and hunted for two full turns. Finally, near breaklight of the third turn Yontar's eyes slitted open, his voice was an angry rasp.

"Just how many times am I going to let that little fuck kill me before I crush his fucking skull?"

They all laughed at that. Lord Yontar was back.

EPILOGUE

Imam Salim had delivered the news himself. Ben had been injured but, Allah the Most Merciful be thanked, would return to his family. Yndi cried for an epi-clik and then straightened up and asked a million questions.

She wanted to go to him but it wasn't practical. She wanted to speak with him, he would see if it could be arranged. She wanted to make sure he would never, ever, be asked to do something like this again. On that, he readily agreed. Ben had served enough.

They went back and forth like that for about a clik and then she finally settled down.

Her husband was alive. That is all that really mattered. Imam Salim didn't know all the details but knew enough to know Ben's injuries had been serious. He did not hide that fact from Ben's wife. Nor did he hide the fact Ben had been named an official member of the Brittle Riders.

She was less than pleased with that bit of news. But he knew of no way to hide it since it was going to be in the Din-La news sheets in a turn or so. He pointed out it was they who had been with him waiting to find out if he would live or not. He knew that much of Ben's brief message the Din-La had passed along.

He thought about it for a moment and then just handed Ben's message to her.

She read it and then softly wept. He knew the last line was what had done it.

"Tell my wife I love her very much, indeed."

Schoolmaster Zk stood over the Kwini-Laku who'd taken a bullet for him. He wasn't sure if he was crazy or brave. The medicos told him he'd live and would be up and around in a turn or so. They also told him his name was

Malehni. Zk made a mental note to honor this one's elders when they got home.

He left his savior in the tender care of the healers and went to find General A'rxk and his flask. The two had become fast friends and seemed to have a lot in common.

It was going to take many turns to clean up this mess and all of the soldiers had agreed to stay on as guards until the work was done. When the flames had finally died out there was no way to tell who or what had been in there, it was all just ashes. However, without the bodies of the super soldiers, no one was taking anything for granted. Zk had shot one of them in the chest three times and all it seemed to do was irritate him.

No, better to be safe than sorry where they were concerned.

He found A'rxk sitting with Oronimus and several others in the cooking tent. They motioned for him to join them and they all seemed to have flasks of ice wine. Looking at the number of injuries seated at the table he could only think of the old joke "yeah, but you should see the other brand."

Douglass Fairwinds sat with D'noma and Pnaard at a small table sharing a bottle of bourbon. Although not a healer Douglass had flown directly into the battle on numerous occasions to rescue the wounded. His efforts had earned him the gratitude of many and three bullet wounds, none serious. He seemed to wear his bandages with pride.

"You once told me I'd only glimpsed hell. Now, having been here, I see what you meant. Forgive me for saying this but this is not something I wish to do ever again."

D'noma smiled wanly.

"None of us want to do this Douglas. This isn't

anyone's idea of fun. At least not anyone I'd ever want to meet. We did what we did because we had to. Evil like Yontar must be stopped. My kind, more than most any other, knows exactly what he would do if he ever regained power. The horrors he inflicted made this battle seem pleasant."

Douglass and Pnaar both shivered at the thought.

The Athabascae Warriors had finally come to the conclusion that none of the brands they'd met were imaginary and asked to open trade. Douglas' brand had asked the same. While they wouldn't leave their homes, no longer would they hide from the world. If danger would come again they wanted to know in advance and be able to prepare.

Douglass had also told them some of their younger clan members wanted to join the army of the Plains. They wanted to learn how to defend themselves for real should an attack come again. D'noma had passed along that request and an emissary was on their way to meet with them.

No matter what the future held D'noma was sure of one thing, the Haliaeetus were going to make a lot of goldens off this bourbon stuff.

Flight Leader Smythe and Bwanuul, Flight Leader of the Columbas, had begun a regular habit of racing to and from specific points. It was a lot of fun for them and their troops joined in by placing wagers on the various outcomes. So far they were about evenly matched.

Oronimus and others got involved and tried to devise courses for them to race. Some of those required skills neither had, like being able to fly through rock, so they had to be careful. After a couple of turns the Succubi and the Haliaeetus joined in and they had some serious competition.

They would hold a race or contest just after everyone had finished their breaklight repast. Corvington enjoyed them and wanted to fly in every one but he knew allowing his troops to participate would bring them closer to their new allies.

Nothing like found fun and lost goldens to draw soldiers together.

The Elders' Council of the Plains was in session and trying to unknot a problem they'd never considered. The war with Kalindor had left them with many prisoners. Unlike the Naradhama there was no way to repatriate them, they had never been part of life here at all.

Ambassadors from the eastern warrens and the Children of the Waters were on their way to help unsnarl this mess and Lord Südermann, herself, was coming.

After several turns of arguing amongst themselves, they knew they had to wait for fresh points of view. On the one hand they didn't want to keep the prisoners but, on the other, they didn't want to send highly trained soldiers back to Kalindor.

There were those who thought they should invite the Exalted Quelnerom and force him to sign a treaty. The problem was no one knew if reptiloids would honor a treaty. They did know they had warred for almost six hundred Suns between themselves just to settle a simple dispute.

When looked at in that light the effectiveness of a treaty seemed questionable.

Finally, all of the invitees had arrived. They sat at a large table in the center of the council and worked out every possible solution and its ramifications. If they kept them imprisoned it would cost the warrens considerable goldens to house them, guard them, and feed them. That was capital they'd rather spend elsewhere.

If they tried to meld them into their societies they were looking at thousands of possible spies living in their midst.

They didn't want to kill them since that set a bad example.

They decided to send them back, but with a letter. That letter would explain, in no uncertain terms, if the Exalted Quelnerom ever tried anything like this again, the combined might of every northern army would descend on him and leave Kalindor a smoking ruin.

In fact, and this was made perspicious, they would not stop until they reached the southern ice lands and then they would melt those.

That letter was signed by every representative. Copies were made for everyone's records and then Lord Südermann, in a moment of whimsy, framed the original for the Exalted Quelnerom. She said she hoped he'd hang it on his wall as a reminder.

That got laughs all around.

They arranged for the prisoners to be taken to the lands of Kalindor and, once there, placed on their train system and sent to the palace. Since the armies were all still there they felt no additional security would be required after they were dropped off.

As long as they were all together they also voted on Geldish's request concerning the makers' facility which had spawned the Named Ones. He'd asked that it be burned to the ground after the Din-La had scavenged any technology they didn't already have. That was unanimously approved.

They would send a patrol of a hundred and the Din-La could send whomever they wanted.

It had been almost thirty turns since the battle. The prisoners were due back next turn and they would be escorted to the train which would take them home. Geldish wandered the camp with Ben, who was ambulatory if not nimble, and they chatted about inconsequential things. Throughout his recovery, his faith had kept him strong. He met some of the Periplaneta's who served under Lord Südermann and found their faith to be a source of hope as well. He would tell his Imam about both the differences and the similarities.

Geldish didn't put too much stock into things like that but he had to admit it seemed to help those who believed.

R'yune and Sland seemed determined to make every action into a drinking game and had conned several of the troops into joining them each even. After the discovery of bourbon they'd been unstoppable. Several troopers looked like they'd rather be shot than spend another even with those two. In fact, one had begged Geldish to do just that.

BraarB had struck up a friendship with General al Rahim. He'd been seriously wounded but she made sure to spend time with him each turn. The two of them would often talk until even-split about anything and everything. Geldish thought it was a sign of good things to come. If two such disparate brands could find common ground then there should be no reason all of them couldn't.

Being thrown together in war was one thing, making it work during peace quite another.

The only one he was truly concerned with was N'leah. She seemed to have reacted badly to something and was now sick almost every breaklight. He'd seen her consulting with Fried-a-liche two turns ago and hoped she would be better soon. He doubted she could ride being ill like that.

He and Ben continued their leisurely stroll and were amazed at how well the troops had done cleaning everything up. The bodies of the allies had been sent home for proper internment and those of the Kalindorians had been burned.

The river had been cleansed of all the bodies and now seemed to be running pure. They both agreed it was a beautiful river and deserved better than the treatment they'd given it.

They stopped when they saw N'leah arguing angrily with Fried-a-liche. They had no idea what the gentle healer could have said to inspire such vitriol. They were joined by D'noma and Pnaar and walked over just in time to hear N'leah scream at her one more time.

"YOU'RE WRONG! This can't be right. You've made a horrible mistake!"

She went on like that for an epi-clik or so but shut up when she realized there was a small crowd standing behind her. Quiet or no, she was still fuming.

Sland and R'yune saw the commotion and were coming over as well just as BraarB was exiting the medicos' tent after visiting with the remaining injured.

"N'leah," said Geldish quietly, "what's wrong? Is there something we can do to help?"

That actually made her laugh, although it wasn't her usual pleasant sound. She just shook her head.

She finally seemed to get control of her emotions and spoke.

"I have not seen P'marna in almost eighty turns. I have never, ever, been with any other Succubus. Not even when I was a prisoner in Anapsida."

They all agreed this was true even if they had no idea what she was driving at or why she was so upset. It was R'yune who took the leap of logic and quickly signed to her questioningly.

"Yes," she sighed and turned to the others, "I'm pregnant and R'yune's the father."

D'noma and Pnaar fainted.

The End of Book Two

Author's note: Al Cech was a real person and is enshrined in the 16" Softball Hall of Fame located in Forest Park Illinois. His son, Little Al, who could bench press a Volvo if irked, is also a pretty neat guy.

Made in the USA
Lexington, KY
29 September 2018